1

DR JEKYLL & MR HYDE, *THE BODY SNATCHER,* & OTHER HORRORS

The Best Horror & Ghost Stories of
ROBERT LOUIS STEVENSON

Edited, Annotated, and Illustrated By
M. GRANT KELLERMEYER, M.A.

☙

— OLDSTYLE TALES PRESS —
Fort Wayne, Indiana

4

EXPAND YOUR SUPERNATURAL FICTION COLLECTION
By Acquiring These
— ANNOTATED AND ILLUSTRATED EDITIONS —

WWW.OLDSTYLETALES.COM

WEIRD FICTION & HORROR BY:
Algernon Blackwood
Robert W. Chambers
F. Marion Crawford
William Hope Hodgson
Arthur Machen
Guy de Maupassant
Fitz-James O'Brien
Edgar Allan Poe
Ambrose Bierce
H. G. Wells

CLASSIC GHOST STORIES BY:
Charles Dickens
Sir Arthur Conan Doyle
W. W. Jacobs
Henry James
J. Sheridan Le Fanu
E. Nesbit
Robert Louis Stevenson
Bram Stoker
Washington Irving
E. T. A. Hoffmann
M. R. James

CLASSIC GOTHIC NOVELS:
Dracula
Frankenstein
The Phantom of the Opera
Dr. Jekyll and Mr. Hyde
The Turn of the Screw
The Invisible Man
The Picture of Dorian Gray
The Hound of the Baskervilles

FIRESIDE HORROR SERIES:
Ghost Stories for Christmas Eve
Victorian Ghost Stories
Supernatural Cats
Demons and the Devil
Mummies and Curses
Pirates and Ghost Ships
Werewolves

OLDSTYLE TALES

This edition published 2016 by
OLDSTYLE TALES PRESS
2424 N. Anthony Blvd
Fort Wayne, Indiana
46805–3604

*For more information, or to request permission
to reprint selections or illustrations from
this book, write to the Editor at*
oldstyletales@gmail.com

NOTES, INTRODUCTIONS, AND ILLUSTRATIONS
COPYRIGHT © 2016 BY MICHAEL GRANT KELLERMEYER

Readers who are interested in further titles from
Oldstyle Tales Press are invited to visit our website at

— WWW.OLDSTYLETALES.COM —

— TABLE *of* CONTENTS —

*Each story comes with introductory and analytical commentary.
Five of the most critically or popularly acclaimed stories also include footnotes.*

— FOREWORD —

IT'S a wonder that there was a time when Robert Louis Stevenson was almost entirely forgotten by the masses. Having died in 1894 in the throws of middle age, the celebrity author's reputation for thrills and chills diminished as the world fell into the Great War and came out of the trenches ready to redefine itself. Branded as juvenile delights, his work was stripped from the common canon of school literature and looked down upon by the Literati.

Perhaps Stevenson's tales didn't speak to the tastes of the shifting society, but another diagnosis is that it all rang too close to home. For his is a body of work that, when grim in tone, festers up fear not from the bleak recesses of the mind, but from the soul – shining a blinding light into our darkest corners. What is the tale of the noble Jekyll and sinister Hyde if not an examination of mankind's continuing struggle to deny it's most carnal urges? Or what of the moral quandary of Fettes and MacFarlane who exhume the dead while burying their own secrets? These are dark stories where the greatest of boogiemen are mere reflections of our own tarnished humanity.

But there is hope. As Olalla, reminds the solider in one of Stevenson's more famous short stories, "We must endure for a little while, until morning returns bringing peace." It is this endurance Stevenson so artfully examines and, after several decades on the fringes, it must have been a part of what drew people back to his stories. For this struggle for civility amidst our inner most evils can be an ugly one, but the fight is always engaging and, in the prose of Stevenson, enriching.

Thanks to Michael Kellermeyer's new anthology, rich undiscovered shades of what makes Robert Louis Stevenson resound with our souls will no doubt be unearthed and I, for one, am ready to explore my soul's darkest corners with a fresh perspective.

Nathan Hartman
Huntington, Indiana, October 2015

CONCERNING WHAT
You Are About To Read

J. M. Barrie, the Scottish playwright and author of *Peter Pan*, once quipped that the initials "R.L.S." are "the best beloved in recent literature." A quick comparison between *Pan* and *Treasure Island, Kidnapped,* or *The Black Arrow* will remove any doubt that the writer was making an impersonal observation. Edmond Gosse agreed that he was "the most beloved of all the authors of our time," and William Gladstone, Prime Minister at the time, stayed up an entire night reading *Treasure Island*, his favorite book. Kipling considered the man "his idol," while Henry James termed him "the only man in England who can write a decent English sentence," and Arthur Conan Doyle blessed him for "all the pleasure you have given me during my lifetime – more than any other living man." G. K. Chesterton and Vladimir Nabokov wrote rhapsodic essays interpreting his works. Chesterton glowed, "he seemed to pick the right word up on the point of his pen, like a man playing [pick-up-sticks]," and Stevenson remains one of the most highly translated authors in the world (ranked 26th) outpacing such literary colossi as Hemingway, Kipling, Wilde, and even Poe.

His writing is frequently associated with adventure literature, historical fiction, and the justly-called "boy's novel." His historical masterpieces *The Black Arrow, The Master of Ballantrae, Kidnapped, Treasure Island*, and *The Wrecker* demonstrate the influence of Washington Irving, Charles Dickens, Sir Walter Scott, Nathaniel Hawthorne, Edgar Allan Poe, Honoré de Balzac, Victor Hugo, and Guy de Maupassant, showing all their range, depth, imagination, and richness of prose. But attentive readers are familiar with the darker side of Stevenson's writing – a side closely linked to Irving, Poe, and Hawthorne's Gothic fiction – and to horror aficionados he remains a tribune in the unholy trinity of British horror fiction: the Irishman, Englishwoman, and Scott whose 19th century novels still remain the greatest influences in horror culture today.

Stevenson's Influence on Gothic Literature

The Gothic horror novel is a relatively uncommon form. The short story is far more efficient in delivering scares, and far easy to create. But when it has appeared on bookshelves, it typically owes a debt to the genre's most influential ancestors: the three S's – Shelley, Stoker, and Stevenson. Collectively they are responsible for nearly all of our modern cultural associations with monsters, vampires, and werewolves, respectively. Some, including Stephen King, have included Henry James' *The Turn of the Screw* on this list to include the novelized ghost story (that rarest of all forms), and it is certainly inaccurate to treat the three as the century's best horror novelists (in actuality, *Turn of the Screw*, J. Sheridan Le Fanu's *Carmilla*, and Arthur Machen's *The Great God Pan*, may be the best examples of the form), but they are unquestionably the three most impactful voices in horror dating from that decade.

The three most influential horror novels of the 19th century – and subsequently the modern age – have generally been accepted as those masterpieces written by the Three S's: Shelley, Stoker, and Stevenson, unholy trinity of terror. There is a reason that in the 1920s *Frankenstein, Dracula,* and *Dr Jekyll and Mr Hyde* were all wildly popular stage-plays, and a reason that between 1931 and 1932 all three were adapted into inexorably iconic monster films (the first two by Universal, the later by Paramount). Collectively they make up the cornerstone of collective cultural imagination on three of Stephen King's five archetypal horrors: the Monster (or, Nameless Thing), the Vampire, and the Werewolf (the Ghost and the Bad Place, or the Haunted House make up the other two). Since perhaps the 1900s, Shelley, Stoker, and Stevenson have been treated like the Peter, Paul and Mary of the horror world – their names synonymous with terror. But one of the trio has a distinctively more diversified portfolio: Mary Shelley wrote *Frankenstein*, and other than a few dark parables ("The Last Man") and a couple supernatural tales ("Transformation"), her career was a one-hit wonder; Stoker was prolific to a degree, conjuring several Poe-esque stories that raise the hair ("The Squaw," "The Burial of the Rats," "The Judge's House") and a clump of awkward novels (the infamous *Lair of the White Worm*), his career was not a one hit wonder, but resulted in only four or five quality pieces, the rest maudlin, farcical, or ignorant; but Stevenson – despite a modest output – produced a wonderful range of high-quality short stories and novelettes that cross both the borderlands of horror and literary fiction.

"Markheim," "The Merry Men," "The Bottle Imp," "The Body Snatcher," "Olalla," and of course *Dr Jekyll and Mr Hyde* are just as likely to appear on the syllabus of a 19th century short story class as on a Good Reads list of favorite horror stories. They brood with rich atmosphere, evocative prose, luscious dialects, mythic symbolism, and stupefying irony. While Shelley proved influential to the basic understanding of the modern horror genre, and Stoker leant his legacy to Anne Rice, Kim Newman, Richard Matheson, and Stephen King (no disrespect meant to any of those best-selling artists), Stevenson became a sounding point for Ernest Hemingway, Berthold Brecht, Henry James, Rudyard Kipling, Jack London, Vladimir Nabokov, J. M. Barrie, G. K. Chesterton, Jorge Luis Borges, Marcel Proust, Joseph Conrad, H. Rider Haggard, F. Scott Fitzgerald, Arthur Conan Doyle, and J. R. R. Tolkien. The potency of his writing – the power of his vision and voice –

extend beyond the horror genre into the universal canon of Western literature – something which the purple prose of Lovecraft and the sentimental rhapsodies of *Dracula*, cannot boast for all of their long-lasting influence.

This diversity of talent suits my purposes very well, because Jekyll and Hyde have been given their own introduction – their legacy, interpretations, and complexity are too great to be dealt with in any way other than individual – but unlike my introductions to Frankenstein and Dracula, I have much more to talk about than the headlining act, and the entirety of Stevenson's speculative oeuvre deserves consideration.

Calvinism and Christianity in Stevenson

Stevenson's fiction continues to thrill and disturb, largely due to its grounding in his childhood imagination. As a boy he was chronically bedridden – a miserable cosmic punishment to a youngster with such a ripe imagination. To keep him still and well behaved, Cummy, his nurse, entertained him with stories that excited him during the day and horrified him at night. A strict Calvinist, Cummy's worldview was bleak, harsh, and cynical, and her stories conveyed that darkness to their young audience. Most often she read the Bible to her ward – especially the gory and doom-ridden Old Testament – but she also treated him to folktales from the Scottish countryside: stories of ghosts, demons, strolling corpses, werewolves, goblins, and supernatural wonders. Many of her legends included meetings with the devil (often depicted as a tall man with coal black skin and fiery eyes), the temptations of evil, and the punishments of a just and merciless God. The grandson of a Presbyterian minister, son to devout parents, and captive to Cummy's vicious theology, Stevenson initially aspired to be a powerful-worded preacher (he would at times play-act giving sermons in his nursery), but Cummy's well-intended lessons eventually soured her ward on religion.

Calvinism and Christianity in general are philosophically crucial to Stevenson's oeuvre, and will come up constantly in the notes and annotations. As such, a short description of the Calvinist worldview is necessary before we delve into the actual stories. Calvinism was a Protestant response to the Reformation begun by Martin Luther. Luther's followers split off and became Anglicans, Lutherans, and Episcopalians – essentially high church, and similar in architecture, liturgy, and performance to Roman Catholics. But a more conservative response to the schism from Rome came from the teachings of John Calvin, whose followers developed into what we now call "evangelical" denominations – Wesleyan, Baptist, Nazarene, Holiness, Pentecostal, Amish, and Mennonite church bodies. Not all of these groups continue to advocate the stringent Calvinism that Stevenson was exposed to, but until the previous century, the tenets of Calvinism were particularly dire.

They viewed mankind as irredeemably bad – prone to sin, hopeless to save, pathetic to consider – and considered salvation an accident of God's precarious grace. Unlike other Protestants, they didn't see salvation as something to be acquired by choice, but as something given without cause or reason. So far this sounds fairly standard, but Calvinists took the theory of election very seriously: we are either saved or damned before we are even born, they thought, and the far majority are damned, and nothing can ever be done to change that fate. They called the saved the Elect – the small group God had predestined for heaven – and felt that the only way to know whether one had been elected was to see whether they were naturally good (not that doing good things could make a difference). So to save face, avoid gossip, and appear elected, Calvinists strained themselves trying to perform well in public. In private, however, it didn't matter – nothing mattered, because you were already either saved or damned, and no sin or good deed could change that. All that mattered was appearing elected, and avoiding social disgrace. The combination of self-consciousness and helplessness led to do a culture of grim dissatisfaction, self-loathing, and paranoia. Concerning the emotional culture of Calvinism, John Keats complained that the Presbyterians "have done Scotland harm. They have banished... love and laughing." Stevenson himself groaned that but "one thing is not to be learned in Scotland, and that is the way to be happy."

Nathaniel Hawthorne was similarly disgusted by the hypocrisy of his own Calvinist (Puritans) descendants, and ruthlessly critiqued their obsession with appearance and disregard for hope in *The Scarlet Letter*, "Young Goodman Brown," "The May-Pole at Merry Mount," and many other stories. Like his American counterpart, Stevenson turned against this religion of guilt and gossip and became a radical atheist as a college student. What began as an expression of youthful rebellion crashed down around him in an avalanche of domestic misery when his father learned of his activities. While at Edinburgh University, Stevenson's cousin Bob co-founded the atheist "Liberty-Justice-Reverence Club," which contained in its constitution a command to "Disregard everything our parents have taught us." To his horror, his father found a copy of the document in his room, which led to a heated argument and a traumatic falling apart: "What a damned curse I am to my parents! As my father said "You have rendered my whole life a failure". As my mother said "This is the heaviest affliction that has ever befallen me". O Lord, what a pleasant thing it is to have damned the happiness of (probably) the only two people who care a damn about you in the world." Stevenson ended his life as an open-minded theist, but his relationship with religion was always rocky, and the scars left by the encounter with his genuinely devoted parents left him fixated on concepts of shame, guilt, and hypocrisy.

Most of Stevenson's quality supernatural fiction was collected in two anthologies, 1887's *The Merry Men and Other Tales and Fables* and 1893 *Island Nights' Entertainments*. The first collection is largely set in Scotland and Europe, while the second, written during his tenure in Samoa, takes place in the Pacific Islands. Besides these anthologies, "The Body Snatcher" and the posthumously published "Waif Woman" (originally planned for *Island Nights' Entertainments*) round out his short supernatural fiction. Our edition of Stevenson's best horror and weird fiction excludes "Will O' the Mill," "The Isle of Voices," and "The Poor Thing" for the sake of brevity and quality, but I would recommend them to your attention if you are interested in further reading.

His stories are famous for their psychological depth, ethical complexity, and luscious prose, and his horror fiction is no exception. *The Merry Men*, a novelette set on the atmospheric Scottish coast has its foundations in Washington Irving and Poe. Like "Thrawn Janet," it features the gorgeous Scots dialect, and a possible appearance by Satan. It concerns itself with an old man whose Calvinist belief in his election has allowed him to justify murdering and robbing a shipwreck survivor. Shadowy treasure hunters, hellish electrical storms, and a doomed romance charges this story – one of Stevenson's most underrated – with the moral complexity and emotional power of *Jekyll & Hyde* in half the pages.

Based on the historical anatomy murders of Burke and Hare, "The Body Snatcher" is probably Stevenson's most famous short story, horror or otherwise. Fettes, a squirrely rogue who spends his days drinking in a purgatorial tavern is greatly disturbed when he sees Macfarlane – an old medical school acquaintance. As students the two knowingly bought murdered corpses for their anatomy college, and revealed in blasphemous arrogance. The horror that they encounter on their way back from graverobbing a cemetery is both Lovecraftian and Hoffmannesque. It remains a staple of supernatural literature, and – alongside "The Judge's House," "The Monkey's Paw," and "The Tell-Tale Heart" – is perhaps one of the best, most anthologized horror stories in the language.

"Markheim" is often cited as the predecessor to *Jekyll & Hyde*, and by all accounts the first draft (which Mrs Stevenson critiqued and her husband theatrically burned) had many of the same character elements. In this story – equal parts *Faust*, "William Wilson," and *Crime and Punishment* – a man kills an unscrupulous pawnbroker as an ethical experiment, and spends the vast majority of the tale alone in the murder room until he is accompanied by a supernatural visitor who may be Satan tempting him to continue down a predestined path of moral degeneration, or his conscience employing reverse psychology.

"Thrawn Janet" – one of the finest tales in this collection – is written almost entirely in Scots, a Germanic language which is similar to English, but unquestionably unique. To the best of my knowledge this book contains the first full translation of this exceedingly underrated ghost story (most anthologies either expect their readers to infer the meaning, or include a small gloss). The title (which translates as "Twisted" or "Throttled Janet") refers to a suspected witch who is reviled by her neighbors but pitied by their new, liberal-minded parson. The Reverend Soulis (yes, the name is telling) hires Janet as a housekeeper, and saves her from a mob of angry women by having her denounce Satan in front of them, but is disturbed when she walks through town the next morning with a wrung neck and a garbled voice. A ghost story, witch story, zombie story, demon possession story, and Hawthornian parable, all rolled into one, "Thrawn Janet" is one of the best horror tales in Victorian literature, and includes one of the genre's most disturbing scenes.

"Olalla" represents one of the crowning accomplishments of Stevenson's career. Despite its anticlimactic ending, it is perhaps one of the best pastiches of Edgar Allan Poe's works that has ever been created. An homage to Poe's tales of cursed women straddling the boundaries between spirituality and mortality, "Olalla" is a wildly erotic, psychologically rich banquet that follows the doomed romance between a handsome British officer and the spiritually precocious daughter of an inbred family who are suggested to be vampires or werewolves. Their monstrous nature is never revealed, though grimly hinted at, but Stevenson is more fascinated with the sexual magnetism between their archetypal dichotomies – the soldier's dominating, homoerotic animus and Olalla's submissive, androgynous anima.

Other than "The Body Snatcher," "The Bottle Imp" is probably Stevenson's most famous short story – a Hawaiian parable based on the "be careful what you wish for." Like "The Monkey's Paw," Hawthrone's adaptation of "King Midas and the Golden Touch," and Irving's "The Devil and Tom Walker," the tale has become synonymous with warnings against wishful thinking. A poor islander buys a diabolical bottle, the imp (or genie, or demon) inside will grant wishes, but must be sold at a loss in order to avoid damnation. While he successfully wishes away his leprosy, the possession of the trinket drags him and his young wife towards eternal destruction.

"The Waif Woman," set in the year that Christianity was introduced to Viking-occupied Iceland, is an adaptation of a grisly ghost story from chapters 50 and 51 of the medieval *Eyrbyggja Saga*. Fanny Stevenson discouraged her husband's plans to include it in *Island Nights' Entertainment*, claiming he had only ripped off the saga, but it brings a nice circularity to this book, ending where *The Merry Men* began – a tale of greed haunted by guilt, the lust for material comforts, and the hideous costs of a selfish life.

Stevenson's stories rotate around several constant themes: the duplicity of mankind, the struggle between morality and indulgence, the hubris of unchecked intellectualism, the deceptive comforts and lurking pitfalls of hypocrisy, and the ever-waiting, ever-watching karmic justice that lurks in the periphery of gloating sinners. The Merry Men watches a man shift from contentment with murder to uncertainty to moral terror when he thinks that the devil (though possibly an African sailor) has come for his soul. "Thrawn Janet" concerns itself with Reverend Soulis (who distinctly recalls Hawthorne's Dimmesdale) and his retreat away from his superstitious parishoners, how he resented their ignorance and judged their stupidity until he realized that they were right all along, and lived the rest of his life a shaken and affected man. "The Body Snatcher" uses the metaphor of "looking it in the face" – of understanding the consequences of one's moral choices – to great effect: Fettes is shaken by the sight of Macfarlane's face (proof that his evil ways were never challenged – that he thrived his way to the top), he is horrified by the face of the murdered girl, whose death he understands to be largely due to his turning a blind eye to Macfarlane, and both he and Macfarlane are terrified when they look the corpse of an old woman in the face only to see the leering features of a man they had previously buried. "Markheim" and *Jekyll* both focus on the struggle to overcome one's corrupted nature, and end with their heroes facing death as a result of having already given too much slack to their carnal senses of entitlement. Even "Olalla," with its lush eroticism and delicious prose is darkened by the struggle between the sensual, atheistic narrator (an emotional vampire) and the sacrificial, pious Olalla (a literal, though latent, vampire) – two halves of the same soul, a masculine animus and a feminine anima, a fleshly yang and a spiritual yin.

Humanity, like nature, is fraught with delicate balances between its warring powers, Stevenson tries to communicate, and the battle is all the easier when a compromise is sought, but far too often the opposing forces crush each other into oblivion. Let me illustrate this with the final episode in *Dr Jekyll and Mr Hyde*: Hyde treats Jekyll like a parasite would (much like Dracula's brides used Jonathan Harker) keeping him weak, submissive, but alive, because Jekyll's exterior was entirely necessary for Hyde to survive. But when the battle had reached the tipping point, Jekyll was destroyed and accidentally lost – his spirit evicted from the fleshly vessel now inhabited solely by Hyde – to Hyde's utmost despair. Hyde spends his last eight days on earth pacing his apartment wildly, sobbing "like a woman" and crying out on God. Hyde does not vanquish Jekyll – they vanquish one another. The balance has been lost.

Throughout his oeuvre, Stevenson continues to desperately illustrate the lessons he learned as a child with the openness he developed as a man: that choices have costs, that man is neither wholly evil (as Calvinists believe) nor wholly good (as some humanists believe), but an amalgam – a soup of emotions, impulses, and desires. His characters struggle to find a balance between their lusts and their peace of mind: Markheim wants to murder and not feel guilty, Keawe wants to cure his leprosy without being damned, Uncle Gordon wants to have fine possessions – even at the cost of murder – and still be among God's Elect, Soulis wants to reject his congregation's superstitions and not have to acknowledge the terrors of the night, and Jekyll – saddest of all, perhaps – just wants to have fun ("pleasures [which] were ... undignified; though I would scarce use a harsher term") and for once in his life not feel like he is disappointing anyone. But each of these characters come to a time of reckoning where they must swallow the medicine they have poured out – and for some the dose is lethal.

In his confession Jekyll writes that "I hazard the guess that man will be ultimately known for a mere polity of multifarious, incongruous and independent denizens." Stevenson knew this full well; he felt the pull of his parents' religion, of his university education, of his Conservative politics, of his radical lifestyle, and of many other forces straining inside his soul. He truly was populated by clashing tribes of "multifarious, incongruous and independent" spirits. We can see much of his own life in Soulis' fate: unconvinced by his faith, unsure of his intellect, belonging to neither church nor university, family nor wider world, he wanders like the Ancient Mariner, hoping that perhaps at least the telling of his tale will make some impact on someone. If he was otherwise distraught over the congested polity that made up his soul, Stevenson could at least take solace in the fact that his tales have done that exactly.

M. Grant Kellermeyer
Fort Wayne, Hallowe'en 2015

DR JEKYLL & MR HYDE,
THE BODY-SNATCHER, AND OTHER HORRORS
The Best Horror & Ghost Stories of
ROBERT LOUIS STEVENSON

STEVENSON was obsessed with the duplicity of man, as each of his horror stories will aptly illustrate. He was fixated on the concept of hypocrisy – the man who loudly espouses a nobler worldview but fails to live up to his own lofty standards. Much of this could be said to emanate from his family's religious background, and in few stories is this religious tension dealt with more directly than "The Merry Men." The story, which takes place on the rugged Scottish coast where shipwrecks are witnessed and sunken treasure reclaimed on becalmed nights, shares much with Stevenson's adventure novels (cf. *Treasure Island* and *Kidnapped*) but maintains a much darker and more philosophical atmosphere stepped in Scotland's theological history. Since the Reformation, the rugged Lowland countryside was a hotbed of Calvinist fervor which often flirted with fanaticism. Strict Calvinists even rejected grave markers and prayers for the souls of the dead as being idolatrous. Catholics – who flourished in the Highlands – were viewed as depraved heretics, and Bonnie Prince Charlie's ill-starred return from exile – viewed romantically even by the English – was the stuff of a bogeyman legend. At the time of the story, the Killing Time (a period during most of the 1680s, when Calvinist rebels called Covenanters hid in the moorland to avoid persecution from Catholic King James's soldiers) is still a matter of local memory, the invasion of James's son Charlie's army still fills Presbyterian hearts with terror, and the satisfying thought of Anglicans, Papists, and Jacobites burning in Damnation was a rare and soothing consolation to the (often destitute) rural, Calvinist peasants. The character of Uncle Gordon in "The Merry Men" is one such fundamentalist. He is quick to pronounce judgement, eager to proscribe hellfire, and sadistic in his delight of watching sailors drown off the coast. And yet he harbors a secret lust for their beautiful possessions which hardly befits a severe Calvinist – not to mention the crime of murder.

The Merry Men
{1882}

Chapter I. Eilean Aros

IT was a beautiful morning in the late July when I set forth on foot for the last time for Aros[1]. A boat had put me ashore the night before at Grisapol[2]; I had such breakfast as the little inn afforded, and, leaving all my baggage till

---

[1] A fictional island based on the Isle of Erraid, which Stevenson featured in *Kidnapped*. The island is in the Inner Hebrides off the west cost of Scotland – a wild and desolate stretch of rocky beaches

[2] Also fictional

I had an occasion to come round for it by sea, struck right across the promontory[1] with a cheerful heart.

I was far from being a native of these parts, springing, as I did, from an unmixed lowland stock[2]. But an uncle of mine, Gordon Darnaway, after a poor, rough youth, and some years at sea, had married a young wife in the islands; Mary Maclean she was called, the last of her family; and when she died in giving birth to a daughter, Aros, the sea-girt farm, had remained in his possession. It brought him in nothing but the means of life, as I was well aware; but he was a man whom ill-fortune had pursued; he feared, cumbered as he was with the young child, to make a fresh adventure upon life; and remained in Aros, biting his nails at destiny. Years passed over his head in that isolation, and brought neither help nor contentment. Meantime our family was dying out in the lowlands; there is little luck for any of that race; and perhaps my father was the luckiest of all, for not only was he one of the last to die, but he left a son to his name and a little money to support it. I was a student of Edinburgh University, living well enough at my own charges, but without kith or kin; when some news of me found its way to Uncle Gordon on the Ross of Grisapol; and he, as he was a man who held blood thicker than water, wrote to me the day he heard of my existence, and taught me to count Aros as my home. Thus it was that I came to spend my vacations in that part of the country, so far from all society and comfort, between the codfish and the moorcocks; and thus it was that now, when I had done with my classes, I was returning thither with so light a heart that July day.

The Ross[3], as we call it, is a promontory neither wide nor high, but as rough as God made it to this day; the deep sea on either hand of it, full of rugged isles and reefs most perilous to seamen—all overlooked from the eastward by some very high cliffs and the great peals of Ben Kyaw. *The Mountain of the Mist*, they say the words signify in the Gaelic tongue; and it is well named. For that hill-top, which is more than three thousand feet in height, catches all the clouds that come blowing from the seaward; and, indeed, I used often to think that it must make them for itself; since when all heaven was clear to the sea level, there would ever be a streamer on Ben

---

[1] Cliff face or a very steep hill

[2] Meaning that he comes from industrial southern Scotland (Edinburgh and Glasgow being the two great cities of the Lowlands) which is more closely aligned with Northern England's sensibilities, industry, culture, and folklore than those of the agrarian, sheep herding Highlanders. Being unmixed, our protagonist claims not to have any Highland blood in him. This will be useful when trying to establish authorial credibility by implying that he is not prone to fantasies or daydreams

[3] Ross is a Gaelic word that means "headland," or a rocky projection that juts into the sea

Kyaw. It brought water, too, and was mossy to the top in consequence. I have seen us sitting in broad sunshine on the Ross, and the rain falling black like crape[1] upon the mountain. But the wetness of it made it often appear more beautiful to my eyes; for when the sun struck upon the hill sides, there were many wet rocks and watercourses that shone like jewels even as far as Aros, fifteen miles away.

The road that I followed was a cattle-track. It twisted so as nearly to double the length of my journey; it went over rough boulders so that a man had to leap from one to another, and through soft bottoms where the moss came nearly to the knee. There was no cultivation anywhere, and not one house in the ten miles from Grisapol to Aros. Houses of course there were—three at least; but they lay so far on the one side or the other that no stranger could have found them from the track. A large part of the Ross is covered with big granite rocks, some of them larger than a two-roomed house, one beside another, with fern and deep heather in between them where the vipers breed. Anyway the wind was, it was always sea air, as salt as on a ship; the gulls were as free as moorfowl over all the Ross; and whenever the way rose a little, your eye would kindle with the brightness of the sea. From the very midst of the land, on a day of wind and a high spring, I have heard the Roost roaring, like a battle where it runs by Aros, and the great and fearful voices of the breakers[2] that we call the Merry Men.

Aros itself—Aros Jay, I have heard the natives call it, and they say it means *the House of God*[3]—Aros itself was not properly a piece of the Ross, nor was it quite an islet. It formed the south-west corner of the land, fitted close to it, and was in one place only separated from the coast by a little gut of the sea, not forty feet across the narrowest. When the tide was full, this was clear and still, like a pool on a land river; only there was a difference in the weeds and fishes, and the water itself was green instead of brown; but when the tide went out, in the bottom of the ebb, there was a day or two in every month when you could pass dryshod from Aros to the mainland. There was some good pasture, where my uncle fed the sheep he lived on; perhaps the feed was better because the ground rose higher on the islet than the main level of the Ross, but this I am not skilled enough to settle. The house was a good one for that country, two storeys high. It

---

[1] Mourning veils

[2] Waves crashing into the shore

[3] Robertson consistently uses mood and Romanticism to suggest that Aros is some sort of capital of the supernatural powers of Heaven and Hell. God and Satan alike are at home in this world which is part dismal rocks and shadow and part brilliant sea and sun. It is a stage set to test the mortals that tread the boards, directed and observed by the Holy and Profane powers that are so native to the rocky, nature-ravaged coastline of West Scotland

looked westward over a bay, with a pier hard by for a boat, and from the door you could watch the vapours blowing on Ben Kyaw.

On all this part of the coast, and especially near Aros, these great granite rocks that I have spoken of go down together in troops into the sea, like cattle on a summer's day. There they stand, for all the world like their neighbours ashore; only the salt water sobbing between them instead of the quiet earth, and clots of sea-pink blooming on their sides instead of heather; and the great sea conger to wreathe about the base of them instead of the poisonous viper of the land[1]. On calm days you can go wandering between them in a boat for hours, echoes following you about the labyrinth; but when the sea is up, Heaven help the man that hears that cauldron boiling.

Off the south-west end of Aros these blocks are very many, and much greater in size. Indeed, they must grow monstrously bigger out to sea, for there must be ten sea miles of open water sown with them as thick as a country place with houses, some standing thirty feet above the tides, some covered, but all perilous to ships; so that on a clear, westerly blowing day, I have counted, from the top of Aros, the great rollers breaking white and heavy over as many as six-and-forty buried reefs. But it is nearer in shore that the danger is worst; for the tide, here running like a mill race, makes a long belt of broken water—a *Roost* we call it—at the tail of the land. I have often been out there in a dead calm at the slack of the tide; and a strange place it is, with the sea swirling and combing up and boiling like the cauldrons of a linn[2], and now and again a little dancing mutter of sound as though the *Roost* were talking to itself. But when the tide begins to run again, and above all in heavy weather, there is no man could take a boat within half a mile of it, nor a ship afloat that could either steer or live in such a place. You can hear the roaring of it six miles away. At the seaward end there comes the strongest of the bubble; and it's here that these big breakers dance together—the dance of death, it may be called—that have got the name, in these parts, of the Merry Men. I have heard it said that they run fifty feet high; but that must be the green water only, for the spray runs twice as high as that. Whether they got the name from their movements, which are swift and antic, or from the shouting they make about the turn of the tide, so that all Aros shakes with it, is more than I can tell.

The truth is, that in a south-westerly wind, that part of our archipelago is no better than a trap. If a ship got through the reefs, and weathered the Merry Men, it would be to come ashore on the south coast of Aros, in

---

[1] Here once more we have a spiritual image of the Holy sea and the Profane land: the sea which symbolizes God and produces the edible eel (a conger was a staple of the Scottish costal diet), and the land which symbolizes Satan and produces the poisonous serpent

[2] A waterfall

Sandag Bay, where so many dismal things befell our family, as I propose to tell. The thought of all these dangers, in the place I knew so long, makes me particularly welcome the works now going forward to set lights upon the headlands and buoys along the channels of our iron-bound, inhospitable islands.

The country people had many a story about Aros, as I used to hear from my uncle's man, Rorie, an old servant of the Macleans, who had transferred his services without afterthought on the occasion of the marriage. There was some tale of an unlucky creature, a sea-kelpie[1], that dwelt and did business in some fearful manner of his own among the boiling breakers of the Roost. A mermaid had once met a piper on Sandag beach, and there sang to him a long, bright midsummer's night, so that in the morning he was found stricken crazy, and from thenceforward, till the day he died, said only one form of words; what they were in the original Gaelic I cannot tell, but they were thus translated: 'Ah, the sweet singing out of the sea.' Seals that haunted on that coast have been known to speak to man in his own tongue, presaging great disasters. It was here that a certain saint first landed on his voyage out of Ireland to convert the Hebrideans[2]. And, indeed, I think he had some claim to be called saint; for, with the boats of that past age, to make so rough a passage, and land on such a ticklish coast, was surely not far short of the miraculous. It was to him, or to some of his monkish underlings who had a cell there, that the islet owes its holy and beautiful name, the House of God[3].

Among these old wives' stories there was one which I was inclined to hear with more credulity. As I was told, in that tempest which scattered the ships of the Invincible Armada[4] over all the north and west of Scotland, one great vessel came ashore on Aros, and before the eyes of some solitary people on a hill-top, went down in a moment with all hands, her colours

---

[1] A shape-shifting water spirit, who like Lorelei or the Sirens, is renowned for luring sailors to their ruin. Often these spirits took the form of a horse or a beautiful man or woman, and are said to "delight in the drowning of travelers." Very nearly every sizable body of water in Scotland has a Kelpie myth attached to it, most notably Loch Ness. The tales likely sprang up as a means of warning children about the dangers of downing, and young women about the perils of strange young men (who very likely might lure a woman towards the water, rape her, and then drown her, exactly like a Kelpie)

[2] Saint Columba (521 – 597), an Irish monk who famously attempted to convert the Picts and founded an abbey in Iona in the Hebrides

[3] Stevenson continues to underscore the importance of this name: God and Satan abide hard by, manifesting in the darkness and storm and sea and light, and the House of God and the Merry Men serve as a proving ground for human souls that happen to tread in the shadows of the deities

[4] Specifically the Spanish Armada, during a failed invasion of England in 1588

flying even as she sank. There was some likelihood in this tale; for another of that fleet lay sunk on the north side, twenty miles from Grisapol. It was told, I thought, with more detail and gravity than its companion stories, and there was one particularity which went far to convince me of its truth: the name, that is, of the ship was still remembered, and sounded, in my ears, Spanishly. The *Espirito Santo*[1] they called it, a great ship of many decks of guns, laden with treasure and grandees[2] of Spain, and fierce soldadoes[3], that now lay fathom deep to all eternity, done with her wars and voyages, in Sandag bay, upon the west of Aros. No more salvos of ordnance[4] for that tall ship, the 'Holy Spirit,' no more fair winds or happy ventures; only to rot there deep in the sea-tangle and hear the shoutings of the Merry Men as the tide ran high about the island. It was a strange thought to me first and last, and only grew stranger as I learned the more of Spain, from which she had set sail with so proud a company, and King Philip, the wealthy king, that sent her on that voyage.

And now I must tell you, as I walked from Grisapol that day, the *Espirito Santo* was very much in my reflections. I had been favourably remarked by our then Principal in Edinburgh College, that famous writer, Dr. Robertson, and by him had been set to work on some papers of an ancient date to rearrange and sift of what was worthless; and in one of these, to my great wonder, I found a note of this very ship, the *Espirito Santo*, with her captain's name, and how she carried a great part of the Spaniard's treasure, and had been lost upon the Ross of Grisapol; but in what particular spot, the wild tribes of that place and period would give no information to the king's inquiries. Putting one thing with another, and taking our island tradition together with this note of old King Jamie's[5] perquisitions after wealth, it had come strongly on my mind that the spot for which he sought in vain could be no other than the small bay of Sandag on my uncle's land; and being a fellow of a mechanical turn, I had ever since been plotting how to weigh that good ship up again with all her ingots[6], ounces, and doubloons, and bring back our house of Darnaway to its long-forgotten dignity and wealth.

---

[1] Spanish for "The Holy Spirit." In Christian theology, the Holy Spirit is the third part of the Trinity – the tri-parte nature of God – which descended onto Jesus while he was dipped under water in baptism. The Holy Spirit is said to communicate between men and God, acting as a messenger and inspiration to those who commune with It. This is relevant to the overall themes and religious motifs of this story

[2] Noblemen and persons of importance

[3] Warriors

[4] "Volleys of cannon-fire"

[5] King James VI of Scotland, I of England – the monarch who followed Elizabeth I to the throne

[6] Bars of gold made to be melted and formed into coinage and jewelry

This was a design of which I soon had reason to repent. My mind was sharply turned on different reflections; and since I became the witness of a strange judgment of God's, the thought of dead men's treasures has been intolerable to my conscience. But even at that time I must acquit myself of sordid greed; for if I desired riches, it was not for their own sake, but for the sake of a person who was dear to my heart—my uncle's daughter, Mary Ellen. She had been educated well, and had been a time to school upon the mainland; which, poor girl, she would have been happier without. For Aros was no place for her, with old Rorie the servant, and her father, who was one of the unhappiest men in Scotland, plainly bred up in a country place among Cameronians, long a skipper sailing out of the Clyde about the islands, and now, with infinite discontent, managing his sheep and a little 'long shore fishing for the necessary bread. If it was sometimes weariful to me, who was there but a month or two, you may fancy what it was to her who dwelt in that same desert all the year round, with the sheep and flying sea-gulls, and the Merry Men singing and dancing in the Roost!

Chapter II. What the Wreck Had Brought to Aros.

It was half-flood when I got the length of Aros; and there was nothing for it but to stand on the far shore and whistle for Rorie with the boat. I had no need to repeat the signal. At the first sound, Mary was at the door flying a handkerchief by way of answer, and the old long-legged serving-man was shambling down the gravel to the pier. For all his hurry, it took him a long while to pull across the bay; and I observed him several times to pause, go into the stern, and look over curiously into the wake. As he came nearer, he seemed to me aged and haggard, and I thought he avoided my eye. The coble had been repaired, with two new thwarts and several patches of some rare and beautiful foreign wood, the name of it unknown to me.

'Why, Rorie,' said I, as we began the return voyage, 'this is fine wood. How came you by that?'

'It will be hard to cheesel,' Rorie opined reluctantly; and just then, dropping the oars, he made another of those dives into the stern which I had remarked as he came across to fetch me, and, leaning his hand on my shoulder, stared with an awful look into the waters of the bay.

'What is wrong?' I asked, a good deal startled.

'It will be a great feesh,' said the old man, returning to his oars; and nothing more could I get out of him, but strange glances and an ominous nodding of the head. In spite of myself, I was infected with a measure of uneasiness; I turned also, and studied the wake. The water was still and transparent, but, out here in the middle of the bay, exceeding deep. For some time I could see naught; but at last it did seem to me as if something dark—a great fish, or perhaps only a shadow—followed studiously in the

27

track of the moving coble[1]. And then I remembered one of Rorie's superstitions: how in a ferry in Morven, in some great, exterminating feud among the clans; a fish, the like of it unknown in all our waters, followed for some years the passage of the ferry-boat, until no man dared to make the crossing.

'He will be waiting for the right man,' said Rorie.

Mary met me on the beach, and led me up the brae and into the house of Aros. Outside and inside there were many changes. The garden was fenced with the same wood that I had noted in the boat; there were chairs in the kitchen covered with strange brocade[2]; curtains of brocade hung from the window; a clock stood silent on the dresser; a lamp of brass was swinging from the roof; the table was set for dinner with the finest of linen and silver; and all these new riches were displayed in the plain old kitchen that I knew so well, with the high-backed settle, and the stools, and the closet bed for Rorie; with the wide chimney the sun shone into, and the clear-smouldering peats[3]; with the pipes on the mantelshelf and the three-cornered spittoons, filled with sea-shells instead of sand, on the floor; with the bare stone walls and the bare wooden floor, and the three patchwork rugs that were of yore its sole adornment—poor man's patchwork, the like of it unknown in cities, woven with homespun, and Sunday black, and sea-cloth polished on the bench of rowing. The room, like the house, had been a sort of wonder in that country-side, it was so neat and habitable; and to see it now, shamed by these incongruous additions, filled me with indignation and a kind of anger. In view of the errand I had come upon to Aros, the feeling was baseless and unjust; but it burned high, at the first moment, in my heart.

'Mary, girl,' said I, 'this is the place I had learned to call my home, and I do not know it.'

'It is my home by nature, not by the learning,' she replied; 'the place I was born and the place I'm like to die in; and I neither like these changes, nor the way they came, nor that which came with them. I would have liked better, under God's pleasure, they had gone down into the sea, and the Merry Men were dancing on them now.'

Mary was always serious; it was perhaps the only trait that she shared with her father; but the tone with which she uttered these words was even graver than of custom.

---

[1] A flat-bottomed, high-bowed fishing boat traditionally used on the northeast coasts of Britain

[2] Patterned fabric, typically shuttle-woven silk

[3] In Scotland, where trees are few, peat – partly decayed vegetable matter – is dug up from bogs, dried in the air, and burned for fuel

'Ay,' said I, 'I feared it came by wreck[1], and that's by death; yet when my father died, I took his goods without remorse.'

'Your father died a clean strae death, as the folk say,' said Mary.

'True,' I returned; 'and a wreck is like a judgment. What was she called?'

'They ca'd her the *Christ-Anna*[2],' said a voice behind me; and, turning round, I saw my uncle standing in the doorway.

He was a sour, small, bilious man, with a long face and very dark eyes; fifty-six years old, sound and active in body, and with an air somewhat between that of a shepherd and that of a man following the sea. He never laughed, that I heard; read long at the Bible; prayed much, like the Cameronians[3] he had been brought up among; and indeed, in many ways, used to remind me of one of the hill-preachers in the killing times[4] before the Revolution. But he never got much comfort, nor even, as I used to think, much guidance, by his piety. He had his black fits when he was afraid of hell; but he had led a rough life, to which he would look back with envy, and was still a rough, cold, gloomy man.

As he came in at the door out of the sunlight, with his bonnet on his head and a pipe hanging in his button-hole, he seemed, like Rorie, to have grown older and paler, the lines were deeplier ploughed upon his face, and

---

[1] Like a body-snatcher, a wreckers had a certain social repugnance in polite society. Wreckers sometimes lured ships by building bonfires (called false lights) that resembled lighthouses, misleading ships and driving them onto rocks. After the ships sank, the flotsam (floating debris) would wash ashore with the corpses, and the wreckers would load the debris into carts and sell it or keep it. They would also rob the corpses of passengers and crew who happened to have rings, watches, or cash on them. While Uncle Gordon did not use false lights to deliberately wreck vessels he is still a wrecker, and his ill-gotten gains are a point of shame to Charles

[2] This is the name of the vessel whose wreckage Gordon has pillaged

[3] Members of a religious sect founded by Richard Cameron in 1680. These fundamentalists refused to recognize any government that didn't owe its powers to God

[4] The killing times were periods of bloody civil war following the Restoration of Charles II, beginning in 1680 with Cameron's rejection of the King's authority and lasting until James II's deposal during the English Revolution of 1688. Charles was suspected of Catholic sympathies, which the Scottish Presbyterians loathed (the Highlanders, on the other hand, were largely Catholic all along). The Killing Time saw thousands slaughtered for refusing to pledge allegiance to the King, follow the Church of England, and rejecting the claims of so-called Covenanters like Cameron

the whites of his eyes were yellow, like old stained ivory[1], or the bones of the dead.

'Ay' he repeated, dwelling upon the first part of the word, 'the *Christ-Anna*. It's an awfu' name.'

I made him my salutations, and complimented him upon his look of health; for I feared he had perhaps been ill.

'I'm in the body,' he replied, ungraciously enough; 'aye in the body and the sins of the body, like yoursel'. Denner,' he said abruptly to Mary, and then ran on to me: 'They're grand braws, thir that we hae gotten, are they no? Yon's a bonny knock, but it'll no gang; and the napery's by ordnar. Bonny, bairnly braws; it's for the like o' them folk sells the peace of God that passeth understanding; it's for the like o' them, an' maybe no even sae muckle worth, folk daunton God to His face and burn in muckle hell; and it's for that reason the Scripture ca's them, as I read the passage, the accursed thing. Mary, ye girzie,' he interrupted himself to cry with some asperity, 'what for hae ye no put out the twa candlesticks?'[2]

'Why should we need them at high noon?' she asked.

But my uncle was not to be turned from his idea. 'We'll bruik[3] them while we may,' he said; and so two massive candlesticks of wrought silver were added to the table equipage, already so unsuited to that rough sea-side farm.

'She[4] cam' ashore Februar' 10, about ten at nicht,' he went on to me. 'There was nae wind, and a sair run o' sea; and she was in the sook o'

---

[1] Stevenson's portrait of a man whose eyes – the windows to the soul – are stained like old ivory, suggests a man whose soul has grown corrupt and jaded with time

[2] *I am in the body , Yes, in the body , and in the sins of the body , as you yourself food... Beautiful things expensive things that we have there, is not it? The clock there is good, but it does not go , and the hanger is also good ; all good , fine things , things for the people to give up the peace of God , which is higher than reason ; Things for the same and for less than the same people defy the Lord God in the face and burn in hell ; and that's why the Scriptures I've read call them cursed things. Mary, your parlor! Why have you not already put out two candlesticks?*

[3] Use

[4] *She came ashore on February 10, about 10 at night. There was no wind and a horrible run of sea; and she was in the quagmire of the Roost, as I suppose. We'd seen her all day, Rorie and me, beating to the wind. She wasn't a handy craft, I suppose, that Christ-Anna; for she'd neither respond to her wheel nor stay put. A hideous day it was for those men; their hands were never off the rigging – constantly working, and it was deadly cold – too cold too even snow; and yes, they would sometimes get a breath of wind, and off they'd go with the false hope that they'd make it. Dear Heavens! But they had a hideous final day on earth! Any*

the Roost, as I jaloose. We had seen her a' day, Rorie and me, beating to the wind. She wasnae a handy craft, I'm thinking, that *Christ-Anna*; for she would neither steer nor stey wi' them. A sair day they had of it; their hands was never aff the sheets, and it perishin' cauld—ower cauld to snaw; and aye they would get a bit nip o' wind, and awa' again, to pit the emp'y hope into them. Eh, man! but they had a sair day for the last o't! He would have had a prood, prood heart that won ashore upon the back o' that.'

'And were all lost?' I cried. 'God held them!'

'Wheesht!' he said sternly. 'Nane shall pray for the deid on my hearth-stane[1].'

I disclaimed a Popish sense for my ejaculation[2]; and he seemed to accept my disclaimer with unusual facility, and ran on once more upon what had evidently become a favourite subject.

'We[3] fand her in Sandag Bay, Rorie an' me, and a' thae braws in the inside of her. There's a kittle bit, ye see, about Sandag; whiles the sook rins strong for the Merry Men; an' whiles again, when the tide's makin' hard an' ye can hear the Roost blawin' at the far-end of Aros, there comes a back-spang of current straucht into Sandag Bay. Weel, there's the thing that got the grip on the *Christ-Anna*. She but to have come in ram-stam an' stern forrit; for the bows of her are aften under, and the back-side of her is clear at hie-water o' neaps. But, man! the dunt that she cam doon wi' when she

---

man who could have made it to shore would have been a proud, proud man for all their efforts.

[1] *Shut your mouth! No one under my roof will be praying to the dead.*

[2] His uncle is suspicious that Charles might be a Catholic – or Popish – because of this exclamation. The strict Covenanters viewed prayers for the dead as a Catholic heresy (Catholics believe that the baptized, even if evil, can have their salvation purchased from them if the living pray for their release from Purgatory. Protestants don't believe in Purgatory and think that salvation is each man's responsibility – not something that can be prayed for by others – and consider praying for the dead, and especially lighting candles for them, to be idolatry)

[3] *We found her in Sandag Bay, Rorie and I, and oh my – all the beautiful things inside her! There's just a sample of it about Sandag. Sometimes the suction runs strong for the Merry Men, and sometimes, when the tide's rushing in and you can hear the Roost roaring at the far end of Aros, there comes a back-wash of current straight into the Bay. Well, that's what grabbed up the Christ-Anna. She had to come in bow-backwards and stern-forwards; for her bows were often swamped, and the stern stuck out of the water. But, my word! The terrible sound that cracked when she came down hard on the water! Lord save us all! But it's a strange life that a sailor leads – a cold, unlucky life. Many's the time that I've pictured myself in the great deep; and why the Lord should have made those weird waters is more than I could ever hope to understand. He made the valleys and pastures, the lovely green fields, the wholesome countryside...*

struck! Lord save us a'! but it's an unco life to be a sailor—a cauld, wanchancy life. Mony's the gliff I got mysel' in the great deep; and why the Lord should hae made yon unco water is mair than ever I could win to understand. He made the vales and the pastures, the bonny green yaird, the halesome, canty land—

And now they shout and sing to Thee,
For Thou hast made them glad,

as the Psalms say in the metrical version. No[1] that I would preen my faith to that clink neither; but it's bonny, and easier to mind. "Who go to sea in ships," they hae't again—

And in
Great waters trading be,
Within the deep these men God's works
And His great wonders see.

Weel[2], it's easy sayin' sae. Maybe Dauvit wasnae very weel acquant wi' the sea. But, troth, if it wasnae prentit in the Bible, I wad whiles be temp'it to think it wasnae the Lord, but the muckle, black deil that made the sea. There's naething good comes oot o't but the fish; an' the spentacle o' God riding on the tempest, to be shure, whilk would be what Dauvit was likely ettling at. But, man, they were sair wonders that God showed to the *Christ-Anna*—wonders, do I ca' them? Judgments, rather: judgments in the mirk nicht among the draygons o' the deep. And their souls—to think o' that—their souls, man, maybe no prepared! The sea—a muckle yett to hell!'

I observed, as my uncle spoke, that his voice was unnaturally moved and his manner unwontedly demonstrative. He leaned forward at these last words, for example, and touched me on the knee with his spread fingers, looking up into my face with a certain pallor, and I could see that his eyes shone with a deep-seated fire, and that the lines about his mouth were drawn and tremulous.

Even the entrance of Rorie, and the beginning of our meal, did not detach him from his train of thought beyond a moment. He condescended, indeed, to ask me some questions as to my success at college, but I thought

---

[1] *Not that I would dare base my faith on that false hope either, but it's lovely and easier to deal with. "Who go to sea in ships," they say again...*

[2] *Well, it's easy to say that. Maybe David wasn't well acquainted with the sea. But, it's surely true, if it wasn't printed there in the Holy Word, I would sometimes be tempted to think it wasn't God at all, but the great, black Devil that made the seas. There's nothing good that comes from them other than fish; and the idea of God riding the tempest was probably what David was getting at. But, my word, there are horrible wonder that God revealed to the Christ-Anna – wonders, I say? No – more like judgments; judgments in the black night among the demons of the deep. And their souls – just imagine! – their souls, I say! – might not have been saved! The sea: it's a great gateway to Hell itself*

it was with half his mind; and even in his extempore grace, which was, as usual, long and wandering, I could find the trace of his preoccupation, praying, as he did, that God would 'remember[1] in mercy fower puir, feckless, fiddling, sinful creatures here by their lee-lane beside the great and dowie waters.'

Soon there came an interchange of speeches between him and Rorie.

'Was it there?' asked my uncle.

'Ou, ay[2]!' said Rorie.

I observed that they both spoke in a manner of aside, and with some show of embarrassment, and that Mary herself appeared to colour, and looked down on her plate. Partly to show my knowledge, and so relieve the party from an awkward strain, partly because I was curious, I pursued the subject.

'You mean the fish?' I asked.

'Whatten fish[3]?' cried my uncle. 'Fish, quo' he! Fish! Your een are fu' o' fatness, man; your heid dozened wi' carnal leir. Fish! it's a bogle!'

He spoke with great vehemence, as though angry; and perhaps I was not very willing to be put down so shortly, for young men are disputatious. At least I remember I retorted hotly, crying out upon childish superstitions.

'And[4] ye come frae the College!' sneered Uncle Gordon. 'Gude kens what they learn folk there; it's no muckle service onyway. Do ye think, man, that

---

[1] *Remember with mercy these four, pour, incompetent, idle, sinful creatures here by their [house on the side of a hill protected from the wind] beside the great and melancholy waters*

[2] *Amen*

[3] *What kind of fish? Fish, you say! Fish your eyes are full of gluttony, man; your hide spoiled with carnal teachings. Fish! No, it's a demon!*

[4] *And you come from the College! God knows what they teach folks there; it's no great service at any rate. Do you think, boy, that there's nothing in that bitter wilderness of a world that was out there, with the sea grasses growing and the sea beasts fighting, and the sun glinting down into it day in and out? No – the sea's like the land but fearsomer. If there's folks ashore there's folks in the sea – dead perhaps, but folks nonetheless; and as for land devils, there's none of them remotely like sea devils. There's no great harm in them, when it's all said and done. Long ago, when I was a kid in the Lowlands, I mind there was an old, bald spirit in the Peewie Moss. I got a glimpse of him myself, siting on his haunches in a hollow, as gray as a tombstone. And by my word, he was a hideous toad. But he didn't bother a soul. No doubt, if any that was a reprobate, any that the Lord hated, had gone by there with his sin still on his heart, no doubt that creature would have leaped up to spirit him away. But there's devil's in the deep sea that would make a captive out of a good Christian! Mark my words: if you had gone down with the poor boys of the Christ-Anne, you would know by now the mercy of the seas. If you had sailed on it for as long as I have, you would despise the*

there's naething in a' yon saut wilderness o' a world oot wast there, wi' the sea grasses growin', an' the sea beasts fechtin', an' the sun glintin' down into it, day by day? Na; the sea's like the land, but fearsomer. If there's folk ashore, there's folk in the sea—deid they may be, but they're folk whatever; and as for deils, there's nane that's like the sea deils. There's no sae muckle harm in the land deils, when a's said and done. Lang syne, when I was a callant in the south country, I mind there was an auld, bald bogle in the Peewie Moss. I got a glisk o' him mysel', sittin' on his hunkers in a hag, as gray's a tombstane. An', troth, he was a fearsome-like taed. But he steered naebody. Nae doobt, if ane that was a reprobate, ane the Lord hated, had gane by there wi' his sin still upon his stamach, nae doobt the creature would hae lowped upo' the likes o' him. But there's deils in the deep sea would yoke on a communicant! Eh, sirs, if ye had gane doon wi' the puir lads in the *Christ-Anna*, ye would ken by now the mercy o' the seas. If ye had sailed it for as lang as me, ye would hate the thocht of it as I do. If ye had but used the een God gave ye, ye would hae learned the wickedness o' that fause, saut, cauld, bullering creature, and of a' that's in it by the Lord's permission: labsters an' partans, an' sic like, howking in the deid; muckle, gutsy, blawing whales; an' fish—the hale clan o' them—cauld-wamed, blind-eed uncanny ferlies. O, sirs,' he cried, 'the horror—the horror o' the sea!'

We were all somewhat staggered by this outburst; and the speaker himself, after that last hoarse apostrophe, appeared to sink gloomily into his own thoughts. But Rorie, who was greedy of superstitious lore, recalled him to the subject by a question.

'You will not ever have seen a teevil of the sea?' he asked.

'No clearly[1],' replied the other. 'I misdoobt if a mere man could see ane clearly and conteenue in the body. I hae sailed wi' a lad—they ca'd him

---

thought of it as I do. If you had but used the eyes God stuck in your head, you would have learned the wickedness of that false, bitter, cold, gurgling creature, and all that's in it by the Lord's permission: lobsters and crabs and the like, burrowing in corpses; great, gusty, blowing whales and fish – the whole clan of them – cold-blooded, blind-eyed, uncanny wonders. O sirs! The horror! The horror of the sea!

[1] Not clearly. I doubt that a mere man could see one clearly and live. I have sailed with a lad – they called him Sandy Gabart; he saw one, sure enough, and sure enough it was the end of him. We were seven days out of the Clyde River – a hard job of it we had – going north with grains and fine goods for the Macleod Clan. We had got in over near under the Cutchull'ns, and had just gone about and were off on a long tack, we thought would maybe hold as far as Copnahow. I was steering the wheel that night; a moon smothered in mist; a fine-going breeze upon the water, but not steady; an – what none of us like to hear – another wind wailing overhead among the fearsome old stone crags of the Cutchull'ns. Well, Sandy was forward with the jib sheet; we couldn't see him because of the

Sandy Gabart; he saw ane, shure eneueh, an' shure eneueh it was the end of him. We were seeven days oot frae the Clyde—a sair wark we had had—gaun north wi' seeds an' braws an' things for the Macleod. We had got in ower near under the Cutchull'ns, an' had just gane about by soa, an' were off on a lang tack, we thocht would maybe hauld as far's Copnahow. I mind the nicht weel; a mune smoored wi' mist; a fine gaun breeze upon the water, but no steedy; an'—what nane o' us likit to hear—anither wund gurlin' owerheid, amang thae fearsome, auld stane craigs o' the Cutchull'ns. Weel, Sandy was forrit wi' the jib sheet; we couldnae see him for the mains'l, that had just begude to draw, when a' at ance he gied a skirl. I luffed for my life, for I thocht we were ower near Soa; but na, it wasnae that, it was puir Sandy Gabart's deid skreigh, or near hand, for he was deid in half an hour. A't he could tell was that a sea deil, or sea bogle, or sea spenster, or sic-like, had clum up by the bowsprit, an' gi'en him ae cauld, uncanny look. An', or the life was oot o' Sandy's body, we kent weel what the thing betokened, and why the wund gurled in the taps o' the Cutchull'ns; for doon it cam'—a wund do I ca' it! it was the wund o' the Lord's anger—an' a' that nicht we foucht like men dementit, and the niest that we kenned we were ashore in Loch Uskevagh, an' the cocks were crawin' in Benbecula.'

'It will have been a merman,' Rorie said.

'A merman!' screamed my uncle with immeasurable scorn. 'Auld wives' clavers! There's nae sic things as mermen[1].'

'But what was the creature like?' I asked.

'What like was it? Gude forbid that we suld ken what like it was! It had a kind of a heid upon it—man could say nae mair[2].'

Then Rorie, smarting under the affront, told several tales of mermen, mermaids, and sea-horses that had come ashore upon the islands and

---

mainsail, that had just begun to be drawn, when all at once he gave a shriek. I jumped for my life, for I thought we were over near Soa; but no, it wasn't that, it was poor Sandy Gabart's dying scream – or near at hand, for he was dead in half an hour. All that he could tell was that a sea devil, or sea bogey, or sea witch or suchlike had climbed up by the bowsprit, and given him one cold, bizaare look. And before the life was out of Sandy's body, we knew well what the thing foretold, and why the wind gurgled in the tops of the Cutchull'ns; for down in came – a wind do I call it? It was the wind of the Lord's anger – and all that night we fought like men demented, and the nearest that we knew we were ashore in Loch Uskevagh, and the cocks were crowing in the Benbecula

[1] *Old lady gossip! There's no such things as mermen*

[2] *God forbid that we should know what kind of a thing it was! It had a kind of head upon it – the man could say nothing else about it*

attacked the crews of boats upon the sea[1]; and my uncle, in spite of his incredulity, listened with uneasy interest.

'Aweel, aweel,' he said, 'it may be sae; I may be wrang; but I find nae word o' mermen in the Scriptures[2].'

'And you will find nae word of Aros Roost, maybe,' objected Rorie, and his argument appeared to carry weight.

When dinner was over, my uncle carried me forth with him to a bank behind the house. It was a very hot and quiet afternoon; scarce a ripple anywhere upon the sea, nor any voice but the familiar voice of sheep and gulls; and perhaps in consequence of this repose in nature, my kinsman showed himself more rational and tranquil than before. He spoke evenly and almost cheerfully of my career, with every now and then a reference to the lost ship or the treasures it had brought to Aros. For my part, I listened to him in a sort of trance, gazing with all my heart on that remembered scene, and drinking gladly the sea-air and the smoke of peats that had been lit by Mary.

Perhaps an hour had passed when my uncle, who had all the while been covertly gazing on the surface of the little bay, rose to his feet and bade me follow his example. Now I should say that the great run of tide at the south-west end of Aros exercises a perturbing influence round all the coast. In Sandag Bay, to the south, a strong current runs at certain periods of the flood and ebb respectively; but in this northern bay—Aros Bay, as it is called—where the house stands and on which my uncle was now gazing, the only sign of disturbance is towards the end of the ebb, and even then it is too slight to be remarkable. When there is any swell, nothing can be seen at all; but when it is calm, as it often is, there appear certain strange, undecipherable marks—sea-runes, as we may name them—on the glassy surface of the bay. The like is common in a thousand places on the coast; and many a boy must have amused himself as I did, seeking to read in them some reference to himself or those he loved. It was to these marks that my uncle now directed my attention, struggling, as he did so, with an evident reluctance.

---

[1] This might surprise modern readers. We have been so enchanted by H. C. Andersen's "The Little Mermaid" that we have forgotten the mythology of merpeople, who were said to use lust, sweet music, and seduction to lure men to their deaths, and who delighted in causing destruction and misery in the human race. More akin to evil fairies and the Greek Sirens, these creatures were viewed as monsters before the romanticism of Andersen and Disney

[2] Our man here is a devoted literalist, expecting to find answers to everything in the Bible. He would likely believe in a Young Earth chronology and might even doubt the roundness of the globe

36

'Do¹ ye see yon scart upo' the water?' he inquired; 'yon ane wast the gray stane? Ay? Weel, it'll no be like a letter, wull it?'

'Certainly it is,' I replied. 'I have often remarked it. It is like a C.'

He heaved a sigh as if heavily disappointed with my answer, and then added below his breath: 'Ay, for the *Christ-Anna*.'

'I used to suppose, sir, it was for myself,' said I; 'for my name is Charles.'

'And² so ye saw't afore?', he ran on, not heeding my remark. 'Weel, weel, but that's unco strange. Maybe, it's been there waitin', as a man wad say, through a' the weary ages. Man, but that's awfu'.' And then, breaking off: 'Ye'll no see anither, will ye?' he asked.

'Yes,' said I. 'I see another very plainly, near the Ross side, where the road comes down—an M.'

'An M,' he repeated very low; and then, again after another pause: 'An' what wad ye make o' that?' he inquired.

'I had always thought it to mean Mary, sir,' I answered, growing somewhat red, convinced as I was in my own mind that I was on the threshold of a decisive explanation³.

But we were each following his own train of thought to the exclusion of the other's. My uncle once more paid no attention to my words; only hung his head and held his peace; and I might have been led to fancy that he had not heard me, if his next speech had not contained a kind of echo from my own.

'I would say naething o' thae clavers⁴ to Mary,' he observed, and began to walk forward.

There is a belt of turf along the side of Aros Bay, where walking is easy; and it was along this that I silently followed my silent kinsman. I was perhaps a little disappointed at having lost so good an opportunity to declare my love; but I was at the same time far more deeply exercised at the change that had befallen my uncle. He was never an ordinary, never, in the strict sense, an amiable, man; but there was nothing in even the worst that I had known of him before, to prepare me for so strange a transformation. It was impossible to close the eyes against one fact; that he had, as the saying goes, something on his mind; and as I mentally ran over the different words which might be represented by the letter M—misery, mercy, marriage,

---

¹ *Do you see all that scribbling on the water? There's one west of the grey stone? Yeah? Does it seem like a letter?*

² *And so you've seen it before? Well, well... my word, that's quite strange. Maybe it's been there waiting, as a man would say, through all the weary ages. Man but that's an awful thought... You wouldn't happen to see another, would you?*

³ Which is to say, he is nervous that admitting that he took these talismanic letters to mean "Charles and Mary" will effectively be outing his secret love for his cousin

⁴ *If I were you, I wouldn't say anything about this foolish chatter to Mary*

money, and the like—I was arrested with a sort of start by the word murder[1]. I was still considering the ugly sound and fatal meaning of the word, when the direction of our walk brought us to a point from which a view was to be had to either side, back towards Aros Bay and homestead, and forward on the ocean, dotted to the north with isles, and lying to the southward blue and open to the sky. There my guide came to a halt, and stood staring for awhile on that expanse. Then he turned to me and laid a hand on my arm.

'Ye think there's naething there?' he said, pointing with his pipe; and then cried out aloud, with a kind of exultation: 'I'll tell ye, man! The deid are down there—thick like rattons[2]!'

He turned at once, and, without another word, we retraced our steps to the house of Aros.

I was eager to be alone with Mary; yet it was not till after supper, and then but for a short while, that I could have a word with her. I lost no time beating about the bush, but spoke out plainly what was on my mind.

'Mary,' I said, 'I have not come to Aros without a hope. If that should prove well founded, we may all leave and go somewhere else, secure of daily bread and comfort; secure, perhaps, of something far beyond that, which it would seem extravagant in me to promise[3]. But there's a hope that lies nearer to my heart than money.' And at that I paused. 'You can guess fine what that is, Mary,' I said. She looked away from me in silence, and that was small encouragement, but I was not to be put off. 'All my days I have thought the world of you,' I continued; 'the time goes on and I think always the more of you; I could not think to be happy or hearty in my life without you: you are the apple of my eye.' Still she looked away, and said never a

---

[1] It is worth pausing to note the obvious influence that "The Scarlet Letter" has had on this imagery. In that book, a supernatural A – once seen shining in the night sky, and later as a stigmata on the chest of one of the characters – is thought to represent different things by different people. At its core, the letter refers to the sin of Adultery, but others interpret it to mean Angel and Able depending on what the viewer is expecting to see. Likewise, the C and M represent a sort of Rorschach test that the characters project their secrets onto: Charles' secret affection for Mary, and his uncle's potential to commit Murder for the gain of Money

[2] *The dead are down there – swarming thick like rats!*

[3] "Daily bread" is one of the phrases used in the Lord's Prayer, where Christ teaches his followers to ask God to provide for their daily lives. It is implied that salvation is what truly sustains men, that it is "something far beyond that." With his rhetoric, Charles is implying to this devoutly religious girl – in a language that will be immediately understood to her – that she is his salvation

word; but I thought I saw that her hands shook. 'Mary,' I cried in fear, 'do ye no like me[1]?'

'O, Charlie man,' she said, 'is this a time to speak of it? Let me be, a while; let me be the way I am; it'll not be you that loses by the waiting!'

I made out by her voice that she was nearly weeping, and this put me out of any thought but to compose her. 'Mary Ellen,' I said, 'say no more; I did not come to trouble you: your way shall be mine, and your time too; and you have told me all I wanted. Only just this one thing more: what ails you?'

She owned it was her father, but would enter into no particulars, only shook her head, and said he was not well and not like himself, and it was a great pity. She knew nothing of the wreck. 'I havenae been near it,' said she. 'What for would I go near it, Charlie lad? The poor souls are gone to their account long syne; and I would just have wished they had ta'en their gear with them—poor souls[2]!'

This was scarcely any great encouragement for me to tell her of the *Espirito Santo*; yet I did so, and at the very first word she cried out in surprise. 'There was a man at Grisapol,' she said, 'in the month of May—a little, yellow, black-avised[3] body, they tell me, with gold rings upon his fingers, and a beard; and he was speiring[4] high and low for that same ship.'

It was towards the end of April that I had been given these papers to sort out by Dr. Robertson: and it came suddenly back upon my mind that they were thus prepared for a Spanish historian, or a man calling himself such, who had come with high recommendations to the Principal, on a mission of inquiry as to the dispersion of the great Armada. Putting one thing with another, I fancied that the visitor 'with the gold rings upon his fingers' might be the same with Dr. Robertson's historian from Madrid. If that were so, he would be more likely after treasure for himself than information for a learned society. I made up my mind, I should lose no time over my undertaking; and if the ship lay sunk in Sandag Bay, as perhaps both he and I supposed, it should not be for the advantage of this ringed adventurer, but

---

[1] The moment is very tender and sweet: at this moment of vulnerability, the Edinburgh-educated student breaks for a brief time into his childhood Scots brogue, saying "do ye no like me" rather than the standard "do you not care for me"

[2] *I haven't been near it… Why would I even want to, Charlie dear? The poor souls have gone to their eternal destination long ago; and I only wish they'd have taken their things with them – poor souls*

[3] *Swarthy.* Literally "dark-visaged." Combined with the tones of yellow, we can assume that his complexion is what we would most likely call "olive" or Mediterranean

[4] *Searching*

for Mary and myself, and for the good, old, honest, kindly family of the Darnaways.

Chapter III. Land and Sea in Sandag Bay

I was early afoot next morning; and as soon as I had a bite to eat, set forth upon a tour of exploration. Something in my heart distinctly told me that I should find the ship of the Armada; and although I did not give way entirely to such hopeful thoughts, I was still very light in spirits and walked upon air. Aros is a very rough islet, its surface strewn with great rocks and shaggy with fernland heather; and my way lay almost north and south across the highest knoll; and though the whole distance was inside of two miles it took more time and exertion than four upon a level road. Upon the summit, I paused. Although not very high—not three hundred feet, as I think—it yet outtops all the neighbouring lowlands of the Ross, and commands a great view of sea and islands. The sun, which had been up some time, was already hot upon my neck; the air was listless and thundery, although purely clear; away over the north-west, where the isles lie thickliest congregated, some half-a-dozen small and ragged clouds hung together in a covey; and the head of Ben Kyaw wore, not merely a few streamers, but a solid hood of vapour. There was a threat in the weather. The sea, it is true, was smooth like glass: even the Roost was but a seam on that wide mirror, and the Merry Men no more than caps of foam; but to my eye and ear, so long familiar with these places, the sea also seemed to lie uneasily; a sound of it, like a long sigh, mounted to me where I stood; and, quiet as it was, the Roost itself appeared to be revolving mischief. For I ought to say that all we dwellers in these parts attributed, if not prescience, at least a quality of warning, to that strange and dangerous creature of the tides.

I hurried on, then, with the greater speed, and had soon descended the slope of Aros to the part that we call Sandag Bay. It is a pretty large piece of water compared with the size of the isle; well sheltered from all but the prevailing wind; sandy and shoal and bounded by low sand-hills to the west, but to the eastward lying several fathoms deep along a ledge of rocks. It is upon that side that, at a certain time each flood, the current mentioned by my uncle sets so strong into the bay; a little later, when the Roost begins to work higher, an undertow runs still more strongly in the reverse direction; and it is the action of this last, as I suppose, that has scoured that part so deep. Nothing is to be seen out of Sandag Bay, but one small segment of the horizon and, in heavy weather, the breakers flying high over a deep sea reef.

From half-way down the hill, I had perceived the wreck of February last, a brig[1] of considerable tonnage, lying, with her back broken, high and dry on the east corner of the sands; and I was making directly towards it, and already almost on the margin of the turf, when my eyes were suddenly arrested by a spot, cleared of fern and heather, and marked by one of those long, low, and almost human-looking mounds that we see so commonly in graveyards. I stopped like a man shot. Nothing had been said to me of any dead man or interment on the island; Rorie, Mary, and my uncle had all equally held their peace; of her at least, I was certain that she must be ignorant; and yet here, before my eyes, was proof indubitable of the fact. Here was a grave; and I had to ask myself, with a chill, what manner of man lay there in his last sleep, awaiting the signal of the Lord in that solitary, sea-beat resting-place? My mind supplied no answer but what I feared to entertain. Shipwrecked, at least, he must have been; perhaps, like the old Armada mariners, from some far and rich land over-sea; or perhaps one of my own race, perishing within eyesight of the smoke of home. I stood awhile uncovered[2] by his side, and I could have desired that it had lain in our religion[3] to put up some prayer for that unhappy stranger, or, in the old classic way, outwardly to honour his misfortune[4]. I knew, although his bones lay there, a part of Aros, till the trumpet sounded, his imperishable soul was forth and far away, among the raptures of the everlasting Sabbath or the pangs of hell; and yet my mind misgave me even

---

[1] Large sailing ship with two fully rigged masts (having square, perpendicular sails), and a gaff sail on the mainmast

[2] With his hat respectfully doffed

[3] Again, Scottish Calvinists were loath to show the dead any form of reverence that approached what they considered Catholicism's idolatry of saints and the baptized dead

[4] The "old classic way" is, surprisingly enough, a reference to tombstones – perhaps shocking for modern readers, who would hardly consider a simple gravestone to be irreligious or heretical, but the staunchest Calvinists would destroy gravemarkers which they considered to be idolatrous

with a fear, that perhaps he was near me where I stood, guarding his sepulchre, and lingering on the scene of his unhappy fate.

Certainly it was with a spirit somewhat over-shadowed that I turned away from the grave to the hardly less melancholy spectacle of the wreck. Her stem was above the first arc of the flood; she was broken in two a little abaft the foremast[1]—though indeed she had none, both masts having broken short in her disaster; and as the pitch of the beach was very sharp and sudden, and the bows lay many feet below the stern[2], the fracture gaped widely open, and you could see right through her poor hull upon the farther side. Her name was much defaced, and I could not make out clearly whether she was called *Christiania*, after the Norwegian city, or *Christiana*, after the good woman, Christian's wife, in that old book the 'Pilgrim's Progress[3].' By her build she was a foreign ship, but I was not certain of her nationality. She had been painted green, but the colour was faded and weathered, and the paint peeling off in strips. The wreck of the mainmast[4] lay alongside, half buried in sand. She was a forlorn sight, indeed, and I could not look without emotion at the bits of rope that still hung about her, so often handled of yore by shouting seamen; or the little scuttle[5] where they had passed up and down to their affairs; or that poor noseless angel of a figure-head[6] that had dipped into so many running billows.

I do not know whether it came most from the ship or from the grave, but I fell into some melancholy scruples, as I stood there, leaning with one hand against the battered timbers. The homelessness of men and even of inanimate vessels, cast away upon strange shores, came strongly in upon my mind. To make a profit of such pitiful misadventures seemed an unmanly and a sordid act; and I began to think of my then quest as of something sacrilegious in its nature. But when I remembered Mary, I took heart again. My uncle would never consent to an imprudent[7] marriage, nor would she, as I was persuaded, wed without his full approval. It behoved me, then,

---

[1] Slightly to the rear of the front mast
[2] The ship is on a steep incline, with its rear rising high above its front
[3] Written by the English Baptist John Bunyan, *Pilgrim's Progress* is an allegorical story of faith, doubt, and persecution which follows Christian on his journey to the Celestial City (Heaven) where he is beset by monsters and other allegorical tribulations symbolizing sin, temptation, and suffering. He is later followed, after safely arriving, by his wife Christiania
[4] The rear mast, which was the larger of the two
[5] A small hatch on the deck
[6] A wooden statue fastened to the front of the ship under the bowsprit. It was seen as a sort of mascot and talisman – the ship's persona – and was often made to resemble its namesake (in this case a female angel named Christiania, Christ-Anna, or Christina)
[7] One without a promise of financial stability

to be up and doing for my wife; and I thought with a laugh how long it was since that great sea-castle, the *Espirito Santo*, had left her bones in Sandag Bay, and how weak it would be to consider rights so long extinguished and misfortunes so long forgotten in the process of time.

I had my theory of where to seek for her remains. The set of the current and the soundings both pointed to the east side of the bay under the ledge of rocks. If she had been lost in Sandag Bay, and if, after these centuries, any portion of her held together, it was there that I should find it. The water deepens, as I have said, with great rapidity, and even close along-side the rocks several fathoms may be found. As I walked upon the edge I could see far and wide over the sandy bottom of the bay; the sun shone clear and green and steady in the deeps; the bay seemed rather like a great transparent crystal, as one sees them in a lapidary's[1] shop; there was naught to show that it was water but an internal trembling, a hovering within of sun-glints and netted shadows, and now and then a faint lap and a dying bubble round the edge. The shadows of the rocks lay out for some distance at their feet, so that my own shadow, moving, pausing, and stooping on the top of that, reached sometimes half across the bay. It was above all in this belt of shadows that I hunted for the *Espirito Santo*; since it was there the undertow ran strongest, whether in or out. Cool as the whole water seemed this broiling day, it looked, in that part, yet cooler, and had a mysterious invitation for the eyes. Peer as I pleased, however, I could see nothing but a few fishes or a bush of sea-tangle, and here and there a lump of rock that had fallen from above and now lay separate on the sandy floor. Twice did I pass from one end to the other of the rocks, and in the whole distance I could see nothing of the wreck, nor any place but one where it was possible for it to be. This was a large terrace in five fathoms of water, raised off the surface of the sand to a considerable height, and looking from above like a mere outgrowth of the rocks on which I walked. It was one mass of great sea-tangles like a grove, which prevented me judging of its nature, but in shape and size it bore some likeness to a vessel's hull. At least it was my best chance. If the *Espirito Santo* lay not there under the tangles, it lay nowhere at all in Sandag Bay; and I prepared to put the question to the proof, once and for all, and either go back to Aros a rich man or cured for ever of my dreams of wealth.

I stripped to the skin, and stood on the extreme margin with my hands clasped, irresolute. The bay at that time was utterly quiet; there was no sound but from a school of porpoises somewhere out of sight behind the point; yet a certain fear withheld me on the threshold of my venture. Sad sea-feelings, scraps of my uncle's superstitions, thoughts of the dead, of the grave, of the old broken ships, drifted through my mind. But the strong sun

---

[1] A gemstone cutter; a jeweler

upon my shoulders warmed me to the heart, and I stooped forward and plunged into the sea.

It was all that I could do to catch a trail of the sea-tangle that grew so thickly on the terrace; but once so far anchored I secured myself by grasping a whole armful of these thick and slimy stalks, and, planting my feet against the edge, I looked around me. On all sides the clear sand stretched forth unbroken; it came to the foot of the rocks, scoured into the likeness of an alley in a garden by the action of the tides; and before me, for as far as I could see, nothing was visible but the same many-folded sand upon the sun-bright bottom of the bay. Yet the terrace to which I was then holding was as thick with strong sea-growths as a tuft of heather, and the cliff from which it bulged hung draped below the water-line with brown lianas. In this complexity of forms, all swaying together in the current, things were hard to be distinguished; and I was still uncertain whether my feet were pressed upon the natural rock or upon the timbers of the Armada treasure-ship, when the whole tuft of tangle came away in my hand, and in an instant I was on the surface, and the shores of the bay and the bright water swam before my eyes in a glory of crimson.

I clambered back upon the rocks, and threw the plant of tangle at my feet. Something at the same moment rang sharply, like a falling coin. I stooped, and there, sure enough, crusted with the red rust, there lay an iron shoe-buckle. The sight of this poor human relic thrilled me to the heart, but not with hope nor fear, only with a desolate melancholy. I held it in my hand, and the thought of its owner appeared before me like the presence of an actual man. His weather-beaten face, his sailor's hands, his sea-voice hoarse with singing at the capstan, the very foot that had once worn that buckle and trod so much along the swerving decks—the whole human fact of him, as a creature like myself, with hair and blood and seeing eyes, haunted me in that sunny, solitary place, not like a spectre, but like some friend whom I had basely injured. Was the great treasure ship indeed below there, with her guns and chain and treasure, as she had sailed from Spain; her decks a garden for the seaweed, her cabin a breeding place for fish, soundless but for the dredging water, motionless but for the waving of the tangle upon her battlements—that old, populous, sea-riding castle, now a reef in Sandag Bay? Or, as I thought it likelier, was this a waif[1] from the disaster of the foreign brig—was this shoe-buckle bought but the other day and worn by a man of my own period in the world's history, hearing the same news from day to day, thinking the same thoughts, praying, perhaps, in the same temple with myself? However it was, I was assailed with dreary thoughts; my uncle's words, 'the dead are down there,' echoed in my ears; and though I determined to dive once more, it was with a strong repugnance that I stepped forward to the margin of the rocks.

---

[1] Stray

A great change passed at that moment over the appearance of the bay. It was no more that clear, visible interior, like a house roofed with glass, where the green, submarine sunshine slept so stilly. A breeze, I suppose, had flawed the surface, and a sort of trouble and blackness filled its bosom, where flashes of light and clouds of shadow tossed confusedly together. Even the terrace below obscurely rocked and quivered. It seemed a graver thing to venture on this place of ambushes; and when I leaped into the sea the second time it was with a quaking in my soul.

I secured myself as at first, and groped among the waving tangle. All that met my touch was cold and soft and gluey. The thicket was alive with crabs and lobsters, trundling to and fro lopsidedly, and I had to harden my heart against the horror of their carrion neighbourhood. On all sides I could feel the grain and the clefts of hard, living stone; no planks, no iron, not a sign of any wreck; the *Espirito Santo* was not there. I remember I had almost a sense of relief in my disappointment[1], and I was about ready to leave go, when something happened that sent me to the surface with my heart in my mouth. I had already stayed somewhat late over my explorations; the current was freshening with the change of the tide, and Sandag Bay was no longer a safe place for a single swimmer. Well, just at the last moment there came a sudden flush of current, dredging through the tangles like a wave. I lost one hold, was flung sprawling on my side, and, instinctively grasping for a fresh support, my fingers closed on something hard and cold. I think I knew at that moment what it was. At least I instantly left hold of the tangle, leaped for the surface, and clambered out next moment on the friendly rocks with the bone of a man's leg in my grasp.

Mankind is a material creature, slow to think and dull to perceive connections. The grave, the wreck of the brig, and the rusty shoe-buckle were surely plain advertisements[2]. A child might have read their dismal story, and yet it was not until I touched that actual piece of mankind that the full horror of the charnel ocean burst upon my spirit. I laid the bone beside the buckle, picked up my clothes, and ran as I was along the rocks towards the human shore. I could not be far enough from the spot; no fortune was vast enough to tempt me back again. The bones of the drowned dead should henceforth roll undisturbed by me, whether on tangle or minted gold. But as soon as I trod the good earth again, and had covered

---

[1] He is clearly morally conflicted with what he considers to be grave robbing – profaning this holy sleeping place of drowned sailors with his vulgar greed for dead men's gold – and like any man who half-heartedly begins to do something he knows is wrong, only to find his way blocked, he is more relieved by the obstruction than disappointed

[2] And the advertisement is "murder"

my nakedness against the sun[1], I knelt down over against the ruins of the brig, and out of the fulness of my heart prayed long and passionately for all poor souls upon the sea. A generous prayer is never presented in vain; the petition may be refused, but the petitioner is always, I believe, rewarded by some gracious visitation. The horror, at least, was lifted from my mind; I could look with calm of spirit on that great bright creature, God's ocean; and as I set off homeward up the rough sides of Aros, nothing remained of my concern beyond a deep determination to meddle no more with the spoils of wrecked vessels or the treasures of the dead[2].

I was already some way up the hill before I paused to breathe and look behind me. The sight that met my eyes was doubly strange.

For, first, the storm that I had foreseen was now advancing with almost tropical rapidity[3]. The whole surface of the sea had been dulled from its conspicuous brightness to an ugly hue of corrugated lead; already in the distance the white waves, the 'skipper's daughters,' had begun to flee before a breeze that was still insensible on Aros; and already along the curve of Sandag Bay there was a splashing run of sea that I could hear from where I stood. The change upon the sky was even more remarkable. There had begun to arise out of the south-west a huge and solid continent of scowling cloud; here and there, through rents in its contexture, the sun still poured a sheaf of spreading rays; and here and there, from all its edges, vast inky streamers lay forth along the yet unclouded sky. The menace was express and imminent. Even as I gazed, the sun was blotted out. At any moment the tempest might fall upon Aros in its might.

The suddenness of this change of weather so fixed my eyes on heaven that it was some seconds before they alighted on the bay, mapped out below my feet, and robbed a moment later of the sun. The knoll which I had just surmounted overflanked a little amphitheatre of lower hillocks sloping towards the sea, and beyond that the yellow arc of beach and the whole extent of Sandag Bay. It was a scene on which I had often looked down, but where I had never before beheld a human figure. I had but just turned my

---

[1] This suggests Adam, the first man, who first became aware of his nakedness (read: shame) after disobeying God and eating the fruit of Knowledge of Good and Evil. Essentially, Stevenson implies that Charles has learned some hidden secret which now causes him to lose part of his innocence and become shocked and disenchanted with his idealistic worldview: his uncle, he suspects, the devout Calvinist, is a murderer

[2] Unlike his uncle, Charles' brief encounter with death is enough to trump his lust for wealth; he understands the cost of the loss in terms of human suffering, and views the search for gold as sacriligous to the memory of the lost men

[3] Storms in the tropics – unlike those in the north – can come out of a purely blue sky in a matter of moments. Storms in, say Scotland, are presaged for days by gloomy, darkening weather

back upon it and left it empty, and my wonder may be fancied when I saw a boat and several men in that deserted spot. The boat was lying by the rocks. A pair of fellows, bareheaded, with their sleeves rolled up, and one with a boathook, kept her with difficulty to her moorings for the current was growing brisker every moment. A little way off upon the ledge two men in black clothes[1], whom I judged to be superior in rank, laid their heads together over some task which at first I did not understand, but a second after I had made it out—they were taking bearings with the compass; and just then I saw one of them unroll a sheet of paper and lay his finger down, as though identifying features in a map. Meanwhile a third was walking to and fro, polling among the rocks and peering over the edge into the water. While I was still watching them with the stupefaction of surprise, my mind hardly yet able to work on what my eyes reported, this third person suddenly stooped and summoned his companions with a cry so loud that it reached my ears upon the hill. The others ran to him, even dropping the compass in their hurry, and I could see the bone and the shoe-buckle going from hand to hand, causing the most unusual gesticulations of surprise and interest. Just then I could hear the seamen crying from the boat, and saw them point westward to that cloud continent which was ever the more rapidly unfurling its blackness over heaven. The others seemed to consult; but the danger was too pressing to be braved, and they bundled into the boat carrying my relics with them, and set forth out of the bay with all speed of oars.

I made no more ado about the matter, but turned and ran for the house. Whoever these men were, it was fit my uncle should be instantly informed. It was not then altogether too late in the day for a descent of the Jacobites[2]; and may be Prince Charlie[3], whom I knew my uncle to detest,

---

[1] The traditional color of choice for scholars, whether academic or clerical

[2] The Jacobites were a faction who supported the lineage of King James II (Jacobus being Latin for "James"), the Catholic monarch who was ousted by the combined forces of Protestants: Anglicans, Puritans, Presbyterians, and other dissenters, in the Glorious Revolution of 1688. The Protestant William of Orange was brought over from Holland, and he and his wife Mary, James' daughter. James' descendents continued to claim that they were the rightful heirs to the throne, even going so far as to invade Scotland in 1715 and 1745 only to be repulsed and defeated by the Hanoverian armies of George I and George II. The Catholic Jacobites were the scourge of devout Calvinists like Charles' uncle

[3] Bonnie Prince Charlie was James II's grandson, and the heir to the Jacobite throne. In 1745 he left his exile in France, famously landing in Scotland in a small boat (hence the reference), and quickly built an army to occupy Scotland, invade England, and dethrone George II. The Prince's campaign was initially very successful, winning several victories over the British, but it hit a few snags as the Duke of Cumberland's army marched north to meet him. The scales tipped at

was one of the three superiors whom I had seen upon the rock. Yet as I ran, leaping from rock to rock, and turned the matter loosely in my mind, this theory grew ever the longer the less welcome to my reason. The compass, the map, the interest awakened by the buckle, and the conduct of that one among the strangers who had looked so often below him in the water, all seemed to point to a different explanation of their presence on that outlying, obscure islet of the western sea. The Madrid historian, the search instituted by Dr. Robertson, the bearded stranger with the rings, my own fruitless search that very morning in the deep water of Sandag Bay, ran together, piece by piece, in my memory, and I made sure that these strangers must be Spaniards in quest of ancient treasure and the lost ship of the Armada. But the people living in outlying islands, such as Aros, are answerable for their own security; there is none near by to protect or even to help them; and the presence in such a spot of a crew of foreign adventurers—poor, greedy, and most likely lawless—filled me with apprehensions for my uncle's money, and even for the safety of his daughter[1]. I was still wondering how we were to get rid of them when I came, all breathless, to the top of Aros. The whole world was shadowed over; only in the extreme east, on a hill of the mainland, one last gleam of sunshine lingered like a jewel; rain had begun to fall, not heavily, but in great drops; the sea was rising with each moment, and already a band of white encircled Aros and the nearer coasts of Grisapol. The boat was still pulling seaward, but I now became aware of what had been hidden from me lower down—a large, heavily sparred, handsome schooner[2], lying to at the south end of Aros. Since I had not seen her in the morning when I had looked around so closely at the signs of the weather, and upon these lone waters where a sail was rarely visible, it was clear she must have lain last night behind the uninhabited Eilean Gour, and this proved conclusively that she was manned by strangers to our coast, for that anchorage, though good enough to look at, is little better than a trap for ships. With such ignorant sailors upon so wild a coast, the coming gale was not unlikely to bring death upon its wings.

Culloden, where the Jacobite army was routed and subsequently slaughter by the Hanoverian forces. Charlie espaced, leaving – again – by small boat for the Isle of Skye, and vowing to return. He never did, but his mythic pledge – not unlike those of King Arthur or Douglas McArthur – became messianic to Scottish Catholics, who waited for his return hopefully, though vainly

[1] Treasure hunters who – by all accounts – have little respect for the legal avenues of recovery might, if disappointed, turn to robbery and rape

[2] A medium-sized ship with two or more gaff-rigged masts (meaning the sails are parallel to the keel, suspended by two spars jutting from the back of the mast)

I found my uncle at the gable end, watching the signs of the weather, with a pipe in his fingers.

'Uncle,' said I, 'there were men ashore at Sandag Bay—'

I had no time to go further; indeed, I not only forgot my words, but even my weariness, so strange was the effect on Uncle Gordon. He dropped his pipe and fell back against the end of the house with his jaw fallen, his eyes staring, and his long face as white as paper. We must have looked at one another silently for a quarter of a minute, before he made answer in this extraordinary fashion: 'Had he a hair kep on?'

I knew as well as if I had been there that the man who now lay buried at Sandag had worn a hairy cap, and that he had come ashore alive[1]. For the first and only time I lost toleration for the man who was my benefactor and the father of the woman I hoped to call my wife.

'These were living men,' said I, 'perhaps Jacobites, perhaps the French, perhaps pirates, perhaps adventurers come here to seek the Spanish treasure ship; but, whatever they may be, dangerous at least to your daughter and my cousin. As for your own guilty terrors, man, the dead sleeps well where you have laid him. I stood this morning by his grave; he will not wake before the trump of doom[2].'

My kinsman looked upon me, blinking, while I spoke; then he fixed his eyes for a little on the ground, and pulled his fingers foolishly; but it was plain that he was past the power of speech.

'Come,' said I. 'You must think for others. You must come up the hill with me, and see this ship.'

He obeyed without a word or a look, following slowly after my impatient strides. The spring seemed to have gone out of his body, and he scrambled heavily up and down the rocks, instead of leaping, as he was wont, from one to another. Nor could I, for all my cries, induce him to make better haste. Only once he replied to me complainingly, and like one in bodily pain: 'Ay, ay, man, I'm coming.' Long before we had reached the top, I had no other thought for him but pity. If the crime had been monstrous the punishment was in proportion.

At last we emerged above the sky-line of the hill, and could see around us. All was black and stormy to the eye; the last gleam of sun had vanished; a wind had sprung up, not yet high, but gusty and unsteady to the point; the rain, on the other hand, had ceased. Short as was the interval, the sea already ran vastly higher than when I had stood there last; already it had begun to break over some of the outward reefs, and already it moaned aloud in the sea-caves of Aros. I looked, at first, in vain for the schooner.

---

[1] His uncle suspects a ghost

[2] The proverbial "last trumpet" which will signal the end of the world

'There she is,' I said at last. But her new position, and the course she was now lying, puzzled me. 'They cannot mean to beat to sea[1],' I cried.

'That's what they mean,' said my uncle, with something like joy[2]; and just then the schooner went about and stood upon another tack[3], which put the question beyond the reach of doubt. These strangers, seeing a gale on hand, had thought first of sea-room[4]. With the wind that threatened, in these reef-sown waters and contending against so violent a stream of tide, their course was certain death.

'Good God!' said I, 'they are all lost.'

'Ay,' returned my uncle, 'a'—a' lost. They[5] hadnae a chance but to rin for Kyle Dona. The gate they're gaun the noo, they couldnae win through an the muckle deil were there to pilot them. Eh, man,' he continued, touching me on the sleeve, 'it's a braw nicht for a shipwreck! Twa in ae twalmonth! Eh, but the Merry Men'll dance bonny!'

I looked at him, and it was then that I began to fancy him no longer in his right mind. He was peering up to me, as if for sympathy, a timid joy in his eyes. All that had passed between us was already forgotten in the prospect of this fresh disaster.

'If it were not too late,' I cried with indignation, 'I would take the coble and go out to warn them.'

'Na[6], na,' he protested, 'ye maunnae interfere; ye maunnae meddle wi' the like o' that. It's His'—doffing his bonnet—'His wull. And, eh, man! but it's a braw nicht for't!'

Something like fear began to creep into my soul and, reminding him that I had not yet dined, I proposed we should return to the house. But no; nothing would tear him from his place of outlook.

---

[1] A ship that is in peril of being dashed on rocks might attempt to sail further out to sea in hopes of surviving the high waves which might be considered more merciful than the breakers that threaten to dash them to pieces

[2] It isn't entirely clear if the joy is due to hope that the ship might escape the Merry Men, or – more likely – lust after the goods that might be recovered if they make the futile decision to run for it, which will only ensure their destruction

[3] That is to say, it was headed in one direction – or tack – when the winds beat them back and turned them around

[4] Unobstructed, wide space at sea necessary to maneuver a ship. In other words they want to get as far from the rocks as possible

[5] *They had no chance but to run for Kyle Dona. The gate they're going to now they couldn't get to even if the great devil were to guide them. Oh, my boy! It's a fine night for a shipwreck! Two in a year! Oh, but the Merry Men'll dance beautifully!*

[6] *No, no! You mustn't interfere; you mustn't meddle with the likes of that. It's His will. And, oh, my boy! But it's a lovely night for [a shipwreck]!*

'I[1] maun see the hail thing, man, Cherlie,' he explained—and then as the schooner went about a second time, 'Eh, but they han'le her bonny!' he cried. 'The *Christ-Anna* was naething to this.'

Already the men on board the schooner must have begun to realise some part, but not yet the twentieth, of the dangers that environed their doomed ship. At every lull of the capricious wind they must have seen how fast the current swept them back. Each tack was made shorter, as they saw how little it prevailed. Every moment the rising swell began to boom and foam upon another sunken reef; and ever and again a breaker would fall in sounding ruin under the very bows of her, and the brown reef and streaming tangle appear in the hollow of the wave. I tell you, they had to stand to their tackle: there was no idle men aboard that ship, God knows. It was upon the progress of a scene so horrible to any human-hearted man that my misguided uncle now pored and gloated like a connoisseur[2]. As I turned to go down the hill, he was lying on his belly on the summit, with his hands stretched forth and clutching in the heather. He seemed rejuvenated, mind and body.

When I got back to the house already dismally affected, I was still more sadly downcast at the sight of Mary. She had her sleeves rolled up over her strong arms, and was quietly making bread. I got a bannock[3] from the dresser and sat down to eat it in silence.

'Are ye wearied, lad?' she asked after a while.

'I am not so much wearied, Mary,' I replied, getting on my feet, 'as I am weary of delay, and perhaps of Aros too. You know me well enough to judge me fairly, say what I like. Well, Mary, you may be sure of this: you had better be anywhere but here.'

'I'll be sure of one thing,' she returned: 'I'll be where my duty is.'

'You forget, you have a duty to yourself,' I said.

'Ay, man[4]?' she replied, pounding at the dough; 'will you have found that in the Bible, now?'

'Mary,' I said solemnly, 'you must not laugh at me just now. God knows I am in no heart for laughing. If we could get your father with us, it would be best; but with him or without him, I want you far away from here, my girl; for your own sake, and for mine, ay, and for your father's too, I want you far—far away from here. I came with other thoughts; I came here as a man comes home; now it is all changed, and I have no desire nor hope but to

---

[1] *I must see the whole thing, Charlie boy... Oh, but they're handling her beautifully*
[2] In the character of Charlie's uncle we may be seeing Stevenson's greatest quibble with the Calvinism of his forefathers: a lack of mercy, a delight in punishment, a sadistic glee at the promise of hell, and the absence of human compassion
[3] Large flatbread
[4] *Is that so, now?*

flee—for that's the word—flee, like a bird out of the fowler's snare[1], from this accursed island.'

She had stopped her work by this time.

'And do you think, now,' said she, 'do you think, now, I have neither eyes nor ears? Do ye think I havenae broken my heart to have these braws (as he calls them, God forgive him!) thrown into the sea? Do ye think I have lived with him, day in, day out, and not seen what you saw in an hour or two? No,' she said, 'I know there's wrong in it; what wrong, I neither know nor want to know. There was never an ill thing made better by meddling, that I could hear of. But, my lad, you must never ask me to leave my father. While the breath is in his body, I'll be with him. And he's not long for here, either: that I can tell you, Charlie—he's not long for here[2]. The mark is on his brow; and better so—maybe better so.'

I was a while silent, not knowing what to say; and when I roused my head at last to speak, she got before me.

'Charlie,' she said, 'what's right for me, neednae be right for you. There's sin upon this house and trouble; you are a stranger; take your things upon your back and go your ways to better places and to better folk, and if you were ever minded to come back, though it were twenty years syne, you would find me aye waiting.'

'Mary Ellen,' I said, 'I asked you to be my wife, and you said as good as yes. That's done for good. Wherever you are, I am; as I shall answer to my God.'

As I said the words, the wind suddenly burst out raving, and then seemed to stand still and shudder round the house of Aros. It was the first squall, or prologue, of the coming tempest, and as we started and looked about us, we found that a gloom, like the approach of evening, had settled round the house.

'God pity all poor folks at sea!' she said. 'We'll see no more of my father till the morrow's morning.'

And then she told me, as we sat by the fire and hearkened to the rising gusts, of how this change had fallen upon my uncle. All last winter he had been dark and fitful in his mind. Whenever the Roost ran high, or, as Mary said, whenever the Merry Men were dancing, he would lie out for hours together on the Head, if it were at night, or on the top of Aros by day, watching the tumult of the sea, and sweeping the horizon for a sail. After

---

[1] A trap for birds. Metaphorically, a temptation that lures the innocent to destruction. The reference, like so many, is biblical: "I will say of the LORD, 'He is my refuge and my fortress, my God, in whom I trust.' Surely he will save you from the fowler's snare and from the deadly pestilence. He will cover you with his feathers, and under his wings you will find refuge; his faithfulness will be your shield and rampart." – Psalm 91:2-4

[2] She believes that he will soon die

February the tenth, when the wealth-bringing wreck was cast ashore at Sandag, he had been at first unnaturally gay, and his excitement had never fallen in degree, but only changed in kind from dark to darker. He neglected his work, and kept Rorie idle. They two would speak together by the hour at the gable end, in guarded tones and with an air of secrecy and almost of guilt; and if she questioned either, as at first she sometimes did, her inquiries were put aside with confusion. Since Rorie had first remarked the fish that hung about the ferry, his master had never set foot but once upon the mainland of the Ross. That once—it was in the height of the springs—he had passed dryshod while the tide was out; but, having lingered overlong on the far side, found himself cut off from Aros by the returning waters. It was with a shriek of agony that he had leaped across the gut, and he had reached home thereafter in a fever-fit of fear. A fear of the sea, a constant haunting thought of the sea, appeared in his talk and devotions, and even in his looks when he was silent.

Rorie alone came in to supper; but a little later my uncle appeared, took a bottle under his arm, put some bread in his pocket, and set forth again to his outlook, followed this time by Rorie. I heard that the schooner was losing ground, but the crew were still fighting every inch with hopeless ingenuity and course; and the news filled my mind with blackness.

A little after sundown the full fury of the gale broke forth, such a gale as I have never seen in summer[1], nor, seeing how swiftly it had come, even in winter. Mary and I sat in silence, the house quaking overhead, the tempest howling without, the fire between us sputtering with raindrops. Our thoughts were far away with the poor fellows on the schooner, or my not less unhappy uncle, houseless on the promontory; and yet ever and again we were startled back to ourselves, when the wind would rise and strike the gable like a solid body, or suddenly fall and draw away, so that the fire leaped into flame and our hearts bounded in our sides. Now the storm in its might would seize and shake the four corners of the roof, roaring like Leviathan[2] in anger. Anon, in a lull, cold eddies of tempest moved shudderingly in the room, lifting the hair upon our heads and passing between us as we sat. And again the wind would break forth in a chorus of melancholy sounds, hooting low in the chimney, wailing with flutelike softness round the house.

It was perhaps eight o'clock when Rorie came in and pulled me mysteriously to the door. My uncle, it appeared, had frightened even his constant comrade; and Rorie, uneasy at his extravagance, prayed me to come out and share the watch. I hastened to do as I was asked; the more

---

[1] The worst storms and hurricanes are in late fall, roughly August through December

[2] A biblical monster referred to in the Book of Job that some identify as a whale, a dragon, a sea-monster, or a hippopotamous

readily as, what with fear and horror, and the electrical tension of the night, I was myself restless and disposed for action. I told Mary to be under no alarm, for I should be a safeguard on her father; and wrapping myself warmly in a plaid[1], I followed Rorie into the open air.

The night, though we were so little past midsummer, was as dark as January. Intervals of a groping twilight alternated with spells of utter blackness; and it was impossible to trace the reason of these changes in the flying horror of the sky. The wind blew the breath out of a man's nostrils; all heaven seemed to thunder overhead like one huge sail; and when there fell a momentary lull on Aros, we could hear the gusts dismally sweeping in the distance. Over all the lowlands of the Ross, the wind must have blown as fierce as on the open sea; and God only knows the uproar that was raging around the head of Ben Kyaw. Sheets of mingled spray and rain were driven in our faces. All round the isle of Aros the surf, with an incessant, hammering thunder, beat upon the reefs and beaches. Now louder in one place, now lower in another, like the combinations of orchestral music, the constant mass of sound was hardly varied for a moment. And loud above all this hurly-burly I could hear the changeful voices of the Roost and the intermittent roaring of the Merry Men. At that hour, there flashed into my mind the reason of the name that they were called. For the noise of them seemed almost mirthful, as it out-topped the other noises of the night; or if not mirthful, yet instinct with a portentous joviality. Nay, and it seemed even human. As when savage men have drunk away their reason, and, discarding speech, bawl together in their madness by the hour; so, to my ears, these deadly breakers shouted by Aros in the night[2].

Arm in arm, and staggering against the wind, Rorie and I won every yard of ground with conscious effort. We slipped on the wet sod, we fell together sprawling on the rocks. Bruised, drenched, beaten, and breathless, it must have taken us near half an hour to get from the house down to the Head that overlooks the Roost. There, it seemed, was my uncle's favourite observatory. Right in the face of it, where the cliff is highest and most

---

[1] A long, woolen cloak – typicaly woven in the Tartan of a family's clan – wrapped in wide swathes around the body

[2] Stevenson offers a glimpse into the metaphorical import of the Merry Men, which are a physical symbol of Uncle Gordon's inhumanity: they laugh at suffering, tingle with glee at destruction, and roar approvingly at the damnation of others. As rocks embedded in the sea, they represent Gordon's purgatorial situation: he is neither a man of the sea (heaven and the realm of the supernatural), nor the earth (mankind and the world of relationships), but an uncommitted denizen of both worlds – both a metaphysical demon and a very physical murderer. The Merry Men delight in violence and suffering – it is, after all, what makes them merry: the crashing waves that drive ships upon the rocks. Likewise, Gordon revels in misery and benefits from suffering

sheer, a hump of earth, like a parapet, makes a place of shelter from the common winds, where a man may sit in quiet and see the tide and the mad billows contending at his feet. As he might look down from the window of a house upon some street disturbance, so, from this post, he looks down upon the tumbling of the Merry Men. On such a night, of course, he peers upon a world of blackness, where the waters wheel and boil, where the waves joust together with the noise of an explosion, and the foam towers and vanishes in the twinkling of an eye. Never before had I seen the Merry Men thus violent. The fury, height, and transiency of their spoutings was a thing to be seen and not recounted. High over our heads on the cliff rose their white columns in the darkness; and the same instant, like phantoms, they were gone. Sometimes three at a time would thus aspire and vanish; sometimes a gust took them, and the spray would fall about us, heavy as a wave. And yet the spectacle was rather maddening in its levity than impressive by its force. Thought was beaten down by the confounding uproar—a gleeful vacancy possessed the brains of men, a state akin to madness; and I found myself at times following the dance of the Merry Men as it were a tune upon a jigging instrument.

I first caught sight of my uncle when we were still some yards away in one of the flying glimpses of twilight that chequered the pitch darkness of the night. He was standing up behind the parapet, his head thrown back and the bottle to his mouth. As he put it down, he saw and recognised us with a toss of one hand fleeringly above his head.

'Has he been drinking?' shouted I to Rorie.

'He will aye be drunk when the wind blows[1],' returned Rorie in the same high key, and it was all that I could do to hear him.

'Then—was he so—in February?' I inquired.

Rorie's 'Ay' was a cause of joy to me. The murder, then, had not sprung in cold blood from calculation; it was an act of madness no more to be condemned than to be pardoned. My uncle was a dangerous madman, if you will, but he was not cruel and base as I had feared. Yet what a scene for a carouse, what an incredible vice, was this that the poor man had chosen! I have always thought drunkenness a wild and almost fearful pleasure, rather demoniacal than human; but drunkenness, out here in the roaring blackness, on the edge of a cliff above that hell of waters, the man's head spinning like the Roost, his foot tottering on the edge of death, his ear watching for the signs of ship-wreck, surely that, if it were credible in any one, was morally impossible in a man like my uncle, whose mind was set upon a damnatory creed and haunted by the darkest superstitions. Yet so it was; and, as we reached the bight of shelter and could breathe again, I saw the man's eyes shining in the night with an unholy glimmer.

---

[1] *He's always drunk when it storms*

56

'Eh, Charlie, man, it's grand!' he cried. 'See to them!' he continued, dragging me to the edge of the abyss from whence arose that deafening clamour and those clouds of spray; 'see to them dancin', man! Is that no wicked?'

He pronounced the word with gusto, and I thought it suited with the scene.

'They're[1] yowlin' for thon schooner,' he went on, his thin, insane voice clearly audible in the shelter of the bank, 'an' she's comin' aye nearer, aye nearer, aye nearer an' nearer an' nearer; an' they ken't, the folk kens it, they ken wool it's by wi' them. Charlie, lad, they're a' drunk in yon schooner, a' dozened wi' drink. They were a' drunk in the *Christ-Anna*, at the hinder end. There's nane could droon at sea wantin' the brandy. Hoot awa, what do you ken?' with a sudden blast of anger. 'I tell ye, it cannae be; they droon withoot it. Ha'e,' holding out the bottle, 'tak' a sowp.'

I was about to refuse, but Rorie touched me as if in warning; and indeed I had already thought better of the movement. I took the bottle, therefore, and not only drank freely myself, but contrived to spill even more as I was doing so. It was pure spirit, and almost strangled me to swallow. My kinsman did not observe the loss, but, once more throwing back his head, drained the remainder to the dregs. Then, with a loud laugh, he cast the bottle forth among the Merry Men, who seemed to leap up, shouting to receive it.

'Ha'e[2], bairns!' he cried, 'there's your han'sel. Ye'll get bonnier nor that, or morning.'

Suddenly, out in the black night before us, and not two hundred yards away, we heard, at a moment when the wind was silent, the clear note of a human voice. Instantly the wind swept howling down upon the Head, and the Roost bellowed, and churned, and danced with a new fury. But we had heard the sound, and we knew, with agony, that this was the doomed ship now close on ruin, and that what we had heard was the voice of her master issuing his last command. Crouching together on the edge, we waited, straining every sense, for the inevitable end. It was long, however, and to us it seemed like ages, ere the schooner suddenly appeared for one brief

---

[1] *They're yowling for yonder schooner! And she's coming still nearer, still nearer ... and they know, the lads know it, they know well that they're donefore. Charlie, lad, they're all drunk in yon schooner, all stupefied with drink. They were all drunk in the Christ-Anna, in the stern. There none that could drown at sea without drandy. Dash it all – what do you know! I tell you, it cannot be; they drown without it. Here: take a swig*

[2] *Here, my children! There's your good luck gift. You'll get an even better one than that before morning comes*

instant, relieved against a tower of glimmering foam. I still see her reefed mainsail[1] flapping loose, as the boom[2] fell heavily across the deck; I still see the black outline of the hull, and still think I can distinguish the figure of a man stretched upon the tiller[3]. Yet the whole sight we had of her passed swifter than lightning; the very wave that disclosed her fell burying her for ever; the mingled cry of many voices at the point of death rose and was quenched in the roaring of the Merry Men. And with that the tragedy was at an end. The strong ship, with all her gear, and the lamp perhaps still burning in the cabin, the lives of so many men, precious surely to others, dear, at least, as heaven to themselves, had all, in that one moment, gone down into the surging waters. They were gone like a dream. And the wind still ran and shouted, and the senseless waters in the Roost still leaped and tumbled as before.

How long we lay there together, we three, speechless and motionless, is more than I can tell, but it must have been for long. At length, one by one, and almost mechanically, we crawled back into the shelter of the bank. As I lay against the parapet, wholly wretched and not entirely master of my mind, I could hear my kinsman maundering to himself in an altered and melancholy mood. Now he would repeat to himself with maudlin iteration, 'Sic a fecht as they had—sic a sair fecht as they had, puir lads, puir lads[4]!' and anon he would bewail that 'a' the gear was as gude's tint,' because the ship had gone down among the Merry Men instead of stranding on the shore; and throughout, the name—the *Christ-Anna*—would come and go in his divagations, pronounced with shuddering awe. The storm all this time was rapidly abating. In half an hour the wind had fallen to a breeze, and the change was accompanied or caused by a heavy, cold, and plumping rain. I must then have fallen asleep, and when I came to myself, drenched, stiff, and unrefreshed, day had already broken, grey, wet, discomfortable day; the wind blew in faint and shifting capfuls, the tide was out, the Roost was at its lowest, and only the strong beating surf round all the coasts of Aros remained to witness of the furies of the night.

---

[1] An extra sail attached to the regular sail in order to increase its power. Reefed sails are used in times when extra speed is absolutely necessary

[2] A spar that pivots on either side of the mast. The bottom of the sail is attached to it

[3] This ship is not driven by a wheel (which, when turned, would tighten and give slack to a series of ropes which would turn the rudder), but a tiller: a long pole or handle that projects outward from the top of the rudder – which would, in this case, run all the way up the stern of the ship – allowing the rudder to be manually turned

[4] *Such a fight as they had – such a horrible fight as they had, poor lads... All the gear was as good as lost*

Rorie set out for the house in search of warmth and breakfast; but my uncle was bent upon examining the shores of Aros, and I felt it a part of duty to accompany him throughout. He was now docile and quiet, but tremulous and weak in mind and body; and it was with the eagerness of a child that he pursued his exploration. He climbed far down upon the rocks; on the beaches, he pursued the retreating breakers. The merest broken plank or rag of cordage was a treasure in his eyes to be secured at the peril of his life. To see him, with weak and stumbling footsteps, expose himself to the pursuit of the surf, or the snares and pitfalls of the weedy rock, kept me in a perpetual terror. My arm was ready to support him, my hand clutched him by the skirt, I helped him to draw his pitiful discoveries beyond the reach of the returning wave; a nurse accompanying a child of seven would have had no different experience.

Yet, weakened as he was by the reaction from his madness of the night before, the passions that smouldered in his nature were those of a strong man. His terror of the sea, although conquered for the moment, was still undiminished; had the sea been a lake of living flames[1], he could not have shrunk more panically from its touch; and once, when his foot slipped and he plunged to the midleg into a pool of water, the shriek that came up out of his soul was like the cry of death. He sat still for a while, panting like a dog, after that; but his desire for the spoils of shipwreck triumphed once more over his fears; once more he tottered among the curded foam; once more he crawled upon the rocks among the bursting bubbles; once more his whole heart seemed to be set on driftwood, fit, if it was fit for anything, to throw upon the fire. Pleased as he was with what he found, he still incessantly grumbled at his ill-fortune.

'Aros[2],' he said, 'is no a place for wrecks ava'—no ava'. A' the years I've dwalt here, this ane maks the second; and the best o' the gear clean tint!'

'Uncle,' said I, for we were now on a stretch of open sand, where there was nothing to divert his mind, 'I saw you last night, as I never thought to see you—you were drunk.'

'Na, na[3],' he said, 'no as bad as that. I had been drinking, though. And to tell ye the God's truth, it's a thing I cannae mend. There's nae soberer

---

[1] Tremendously suggestive. The Bible describes Satan and Death as being thrown into the Lake of Fire in Hell at the end of time. Stevenson implies that the devout Calvinist is willing to brave damnation for the sake of his pretty "braws," but is terrified by contact with the sea which reminds him – the earthbound Self – of his crimes against God and Man

[2] *Aros is not at all a place for shipwrecks – not at all. All the years I've lived here, this one makes the second; and the best of the gear clean lost!*

[3] *No, no... Not as bad as all that. I'd been drinking, though. And to tell you the God's-honest truth, it's something that I just can't overcome. There's no more*

man than me in my ordnar; but when I hear the wind blaw in my lug, it's my belief that I gang gyte.'

'You are a religious man,' I replied, 'and this is sin'.

'Ou[1],' he returned, 'if it wasnae sin, I dinnae ken that I would care for't. Ye see, man, it's defiance. There's a sair spang o' the auld sin o' the warld in you sea; it's an unchristian business at the best o't; an' whiles when it gets up, an' the wind skreights—the wind an' her are a kind of sib, I'm thinkin'—an' thae Merry Men, the daft callants, blawin' and lauchin', and puir souls in the deid thraws warstlin' the leelang nicht wi' their bit ships— weel, it comes ower me like a glamour. I'm a deil, I ken't. But I think naething o' the puir sailor lads; I'm wi' the sea, I'm just like ane o' her ain Merry Men.'

I thought I should touch him in a joint of his harness. I turned me towards the sea; the surf was running gaily, wave after wave, with their manes blowing behind them, riding one after another up the beach, towering, curving, falling one upon another on the trampled sand. Without, the salt air, the scared gulls, the widespread army of the sea-chargers, neighing to each other, as they gathered together to the assault of Aros; and close before us, that line on the flat sands that, with all their number and their fury, they might never pass.

'Thus far shalt thou go,' said I, 'and no farther.' And then I quoted as solemnly as I was able a verse that I had often before fitted to the chorus of the breakers:—

But yet the Lord that is on high,
  Is more of might by far,
Than noise of many waters is,
  As great sea billows are[2].

'Ay[3],' said my kinsinan, 'at the hinder end, the Lord will triumph; I dinnae misdoobt that. But here on earth, even silly men-folk daur Him to

---

sober man than me when I'm my usual self; but when I hear the wind blow in my ear, it's my belief that I go mad

[1] *Alas... if it wasn't a sin, I don't know that I'd care for it. You see, lad, it's defiance. There a horrible degree of the old sin of the world in the sea; it's an unchristian business at the best times; an otherwise when it gets up, and the wind shrieks – the wind and her are a kind of family, I'm thinking – and the Merry Men, the daft lads, blowing and laughing, and poor souls in the dead throws wrestling the whole night with their wee ships – well it comes over me like an enchantment. I'm a demon, I know it. But I think nothing of the poor sailor lads; I'm with the sea, I'm just like one of her own Merry Men*

[2] Psalm 93 in the 1650 Scottish Psalter

[3] *Aye... At the end of time the Lord will triumph. I have no doubt of that. But here on earth, even silly men-folk dare him to his face. It is not wise; I'm not saying*

His face. It is nae wise; I am nae sayin' that it's wise; but it's the pride of the eye, and it's the lust o' life, an' it's the wale o' pleesures.'

I said no more, for we had now begun to cross a neck of land that lay between us and Sandag; and I withheld my last appeal to the man's better reason till we should stand upon the spot associated with his crime. Nor did he pursue the subject; but he walked beside me with a firmer step. The call that I had made upon his mind acted like a stimulant, and I could see that he had forgotten his search for worthless jetsam[1], in a profound, gloomy, and yet stirring train of thought. In three or four minutes we had topped the brae and begun to go down upon Sandag. The wreck had been roughly handled by the sea; the stem[2] had been spun round and dragged a little lower down; and perhaps the stern had been forced a little higher, for the two parts now lay entirely separate on the beach. When we came to the grave I stopped, uncovered my head in the thick rain, and, looking my kinsman in the face, addressed him.

'A man,' said I, 'was in God's providence suffered to escape from mortal dangers; he was poor, he was naked, he was wet, he was weary, he was a stranger; he had every claim upon the bowels[3] of your compassion; it may be that he was the salt of the earth[4], holy, helpful, and kind; it may be he was a man laden with iniquities to whom death was the beginning of torment. I ask you in the sight of heaven: Gordon Darnaway, where is the man for whom Christ died[5]?'

He started visibly at the last words; but there came no answer, and his face expressed no feeling but a vague alarm.

'You were my father's brother,' I continued; 'You, have taught me to count your house as if it were my father's house; and we are both sinful men walking before the Lord among the sins and dangers of this life. It is by our evil that God leads us into good; we sin, I dare not say by His temptation, but I must say with His consent; and to any but the brutish man his sins are the beginning of wisdom. God has warned you by this crime; He warns you still by the bloody grave between our feet; and if there shall follow no

---

that it's wise; but it's the pride of the eye, and it's the lust of life, and it's having the pick of pleasures

[1] Wreckage that has washed ashore

[2] The prow, or the front portion

[3] Far longer than the heart, the bowels have been considered the source of feelings and compassion. Polite Victorian society, not wishing to dwell on digestion, diverted this locus to the heart, but in rural Scotland the synecdoche would remain unshadowed

[4] A Christian

[5] This is suggestive of God's query to Cain: full knowing the answer, God asked Cain "Where is your brother Able?" Cain, of course, had murdered his brother

repentance, no improvement, no return to Him, what can we look for but the following of some memorable judgment[1]?'

Even as I spoke the words, the eyes of my uncle wandered from my face. A change fell upon his looks that cannot be described; his features seemed to dwindle in size, the colour faded from his cheeks, one hand rose waveringly and pointed over my shoulder into the distance, and the oft-repeated name fell once more from his lips: 'The *Christ-Anna!*'

I turned; and if I was not appalled to the same degree, as I return thanks to Heaven that I had not the cause, I was still startled by the sight that met my eyes. The form of a man stood upright on the cabin-hutch[2] of the wrecked ship; his back was towards us; he appeared to be scanning the offing with shaded eyes, and his figure was relieved to its full height, which was plainly very great, against the sea and sky. I have said a thousand times that I am not superstitious; but at that moment, with my mind running upon death and sin, the unexplained appearance of a stranger on that sea-girt, solitary island filled me with a surprise that bordered close on terror. It seemed scarce possible that any human soul should have come ashore alive in such a sea as had rated last night along the coasts of Aros; and the only vessel within miles had gone down before our eyes among the Merry Men. I was assailed with doubts that made suspense unbearable, and, to put the matter to the touch at once, stepped forward and hailed the figure like a ship.

He turned about, and I thought he started to behold us. At this my courage instantly revived, and I called and signed to him to draw near, and he, on his part, dropped immediately to the sands, and began slowly to approach, with many stops and hesitations. At each repeated mark of the man's uneasiness I grew the more confident myself; and I advanced another step, encouraging him as I did so with my head and hand. It was plain the castaway had heard indifferent accounts of our island hospitality; and indeed, about this time, the people farther north had a sorry reputation[3].

'Why,' I said, 'the man is black!'

And just at that moment, in a voice that I could scarce have recognised, my kinsman began swearing and praying in a mingled stream[4]. I looked at

---

[1] Brilliant employment of Calvinist rhetoric

[2] The protecting doorway structure that leads down into the captain's cabin

[3] That is, in the Highlands

[4] The "Black Man" was a euphemism employed in European folklore to describe Satan, who was said to manifest as a black man – not an African, but a tall, imposing man with coal black skin and glowing eyes. This figure appears regularly in both literature and folklore, especially in the stories of Washington Irving, Nathaniel Hawthorne, and others who write about New England during the Puritan years, where the "Black Man in the woods" was a frequently discussed supernatural terror

him; he had fallen on his knees, his face was agonised; at each step of the castaway's the pitch of his voice rose, the volubility of his utterance and the fervour of his language redoubled. I call it prayer, for it was addressed to God; but surely no such ranting incongruities were ever before addressed to the Creator by a creature: surely if prayer can be a sin, this mad harangue was sinful. I ran to my kinsman, I seized him by the shoulders, I dragged him to his feet.

'Silence, man,' said I, 'respect your God in words, if not in action. Here, on the very scene of your transgressions, He sends you an occasion of atonement[1]. Forward and embrace it; welcome like a father yon creature who comes trembling to your mercy[2].'

With that, I tried to force him towards the black; but he felled me to the ground, burst from my grasp, leaving the shoulder of his jacket, and fled up the hillside towards the top of Aros like a deer. I staggered to my feet again, bruised and somewhat stunned; the negro had paused in surprise, perhaps in terror, some halfway between me and the wreck; my uncle was already far away, bounding from rock to rock; and I thus found myself torn for a time between two duties. But I judged, and I pray Heaven that I judged rightly, in favour of the poor wretch upon the sands; his misfortune was at least not plainly of his own creation; it was one, besides, that I could certainly relieve; and I had begun by that time to regard my uncle as an incurable and dismal lunatic. I advanced accordingly towards the black, who now awaited my approach with folded arms, like one prepared for either destiny. As I came nearer, he reached forth his hand with a great gesture, such as I had seen

---

[1] Charlie may not understand the import of his words: he sees a stranded sailor who offers Gordon an opportunity to atone for his murder by showing him hospitality – a decidedly New Testament, Anglican view of God, a God who provides opportunities to repent. But Gordon – perhaps correctly – sees a very different means of atonement: he sees the devil, who has come from the bowels of the sea (the locus of supernatural activity and the dwelling place of God and Satan) to drag him to damnation as a means of repentance – a decidedly Old Testament, Calvinist view of God, a God who does not suffer sinners, who punishes sin and humiliates the proud. This is the "eye for an eye" God whom Gordon has prayed to his whole life, and where Charlie sees a divine gesture which offers a chance to be redeemed, Gordon sees a divine condemnation which provides the machinery of his damnation

[2] If the Black Man is indeed a demon come to drag Gordon to hell, then this comment drips with all the hideous irony of an M. R. James ghost story (his phantoms frequently embraced their victims with their skeletal arms, dragging them to the ground dead). Speaking as he does of fathers, Charlie calls to mind the fatherliness of God-the-Father, who may be the loving parent who didn't spare his Son, so that mankind might live, or he may be the just patriarch who punishes his rebellious offspring to the seventh generation

from the pulpit, and spoke to me in something of a pulpit voice, but not a word was comprehensible[1]. I tried him first in English, then in Gaelic, both in vain; so that it was clear we must rely upon the tongue of looks and gestures. Thereupon I signed to him to follow me, which he did readily and with a grave obeisance like a fallen king[2]; all the while there had come no shade of alteration in his face, neither of anxiety while he was still waiting, nor of relief now that he was reassured; if he were a slave, as I supposed, I could not but judge he must have fallen from some high place in his own country, and fallen as he was, I could not but admire his bearing. As we passed the grave, I paused and raised my hands and eyes to heaven in token of respect and sorrow for the dead; and he, as if in answer, bowed low and spread his hands abroad[3]; it was a strange motion, but done like a thing of common custom; and I supposed it was ceremonial in the land from which he came. At the same time he pointed to my uncle, whom we could just see perched upon a knoll, and touched his head to indicate that he was mad.

We took the long way round the shore, for I feared to excite my uncle if we struck across the island; and as we walked, I had time enough to mature the little dramatic exhibition by which I hoped to satisfy my doubts. Accordingly, pausing on a rock, I proceeded to imitate before the negro the action of the man whom I had seen the day before taking bearings with the compass at Sandag. He understood me at once, and, taking the imitation out of my hands, showed me where the boat was, pointed out seaward as if to indicate the position of the schooner, and then down along the edge of the rock with the words 'Espirito Santo,' strangely pronounced, but clear enough for recognition. I had thus been right in my conjecture; the pretended historical inquiry had been but a cloak for treasure-hunting; the man who had played on Dr. Robertson was the same as the foreigner who visited Grisapol in spring, and now, with many others, lay dead under the Roost of Aros: there had their greed brought them, there should their bones be tossed for evermore. In the meantime the black continued his imitation of the scene, now looking up skyward as though watching the approach of the storm now, in the character of a seaman, waving the rest to come aboard; now as an officer, running along the rock and entering the boat; and anon bending over imaginary oars with the air of a hurried

---

[1] In maritime folklore, it is not uncommon for the sole survivor of a shipwreck to speak an otherworldly language that none know, before revealing himself to be supernatural in origin. Stevenson deftly avoids removing all doubt (perhaps it is an African tongue or Arabic or Sanskrit), but the suggestion is that this is the backwards language of Hell

[2] Suggestive of Lucifer, who was of course a high ranking fallen angel and the King of Darkness

[3] While Charlie appeals to Heaven, the black man could be interpreted as praying to hell

boatman; but all with the same solemnity of manner, so that I was never even moved to smile. Lastly, he indicated to me, by a pantomime not to be described in words, how he himself had gone up to examine the stranded wreck, and, to his grief and indignation, had been deserted by his comrades; and thereupon folded his arms once more, and stooped his head, like one accepting fate.

The mystery of his presence being thus solved for me, I explained to him by means of a sketch the fate of the vessel and of all aboard her. He showed no surprise nor sorrow, and, with a sudden lifting of his open hand, seemed to dismiss his former friends or masters (whichever they had been) into God's pleasure. Respect came upon me and grew stronger, the more I observed him; I saw he had a powerful mind and a sober and severe character, such as I loved to commune with; and before we reached the house of Aros I had almost forgotten, and wholly forgiven him, his uncanny colour[1].

To Mary I told all that had passed without suppression, though I own my heart failed me; but I did wrong to doubt her sense of justice.

'You did the right,' she said. 'God's will be done.' And she set out meat for us at once.

As soon as I was satisfied, I bade Rorie keep an eye upon the castaway, who was still eating, and set forth again myself to find my uncle. I had not gone far before I saw him sitting in the same place, upon the very topmost knoll, and seemingly in the same attitude as when I had last observed him. From that point, as I have said, the most of Aros and the neighbouring Ross would be spread below him like a map; and it was plain that he kept a bright look-out in all directions, for my head had scarcely risen above the summit of the first ascent before he had leaped to his feet and turned as if to face me. I hailed him at once, as well as I was able, in the same tones and words as I had often used before, when I had come to summon him to dinner. He made not so much as a movement in reply. I passed on a little farther, and again tried parley, with the same result. But when I began a second time to advance, his insane fears blazed up again, and still in dead silence, but with incredible speed, he began to flee from before me along

---

[1] Charlie is not necessarily a raving racist. The implication from his first exclamation – "Why, the man is black!" – is surprise at the literal blackness of his color. Black sailors were tremendously common in ships' crews, regardless of the national origin of the vessel. Spanish ships in particular, with their relationship to the Moors and their closeness to North Africa, could virtually be expected to include a high ratio of blacks to whites. So it is unlikely that Charlie is surprised to see an African, and more likely that the figure is the exact color of soot, which is the case of the Black Man in Puritan folklore: he is a man with coal-black skin (not a man of African ancestry) – skin blackened by the fires of Hell. It is this diabolical association which requires "forgiving," not his ethnicity

the rocky summit of the hill. An hour before, he had been dead weary, and I had been comparatively active. But now his strength was recruited by the fervour of insanity, and it would have been vain for me to dream of pursuit. Nay, the very attempt, I thought, might have inflamed his terrors, and thus increased the miseries of our position. And I had nothing left but to turn homeward and make my sad report to Mary.

She heard it, as she had heard the first, with a concerned composure, and, bidding me lie down and take that rest of which I stood so much in need, set forth herself in quest of her misguided father. At that age it would have been a strange thing that put me from either meat or sleep; I slept long and deep; and it was already long past noon before I awoke and came downstairs into the kitchen. Mary, Rorie, and the black castaway were seated about the fire in silence; and I could see that Mary had been weeping. There was cause enough, as I soon learned, for tears. First she, and then Rorie, had been forth to seek my uncle; each in turn had found him perched upon the hill-top, and from each in turn he had silently and swiftly fled. Rorie had tried to chase him, but in vain; madness lent a new vigour to his bounds; he sprang from rock to rock over the widest gullies; he scoured like the wind along the hill-tops; he doubled and twisted like a hare before the dogs; and Rorie at length gave in; and the last that he saw, my uncle was seated as before upon the crest of Aros. Even during the hottest excitement of the chase, even when the fleet-footed servant had come, for a moment, very near to capture him, the poor lunatic had uttered not a sound. He fled, and he was silent, like a beast; and this silence had terrified his pursuer.

There was something heart-breaking in the situation. How to capture the madman, how to feed him in the meanwhile, and what to do with him when he was captured, were the three difficulties that we had to solve.

'The black,' said I, 'is the cause of this attack. It may even be his presence in the house that keeps my uncle on the hill. We have done the fair thing; he has been fed and warmed under this roof; now I propose that Rorie put him across the bay in the coble, and take him through the Ross as far as Grisapol.'

In this proposal Mary heartily concurred; and bidding the black follow us, we all three descended to the pier. Certainly, Heaven's will was declared against Gordon Darnaway; a thing had happened, never paralleled before in Aros; during the storm, the coble had broken loose, and, striking on the rough splinters of the pier, now lay in four feet of water with one side stove in. Three days of work at least would be required to make her float. But I was not to be beaten. I led the whole party round to where the gut was narrowest, swam to the other side, and called to the black to follow me. He signed, with the same clearness and quiet as before, that he knew not the art; and there was truth apparent in his signals, it would have occurred to none of us to doubt his truth; and that hope being over, we must all go back even as we came to the house of Aros, the negro walking in our midst without embarrassment.

All we could do that day was to make one more attempt to communicate with the unhappy madman. Again he was visible on his perch; again he fled in silence. But food and a great cloak were at least left for his comfort; the rain, besides, had cleared away, and the night promised to be even warm. We might compose ourselves, we thought, until the morrow; rest was the chief requisite, that we might be strengthened for unusual exertions; and as none cared to talk, we separated at an early hour.

I lay long awake, planning a campaign for the morrow. I was to place the black on the side of Sandag, whence he should head my uncle towards the house; Rorie in the west, I on the east, were to complete the cordon, as best we might. It seemed to me, the more I recalled the configuration of the island, that it should be possible, though hard, to force him down upon the low ground along Aros Bay; and once there, even with the strength of his madness, ultimate escape was hardly to be feared. It was on his terror of the black that I relied; for I made sure, however he might run, it would not be in the direction of the man whom he supposed to have returned from the dead[1], and thus one point of the compass at least would be secure.

When at length I fell asleep, it was to be awakened shortly after by a dream of wrecks, black men, and submarine adventure[2]; and I found myself so shaken and fevered that I arose, descended the stair, and stepped out before the house. Within, Rorie and the black were asleep together in the kitchen; outside was a wonderful clear night of stars, with here and there a cloud still hanging, last stragglers of the tempest. It was near the top of the flood, and the Merry Men were roaring in the windless quiet of the night. Never, not even in the height of the tempest, had I heard their song with greater awe. Now, when the winds were gathered home, when the deep was dandling itself back into its summer slumber, and when the stars rained their gentle light over land and sea, the voice of these tide-breakers was still raised for havoc. They seemed, indeed, to be a part of the world's evil and the tragic side of life. Nor were their meaningless vociferations[3] the only sounds that broke the silence of the night. For I could hear, now shrill and thrilling and now almost drowned, the note of a human voice that accompanied the uproar of the Roost. I knew it for my kinsman's; and a

---

[1] Gordon believes that the black man is the spirit of the man he murdererd, returned from the dead in the form of a demon

[2] In an age before submarines could make a human's underwater experience last longer than their lungs would allow, a "submarine adventure" brings to mind the ghoulish experiences of the drowned dead rather than any merfolk shenanigans

[3] Loud cries

great fear fell upon me of God's judgments[1], and the evil in the world. I went back again into the darkness of the house as into a place of shelter, and lay long upon my bed, pondering these mysteries.

It was late when I again woke, and I leaped into my clothes and hurried to the kitchen. No one was there; Rorie and the black had both stealthily departed long before; and my heart stood still at the discovery. I could rely on Rorie's heart, but I placed no trust in his discretion. If he had thus set out without a word, he was plainly bent upon some service to my uncle. But what service could he hope to render even alone, far less in the company of the man in whom my uncle found his fears incarnated? Even if I were not already too late to prevent some deadly mischief, it was plain I must delay no longer. With the thought I was out of the house; and often as I have run on the rough sides of Aros, I never ran as I did that fatal morning. I do not believe I put twelve minutes to the whole ascent.

My uncle was gone from his perch. The basket had indeed been torn open and the meat scattered on the turf; but, as we found afterwards, no mouthful had been tasted; and there was not another trace of human existence in that wide field of view. Day had already filled the clear heavens; the sun already lighted in a rosy bloom upon the crest of Ben Kyaw; but all below me the rude knolls of Aros and the shield of sea lay steeped in the clear darkling twilight of the dawn.

'Rorie!' I cried; and again 'Rorie!' My voice died in the silence, but there came no answer back. If there were indeed an enterprise afoot to catch my uncle, it was plainly not in fleetness of foot, but in dexterity of stalking, that the hunters placed their trust. I ran on farther, keeping the higher spurs[2], and looking right and left, nor did I pause again till I was on the mount above Sandag. I could see the wreck, the uncovered belt of sand, the waves idly beating, the long ledge of rocks, and on either hand the tumbled knolls, boulders, and gullies of the island. But still no human thing.

At a stride the sunshine fell on Aros, and the shadows and colours leaped into being. Not half a moment later, below me to the west, sheep began to scatter as in a panic[3]. There came a cry. I saw my uncle running. I saw the

---

[1] Initially suspecting that God had been merciful in offering Gordon a chance at redemption, Charlie is increasingly skeptical that anything other than the wrath of the Old Testament God awaits his hypocritical uncle

[2] That is, staying on the higher peaks – so as to have a more commanding view of the scenery

[3] This is a reference to the biblical passage "smite the shepherd and the sheep shall be scattered," a reference to the capture of Christ, and His subsequent abandonment by his terrified disciples. This seems to imply that a shepherd has indeed been struck down: the guilt-ridden patriarch of the family

black jump up in hot pursuit; and before I had time to understand, Rorie also had appeared, calling directions in Gaelic[1] as to a dog herding sheep.

I took to my heels to interfere, and perhaps I had done better to have waited where I was, for I was the means of cutting off the madman's last escape. There was nothing before him from that moment but the grave, the wreck, and the sea in Sandag Bay. And yet Heaven knows that what I did was for the best.

My uncle Gordon saw in what direction, horrible to him, the chase was driving him. He doubled, darting to the right and left; but high as the fever ran in his veins, the black was still the swifter. Turn where he would, he was still forestalled, still driven toward the scene of his crime. Suddenly he began to shriek aloud, so that the coast re-echoed; and now both I and Rorie were calling on the black to stop. But all was vain, for it was written otherwise[2]. The pursuer still ran, the chase still sped before him screaming; they avoided the grave, and skimmed close past the timbers of the wreck; in a breath they had cleared the sand; and still my kinsman did not pause, but dashed straight into the surf; and the black, now almost within reach, still followed swiftly behind him. Rorie and I both stopped, for the thing was now beyond the hands of men, and these were the decrees of God that came to pass before our eyes. There was never a sharper ending. On that steep beach they were beyond their depth at a bound[3]; neither could swim; the black rose once for a moment with a throttling cry; but the current had them, racing seaward; and if ever they came up again, which God alone can tell, it would be ten minutes after, at the far end of Aros Roost, where the seabirds hover fishing.

---

[1] It should be noted that Gaelic is different from Scots. Scots is a Germanic language with ties to English, while Gaelic is a Celtic language that bears no resemblance to English. Compare:
    ENGLISH: Good day to you! What's your name? Where do you come from?
    SCOTS: Gudday t'ye! Whit's yer name? Whaur dae ye come fae?
    GAELIC: Latha math. Dè an t-ainm a tha oirbh? Cò as a tha thu?
[2] Charlie is fairly convinced that, devil or man, the black man was destined to serve divine justice to his uncle in the form of destruction
[3] Meaning, the beach is so steep that it only takes a mere bound to be in water deeper than one is tall

SO many of Stevenson's horror stories float around the karmic debts accrued by a life of hypocrisy, and "The Merry Men" – perhaps even more so than "Jekyll" – demonstrates the sickening depths to which a man can bifurcate his own soul. Jekyll, after all, was misguided. Vain, perhaps, egoistical, perhaps, childish, pompous, and indulgent, even. But at the heart of his experiment lay an underdeveloped grain of nobility: the hope that a man might be able to extract and contain his weaknesses – to channel them away from his Ego and use the excess energy in the name of good. His thesis was obviously flawed (he underrated the power of the Id), but Gordon's sins are far baser those of Jekyll – and Gordon's murder is accomplished with the help of a far commoner libation than the potion which raises Hyde from Jekyll: whiskey. He is no handwringing socialite: even when he is as sober as a judge he relishes fantasies of human suffering, gloats in notions of divine punishment, and practically tingles with repressed arousal at the idea of sinners being dragged to death and hell. Stevenson was disgusted by what he saw as the two-faced hypocrisy of his family's Calvinist background – one which was fundamentally pessimistic, lorded punishment over the remorseful, and found delicious refreshment in the concept of hellfire, but allowed its adherents to privately nurture a smug, self-satisfaction and a deep sense of superiority to other men. Gordon hates Catholics, loathes Jacobites, and has no mercy for the dead. He ignores his complicity in the death of the sailor, has no pity for the floundering crews of shipwrecks, and sees all human suffering as God's justice – and yet he considers *himself* above punishment because he is one of the Elect (those chosen by God to be saved).

II.

Herein lies another problem that Stevenson harbored towards Calvinism: the concept of election. Calvinists believed that God chose whom to save and whom to damn. Salvation was less a matter of faith or grace and repentance, and more one of predestined superiority. There was no way to tell for sure whether you were among the Elect: it wasn't faith *or* good works that determined salvation, merely God's selection. Indeed, a Calvinist could be a horrible sinner their whole life, but if God had chosen them, they were assured salvation over – say – a devout Catholic who tended to the poor tirelessly. The Catholic would burn in hell for lack of being selected and the Calvinist would ascend to heaven despite their evil. To avoid being judged or considered un-elected by the members of their church, Calvinists would work strenuously to cultivate a good public image (think Jekyll), to make their neighbors think that the good behavior signaled a natural member of the Elect. This was not done as a means of gaining salvation (after all, good works meant nothing in and of themselves; they were but a SYMPTOM of election), but rather in hopes of convincing *others* of their election. But behind closed doors, actions did not matter and whatever wickedness had been pent up during the daytime could be unleashed without a care (think Hyde). Calvinists believed that there was no good in man (see: the doctrine of Total Depravity), so wickedness was to be expected, and as long as a person was a churchgoing member of the Elect, no amount of evil could derail them: it was just the human condition and there was no use restraining it (except to avoid gossip).

III.

Herein, now, lies the problem of *Gordon*: he does not remotely regret his murder: if he has been elected, it cannot prevent his salvation, and what else is expected of mankind besides evil? Stevenson, however, holds him to a higher standard of self-regulation: to strive to *become* good and to avoid acts of evil (again impossible: humans only do evil, except when God manipulates their actions). Gordon is finally struck with fear when the Black Man (a famous representation of Satan in Calvinist lore) comes for him, suggesting that he is not one of the Elect. Stevenson beautifully refuses to clarify whether the sailor is a mere foreigner or the genuine devil, and the supernatural nature of the tale is ambiguous. But regardless of his tartarian origins, the Black Man represents far more to Gordon than a paranormal visitor: he represents the ramifications of sin. No longer can Gordon say "it's not my fault; the devil made me do it," because the devil has manifested outside of him, and the fault falls squarely on his shoulders. Terrified at the prospect that the murder, the selfishness, the lust for finery, and the delight in suffering was internalized by his own soul (not externalized by Satan) – that sin could have been avoided, and that it was his conscious choice – Gordon consigns himself to the Merry Men (the symbolic realm of a wrathful God), hoping to receive mercy. Alas, the Black Man follows him into the water, and it becomes clear: to him that shows no mercy, no mercy shall be allotted, and both the terrified Calvinist and the strange Black Man are consumed in the mystical waters that crash into the Merry Men.

ROBERT Louis Stevenson was raised in a devout Presbyterian household, his father was a devoted Tory, and his family was proud of his trajectory to join the law profession, but in 1867 he attended Edinburgh University, and his parents' love was deeply tested as their son became increasingly attracted to what they considered radical philosophies. Things came to a boil in 1873 when his father was crushed to learn that his son – a self-described "red-hot socialist" – had embraced atheism, and belonged to a radical students' club, whose constitution was founded on the chief principle to "disregard everything our parents have taught us." The Stevenson family was genuinely loving and close, and Stevenson later groused that his decision to clandestinely spurn his upbringing and mock his parents crushed them. After being confronted by his father with a copy of the club's constitution, a sour, self-loathing Stevenson wrote "What a damned curse I am to my parents! As my father said 'You have rendered my whole life a failure.' As my mother said 'This is the heaviest affliction that has ever befallen me.' O Lord, what a pleasant thing it is to have damned the happiness of (probably) the only two people who care a damn about you in the world." University proved to be both a source of growth and misery, placing him at odds with his devoted family, and with the internalized Calvinist morality that so frequently shook his self-confidence. This cognitive dissonance between his adopted secular humanism and his inherited Protestant ethics generated most of his best literature, which largely followed cultural conflicts between material selfishness and spiritual discipline. Despite his youthful radicalism, Stevenson was at heart a cynic, and by 26 he looked back with wistful nostalgia at his secular militancy: "For my part, I look back to the time when I was a Socialist with something like regret. I have convinced myself (for the moment) that we had better leave these great changes to what we call great blind forces: their blindness being so much more perspicacious than the little, peering, partial eyesight of men [...] Now I know that in thus turning Conservative with years, I am going through the normal cycle of change and travelling in the common orbit of men's opinions. I submit to this, as I would submit to gout or gray hair, as a concomitant of growing age or else of failing animal heat; but I do not acknowledge that it is necessarily a change for the better—I dare say it is deplorably for the worse." He wrote these words in 1877, four years before penning the following ghost story. At its heart is a sorrowful sense of disjointed existence: a protagonist who is ultimately neither acceptable to his humanist mentors nor compatible with his religious upbringing – a castaway, cut adrift between two stable continents, and floating alone at the command of purposeless currents.

Thrawn Janet; or, Twisted Janet
{1887}

Translator's Note:

"THRAWN Janet" is one of the most ghoulish and (dare I say) twisted horror stories to come from a Victorian pen. It is one of Stevenson's best supernatural stories, and it is an underrated classic, forged in a deeply Hawthornian tradition of social responsibility, fear of the unconventional, and the battle waging between nature and civilization, reason and impulse, discipline and indulgence. There is only one problem: most 21st century English-speaking readers can only infer much of the plot through context clues, homophones, and detective work. This is because Stevenson wrote all but the first two paragraphs in the beautiful Scots dialect. Those who understand Scots will testify to its charm, and will support most editors' choice to preserve it in the original Scots (I have not yet found one who didn't). And yet, those who speak this rich and robust Germanic dialect only total about 1.5 million, including a mere 99,000 native speakers. While we hope to preserve the eloquent beauty of this dialect, it behooves us to understand it better by having a reference point: just as Shakespeare, Milton, and Spenser benefit dramatically from the inclusion of a gloss, so too will this story be more deeply appreciated by having an English language translation. And that is what I have done. My background in Scots is not formal, but it is passionate. In middle school I cut my teeth on the gorgeous poetry of Robert Burns and Robert Fergusson, the Romances of Sir Walter Scott and Stevenson, and the Scottish stories of Mrs Oliphant and Sir Arthur Conan Doyle which were peppered with the vernacular. Scots seemed to pop up in many of the historical fiction I read, and I found myself growing comfortable and familiar with the sound of it in my head, eventually requiring a gloss less and less. Having a combined five years of German study under my belt, the Scots vocabulary and grammar was familiar and easy to pick out (here are some homophones in English, German, and Scots respectively: night/Nacht/nicht, church/Kirche/kirk, light/Licht/lecht, old/alt/aulde, people/Volk/fowk, daughter/Tochter/dochter, etc.), and this was helpful in graduate school when I wrote my thesis on the Scottish Enlightenment, and the dialectics of nationhood generated by the Edinburgh school during the 18th century. In translating the following tale, I used a good deal of personal knowledge, consulting with a brace of dictionaries when in doubt: Charles Mackay's *The Auld Scots Dictionary of Lowland Scots*, and Crorbett and McClure's *The Edinburgh Companion to Scots*.

The following side-by-side translation is as approximate as we can make it. Some words and phrases are rendered in their original context, while others are updated to our modern vernacular. Notes are printed at the end of the story so as not to interfere with the flow of the twin texts. As the story progresses, the translation naturally begins to outpace the Scots text as single words are necessarily replaced by phrases (*spunk*: brimstone fire) and the characteristically short Scots phrases are necessarily lengthened (*come forrit*: come to take communion). In order to keep the text comparable I have underlined two phrases on each page – one on the Scots side and one on the English – which approximate each other. Should you get lost, that will be your point of comparison on that page to regain your bearings

– M.G.K.

THE Reverend Murdoch Soulis[1] was long minister of the moorland parish of Balweary[2], in the vale of Dule[3]. A severe, bleak-faced old man, dreadful to his hearers, he dwelt in the last years of his life, without relative or servant or any human company, in the small and lonely manse[4] under the Hanging Shaw[5]. In spite of the iron composure of his features, his eye was wild, scared, and uncertain[6]; and when he dwelt, in private admonitions, on the future of the impenitent, it seemed as if his eye pierced through the storms of time to the terrors of eternity. Many young persons, coming to prepare themselves against the season of the holy communion[7], were dreadfully

---

[1] The name is a real Scotch surname, but – as this story will easily demonstrate – Stevenson had a knack for lending significance to his place and people names, and the homonym of "soulless" should not be sneezed at. Stevenson here implies that something has happened to Soulis which has robbed him of his essential essence: in this case, his faith in humanity and his mercy

[2] Having the intentional severe meaning "place of the weary," or "weary place." The place is fictionional, though Stevenson may have gotten the name from an area near Kirkcaldy in Fife that has given the name Balwearie to a high school and a series of streets

[3] Similarly named: the valley of suffering, or the valley of sorrow, misery, grief, or mourning. Important to note: in North Britain a Dule Tree is a tree used as a gallows for public executions

[4] The parsonage of a Presbyterian minister, most specifically in Scotland or New England

[5] A shaw is a wood or copse. Its name indicates what variety of fruit tended to dangle from its branches, and serves as an important sign of woe, doom, and death throughout the tale

[6] The theme of intellectual humiliation and uncertainty – of personal failure and devastated confidence – will prove critical to his character, and presents the main theme of the story

[7] When Christians consume the wine and the bread offered at communion – the Eucharist – they symbolically remember the suffering of Christ and pledge to cleanse themselves of their sin as they await His return. While most homilies for the Eucharist (which literally means thanksgiving) focus on giving thanks and

affected by his talk. He had a sermon on I Pet. V. 8[1], "The devil as a roaring lion," on the Sunday after every 17th of August, and he was accustomed to surpass himself upon that text both by the appalling nature of the matter and the terror of his bearing in the pulpit. The children were frightened into fits, and the old looked more than usually oracular[2], and were, all that day, full of those hints that Hamlet deprecated[3]. The manse itself, where it stood by the water of Dule among some thick trees, with the Shaw overhanging it on the one side, and on the other many cold, moorish hilltops rising toward the sky, had begun, at a very early period of Mr. Soulis's ministry, to be avoided in the dusk hours by all who valued themselves upon their prudence; and guidmen[4] sitting at the clachan[5] alehouse shook their heads together at the thought of passing late by that uncanny neighbourhood. There was one spot, to be more particular, which was regarded with especial awe. The manse stood between the highroad and the water of Dule, with a gable to each; its bank was toward the kirktown[6] of Balweary, nearly half a mile away; in front of it, a bare garden, hedged with thorn, occupied the land between the river and the road[7]. The house was two stories high, with two large rooms on each. It opened not directly on the garden, but on a causewayed path, or passage, giving on the road on the one hand, and closed on the other by the tall willows and elders that bordered on the stream. And it was this strip of causeway that enjoyed among the young parishioners of Balweary so infamous a reputation. The minister walked there often after dark, sometimes groaning aloud in the instancy of his unspoken prayers; and when he was from home, and the manse door was

---

gratitude, this fire and brimstone, shame-based, sin-focused, soul-cleansing interpretation is also fitting if somewhat glum

[1] The text, which has inspired religious zealots and horror writers alike follows thus: *Be sober, be vigilant; because your adversary the devil, as a roaring lion, walketh about, seeking whom he may devour.* It is a fitting text for a man who – as we will see – feels that he has been hoodwinked by Satan

[2] As an oracle – having second sight perception, gifts of prophecy, etc.

[3] The benighted prince of Denmark actually responded very positively to omens, accepting the story of his father's ghost as truth without argument. Even philosophical Horatio treats them seriously when recounting the portents that heralded the assassination of Julius Caesar

[4] Gentlemen

[5] Village

[6] A country hamlet in the immediate neighborhood of the parish church

[7] Symbolically a region lost between civilization and nature, reason and impulse, discipline and indulgence, moral order and moral relativism

locked, the more daring school-boys ventured, with beating hearts, to "follow my leader[1]" across that legendary spot.

This atmosphere of terror, surrounding, as it did, a man of God of spotless character and orthodoxy, was a common cause of wonder and subject of inquiry among the few strangers who were led by chance or business into that unknown, outlying country. But many even of the people of the parish were ignorant of the strange events which had marked the first year of Mr. Soulis's ministrations; and among those who were better informed, some were naturally reticent, and others shy of that particular topic. Now and again, only, one of the older folk would warm into courage over his third tumbler, and recount the cause of the minister's strange looks and solitary life...

---

[1] A game of dares in which the followers must copy every daring act committed by the leader

FIFTY YEARS SYNE, WHEN MR.
SOULIS cam' first into Ba'weary, he
was still a young man,--a callant,
the folk said,--fu' o' book-learnin'
and grand at the exposition, but, as
was natural in sae young a man, wi'
nae leevin' experience in religion.
The younger sort were greatly taken
wi' his gifts and his gab; but auld,
concerned, serious men and women
were moved even to prayer for the
young man, whom they took to be a
self-deceiver, and the parish that
was like to be sae ill supplied. It was
before the days o' the Moderates--
weary fa' them; but ill things are
like guid--they baith come bit by bit,
a pickle at a time; and there were
folk even then that said the Lord had
left the college professors to their
ain devices, an' the lads that went to
study wi' them wad hae done mair
and better sittin' in a peat-bog, like
their forebears of the persecution,
wi' a Bible under their oxter and a
speerit o' prayer in their heart.
There was nae doubt, onyway, but
that Mr. Soulis had been ower-lang
at the college. He was careful and
troubled for mony things besides the
ae thing needful. He had a feck o'
books wi' him--mair than had ever
been seen before in a' that
presbytery; and a sair wark the
carrier had wi' them, for they were
a' like to have smoored in the Deil's
Hag between this and Kilmackerlie.
They were books o' divinity, to be
sure, or so they ca'd them; but the
serious

FIFTY YEARS AGO, WHEN MR
SOULIS first came into Balweary, he
was still a young man – just a kid,
the people said – full of book
learning and wonderful at
exposition, but, as was natural in so
young a man, with no life
experience in religion[1]. The younger
sort were greatly taken with his gifts
and his eloquence; but the older,
concerned, serious men and women
were moved even to prayer for the
young man, whom they took to be a
self-deceiver, and the parish that
was like to be so ill supplied. It was
before the days of the Moderates[2] –
dismal for them; but bad things are
like the good – they both come bit
by bit, a small bit at a time; and
there were people even then that
said the Lord had left the college
professors to their own devices, and
the lads that went to study with them
would have done more and better
sitting in a peat-bog, like their
forebears of the persecution[3], with a
Bible under their armpit and a spirit
of prayer in their heart. There was
no doubt, anyway, but that Mr
Soulis had been at the college for far
too long. We was careful and
troubled for many things besides the
one thing needful. He had a load of
books with him – more than had
ever been seen before in all the
parish; and a miserable chore the
carrier had with them, for they were
likely to have crushed the Devil's ox
between this and Kilmackerlie.

were o' opinion there was little service for sae mony, when the hail o' God's Word would gang in the neuk of a plaid. Then he wad sit half the day and half the nicht forby, which was scant decent--writin', nae less; and first they were feard he wad read his sermons; and syne it proved he was writin' a book himsel', which was surely no fittin' for ane of his years an' sma' experience.___

Onyway, it behooved him *to get an auld, decent wife to keep the manse for him an' see to his bit denners; and he was recommended to an auld limmer,--Janet M'Clour, they ca'd her,--and sae far left to himsel' as to be ower-persuaded. There was mony advised him to the contrar', for Janet was mair than suspeckit by the best folk in Ba'weary. Lang or that, she had had a wean to a dragoon; she hadnae come forrit for maybe thretty year; and bairns had seen her mumblin' to hersel' up on Key's Loan in the gloamin', whilk was an unco time an' place for a God-fearin' woman. Howsoever, it was the laird himsel' that had first tauld the minister o' Janet; and in thae days he wad have gane a far gate to pleesure the laird. When folk tauld him that Janet was sib to the deil, it was a' superstition by his way of it; and' when they cast up the Bible to him, an' the witch of Endor, he wad threep it doun their thrapples that thir days were a' gane*

They were books of divinity, to be sure, or so they called them; but the serious were of the opinion that there was little need for so many when the whole of God's Word would fit in the folds of a plaid cloak[4]. Then he would sit half the day and half the night as well, which was hardly decent – writing no less; and first they were afraid he would read his sermons; and since then it proved he was writing a book himself, which was surely not proper for anyone of his years and slight experience…

Anyway, it behooved him to get an old, decent biddy[5] to order the parsonage for him and to cook his small dinners; and he was recommended to an old hussy[6] – Janet McClour, they called her – and so far left to himself as to be over-persuaded. There were many who advised him against it, for Janet was more than suspected by the best citizens in Balweary. Long ago she had given birth to a dragoon's brat[7]; she hadn't taken communion for maybe thirty years; and children had seen her mumbling to herself up on Key's Loan in the twilit hollow – an uncouth time and place for a God-fearing woman. Howsoever, it was the squire himself that had first told the minister of Janet; and in those days he would have gone far out of his way to please the squire[8]. When the people told him that Janet was kin to the devil, he wrote it all off

*by, and the deil was mercifully
restrained.*

***Weel, when it got** about the clachan
that Janet M'Clour was to be
servant at the manse, the folk were
fair mad wi' her an' him thegether;
and some o' the guidwives had nae
better to dae than get round her
door-cheeks and chairge her wi' a'
that was kent again' her, frae the
sodger's bairn to John Tamson's twa
kye. She was nae great speaker; folk
usually let her gang her ain gait, an'
she let them gang theirs, wi' neither
fair guid-e'en nor fair guid-day; but
when she buckled to, she had a
tongue to deave the miller. Up she
got, an' there wasnae an auld story
in Ba'weary but she gart somebody
lowp for it that day; they couldnae
say ae thing but she could say twa to
it; till, at the hinder end, the
guidwives up and claucht haud of
her, and clawed the coats aff her
back, and pu'd her doun the clachan
to the water o' Dule, to see if she
were a witch or no, soum or droun.
The carline skirled till ye could hear
her at the Hangin' Shaw, and she
focht like ten; there was mony a
guid wife bure the mark of her neist
day an' mony a lang day after; and
just in the hettest o' the
collieshangie, wha suld come up
(for his sins) but the new minister.*

*"Women," said he (and he had a
grand voice), "I charge you in the
Lord's name to let her go."*

as superstition; and when they
showed him the Bible, and the
Witch of Endor[9], he would argue it
back down their throats – that those
days were all bygone, and that God
had bound the devil.

Well, when word got out to the
village that Janet McClour was to be
the parsonage servant, the people
were very cross with her and him
both, and some of the ladies had
nothing better to do than get around
her doorposts and accuse her of all
that was known against her, from
the soldier's bastard to John
Tamson's two cows. She was no
great speaker; people usually let her
go her own pace and she let them go
theirs, with neither a kind "good
evening," nor a kind "good day;"
but when she opened up, she had a
tongue that would deafen a miller[10].
Up she got, and there wasn't an old
story in Balweary but she would
force someone to listen to that day;
they couldn't say a thing but she
could say two in response; till, at the
end of the day, the ladies up and
caught hold of her, and clawed the
coats off her back, and pulled her
down the town to the water of Dule,
to see if she was a witch or not –
swim or drown. The crone shrieked
till you could hear her at the
Hanging Wood, and she fought like
ten; there was a good many ladies
who wore bruises the next day, and
many for longer, and just at the

Janet ran to him--she was fair wud wi' terror--an' clang to him, an' prayed him, for Christ's sake, save her frae the cummers; an' they, for their pairt, tauld him a' that was kent, and maybe mair.

"Woman," says he to Janet, "is this true?"

"As the Lord sees me," says she, "as the Lord made me, no a word o' 't. Forby the bairn," says she, "I've been a decent woman a' my days."

"Will you," says Mr. Soulis, "in the name of God, and before me, His unworthy minister, renounce the devil and his works?"

Weel, it wad appear that, when he askit that, she gave a girn that fairly frichtit them that saw her, an' they could hear her teeth play dirl thegether in her chafts; but there was naething for it but the ae way or the ither; an' Janet lifted up her hand and renounced the deil before them a'.

"And now," says Mr. Soulis to the guidwives, "home with ye, one and all, and pray to God for His forgiveness."

And he gied Janet his arm, though she had little on her but a sark, and took her up the clachan to her ain door like a leddy of the land, an' her scrieghin' and laughin' as was a scandal to be heard.

fiercest of the fighting, who should come up (for his sins) but the new minister.

"Women," said he (and he had a grand voice), "I tell you in the Lord's name to let her go."

Janet ran to him – she was totally wild with terror – and clung to him and begged him, for Christ's sake, save her from the bitches; and they, for their part, told him all that was known, and maybe more.

"Woman," says he to Janet, "is this true?"

"As the Lord sees me," says she, "as the Lord made me, not a word of it. Other than the baby," says she, "I've been a decent woman all my days."

"Will you," says Mr Soulis, "in the name of God, and before me, His unworthy mister, renounce the devil and his works?"

Well, it would appear that, when he asked that, she gave a grin that thoroughly terrified those that saw her, and they could hear her teeth grinding together in her cheeks; but there was nothing to account for it one way or the other; and Janet lifted up her hand and renounced the devil before them all

"And now," says Mr Soulis to the ladies, "Get back home, one and all, and pray to God for his forgiveness."

***There were mony** grave folk lang*
ower their prayers that nicht; but
when the morn cam' there was sic a
fear fell upon a' Ba'weary that the
bairns hid theirsel's, and even the
men folk stood and keekit fraetheir
doors. For there was Janet comin'
doun the clachan,--her or her
likeness, nane could tell,--wi' her
neck thrawn, and her heid on ae
side, like a body that has been
hangit, and a girn on her face like
an unstreakit corp. By-an'-by they
got used wi' it, and even speered at
her to ken what was wrang; but frae
that day forth she couldnae speak
like a Christian woman, but
slavered and played click wi' her
teeth like a pair o' shears; and frae
that day forth the name o' God cam'
never on her lips. Whiles she wad
try to say it, but it michtnae be.
Them that kenned best said least;
but they never gied that Thing the
name o' Janet M'Clour; for the auld
Janet, by their way o' 't, was in
muckle hell that day. But the
minister was neither to haud nor to
bind; he preached about naething
but the folk's cruelty that had gien
her a stroke of the palsy; he skelpt
the bairns that meddled her; and he
had her up to the manse that same
nicht, and dwalled there a' his lane
wi' her under the Hangin' Shaw.

Weel, time gaed by, and the idler
sort commenced to think mair lichtly
o' that black business. The minister
was weel thocht o'; he was aye late
at the writing--folk wad see

And he gave Janet his arm, though
she had little more on than a
chemise[11], and he took her up the
village to her own door like a proper
lady, and her screeching and
laughing was scandalous.

There were many grave people
busy praying that night; but when
morning came, there was such a fear
that fell over all Balweary that the
kids hid themselves, and even the
men stood and peeked through their
doors. For there was Janet coming
down the town – her or her likeness,
none could tell – with her neck
twisted and her head on one side,
like a body that has been hanged,
and a grin on her face like a hanged
corpse cut down[12]. By and by they
got used to it, and even asked her to
tell them what was wrong; but from
that day forth she couldn't speak
like a Christian woman, but slavered
and gnashed her teeth like a pair of
shears[13]; and from that day forth the
name of God never came to her lips.
As much as she would try to say it,
it wouldn't work[14]. Those that knew
best said least; but they never gave
that Thing the name of Janet
McClour; for the old Janet, by their
way of seeing it, was in the middle
of hell that day. But the minster was
neither going to hold up or restrain
himself; he preached about nothing
but the people's cruelty that had
given her a stroke of the palsy; he
belted the children that tormented
her; and he had her up

his can'le doon by the Dule Water after twal' at e'en; and he seemed pleased wi' himsel' and upsitten as at first, though a' body could see that he was dwining. As for Janet, she cam' an' she gaed; if she didnae speak muckle afore, it was reason she should speak less then; she meddled naebody; but she was an eldritch thing to see, an' nane wad hae mistrysted wi' her for Ba'weary glebe.

***About the end o' July** there cam' a spell o' weather, the like o' 't never was in that countryside; it was lown an' het an' heartless; the herds couldnae win up the Black Hill, the bairns were ower-weariet to play; an' yet it was gousty too, wi' claps o' het wund that rummled in the glens, and bits o' shouers that slockened naething. We aye thocht it but to thun'er on the morn; but the morn cam', an' the morn's morning, and it was aye the same uncanny weather; sair on folks and bestial. Of a' that were the waur, nane suffered like Mr. Soulis; he could neither sleep nor eat, he tauld his elders; an' when he wasnae writin' at his weary book, he wad be stravaguin' ower a' the country-side like a man possessed, when a' body else was blithe to keep caller ben the house.*

Abune Hangin' Shaw, in the bield o' the Black Hill, there's a bit enclosed grund wi' an iron yert; and it seems, in the auld days, that was

to the parsonage that same night, and lingered there at his lane with her under the Hanging Wood.

Well, time went by, and the idler sort commenced to think more lightly of that black business. The minister was well regarded; he was always writing – the people would see his candle shining down by the Dule Water after twilight at evening; and he seemed pleased with himself and lackadaisical once again, though anybody could see that he was dwindling. As for Janet, she came and she went; if she didn't speak a great deal before, it was reasonable that she should speak less now; she bothered no one; but she was a hideous and frightful thing to see, and none would have offended her for all of Balweary.

Around the end of July there came a strange period of weather unlike any ever seen in that countryside; it was cloudless and hot and heartless; the herds couldn't climb up the Black Hill, the kids were too exhausted to play, and yet it was gusty too, with bursts of hot wind that rumbled in the glens, and bits of showers that quenched nothing. We always thought it was simply thundering in the morning; but the morning came, and the next morning, and it was always the same uncanny weather; oppressing man and beast alike. Of all that had it bad, no one suffered like Mr

the kirkyaird o' Ba'weary, and consecrated by the papists before the blessed licht shone upon the kingdom. *It was a great howff, o' Mr. Soulis's onyway*; there would sit an' consider his sermons' and inded it's a bieldy bit. Weel, as he came ower the wast end o' the Black Hill, ae day, he saw first twa, an' syne fower, an' syne seeven corbie craws fleein' round an' round abune the auld kirkyaird. They flew laigh and heavy, an' squawked to ither as they gaed; and it was clear to Mr. Soulis that something had put them frae their ordinar. He wasna easy fleyed, an' gaed straucht up to the wa's; and what suld he find there but a man, or the appearance of a man, sittin' in the inside upon a grave. He was of a great stature, an' black as hell, and his een were singular to see. Mr. Soulis had heard tell o' black men, mony's the time; but there was something unco abut this black man that daunted him. Het as he was, he took a kind o' cauld grue in the marrow o' his banes; but up he spak' for a' that; an' says he, "My friend, are you a stranger in this place?" The black man answered never a word; he got upon his feet, an' begude to hirsel to the wa' on the far side; but he aye lookit at the minister; an' the minister stood an' lookit back; till a' in a meenute the black man was ower the wa' an' rinnin' for the bield o' the trees. Mr. Soulis, he hardly kenned why, ran

Soulis; he could neither sleep nor eat, he told his elders; and when he wasn't writing at his weary book, he would be roaming aimlessly over all the countryside like a man possessed, when anybody else was more than happy to keep cool indoors[15].

Above Hanging Wood, in the protection of the Black Hill, there's a small plot enclosed with an iron fence; and it seems, in the olden days, that was the graveyard of Balweary, and consecrated by the Papists before the blessed light shone down upon the kingdom[16]. **It was a favorite haunt** of Mr Soulis' anyway; there he would sit and consider his sermons, and indeed it's a cozy spot. Well, as he came over the west end of the Black Hill one day, he saw first two, and then four, and then seven carrion crows flying round and round above the old graveyard. They flew light and heavy and squawked to each other as they went; and it was clear to Mr Soulis that something had excited them from their routine. He wasn't easily frightened, and went straight up to the wall; and what should he find there but a man, or the appearance of a man, sitting inside on top of a grave. He was of a great stature, and black as hell, and his eyes were extraordinary to see. Mr Soulis had often heard of black men; but there was something off about this black man that daunted him[17]. Hot as he was, *after him; but he was sair forjaskit wi' his walk an' the het, unhalesome weather; and rin as he likit, he got nae mair than a glisk o' the black man amang the birks, till he won doun to the foot o' the hillside, an' there he saw him ance mair, gaun, hap, step, an' lowp, ower Dule Water to the manse.*

Mr. Soulis wasna weel *pleased that this fearsome gangrel suld mak' sae free wi' Ba'weary manse; an' he ran the harder, an' wet shoon, ower the burn, an' up the walk; but the deil a black man was there to see. He stepped out upon the road, but there was naebody there; he gaed a' ower the gairden, but na, nae black man. At the hinder end, and a bit feard as was but natural, he lifted the hasp and into the manse; and there was Janet M'Clour before his een, wi' her thrawn craig, and nane sae pleased to see him. And he aye minded sinsyne, when first he set his een upon her, he had the same cauld and deidy grue.__*

"Janet," says he, "have you seen a black man?"

"A black man?" quo' she. "Save us a'! Ye 're no wise, minister. There's nae black man in a' Ba'weary."

But she didna speak plain, ye maun understand; but yam-yammered, like a powny wi' the bit in its moo.

he took a kind of cold shiver in the marrow of his bones; but he spoke

up in spite of it, saying "My friend, are you a stranger in this place?" The black man answered never a word; he stood up, and lumbered towards the wall on the far side; but he always looked at the minister; and the minister stood and looked back; till in the blink of an eye the black man was over the wall and running for the shelter of the trees. Mr Soulis, he hardly knew why, ran after him; but he was sorely fatigued with his walk and the hot, unwholesome weather; and run as he would, he got no more than a glimpse of the black man among the birches, till he wound down to the foot of the hillside, and there he saw him once more, going hop, step, and jump over Dule Water to the parsonage.

Mr Soulis wasn't too pleased that this fearsome vagrant should be so familiar with Balweary parsonage; and he ran all the harder, in wet shoes, over the stream, and up the walk; but nothing of that devil of a black man was there to see. He stepped out upon the road, but there was nobody there; he went all over the garden, but no, no black man. At the back end – and a bit frightened as was natural – he lifted the hasp and entered the parsonage; and there was Janet McClour before his eyes, with her twisted gullet, and not so pleased to see him. Since then he has always remember that when he first set

"Weel," says he, "Janet, if there was nae black man, I have spoken with the Accuser of the Brethren."

And he sat down like ane wi' a fever, an' his teeth chittered in his heid.

"Hoots!" says she, "think shame to yoursel', minister," an' gied him a drap brandy that she keept aye by her.

__Syne Mr. Soulis gaed__ into his study amang a' his books. It's a lang, laigh, mirk chalmer, perishin' cauld in winter, an' no very dry even in the top o' the simmer, for the manse stands near the burn. Sae doun he sat, and thocht of a' that had come an' gane since he was in Ba'weary, an' his hame, an' the days when he was a bairn an' ran daffin' on the braes; and that black man aye ran in his heid like the owercome of a sang. Aye the mair he thocht, the mair he thocht o' the black man. He tried the prayer, an' the words wouldnae come to him; an' he tried, they say, to write at his book, but he couldnae mak' nae mair o' that. There was whiles he thocht the black man was at his oxter, an' the swat stood upon him cauld as well-water; and there was other whiles when he cam' to himsel' like a christened bairn and minded naething.

The upshot was that he gaed to the window an' stood glowrin' at Dule Water. The trees are unco thick, an'

eyes on her, he had cold and mischievous shiver—

"Janet," says he, "have you seen a black man?"

"A black man?" she said. "Save us all! You're out of your mind, minister. There's no black man in all Balweary."

But she didn't speak plain, you most understand; but grumble-mumbled like a pony with a bit in its mouth[18].

Well," he says, "Janet, if there was no black man, I have spoken with the Accuser of the Saints[19]."

And he sat down like one with fever, and his teeth chattered in his head.

"Bollocks!" says she, "shame on you, minister," giving him a splash of the brandy which was always on her.

Then Mr Soulis went into his study among all of his books. It's a long, low, murky chamber, deadly cold in winter, and not very dry even in the peak of summer, for the parsonage stands near the stream. So down he sat, and thought of all who had come and gone since he was in Balweary, and his hometown, and the days when he was a kid and ran merrily on the hilltops[20]; and that black man always ran in his head like the chorus of a song. All the more he thought, the more he the water lies deep an' black under the manse; and there was Janet washing' the cla'es wi' her coats kilted.

She had her back _to the minister, an' he for his pairt, hardly kenned what he was lookin' at. Syne she turned round, an' shawed her face; Mr. Soulis had the same cauld grue as twice that day afore, an' it was borne in upon him what folk said, that Janet was deid lang syne, an' this was a bogle in her clay-cauld flesh. He drew back a pickle and he scanned her narrowly. She was tramp-trampin' in the cla'es, croonin' to hersel'; and eh! Gude guide us, but it was a fearsome face. Whiles she sang louder, but there was nae man born o' woman that could tell the words o' her sang; an' whiles she lookit sidelang doun, but there was naething there for her to look at. There gaed a scunner through the flesh upon his banes; and that was Heeven's advertisement. But Mr. Soulis just blamed himsel', he said, to think sae ill of a puir auld afflicted wife that hadnae a freend forby himsel'; an' he put up a bit prayer for him an' her, an' drank a little caller water,-- for his heart rose again' the meat,-- an' gaed up to his naked bed in the gloaming._

That was a nicht that has never been forgotten in Ba'weary, the

thought of the black man. He tried the Lord's Prayer, and the words wouldn't come to him; and he tried, they say, to write at his book, but he couldn't come up with anything[21]. There was a time when he thought the black man was at his elbow, and the sweat stood upon him as cold as well water; and there was other times when he came to himself like a christened babe and was troubled by nothing.

The upshot was that he went to the window and stood glowering at Dule Water. The trees were unnaturally thick, and the water lies deep and black under the manse; and there was Janet washing the clothes with her cloak pinned up in kilt fashion.

She had her back to the minister, and he for his part, hardly knew what he was looking at. Then she turned around and showed her face; Mr Soulis had the same cold shiver as twice that day before, and it dawned upon him what the people said: that Janet had died long ago, that this was a walking revenant in her clay-cold flesh[22]. He drew back a bit and scanned her narrowly. She was stomp-stomping the clothes, crooning to herself; and oh! God preserve us, but it was a fearsome face. Soon she sang louder, but there was no man born of woman that could tell the words of her song[23]; and all the while she looked sideways down,

__nicht o' the seeventeenth__ of August,
seventeen hun'er' an' twal'. It had
been het afore, as I hae said, but
that nicht it was hetter than ever.
The sun gaed doun amang unco-
lookin' clouds; it fell as mirk as the
pit; no a star, no a breath o' wund;
ye couldnae see your han' afore
your face, and even the auld folk
cuist the covers frae their beds and
lay pechin' for their breath. Wi' a'
that he had upon his mind, it was
gey and unlikely Mr. Soulis wad get
muckle sleep. He lay an' he
tummled; the gude, caller bed that
he got into brunt his very banes;
whiles he slept, and whiles he
waukened; whiles he heard the time
o' nicht, and whiles a tike yowlin' up
the muir, as if somebody was deid;
whiles he thocht he heard bogles
claverin' in his lug, an' whiles he
saw spunkies in the room. He
behooved, he judged, to be sick; an'
sick he was--little he jaloosed the
sickness.

At the hinder end, he got a clearness
in his mind, sat up in his sark on the
bedside, and fell thinkin' ance mair
o' the black man an' Janet. He
couldnae weel tell how,--maybe it
was the cauld to his feet,--but it
cam' in upon him wi' a spate that
there was some connection between
thir twa, an' that either or baith o'
them were bogles. And just at that
moment, in Janet's room, which was
neist to his, there cam' a stamp o'
feet as if men were wars'lin', an'
then a loud

but there was nothing there for her
to look at. There came a nauseated
disgust through the flesh upon his
bones; and that was heaven's
advertisement. But Mr Soulis just
blamed himself, he said to think so
ill of a poor, old, afflicted biddy,
that hadn't a friend in the world
other than himself; and he prayed a
little prayer for him and her, and
drank a little fresh water – suffering
as he did from heartburn – and went
to his naked bed in the twilight.

That was a night that has never been
forgotten in Balweary, **the night of
the seventeenth** of August, 1712. It
had been hot before, as I have said,
but that night was hotter than ever.
The sun went down among
unnatural-looking clouds; it was as
dark as hell; not a star, not a breath
of wind; you couldn't see your hand
before your face, and even the old
folks threw the covers from their
beds and lay gasping for their
breath. With all that he had upon his
mind, it was very unlikely Mr Soulis
would get much sleep. He lay and
he tossed and turned; the good, cool
bed that he got into burned his very
bones; sometimes he slept and
sometimes he woke; sometimes he
heard the time of night, and
sometimes a hound yowling up the
moor, as if somebody was dead;
sometimes he thought he heard
ghosts chattering in his ear, and
sometimes he saw phantom lights in
the room. He

bang; an' then a wund gaed reishling round the fower quarters of the house; an' then a' was ance mair as seelent as the grave.

Mr. Soulis was *feard for neither man nor deevil. He got his tinder-box, an' lit a can'le, an' made three steps o' 't ower to Janet's door.*

It was on the hasp, an' he pushed it open, an' keeked bauldly in. It was a big room, as big as the minister's ain, an' plenished wi' grand, auld, solid gear, for he had naething else. There was a fower-posted bed wi' auld tapestry; and a braw cabinet of aik, that was fu' o' the minister's divinity books, an' put there to be out o' the gate; an' a wheen duds o' Janet's lying here and there about the floor. But nae Janet could Mr. Soulis see, nor ony sign of a contention. In he gaed (an' there's few that wad hae followed him), an' lookit a' round, an' listened. But there was naethin' to be heard neither inside the manse nor in a' Ba'weary parish, an' naethin' to be seen but the muckle shadows turnin' round the can'le. An' then a' at aince the minister's heart played dunt an' stood stock-still, an' a cauld wund blew amang the hairs o' his heid. Whaten a weary sicht was that for the puir man's een! For there was Janet hangin' frae a nail beside the auld aik cabinet; her heid aye lay on her shouther, her een were steeked, the tongue projecket

behooved, he judged, to be sick; and sick he was – little he suspected the cause of the sickness.

As the night waned, he got a clearness of mind, sat up in his nightshirt on the bedside, and began to once more think of the black man and Janet. He couldn't well explain why – maybe it was the chill in his feet – but it came to him like a flood that there was some connection between the two, and that either or both of them were specters. And just at that moment, in Janet's room, which was nearest to his, there came a stamp of feet as if men were wrestling, and then a loud bang; and then a wind went rushing around the four quarters of the house; and then all was once more as silent as the grave[24].

Mr Soulis was afraid of neither man nor devil. He got his tinder box[25], and lit a candle, and was over to Janet's door in three bounds.

It was unlocked, and he pushed it open, and peeked boldly in. It was a big room, as big as the minister's own, and provided with grand, old solid furniture, for he had nothing else. There was a four-poster bed with antique tapestries; and a beautiful cabinet of oak, that was full of the minister's divinity books, and put there to be out of the way[26]; and a few of Janet's togs

frae her mouth, and her heels were twa feet clear abune the floor.

89

"God forgive us all!" thocht Mr. Soulis, "poor Janet's dead."

He cam' a step nearer to the corp; an' then his heart fair whammled in his inside. For--by what cantrip it wad ill beseem a man to judge—she was hingin' frae a single nail an' by a single wursted thread for darnin' hose.

It's an awfu' thing to be your lane at nicht wi' siccan prodigies o' darkness; but Mr. Soulis was strong in the Lord. He turned an' gaed his ways oot o' that room, and locket the door ahint him; and step by step doon the stairs, as heavy as leed; and set doon the can'le on the table at the stair-foot. He couldnae pray, he couldnae think, he was dreepin' wi' caul' swat, an' naething could he hear but the dunt-dunt-duntin' o' his ain heart. He micht maybe have stood there an hour, or maybe twa, he minded sae little; when a' o' a sudden he heard a laigh, uncanny steer upstairs; a foot gaed to an' fro in the cham'er whair the corp was hingin'; syne the door was opened, though he minded weel that he had lockit it; an' syne there was a step upon the landin', an' it seemed to him as if the corp was lookin' ower the tail and doun upon him whaur he stood.

He took up the can'le again (for he couldnae want the licht), and, as

were lying here and there about the floor. But no Janet could Mr Soulis see, nor any sign of a struggle. In he went (and there's few who would have followed him), and looked all around and listened. But there was nothing to be heard inside the parsonage nor in all Balweary parish, and nothing to be seen but the great shadows turning around the candle. And then all at once the minister's heart knocked loudly and stood stock-still, and a cold wind blew among the hairs of his head. What a hideous sight it was for the poor man's eyes! For there was Janet hanging from a nail beside the old oak cabinet; her head always lay on her shoulder, her eyes bulged out, the tongue protruded from her mouth, and her heels were two feet clear above the floor[27].

"God forgive us all!" thought Mr Soulis, "poor Janet's dead."

He came a step nearer to the corpse; and then his heart nearly tottered inside his chest. For – by what contraption it would hardly seem fit for a man to judge – she was hanging from a single nail and by a single worsted thread for darning hose[28].

It's an awful thing to be alone at night with such prodigies of darkness; but Mr Soulis was strong in the Lord. He turned and went his way out of that room, and locked

__saftly as ever he could__, gaed straucht out o' the manse an' to the far end o' the causeway. It was aye pit-mirk; the flame o' the can'le, when he set it on the grund, brunt steedy and clear as in a room; naething moved, but the Dule Water seepin' and sabbin' doon the glen, an' yon unhaly footstep that cam' plodding' doun the stairs inside the manse. He kenned the foot ower-weel, for it was Janet's; and at ilka step that cam' a wee thing nearer, the cauld got deeper in his vitals. He commended his soul to Him that made an' keepit him; "and, O Lord," said he, "give me strength this night to war against the powers of evil."

By this time the foot was comin' through the passage for the door; he could hear a hand skirt alang the wa', as if the fearsome thing was feelin' for its way. The saughs tossed an' maned thegether, a long sigh cam' ower the hills, the flame o' the can'le was blawn aboot; an' there stood the corp of Thrawn Janet, wi' her grogram goun an' her black mutch, wi' the heid aye upon the shouther, an' the girn still upon the face o' 't,--leevin', ye wad hae said--deid, as Mr. Soulis weel kenned,--upon the threshold o' the manse.

It's a strange thing that the saul of man should be thirled into his perishable body; but the minister saw that, an' his heart didnae break.

the door behind him; and step by step down the stairs, as heavy as lead; and set down the candle on the table of the stair-foot. He couldn't pray, he couldn't think, he was dripping with cold sweat, and nothing could he hear but the dunt-dunt-dunting of his own heart. He might maybe have stood there an hour, or maybe two, he minded so little; when all of a sudden he heard a low, unnatural bustle upstairs; a foot went to and fro in the chamber where the corpse was hanging; then the door was opened though he knew well that he had locked it; and then there was a step upon the landing, and it seemed to him as if the corpse was looking over the rail and down upon him where he stood.

He took up the candle again (for he couldn't bear to be without the light), and, as **softly as he could,** went straight out of the parsonage and to the far end of the causeway. It was still dark as hell outside[29]; the flame of the candle, when he set it on the ground, burnt steady and clear as in a room; nothing moved, but the Dule Water seeping and sobbing down the glen, and those same unholy footsteps that came plodding down the stairs inside the parsonage. He knew the foot all too well, for it was Janet's; and at each step that came a bit nearer, his blood grew colder. He commended his soul to Him that made and kept him; "and, O Lord," said he, "give

__She didnae stand__ there lang; she began to move again, an' cam' slowly toward Mr. Soulis whaur he stood under the saughs. A' the life o' his body, a' the strength o' his speerit, were glowerin' frae his een. It seemed she was gaun to speak, but wanted words, an' made a sign wi' the left hand. There cam' a clap o' wund, like a cat's fuff; oot gaed the can'le, the saughs skrieghed like folk' an' Mr. Soulis kenned that, live or die, this was the end o' 't.

"Witch, beldam, devil!" he cried, "I charge you, by the power of God, begone--if you be dead, to the grave; if you be damned, to hell."

An' at that moment the Lord's ain hand out o' the heevens struck the Horror whaur it stood; the auld, deid, desecrated corp o' the witch-wife, sae lang keepit frae the grave and hirselled round by deils, lowed up like a brunstane spunk and fell in ashes to the grund; the thunder followed, peal on dirling peal, the rairing rain upon the back o' that; and Mr. Soulis lowped through the garden hedge, and ran, wi' skelloch upon skelloch, for the clachan.

That same mornin' John Christie saw the black man pass the Muckle Cairn as it was chappin' six; before eicht, he gaed by the change-house at Knockdow; an' no lang after, Sandy M'Lellan saw him gaun linkin' doun the braes frae Kilmackerlie. There's little doubt

me strength this night to battle the powers of evil."

By this time the step was coming through the passage of the door; he could hear a hand sweep along the wall, as if the fearsome thing was feeling for its way. The willows tossed and moaned together, a long sigh came over the hills, the flame of the candle was blown about; and there stood the corpse of Twisted Janet, with her grosgrain[30] gown and her black nightcap with the head still upon the shoulder, and the grin still upon the face of it – living, you would have thought – but dead, as Mr Soulis well knew – upon the threshold of the parsonage.

It's a strange thing that the soul of man should be woven into his perishable body[31]; but the minister saw that, and his heart didn't break.

She didn't stand there long; she began to move again, and came slowly toward Mr Soulis where he stood under the willows. All the life of his body, all the strength of his spirit, were glowering from his eyes. It seemed she was going to speak, but lack words, and made a sign with the left hand[32]. There came a clap of wind, like a cat's spitting hiss; out went the candle, the willows screamed like living people and Mr Soulis knew that, live or die, this was the end of it.

but it was him that dwalled sae lang in Janet's body; but he was awa' at *last; and sinsyne the deil has never fashed us in Ba'weary.*

But it was a sair *dispensation for the minister; lang, lang he lay ravin' in his bed; and frae that hour to this, he was the man ye ken the day.*

"Witch, crone, devil!" he cried, "I charge you by the power of God[33], begone – if you be dead, to the grave; if you be damned, to hell."

And at that moment the Lord's own hand out of the heavens struck the Horror where it stood; the old, dead, desecrated corpse of the witch-biddy, so long kept from the grave and herded around by demons, flared up like sulfur fire and fell in ashes to the ground; the thunder followed, peal on throbbing peal, the roaring rain upon the back of that; and Mr Soulis leapt through the garden hedge and ran, with scream upon scream, for the village.

That same morning John Christie saw the black man pass the great tomb just before six; before eight he went by the change-house at Knockdow, and not long afterwards, Sandy McLellan saw him rushing smartly down the hills from Kilmackerlie. There's little doubt that it was him that dwelt so long in Janet's body; but he was away at last; and since then the devil has never troubled us in Balweary.

But it was a bitter dispensation for the minister; long, long he lay raving in his bed; and from that hour to this, he was the man you know today[34].

1. Reflecting, perhaps, Stevenson's own break from Christianity and his reliance on theoretical philosophies that he learned at college. In any case, Soulis is separated from his congregation by their respective values: he upholds education, logic, and theory, while they trust experience and intuition. It represents a break between a worldview – essentially optimistic – that places its faith in predictable laws of nature, and one – essentially cynical – which is sure of nothing save the wisdom of experience and intuition. Soulis can also be seen as representing the Enlightenment-era which was defined by a humanist ethic, distrust in religion, and optimism for the reformation of humanity. Like the French Revolution, which proved the great disaster of the Enlightenment, Soulis' faith in Janet and his dismissal of his congregants' distrust will prove the death of his optimism, ushering in the reign of bitter wisdom and soulless (Soulis?) disappointment.
2. The Moderates were Presbyterians who – unlike the radical Covenanters – allied themselves with the traditions, theology, and ornamentations of the Anglican Church
3. During the Killing Time, outlaw Covenanters fled to the moors and wastes of the Scottish countryside. Those who were captured were persecuted – sometimes executed, sometimes lynched – and those who survived did so by hiding from soldiers in the bogs. Again we see the theme of "suffering and experience as the key to wisdom." His older congregants are suspicious of the minister whose new theories and fresh view of religion have never been tested by trials
4. True Calvinists, his parishioners are suspicious of any learning that comes from somewhere other than the Bible (especially religious learning), and his massive cartload of books do nothing to inspire confidence
5. Ministers who were not married typically hired an old (and preferably ugly) widow woman to live in the parsonage and do the chores around the house. After marriage, most ministers continued to retain a housekeeper/cook, but after marriage the threat of scandal was less likely, and it was not so important that the woman be very old and ugly
6. As a "limmer" or hussy, she doesn't have the sort of reputation which is well suited to a reverend's household
7. A dragoon is a mounted infantryman – a soldier who can fight just as ably on foot as on horseback. Dragoons were the scouts of the army and were usually the first sign of the presence of a fighting force. They skirmished, forged, and hunted down prisoners. The most damning part of this fact isn't Janet's premarital pregnancy: if the father was a trooper, he was a government soldier, and if the time was considered long ago in 1712, it is not a leap to suspect that he may have been a British soldier during the Killing Time. In a Calvinist community, having a bastard with a British dragoon during the 1680s would have been like a French woman being impregnated by a Nazi officer from the SS in a village where Jews had been hauled away to the death camps.

8. The local gentry and the local clergy of a small country town had a close relationship. The clergy especially looked to the gentry as a source of patronage, particularly in poor communities with few well-off parishioners. Those who have read Jane Austen will be reminded of the Reverend Mr. Collins' pathetic brown-nosing of Lady Catherine

9. In the Bible, the possibly schizophrenic King Saul has watched his nation turn against him, and desperately pays a visit to the Witch of Endor – a necromancer and conjuror. Terrified at first, for Saul had made witchcraft a capital crime, she is eventually laid at ease and summons the spirit of the prophet Samuel to counsel the troubled tyrant. The news is grave, and Saul leaves Endor to face his foretold death in an upcoming battle

10. Mills are horribly noisy because of their machinery and the rumble of the grinding stones rolling over one another

11. A long undershirt analogous to underwear or a slip. This is the first of several descriptions which suggest that there is an odd sexuality about his relationship with Janet that – in spite of her age – might be inappropriate. Certainly taking the arm of a woman wearing nothing other than a nightshirt and walking her to her house in broad daylight would shock the community

12. This is a reference to the "rictus smile" – a contortion of the facial muscles after death as the muscles dehydrate and stiffen, which resembles a gruesome smirk

13. What appears to have happened is this: having disavowed the Devil in public, Janet has been hanged by her master for treason – her throat wrenched by the noose, and her neck broken by the fall – and her dead body has been possessed by demons. Having no air in her lungs, the animating spirits struggle to make her speak, resulting in the garbled, husky slobbering that passes for speech

14. While a human in league with the Devil, she could fake her allegiance to God, but the demons that now activate her zombie corpse are incapable of speaking the holy name

15. Soulis suffers by himself while the rest of the village congregates indoors, staying cool. Pouring into his "weary book" can be seen as a form of severe self-absorption: he shuns the cool comfort of his neighbors' houses to wander by himself in the sweltering heat of untamed nature, and when he isn't under the sun he's locked up in his study writing. This reclusion is the result of resentment for his under-educated communicants: rather than biding his time with the peasants in his flock, he chooses the bloodless, pulseless books in his library – and the equally bloodless and pulseless witch who makes his lonely suppers. Like Jekyll and Fettes, he is a victim of his own intellectual hubris and trust in his ability to thrive outside of the human community. Too much trust in individual intellect, too much spite for the fellowship of his superstitious community, and too little healthy fear of his vulnerable isolation has combined to expose him to predatory psychological and supernatural forces

16. Papists, or Catholics, consecrated graveyards and erected headstones to mark the site of burial. Iconoclastic Calvinists not only avoided formally consecrating anything, but banned tombstones as being idolatrous.

17. The "Black Man" – whom we first met as an object of terror in "The Merry Men" – was a euphemism employed in European folklore to describe Satan, who was said to manifest as a black man – not an African, but a tall, imposing man with coal black skin

96

and glowing eyes. This figure appears regularly in both literature and folklore, especially in the stories of Washington Irving, Nathaniel Hawthorne, and others who write about New England during the Puritan years, where the "Black Man in the woods" was a frequently discussed supernatural terror

18. This is a particularly chilling simile: it suggests that – like a pony who is guided with the bit in its mouth by the master riding it – Janet is being manipulated and forced to say things which someone else wants her to

19. The name "Satan" literally means "the Accuser." The idea is that Satan will accuse the saved in front of God at the end of time, like a prosecutor arguing why they should be damned. He will bring up every sin that they have committed, and Jesus – who is called the "Wonderful Counsellor" – will act in their defense, vouching for those who have accepted His salvation

20. Soulis recalls his childhood, and presumably his superstitious upbringing, which certainly included warnings of the "Black Man on the moor." These scenes of childhood seem to challenge the worldview-shifting enlightenment of his college education

21. Whether he truly represents the Devil or is merely a figment of Soulis' imagination, or a dark-skinned mortal, the appearance of the Black Man is a deep blow to Soulis' humanist philosophy – as crippling to him as it would be for a devout Evangelical to experience supernatural proof that the Christian God is a myth. Having been confronted with this potential proof of his community's superstitions he is neither able to produce the Lord's Prayer (the only scripture more fundamental to Christian theology and teaching than John 3:16, and a representation of the last tangible link between his religious – and likely fundamentalist – childhood and his clerical – and borderline secular – adulthood), nor bring to mind ideas for his book (which represents his intellectual elitism as well as his self-identity: he literally – and this is crucial – <u>does not know himself or who he is now</u>. His worldview is rocked and he loses all confidence in himself

22. It has been noted by several scholars that Scottish and Gaelic folklore leave a narrow breadth between the natural and supernatural. The undead may appear uncanny, but they are often corporeal, commonplace, and interactive. Rather than a misty vision, Janet is a tottering zombie, washing the reverend's clothes with her awful, dead hands

23. This is, presumably, the diabolical language of Hell. Another, perhaps even likelier possibility is that she is singing backwards. A common rite of witchcraft in European folklore is the perversion of Holy rituals by doing them topsy-turvy: upside-down crucifixes and the sort. Janet may actually be singing a Christian hymn, but backwards, making an uncouth rattle with her dead chops, e.g.: "Htrae eht lla ni eman ruoy si citsejam woh, drol ruo, drol o!"

24. It is still not clear to me what this sound represents, but the facts are suggestive: there is the sound of struggle in Janet's room, followed by a violent crash, after which winds seem to rush around the four corners of the manse, almost possessively. This all occurs, it should be noted, after the Black Man appeared in town and disappeared into the manse. My best guess is that the Devil, who has been masquerading in Janet's skin by day, has just exited her body (a loud and violent process), and hanged her back up on her peg on the wall. With nightfall he has no need of a disguise, and

so he rushes out (the winds) to do mischief, leaving his host body at home while he runs wild in the countryside

25. In the centuries before the invention of the sulfur match (ca. 1805), candles were lit by starting a small fire with flint, a steel striker, and a little nest of dried hay, strips of wool, and lint

26. It is nothing if not suggestive that Janet – an undead witch possessed by Satan – shares a room with Soulis' divinity books. The implication is that they do him absolutely no good if they don't lead him to suspect Janet of witchcraft, and if anything his intellectual skepticism has assisted rather than deterred the forces of Darkness. In short, Janet and Soulis' school books make fine bedfellows

27. This, then, is the gruesome end that made Janet "thrawn": she is hanging from a nail with her face distorted exactly like a victim of hanging – eyes bugging, tongue swollen, face wrenched into a stiff grin

28. This single thread is used for darning hose, or close-fitting stockings, and as such would hardly be expected to support the weight of a woman – old or not. Janet hasn't been hanged just now – the rope that wrung life from her was much stouter – but is hanging in place like a coat hung up after use. This might be exactly the metaphor that Stevenson is hoping us to picture: Janet is nothing more than the garment worn by the Devil during the day and hung up by him at night. Here she hangs until he comes for her again when he needs a more suitable exterior (everyone who sees a Black Man with glowing eyes will immediately know whom they are seeing)

29. Because Hell has literally taken up its throne in the manse of Balweary. Hell reigns in the community, and – in case you haven't already guessed – this also accounts for the unnaturally high temperatures that have been so smothering for "man and beast" since Janet's apparent death at the hands of Satan

30. A ribbed, plain-weaved, corded fabric

31. An important concept: Stevenson the skeptic depicts mankind as neither soulless (Soulis) nor as having a separate soul and the body it inhabits (Christian orthodoxy), but – like Soulis and Janet who are suspended between two realms: individualism and collectivism and life and death respectively – Stevenson defies both Christian teaching and secular humanism by suggesting a third alternative: the soul is interwoven into the very fabric of the body, and the two commune together, support one another, and pollute one another. Hence Janet is a corpse with a spirit and Soulis is a living man with a dead heart

32. The left side is traditionally associated with evil. In fact the word "sinister" comes from the Latin for "left." Evil spells were often done with the left hand in rituals of folk-magic

33. Stevenson's tale is no simple Christian morality play: it is not as important that he calls to the Christian diety for support than it is that he acknowledges that he is beyond controlling – and far more importantly, beyond understanding – the situation he is placed in. Instead, he surrenders his pride, admits being utterly confounded, and submits to powers outside of his influence. By relinquishing his hold on Janet and admitting that he cannot explain who or what she is, he breaks the spell she has had over him

34. The saddest part of this story is how the experience makes Soulis himself "thrawn."
    He is twisted and misshapen by his encounter, both physically and spiritually. His
    eyes are spectral – "wild, scared, and uncertain" – his face craggy like iron, and his
    words are "dreadful to his hearers" much like Janet's unnatural, slobbery speech
    terrified those who heard it. Like Janet, too, he is suspended between two worlds:
    she between earth and hell, he between earth and heaven. Soulis is not reintroduced
    to the community after his conversion from rational skepticism to uncertain awe. He
    has not become one of them, but rather remains perched above them like the icon of
    a saint or a martyr. He is a living sermon, like the Ancient Mariner or the Wandering
    Jew: more of a story than a person, and more of a legend than a man. He remains
    voluntarily removed from the community that he had first spurned for their
    supersitiousness, but now as an act of penance, willingly accepting the suffering of an
    inhuman, asocial life in hopes that his story will be a reminder to his congregants of
    the perils of individualism and hubris

"THRAWN Janet" could be viewed as Stevenson's own confession or a form of
penance written to his parents – or to the internalized version of them that
managed his robust Presbyterian Superego. Soulis, with his suggestive name
(soulless), intellectual hubris, and thinly veiled disgust for his under-
educated parishioners, is a natural stand-in for a younger, radical Stevenson,
who resented the politics and morality of his Tory parents. Convinced that
the old women are being made fools by their narrow-mindedness, he leaps
to defend Janet less out of humanitarianism than from self-righteous pride.
The villagers resent the fact that their minister's faith is based in book
learning rather than practical experience, and Soulis begrudges them for
being ignorant and gullible. He identifies with Janet, another outsider, and
forms an alliance with her more to publicly illustrate his resistance to their
superstitious worldview than as an act of Christian charity. This kinship
draws him further and further from the security of the insulated
community, until he realizes that in sheltering Janet and resisting his
parishioners' prejudice, he has been gradually exposing himself to an
intimate danger. The tale is intensely Hawthornesque, complete with an
isolated religious community, a spiritual threat from within, the presence of
a Satanic "black man," and a minister whose isolation from his flock leads to
supernatural torment and psychological misery. Like Reverend Dimmesdale
in *The Scarlet Letter*, Soulis exposes himself to temptation and torment by
taking in a social outcast – an outcast who, like the diabolical Chillingworth
– is exactly what they seem: a personal tormentor. There are subtle, sexual
implications about the relationship between the ugly witch and the
untested minister which suggest the unnaturalness of their association. A
loose woman – known to liberally breed and abandon bastard children –
Janet is hardly an appropriate inmate for a minister's household, and their

bedroom confrontation is suggestive. Soulis literally and figuratively must come to terms with the oddity of his chosen bedfellow: a skeptical (and borderline agnostic) minister who harbors a genuine witch. Symbolically Soulis represents a man who tries to distance himself from his upbringing, only to find himself thrust violently into his parents' conservatism after spending too much time in the company of the very threats that they dreaded; rather than disproving their philosophies, he accidentally confirms them. Like Jekyll and Fettes, he is a victim of his own intellectual hubris and trust in his ability to thrive outside of the human community: too much faith in individual intellect, too much spite for the fellowship of his superstitious community, and too little healthy fear of his own social and spiritual vulnerability has combined to expose him to these predatory psychological and supernatural forces. And yet, it is not enough to rescind his alliance with Janet. After having ushered her zombie corpse back to hell, he continues to be burdened by his complicity in her diabolical mission. To serve penance for his hubris, he is doomed to dwell in a sort of philosophical purgatory: neither able to return to his youthful idealism, nor capable of being incorporated by his devout congregation. Instead, like Janet who is both alive and dead – a fleshy ghost – he is both damned and saved, both sinner and saint. Like the Ancient Mariner, the Wandering Jew, or Hawthorne's minister in the black veil, Soulis is a living sermon to others: condemned to remain apart from humanity, his testimony being his only means of connecting with his congregation. And so, each year he delivers a hideous discourse – like the Mariner who cannot stop to rest, except to relate his sins and warn a new generation – and then returns to his Manse (positioned so poetically on the river which divides the world of rational intellect from that of supernatural wonder, and individualism from community), like a ghost to its graveyard, rising only to relate the story of how he rejected those closest to him, and how as a result he must now walk alone in the world, accepted by neither party – doomed to be forever inconsistent with his upbringing, with his education, and with his own conflicted, self-loathing spirit.

OTHER than "Jekyll and Hyde," none of Stevenson's horror tales have been more celebrated as "The Body Snatcher." It has a habit of regularly appearing in anthologies of classic terror beside "The Judge's House," "The Black Cat," and "The Monkey's Paw." The story truly belongs in the canon of weird fiction, for it is not easily classifiable. The supernatural manifestation cannot be conclusively called a ghost, a vision, a vampire, or a zombie, and the very physical transformation challenges natural explanations, landing it in the hazy genre of "speculative fiction." The story, like "Jekyll," also doubles as a literary parable, complete with Faustian imagery, psychological depth, and ethical labyrinths. Stevenson's habit of writing moral exercises in the form of horror stories has prevented his supernatural fiction from being written off as mere stylistic folktales and preserved its reputation in academic circles. "The Body Snatcher" may be the most eloquent of his short horror fiction – a philosophical treatise as alarming as *Crime and Punishment*, as metaphysical as *Paradise Lost*, and as tragic as *Frankenstein*. The last of these novels was *undoubtedly* an influence on Stevenson's tale, which also featured an ethically apathetic medical student eschewing social mores in his search for professional ambition. Both protagonists spend more time amongst the dead than the living, and both violate the widely recognized laws of God and man alike, with little regard for the effect that their crimes will have on their souls. Ultimately both Shelley's Frankenstein and Stevenson's Fettes end up bringing something to life which they had created out of death, and dearly regret their blasphemous aspirations. Fettes also shares much in common with Marlowe's vulgar Doctor Faustus (more so than with Goethe's noble, soul-searching interpretation of the character) while his tempter, Macfarlane, has a forefather in the insidious Mephistopheles: both *Fettes* and *Faust* are inspired by self-serving moral relativism and a lust for power, while *Macfarlane* and *Mephistopheles* each tempt their prey into losing their humanity by luring them with promises of greatness, renown, and financial security. Ultimately, Stevenson hopes to warn us all against the desensitization of ethical apathy and greed, demonstrating the fate of all who attempt to leave their sins behind them without settling accounts, for sooner or later – he shows us on no fewer than three occasions – *we must look our crimes in the face.*

The Body Snatcher[1]

---

[1] A person who illegally sells a dead body to medical schools for dissection. Before the Anatomy Act of 1832, only executed murderers were legally allowed to be dissected. As science advanced during the Enlightenment – and as the execution rate dropped drastically in the 1800s – the demand for bodies soared, and schools would pay roughs and thugs to dig up recently buried corpses, or students would do it themselves (as depicted in the opening of Boris Karloff's

{1884}

EVERY night in the year, four of us sat in the small parlour of the George[1] at Debenham[2]—the undertaker, and the landlord, and Fettes[3], and myself. Sometimes there would be more; but blow high, blow low, come rain or snow or frost, we four would be each planted in his own particular arm-chair. Fettes was an old drunken Scotchman, a man of education obviously, and a man of some property, since he lived in idleness[4]. He had come to Debenham years ago, while still young, and by a mere continuance of living had grown to be an adopted townsman. His blue camlet cloak[5] was a local antiquity, like the church-spire. His place in the parlour at the George, his absence from church, his old, crapulous, disreputable vices, were all things of course in Debenham. He had some vague Radical[6] opinions and some fleeting infidelities[7], which he would now and again set forth and emphasise with tottering slaps upon the table. He drank rum— five glasses regularly every evening[8]; and for the greater portion of his nightly visit to the George sat, with his glass in his right hand, in a state of melancholy alcoholic saturation. We called him the Doctor, for he was supposed to have some special knowledge of medicine, and had been known, upon a pinch, to set a fracture or reduce a dislocation; but beyond

---

Frankenstein). Dissections were necessary for both long term medical research and in order to teach individual students medicine, but with fewer bodies available and the need growing, body snatchers raided cemeteries regularly, selling unearthed cadavers and pocketing a fair sum (around $900 - $11,00 in 2015 currency for a well-preserved specimen)

[1] A common name for inns and taverns (e.g., The Royal George, The King George Inn), especially during 18th and 19th centuries, named after one or more of the four King Georges that reigned over Britain 1714 - 1730

[2] A village of some 1,700 persons in central Suffolk in the southeast of England

[3] This Scottish surname is shared with a highly renowned Edinburgh boarding school, and may suggest a promising, precocious future, such as that once expected of Fettes himself

[4] Since Fettes can afford to loaf about the inn and drink aimlessly (shades of Billy Bones), he is understood to be a man of means – a gentleman in the financial sense if not socially

[5] A woven fabric made to appear oriental (as if made from camel hair), though it is likely wool

[6] Like Robert Knox himself (more on him later), the now cynical Fettes began his career as an philosophical idealist and a political radical

[7] Stevenson hints at treasonous and blasphemous outbursts against conventional politics and religion

[8] Once more the similarities with Billy Bones increase (not to mention similarities with Stevenson's own taste for strong drink)

these slight particulars, we had no knowledge of his character and antecedents.

One dark winter night—it had struck nine some time before the landlord joined us—there was a sick man in the George, a great neighbouring proprietor suddenly struck down with apoplexy[1] on his way to Parliament; and the great man's still greater London doctor had been telegraphed to his bedside. It was the first time that such a thing had happened in Debenham, for the railway was but newly open, and we were all proportionately moved by the occurrence.

'He's come,' said the landlord, after he had filled and lighted his pipe.

'He?' said I. 'Who?—not the doctor?'

'Himself,' replied our host.

'What is his name?'

'Doctor Macfarlane,' said the landlord.

Fettes was far through his third tumbler, stupidly fuddled, now nodding over, now staring mazily[2] around him; but at the last word he seemed to awaken, and repeated the name 'Macfarlane' twice, quietly enough the first time, but with sudden emotion at the second.

'Yes,' said the landlord, 'that's his name, Doctor WolfMacfarlane.'

Fettes became instantly sober; his eyes awoke, his voice became clear, loud, and steady, his language forcible and earnest. We were all startled by the transformation, as if a man had risen from the dead[3].

'I beg your pardon,' he said, 'I am afraid I have not been paying much attention to your talk. Who is this WolfMacfarlane?' And then, when he had heard the landlord out, 'It cannot be, it cannot be,' he added; 'and yet I would like well to see him face to face[4].'

'Do you know him, Doctor?' asked the undertaker, with a gasp.

'God forbid!' was the reply. 'And yet the name is a strange one; it were too much to fancy two. Tell me, landlord, is he old?'

'Well,' said the host, 'he's not a young man, to be sure, and his hair is white; but he looks younger[5] than you.'

'He is older, though; years older. But,' with a slap upon the table, 'it's the rum you see in my face—rum and sin. This man, perhaps, may have an easy

---

[1] A stroke

[2] Confused, disoriented – literally like one who is lost in a maze

[3] Mark the phrase well: the resurrection man has been himself resurrected, awakening from the death of his soul while his body lived (and drank) on, to confront Macfarlane, spirit to spirit, just as Gray will do in the conclusion

[4] Again, this foreshadows Gray's similar manifestation – face to face with his killer

[5] Like the amoral Hyde, Macfarlane's lack of a conscience has allowed his aging to be mellowed

conscience[1] and a good digestion. Conscience! Hear me speak. You would think I was some good, old, decent Christian, would you not? But no, not I; I never canted[2]. Voltaire might have canted if he'd stood in my shoes; but the brains'—with a rattling fillip on his bald head—'the brains were clear and active, and I saw and made no deductions[3].'

'If you know this doctor,' I ventured to remark, after a somewhat awful pause, 'I should gather that you do not share the landlord's good opinion.'

Fettes paid no regard to me.

'Yes,' he said, with sudden decision, 'I must see him face to face.'

There was another pause, and then a door was closed rather sharply on the first floor, and a step was heard upon the stair.

'That's the doctor,' cried the landlord. 'Look sharp, and you can catch him.'

It was but two steps from the small parlour to the door of the old George Inn; the wide oak staircase landed almost in the street; there was room for a Turkey rug and nothing more between the threshold and the last round of the descent; but this little space was every evening brilliantly lit up, not only by the light upon the stair and the great signal-lamp below the sign, but by the warm radiance of the bar-room window. The George thus brightly advertised itself to passers-by in the cold street. Fettes walked steadily to the spot, and we, who were hanging behind, beheld the two men meet, as one of them had phrased it, face to face[4]. Dr. Macfarlane was alert and vigorous. His white hair set off his pale and placid, although energetic, countenance. He was richly dressed in the finest of broadcloth and the whitest of linen, with a great gold watch-chain, and studs and spectacles of the same precious material. He wore a broad-folded tie, white and speckled with lilac, and he carried on his arm a comfortable driving-coat of fur. There was no doubt but he became his years, breathing, as he did, of wealth and consideration; and it was a surprising contrast to see our parlour sot—bald, dirty, pimpled, and robed in his old camlet cloak—confront him at the bottom of the stairs.

---

[1] Or lack thereof

[2] He is referring to a conversion from materialism and atheism, which he claims to have never abandoned even when he has seen things that he claims would have brought Voltaire, the infamous atheist, to his knees in reverence

[3] A consummate Victorian intellectual (like the Materialistic Dr Lanyon), Fettes clings to his objectivity, claiming that even when he saw something that proved the existence of the afterlife, he resisted drawing conclusions and merely observed

[4] Robertson is not being subtle: he wants us to remember this concept – the picture of moral curiosity, of staring into the visage of wickedness in order to verify its existence – and of course it will play out in Gray's confrontational manifestation

'Macfarlane!' he said somewhat loudly, more like a herald than a friend.

The great doctor pulled up short on the fourth step, as though the familiarity of the address surprised and somewhat shocked his dignity.

'Toddy Macfarlane!' repeated Fettes.

The London man almost staggered. He stared for the swiftest of seconds at the man before him, glanced behind him with a sort of scare, and then in a startled whisper, 'Fettes!' he said, 'You!'

'Ay,' said the other, 'me! Did you think I was dead too? We are not so easy shut of our acquaintance.'

'Hush, hush!' exclaimed the doctor. 'Hush, hush! this meeting is so unexpected—I can see you are unmanned[1]. I hardly knew you, I confess, at first; but I am overjoyed—overjoyed to have this opportunity. For the present it must be how-d'ye-do and good-bye in one, for my fly is waiting, and I must not fail the train; but you shall—let me see—yes—you shall give me your address, and you can count on early news of me. We must do something for you, Fettes. I fear you are out at elbows[2]; but we must see to that for auld lang syne, as once we sang at suppers[3].'

'Money!' cried Fettes; 'money from you! The money that I had from you is lying where I cast it in the rain.'

Dr. Macfarlane had talked himself into some measure of superiority and confidence, but the uncommon energy of this refusal cast him back into his first confusion.

A horrible, ugly look came and went across his almost venerable countenance. 'My dear fellow,' he said, 'be it as you please; my last thought is to offend you. I would intrude on none. I will leave you my address, however—'

'I do not wish it—I do not wish to know the roof that shelters you,' interrupted the other. 'I heard your name; I feared it might be you; I wished to know if, after all, there were a God; I know now that there is none[4]. Begone!'

---

[1] To be jolted out of self-control, decorum, and respectability by a shock

[2] In a poor state – literally suggesting that the elbows in one's jacket have become threadbare from use and disrepair and have given "out"

[3] *"For old times' sake."* Still popular at New Year's Eve, "Auld Lang Syne" – literally "Old Long Since," or, roughly, "Old Times Long Gone By" – contains text from the eponymous Robert Burns poem from 1788, and is a popular anthem is Scotland and in Scottish culture, associated with friendship, fidelity, and well-aging camaraderie – quite unlike the poorly aged relationship between these two

[4] As, by his estimations, were there a God, that God would have either slain Macfarlane or led him to a life of ruin (like that of Fettes), but since he thrives in society and is a doctor to esteemed members of Parliament, Fettes' atheism is unchallenged

He still stood in the middle of the rug, between the stair and doorway; and the great London physician, in order to escape, would be forced to step to one side. It was plain that he hesitated before the thought of this humiliation[1]. White as he was, there was a dangerous glitter in his spectacles; but while he still paused uncertain, he became aware that the driver of his fly was peering in from the street at this unusual scene and caught a glimpse at the same time of our little body from the parlour, huddled by the corner of the bar. The presence of so many witnesses decided him at once to flee. He crouched together, brushing on the wainscot, and made a dart like a serpent, striking for the door. But his tribulation was not yet entirely at an end, for even as he was passing Fettes clutched him by the arm and these words came in a whisper, and yet painfully distinct, 'Have you seen it again?'

The great rich London doctor cried out aloud with a sharp, throttling cry; he dashed his questioner across the open space, and, with his hands over his head, fled out of the door like a detected thief[2]. Before it had occurred to one of us to make a movement the fly was already rattling toward the station. The scene was over like a dream, but the dream had left proofs and traces of its passage. Next day the servant found the fine gold spectacles broken on the threshold, and that very night we were all standing breathless by the bar-room window, and Fettes at our side, sober, pale, and resolute in look.

'God protect us, Mr. Fettes!' said the landlord, coming first into possession of his customary senses. 'What in the universe is all this? These are strange things you have been saying.'

Fettes turned toward us; he looked us each in succession in the face. 'See if you can hold your tongues,' said he. 'That man Macfarlane is not safe to cross; those that have done so already have repented it too late.'

And then, without so much as finishing his third glass, far less waiting for the other two, he bade us good-bye and went forth, under the lamp of the hotel, into the black night.

We three turned to our places in the parlour, with the big red fire and four clear candles; and as we recapitulated what had passed, the first chill of our surprise soon changed into a glow of curiosity. We sat late; it was the latest session I have known in the old George. Each man, before we parted,

---

[1] For a rascally drunk to force a gentleman to walk around him rather than stepping to the side truly was a humiliating act of disrespect and contempt that most men would have resisted enduring in the absence of a physical threat. But Fettes' threat is moral, not physical: it is Macfarlane's reputation and dignity that he wishes to injure, not his flesh

[2] We are left to presume that Macfarlane – unremorseful and feeding off the rewards of his murderous past – has indeed suffered the sight of "it" in the time that has passed

had his theory that he was bound to prove; and none of us had any nearer business in this world than to track out the past of our condemned companion, and surprise the secret that he shared with the great London doctor. It is no great boast, but I believe I was a better hand at worming out a story[1] than either of my fellows at the George; and perhaps there is now no other man alive[2] who could narrate to you the following foul and unnatural events.

In his young days Fettes studied medicine in the schools of Edinburgh[3]. He had talent of a kind, the talent that picks up swiftly what it hears and readily retails it for its own. He worked little at home; but he was civil, attentive, and intelligent in the presence of his masters. They soon picked him out as a lad who listened closely and remembered well; nay, strange as it seemed to me when I first heard it, he was in those days well favoured, and pleased by his exterior. There was, at that period, a certain extramural teacher of anatomy, whom I shall here designate by the letter K. His name was subsequently too well known[4]. The man who bore it

---

[1] This phrase has been a source of confusion to many readers, including myself when I first read the tale. Is the narrator bragging that he is the best storyteller of the group? Is what follows then merely the content of his made-up conjecture? In fact, no. The key here is the word "Worming." In artillery vocabulary, a worm is a pole with an iron corkscrew-like coil attached to the top. After firing a canon, first a wet sponge was plunged into the cavity to extinguish any lingering embers, then the worm was thrust in and twisted to catch and extract any material debris. To "worm" something, then, is to probe a dark, inaccessible space with a mind to recover what lies hidden there. To "worm" out a story, then, is to convince a story teller to spill the beans, and so the narrator is informing us that he has already "wormed" this story out of Fettes, and is now ("perhaps") the only person alive who knows the tale, Macfarlane and Fettes being dead in all likelihood

[2] The implication being that Fettes either died (presumably that night) or that he disappeared (presumably that night as well). In either case, Fettes metaphorically (and perhaps literally) rose from the purgatorial tavern and willingly consigned himself to the hell represented by the "black night" that he crosses into after bidding his fellow inmates of Purgatory a goodbye that smacks of finality. Fettes' fate and his reasons for leaving (again, we presume to his death or damnation) are discussed in the follow-up note at the end of this story

[3] No university on earth had as fine a reputation for its medical school during the Victorian era. Edinburgh was the pinnacle of research and scholarship and was renowned for its excellent faculty

[4] There is no question that the professor in question is Robert Knox (1791 – 1862), a Scottish anatomist and physician who taught at Edinburgh and is most closely associated with his infamous involvement with the Burke and Hare body snatching murders (in which the two rogues – upon realizing that they could

skulked through the streets of Edinburgh in disguise, while the mob that applauded at the execution of Burke called loudly for the blood of his employer[1]. But Mr. K— was then at the top of his vogue[2]; he enjoyed a popularity due partly to his own talent and address, partly to the incapacity of his rival, the university professor. The students, at least, swore by his name, and Fettes believed himself, and was believed by others, to have laid the foundations of success when he had acquired the favour of this meteorically famous man. Mr. K— was a *bon vivant*[3] as well as an accomplished teacher; he liked a sly illusion no less than a careful preparation. In both capacities Fettes enjoyed and deserved his notice, and

---

make money by selling bodies – murdered and sold sixteen people over ten months before they were caught in 1828). Knox bought the bodies, and while he was never charged, and was said to know nothing of their source, his reputation as a heartless dealer in death was well established

[1] William Burke and William Hare were the serial killers responsible for what came to be known as the body snatching murders or the West Port murders – a series of sixteen slayings. After a tenant of their boardinghouse died unexpectedly, the two stumbled onto the idea of killing for profit when they sold the corpse to Knox's surgery for a high sum. Over the next ten months they smothered their victims – mostly borders, drunks, the infirm, the mentally disabled, and the impoverished; the perfect targets since their disappearance would go unnoticed – and sold the suffocated cadavers to Knox's students. On more than one occasion, students, attendants, and doctors recognized the victims (particularly a young, mentally challenged man called "Daft Jamie"), and Knox brushed the suspicions under the rug, even going so far as to disfigure a corpse's face before public dissection. The criminals were found out when two of their lodgers became suspicious and alerted the police, who quickly discovered a smothered body, and wormed a confession out of the pair. Hare, who was seen as more mentally feeble and brutish turned state's evidence against his accomplice Burke, who was seen as the brains behind the operation, and was hanged in a widely publicized execution. Knox became a social pariah, although he was not arrested since he never personally dealt with the killers, and his house was stormed by outraged peasants in a violent riot. Knox was forced to skulk through the streets of Edinburgh in disguise, and was eventually ousted from his position at the school. A nursery rhyme derived from the events succinctly describes the popular sentiments of the day: "Burke's the butcher, Hare's the thief / Knox is the boy who buys the beef"

[2] Indeed, in spite of the scandal (or rather, because of it), Knox's lectures – already popular due to his charisma and sensational love of gore – became more popular than ever with students

[3] One who lives and almost shamelessly luxuriant lifestyle

by the second year of his attendance he held the half-regular position of second demonstrator or sub-assistant[1] in his class.

In this capacity the charge of the theatre and lecture-room devolved in particular upon his shoulders. He had to answer for the cleanliness of the premises and the conduct of the other students, and it was a part of his duty to supply, receive, and divide the various subjects. It was with a view to this last—at that time very delicate—affair that he was lodged by Mr. K— in the same wynd[2], and at last in the same building, with the dissecting-rooms. Here, after a night of turbulent pleasures, his hand still tottering, his sight still misty and confused, he would be called out of bed in the black hours before the winter dawn by the unclean and desperate interlopers who supplied the table[3]. He would open the door to these men, since infamous throughout the land[4]. He would help them with their tragic burden, pay them their sordid price, and remain alone, when they were gone, with the unfriendly relics of humanity[5]. From such a scene he would return to snatch another hour or two of slumber, to repair the abuses of the night, and refresh himself for the labours of the day.

Few lads could have been more insensible to the impressions of a life thus passed among the ensigns of mortality. His mind was closed against all general considerations. He was incapable of interest in the fate and

---

[1] Assistants would perform some procedures while the lecturer spoke, provide him with instruments, and move the body or extracted body parts. Sub-assistants worked behind the scenes, preparing instruments, chemicals, and cleaning away the gore. They would handle the receipt of specimens, catalog them, and do petty research, and acted as ushers to the laboratory, taking tickets from the audience, monitoring their behavior, and maintaining a clean and gentlemanly premisis

[2] A narrow lane between houses (To Americans: it is worth noting that the British say "in ____ Street" rather than "on _____ Street." Fettes was not literally living in the wynd)

[3] With bodies. Stevenson is making a pun here: to "supply the table" is a phrase equivalent to "bringing home the bacon" or "being a bread-winner," except that the table in this situation is a dissecting table

[4] There is no question that the men are grave robbers or even murderers, even though Fettes attempts to avoid the fact. They are of course infamous because of the Burke and Hare trial which, seemingly, had been within a year or even months of the current story. Whatever the case, the bodies they are delivering are not legally procured

[5] This portrayal of Fettes – a man who callously collects disinterred corpses without regard for their families, who neither pities nor judges the lives of the desperate and conniving men who are bringing them, and who then isolates himself with only the cadavers as company – is profoundly misanthropic and almost inhuman, robotic

fortunes of another, the slave of his own desires and low ambitions. Cold, light, and selfish in the last resort, he had that modicum of prudence, miscalled morality, which keeps a man from inconvenient drunkenness or punishable theft[1]. He coveted, besides, a measure of consideration from his masters and his fellow-pupils, and he had no desire to fail conspicuously in the external parts of life. Thus he made it his pleasure to gain some distinction in his studies, and day after day rendered unimpeachable eye-service to his employer, Mr. K—. For his day of work he indemnified himself by nights of roaring, blackguardly enjoyment; and when that balance had been struck, the organ that he called his conscience declared itself content[2].

The supply of subjects was a continual trouble to him as well as to his master. In that large and busy class, the raw material of the anatomists kept perpetually running out; and the business thus rendered necessary was not only unpleasant in itself, but threatened dangerous consequences to all who were concerned[3]. It was the policy of Mr. K— to ask no questions in his dealings with the trade. 'They bring the body, and we pay the price,' he used to say, dwelling on the alliteration—'quid pro quo.' And, again, and somewhat profanely, 'Ask no questions,' he would tell his assistants, 'for conscience' sake.' There was no understanding that the subjects were provided by the crime of murder. Had that idea been broached to him in words, he would have recoiled in horror[4]; but the lightness of his speech upon so grave a matter was, in itself, an offence against good manners, and

---

[1] Fettes follows a brand of morality which the psychologist Lawrence Kohlberg called "pre-conventional," specifically the lowest of this branch (which is itself the lowest of the three branches) – "obedience and punishment orientation," or the "how can I avoid punishment?" stage. This lowest of low modes of moralization follows the code that one should only avoid those crimes which pose the chance of being caught. All other sins are perfectly acceptable. This childish worldview follows this train of thought: Mom: "Johnny, why is it bad to steal?" Johnny: "Because if I get caught I'll be in trouble." Fettes is hardly a heroic character, although – as we will see – Macfarlane is essentially sociopathic
[2] We have here a specter of hypocrisy that is perhaps even more disturbing than Hyde: a man who by day suckles at the teat of those who could advance his career – doing whatever they deem necessary to forward it – and by night engages in whatever debaucheries he so chooses.
[3] Involvement with body snatching was a misdemeanor, and while this only resulted in a fine or petty jail time, and thus of little consequence to thugs and members of criminal circles, it could be a social and professional disaster for gentlemen
[4] Indeed, as Stevenson points out, Knox was a rogue and a greasy sort, but he was no murderer: he had no idea that the bodies of the Burke and Hare victims had been suffocated, believing them to merely be disinterred paupers

a temptation to the men with whom he dealt[1]. Fettes, for instance, had often remarked to himself upon the singular freshness of the bodies. He had been struck again and again by the hang-dog, abominable looks of the ruffians who came to him before the dawn; and putting things together clearly in his private thoughts, he perhaps attributed a meaning too immoral and too categorical to the unguarded counsels of his master. He understood his duty, in short, to have three branches: to take what was brought, to pay the price, and to avert the eye from any evidence of crime.

One November morning[2] this policy of silence was put sharply to the test. He had been awake all night with a racking toothache[3]—pacing his room like a caged

beast or throwing himself in fury on his bed—and had fallen at last into that profound, uneasy slumber that so often follows on a night of pain, when he was awakened by the third or fourth angry repetition of the concerted signal. There was a thin, bright moonshine; it was bitter cold, windy, and frosty; the town had not yet awakened, but an indefinable stir already preluded the noise and business of the day. The ghouls had come later than usual, and they seemed more than usually eager to be gone. Fettes, sick with sleep, lighted them upstairs. He heard their grumbling Irish voices[4] through a dream; and as they stripped the sack from their sad merchandise he leaned dozing, with his shoulder propped against the wall; he had to shake himself to find the men their money. As he did so his eyes lighted on the dead face. He started; he took two steps nearer, with the candle raised.

'God Almighty!' he cried. 'That is Jane Galbraith!'

The men answered nothing, but they shuffled nearer the door.

------

[1] Stevenson still casts blame on Knox, however: while he may not have meant to condone cold-blooded murder, it was the levity and casualness of his instructions that led his assistants to accept body after body from Burke without question in spite of the obvious implications of his visits

[2] It may be merely coincidental, but I can't help but note that the grand-daddy of all anatomical students/body-snatchers came to terms with his great horror in the dark wee hours of a dreary November morning as well: Victor Frankenstein

[3] Freud viewed the tooth as a symbol of virility and phallic potency, and decay in the tooth represented sexual frustration or repression. Jung saw tooth loss as a sign of an approaching change or transformation. Common folk psychology views toothaches, decay, or loss as symbolic of a disquiet character (the teeth symbolize strength, youth, innocence, bravery, and – when all is said – one's moral character), and for one to be burdened with rot is to suggest that the conscience is burdened with guilt, disquietude, or sin

[4] Burke and Hare were Irish immigrants, and the whole debacle became a *cause celebre* for anti-immigration and anti-Irish factions

'I know her, I tell you,' he continued. 'She was alive and hearty yesterday. It's impossible she can be dead; it's impossible you should have got this body fairly.'

'Sure, sir, you're mistaken entirely,' said one of the men.

But the other looked Fettes darkly in the eyes, and demanded the money on the spot.

It was impossible to misconceive the threat or to exaggerate the danger. The lad's heart failed him. He stammered some excuses, counted out the sum, and saw his hateful visitors depart. No sooner were they gone than he hastened to confirm his doubts. By a dozen unquestionable marks he identified the girl he had jested with the day before. He saw, with horror, marks upon her body that might well betoken violence. A panic seized him, and he took refuge in his room. There he reflected at length over the discovery that he had made; considered soberly the bearing of Mr. K—'s instructions and the danger to himself of interference in so serious a business[1], and at last, in sore perplexity, determined to wait for the advice of his immediate superior, the class assistant.

This was a young doctor, Wolf Macfarlane, a high favourite among all the reckless students, clever, dissipated, and unscrupulous to the last degree. He had travelled and studied abroad. His manners were agreeable and a little forward. He was an authority on the stage, skilful on the ice or the links with skate or golf-club; he dressed with nice audacity, and, to put the finishing touch upon his glory, he kept a gig[2] and a strong trotting-horse. With Fettes he was on terms of intimacy; indeed, their relative positions called for some community of life; and when subjects were scarce the pair would drive far into the country in Macfarlane's gig, visit and desecrate some lonely graveyard, and return before dawn with their booty to the door of the dissecting-room.

On that particular morning Macfarlane arrived somewhat earlier than his wont. Fettes heard him, and met him on the stairs, told him his story, and showed him the cause of his alarm. Macfarlane examined the marks on her body.

---

[1] Once again, Fettes' moral code dictates that wrongness is determined by the trouble it could land him in, and he seems more afraid of "interfering" with school business than of being an accessory to murder. In fact, his two choices are engineered around whom he fears more: Knox, or the police, and although he suffers some genuine sorrow for the girl's violent end, he concludes that rocking his professional boat is more troublesome than alerting the authorities and waits to conference with Macfarlane

[2] A light, two-wheeled carriage drawn by one horse. Built for speed, casual affairs (such as a quick dash into town), or leisurely drives in fair weather, the gig was the motorcycle of the day, and was second only to riding on horseback when some shady, covert operation required doing

'Yes,' he said with a nod, 'it looks fishy.'

'Well, what should I do?' asked Fettes.

'Do?' repeated the other. 'Do you want to do anything? Least said soonest mended, I should say.'

'Some one else might recognise her[1],' objected Fettes. 'She was as well known[2] as the Castle Rock[3].'

'We'll hope not,' said Macfarlane, 'and if anybody does—well, you didn't, don't you see, and there's an end. The fact is, this has been going on too long. Stir up the mud, and you'll get K— into the most unholy trouble; you'll be in a shocking box yourself[4]. So will I, if you come to that. I should like to know how any one of us would look, or what the devil we should have to say for ourselves, in any Christian witness-box. For me, you know there's one thing certain—that, practically speaking, all our subjects have been murdered.'

'Macfarlane!' cried Fettes.

'Come now!' sneered the other. 'As if you hadn't suspected it yourself!'

'Suspecting is one thing—'

'And proof another. Yes, I know; and I'm as sorry as you are this should have come here,' tapping the body with his cane. 'The next best thing for me is not to recognise it; and,' he added coolly, 'I don't. You may, if you please. I don't dictate, but I think a man of the world[5] would do as I do; and I may add, I fancy that is what K— would look for at our hands. The

---

[1] Knox's lectures (as were all) were attended by the public, although admission required buying a ticket – students included

[2] The strong implication here is that Jane was a prostitute. Called a "girl," she was jesting familiarly with Fettes – a youngster, but still a gentleman – at nighttime when he was (as is implied) drinking heavily, and is said to be a fixture of the Edinburgh streets as much as the Castle Rock in spite of her presumed youth. No respectable woman would match one or any of these descriptors, and we may assume that Fettes was one of her johns

[3] A volcanic crag on which Edinburgh Castle is built. The castle dominates and defines the Edinburgh skyline and is to the Scottish capital what the Washington Monument, the Eiffel Tower, Big Ben, and the Sydney Opera House are to their respective cities

[4] *"What can I do to avoid trouble?"* Fettes' infantile moral code is pricked by Macfarlane's rhetoric

[5] Which Macfarlane most certainly is. The common use of this term denotes a savvy, well-experienced man of hard won wisdom, but Stevenson may also be alluding to the biblical injunction to "be not conformed to this world: but be ye transformed by the renewing of your mind, that ye may prove what *is* that good, and acceptable, and perfect, will of God" (Romans 12:2), and I am personally reminded of Marley's woefully injunction against the callous, hypocritical Scrooge: "Man of the worldly mind! Do you believe in me or not?"

question is, Why did he choose us two for his assistants? And I answer, because he didn't want old wives.'

This was the tone of all others to affect the mind of a lad like Fettes[1]. He agreed to imitate Macfarlane. The body of the unfortunate girl was duly dissected, and no one remarked or appeared to recognise her.

One afternoon, when his day's work was over, Fettes dropped into a popular tavern and found Macfarlane sitting with a stranger. This was a small man, very pale and dark, with coal-black eyes. The cut of his features gave a promise of intellect and refinement which was but feebly realised in his manners, for he proved, upon a nearer acquaintance, coarse, vulgar, and stupid[2]. He exercised, however, a very remarkable control over Macfarlane; issued orders like the Great Bashaw[3]; became inflamed at the least discussion or delay, and commented rudely on the servility with which he was obeyed. This most offensive person took a fancy to Fettes on the spot, plied him with drinks, and honoured him with unusual confidences on his past career. If a tenth part of what he confessed were true, he was a very loathsome rogue; and the lad's vanity was tickled by the attention of so experienced a man[4].

'I'm a pretty bad fellow myself,' the stranger remarked, 'but Macfarlane is the boy—Toddy[5] Macfarlane I call him. Toddy, order your friend another glass.' Or it might be, 'Toddy, you jump up and shut the door.' 'Toddy hates me,' he said again. 'Oh yes, Toddy, you do!'

'Don't you call me that confounded name,' growled Macfarlane.

'Hear him! Did you ever see the lads play knife[6]? He would like to do that all over my body,' remarked the stranger.

---

[1] Being singled out, given accolade – such are the deepest desires of Fettes' cold albeit boyish heart. His craving for approval and his disdain for collective morality certainly do single him out as a fitting criminal accomplice

[2] Gray represents sin and temptation, and is something of a devil – a Mephistopheles-type character who tempts the Faustian Macfarlane. From a distance he appears rational, attractive, and engaging, but once seen in the full light of day, he is foolish, grotesque, and repulsive, like sin

[3] Or "pasha" – a Turkish dignitary akin to a prince or a governor

[4] Fettes is drawn to greatness of any kind or caliber, be it a renowned surgeon like Knox or a colorful criminal like Gray, it matters not. So long as there is approval to gain and favor to earn, the sycophantic Fettes is at their service and ready to perform

[5] A tod or toddy is a baby fox in Scots (one could say Puppy in English), and Gray uses it as a humiliating infantilization of Macfarlane's more masculine, aggressive Christian name: Wolfe. You are no wolf to be, he is taunting, just a wee pup

[6] That is, the "knife game," a dangerous childhood pastime wherein the player places his palm flat on a table, fingers spread, and rapidly stabs at the spaces between them in a proscribed sequence with increasing speed

'We medicals have a better way than that,' said Fettes. 'When we dislike a dead friend of ours, we dissect him.'

Macfarlane looked up sharply, as though this jest were scarcely to his mind.

The afternoon passed. Gray[1], for that was the stranger's name, invited Fettes to join them at dinner, ordered a feast so sumptuous that the tavern was thrown into commotion, and when all was done commanded Macfarlane to settle the bill. It was late before they separated; the man Gray was incapably drunk. Macfarlane, sobered by his fury, chewed the cud of the money he had been forced to squander and the slights he had been obliged to swallow[2]. Fettes, with various liquors singing in his head[3], returned home with devious footsteps and a mind entirely in abeyance. Next day Macfarlane was absent from the class, and Fettes smiled to himself as he imagined him still squiring the intolerable Gray from tavern to tavern. As soon as the hour of liberty had struck he posted from place to place in quest of his last night's companions. He could find them, however, nowhere; so returned early to his rooms, went early to bed, and slept the sleep of the just[4].

At four in the morning he was awakened by the well-known signal. Descending to the door, he was filled with astonishment to find Macfarlane with his gig, and in the gig one of those long and ghastly packages with which he was so well acquainted.

'What?' he cried. 'Have you been out alone? How did you manage?'

But Macfarlane silenced him roughly, bidding him turn to business. When they had got the body upstairs and laid it on the table, Macfarlane made at first as if he were going away. Then he paused and seemed to hesitate; and then, 'You had better look at the face,' said he, in tones of some constraint. 'You had better,' he repeated, as Fettes only stared at him in wonder.

'But where, and how, and when did you come by it?' cried the other.

---

[1] Gray, as it so happens, was the surname of the couple that alerted the police to Burke and Hare

[2] There is no question for the narrator that – as Utterson suspected of Hyde – Gray is a blackmailer

[3] In 19th century Edinburgh, the most common liquors would be whisky, gin, brandy, and rum

[4] Fettes genuinely believes that he is guiltless in this situation: so long as he is umbrella-ed by masters like Knox, Macfarlane, and even Gray, he imagines that the blame belongs on them as he is a mere follower, a mere executor of orders. This tale is chiefly concerned with the concept of moral responsibility and the consequences of ethical denial, a sin which Fettes is constantly commits

'Look at the face[1],' was the only answer.

Fettes was staggered; strange doubts assailed him. He looked from the young doctor to the body, and then back again. At last, with a start, he did as he was bidden[2]. He had almost expected the sight that met his eyes, and yet the shock was cruel. To see, fixed in the rigidity of death and naked on that coarse layer of sackcloth, the man whom he had left well clad and full of meat and sin upon the threshold of a tavern, awoke, even in the thoughtless Fettes, some of the terrors of the conscience[3]. It was a *cras tibi*[4] which re-echoed in his soul, that two whom he had known should have come to lie upon these icy tables. Yet these were only secondary thoughts. His first concern regarded Wolfe. Unprepared for a challenge so momentous, he knew not how to look his comrade in the face. He durst not meet his eye, and he had neither words nor voice at his command.

It was Macfarlane himself who made the first advance. He came up quietly behind and laid his hand gently but firmly on the other's shoulder.

'Richardson,' said he, 'may have the head.'

Now Richardson was a student who had long been anxious for that portion of the human subject to dissect. There was no answer, and the

---

[1] Once again – as in the beginning, and as will occur in the end – we see the theme of looking something distasteful in the face. This motif symbolizes moral accountability and suggests that the person who does the looking carries away the horror with them as penance for their complicity. Fettes looks Macfarlane in the face in the beginning and is horrorstruck to see that he is flourishing in society due to Fettes' drunken retirement from respectable life. The responsibility, therefore, is Fettes: had he come forward and admitted their crimes, this would not have occurred, and he totters away into the night, stunned by the encounter, and possibly driven to death. In this incident, Macfarlane – who is an unconscionable sociopath – wishes Fettes to share his burden, and rightly so: if Fettes had reported the murders when he first detected them, Macfarlane could not have processed Gray through the dissecting school. But he took Macfarlane's advice, and now both of them share culpability in the murder – a revelation that Fettes understands when he looks Gray's corpse in the face, dashing the protracted denial of his guilt, and bringing the burden of the deed to weigh on his budding conscience

[2] A habit which has gotten him into this mess in the first place

[3] Fettes, although he is indeed one step nearer to being "in trouble," does not appear to cringe from the sight for any reason other than a moral revulsion, and this marks a change in his ethical worldview – the development of "wrongness" – which didn't occur until he looked the body in the face – until he personally witnessed the human consequences of his moral dereliction

[4] An abbreviation of the Latin phrase "Hodie mihi, cras tibi": "Today it is me, but tomorrow it is you," a phrase used to counter thoughtless hubris and to inspire mercy and pity

murderer resumed: 'Talking of business, you must pay me; your accounts, you see, must tally.'

Fettes found a voice, the ghost of his own: 'Pay you!' he cried. 'Pay you for that?'

'Why, yes, of course you must. By all means and on every possible account, you must,' returned the other. 'I dare not give it for nothing, you dare not take it for nothing; it would compromise us both[1]. This is another case like Jane Galbraith's. The more things are wrong the more we must act as if all were right. Where does old K— keep his money?'

'There,' answered Fettes hoarsely, pointing to a cupboard in the corner.

'Give me the key, then,' said the other, calmly, holding out his hand.

There was an instant's hesitation, and the die was cast[2]. Macfarlane could not suppress a nervous twitch, the infinitesimal mark of an immense relief, as he felt the key between his fingers. He opened the cupboard, brought out pen and ink and a paper-book that stood in one compartment, and separated from the funds in a drawer a sum suitable to the occasion.

'Now, look here,' he said, 'there is the payment made—first proof of your good faith: first step to your security. You have now to clinch it by a second. Enter the payment in your book, and then you for your part may defy the devil.'

The next few seconds were for Fettes an agony of thought; but in balancing his terrors it was the most immediate that triumphed. Any future difficulty seemed almost welcome if he could avoid a present quarrel with Macfarlane[3]. He set down the candle which he had been carrying all this time, and with a steady hand entered the date, the nature, and the amount of the transaction.

---

[1] There are two points here that are of extreme interest: firstly, Macfarlane is bound and determined to make Fettes as complicit as he possibly can, and makes him do as much as he can make him do to participate in the murder (Look at the face! Pay me! Show me the cabinet! Give me the key!), and secondly, the exchange of money is doubly damning, especially as the battering of human flesh is a particularly heinous crime, and one associated with the sale of Jesus by Judas for thirty silver pieces, giving the action an unusually hellish tint

[2] He had only this last chance to make the choice that Markheim ultimately does: to save his soul by surrendering his life (in this case, either Macfarlane would attempt to kill him, or Fettes' career would end in disgrace if he publicized the scandal), but he hands the key over, effectively selling his soul for the price of Gray's corpse

[3] Conscience awakened though it may be, it is still enslaved to a childish morality that chooses avoiding an awkward quarrel over enabling a murderer

'And now,' said Macfarlane, 'it's only fair that you should pocket the lucre[1]. I've had my share already. By the bye, when a man of the world falls into a bit of luck, has a few shillings extra in his pocket—I'm ashamed to speak of it, but there's a rule of conduct in the case[2]. No treating, no purchase of expensive class-books, no squaring of old debts; borrow, don't lend.'

'Macfarlane,' began Fettes, still somewhat hoarsely, 'I have put my neck in a halter[3] to oblige you.'

'To oblige me?' cried Wolfe[4]. 'Oh, come! You did, as near as I can see the matter, what you downright had to do in self-defence. Suppose I got into trouble, where would you be? This second little matter flows clearly from the first. Mr. Gray is the continuation of Miss Galbraith. You can't begin and then stop. If you begin, you must keep on beginning; that's the truth. No rest for the wicked[5].'

A horrible sense of blackness and the treachery of fate[6] seized hold upon the soul of the unhappy student.

'My God!' he cried, 'but what have I done? and when did I begin? To be made a class assistant—in the name of reason, where's the harm in that? Service wanted the position; Service might have got it. Would *he* have been where *I* am now[7]?'

---

[1] Ill-gotten money, loot, payment for a dishonorable deed. Macfarlane really is desperate to force Fettes into an alliance: if he pockets the money from his murder, then there really is no argument whatsoever that Fettes is morally responsible, and a bound accomplice

[2] Macfarlane has done this before, and is warning Fettes on how to avoid detection. It is also worthy to note the now unmistakable meaning of his phrase "a man of the world": a damned man

[3] A hangman's noose

[4] Stevenson drops his symbolically significant first name here as his predatory nature becomes unmistakably apparent

[5] Indeed. Commentary is hardly needed here even though Macfarlane's philosophical retort is one of the most important lines in the text, but a brief note will suffice: if Fettes wanted to avoid a life of miserable criminality, guilt, and fear, then he should have risen above his corrupt superiors and resisted their ethical indiscretions

[6] Rather than evil, wickedness, or treachery, Stevenson indicts fate, as though Macfarlane is not a free agent of moral choice but a decided client of wrong – an almost Satanic employee of the dark side, as it were. As previously mentioned, there is something undeniably Mephistophelean about Macfarlane's methodical corruption of the impressionable Fettes

[7] Once again evoking the pathos of the "Today it is me, tomorrow you" philosophy, Fettes almost seems like a protagonist from a Greek or Shakespearean tragedy, wondering if fate has conspired against him, or if the

'My dear fellow,' said Macfarlane, 'what a boy you are! What harm *has* come to you? What harm *can* come to you if you hold your tongue? Why, man, do you know what this life is? There are two squads of us—the lions and the lambs[1]. If you're a lamb, you'll come to lie upon these tables like Gray or Jane Galbraith; if you're a lion, you'll live and drive a horse like me, like K—, like all the world with any wit or courage. You're staggered at the first. But look at K—! My dear fellow, you're clever, you have pluck. I like you, and K— likes you. You were born to lead the hunt; and I tell you, on my honour and my experience of life, three days from now you'll laugh at all these scarecrows like a High School boy at a farce.'

And with that Macfarlane took his departure and drove off up the wynd in his gig to get under cover before daylight. Fettes was thus left alone with his regrets. He saw the miserable peril in which he stood involved. He saw, with inexpressible dismay, that there was no limit to his weakness, and that, from concession to concession, he had fallen from the arbiter of Macfarlane's destiny to his paid and helpless accomplice[2]. He would have given the world to have been a little braver at the time, but it did not occur to him that he might still be brave. The secret of Jane Galbraith and the cursed entry in the day-book closed his mouth.

Hours passed; the class began to arrive; the members of the unhappy Gray were dealt out to one and to another, and received without remark. Richardson was made happy with the head; and before the hour of freedom rang Fettes trembled with exultation to perceive how far they had already gone toward safety.

For two days he continued to watch, with increasing joy, the dreadful process of disguise.

---

universe and human will are meaningless. It is worth mentioning that many pitied Knox and the ruination of his good name, noting that had Burke and Hare arrived on another day of the week, they might have been associated with another doctor's patronage, and that it was more a systemic flaw in the school than a personal weakness in Knox which permitted the killings

[1] This evokes two strains of Bible imagery: firstly, Christ's warning that humanity will be sifted – the lambs (or the penitent saved) from the goats (the corrupt damned), and secondly Peter's warning that "the devil prowls about like a roaring lion looking for someone to devour" (1 Peter 5:8). No literate Victorian would fail to notice the symbolism, and the horror of Macfarlane's reversal (what decent man would want to be on the other side of this divide?) would have been utterly chilling, like suggesting today that there are two types of people: rapists and the raped. Macfarlane's dichotomy would have been equally disgusting and hateful to a typically Victorian reader

[2] One moral allowance has led to another, and thence to many, and thence to corruption. It evokes the alcoholic maxim: "first the man takes the drink, then the drink takes a drink, then the drink takes the man"

On the third day Macfarlane made his appearance. He had been ill, he said; but he made up for lost time by the energy with which he directed the students. To Richardson in particular he extended the most valuable assistance and advice, and that student, encouraged by the praise of the demonstrator, burned high with ambitious hopes, and saw the medal already in his grasp[1].

Before the week was out Macfarlane's prophecy had been fulfilled. Fettes had outlived his terrors and had forgotten his baseness. He began to plume himself upon his courage, and had so arranged the story in his mind that he could look back on these events with an unhealthy pride. Of his accomplice he saw but little. They met, of course, in the business of the class; they received their orders together from Mr. K—. At times they had a word or two in private, and Macfarlane was from first to last particularly kind and jovial. But it was plain that he avoided any reference to their common secret; and even when Fettes whispered to him that he had cast in his lot with the lions and foresworn the lambs[2], he only signed to him smilingly to hold his peace.

At length an occasion arose which threw the pair once more into a closer union. Mr. K— was again short of subjects; pupils were eager, and it was a part of this teacher's pretensions to be always well supplied. At the same time there came the news of a burial in the rustic graveyard of Glencorse[3]. Time has little changed the place in question. It stood then, as now, upon a cross road, out of call of human habitations, and buried fathom deep in the foliage of six cedar trees. The cries of the sheep upon the neighbouring hills, the streamlets upon either hand, one loudly singing among pebbles, the other dripping furtively from pond to pond, the stir of the wind in mountainous old flowering chestnuts, and once in seven days the voice of the bell and the old tunes of the precentor, were the only sounds that disturbed the silence around the rural church. The Resurrection Man[4]—to use a byname of the period—was not to be deterred by any of the sanctities of customary piety. It was part of his trade to

---

[1] Recognizing a potential enemy in Richardson (should he recognize the visage on his head), Macfarlane – slick as oil – is quick to corrupt him as well with visions of social elevation and status

[2] Although the foreswearing is surely rhetorical, the use of the phrase – like the Judas-esque exchange of the coins – demonstrates that he has symbolically renounced God (or goodness/the light side), and sworn his soul over to Darkness

[3] Established in 1665, Glencorse Parish Church lies some eight miles south of Edinburgh University, near Roslin, Scotland. The church and its graveyard are still in place, and can be seen on Google Maps. It is a small, sturdy stone building surrounded by fields and trees – still a "rustic" locale

[4] If still unclear, this was a coy euphemism for a body snatcher

despise and desecrate the scrolls and trumpets[1] of old tombs, the paths worn by the feet of worshippers and mourners, and the offerings and the inscriptions of bereaved affection. To rustic neighbourhoods, where love is more than commonly tenacious, and where some bonds of blood or fellowship unite the entire society of a parish, the body-snatcher, far from being repelled by natural respect, was attracted by the ease and safety of the task. To bodies that had been laid in earth, in joyful expectation of a far different awakening, there came that hasty, lamp-lit, terror-haunted resurrection of the spade and mattock[2]. The coffin was forced, the cerements[3] torn, and the melancholy relics, clad in sackcloth, after being rattled for hours on moonless byways, were at length exposed to uttermost indignities before a class of gaping boys.

Somewhat as two vultures may swoop upon a dying lamb, Fettes and Macfarlane were to be let loose upon a grave in that green and quiet resting-place. The wife of a farmer, a woman who had lived for sixty years, and been known for nothing but good butter and a godly conversation, was to be rooted from her grave at midnight and carried, dead and naked, to that far-away city that she had always honoured with her Sunday's best[4]; the place beside her family was to be empty till the crack of doom; her innocent and almost venerable members to be exposed to that last curiosity of the anatomist.

---

[1] Scrolls and trumpets are images employed in the Book of Revelation, which describes the dead rising from their graves as a series of seals are broken on a scroll – amidst the peal of trumpets – which, when opened and revealed will herald the End of Times. Stevenson suggests that – like Frankenstein – the body snatchers are defying the natural order by hastening the resurrection of the body before the trumpets and scrolls depicted on the tombstones have ordained their revival

[2] A heavy hoe-like instrument (such as the flat bill on a pickaxe) used to break up earth

[3] Waxed sackcloth body bags or winding cloths that protected corpses from decay before burial

[4] Eight miles was still far for a farmer's wife, who would probably only visit Edinburgh once a month or once a quarter, or even once a year depending on how much business their farm dealt in the capital city. Since the farmer was likely to handle any business, she was likely to travel there only to gather non-agrarian supplies such as buckles, cloth, silver, ironwork, books, medicine, or ribbons, and even then, this was likely to be an infrequent pilgrimage since many of these goods could be bought from peddlers. But when she did drive to town, she was sure to wear her finest clothes in the same way that an empty-nesting matron from Ohio would scrounge up her finest dress if her husband took her to New York City to see a Broadway play for their fortieth anniversary

Late one afternoon the pair set forth, well wrapped in cloaks and furnished with a formidable bottle[1]. It rained without remission—a cold, dense, lashing rain. Now and again there blew a puff of wind, but these sheets of falling water kept it down. Bottle and all, it was a sad and silent drive as far as Penicuik[2], where they were to spend the evening. They stopped once, to hide their implements in a thick bush not far from the churchyard, and once again at the Fisher's Tryst[3], to have a toast before the kitchen fire and vary their nips of whisky with a glass of ale. When they reached their journey's end the gig was housed, the horse was fed and comforted, and the two young doctors in a private room sat down to the best dinner and the best wine the house afforded. The lights, the fire, the beating rain upon the window, the cold, incongruous work that lay before them, added zest to their enjoyment of the meal. With every glass their cordiality increased. Soon Macfarlane handed a little pile of gold to his companion.

'A compliment,' he said. 'Between friends these little d----d accommodations ought to fly like pipe-lights.'

Fettes pocketed the money[4], and applauded the sentiment to the echo. 'You are a philosopher,' he cried. 'I was an ass till I knew you[5]. You and K— between you, by the Lord Harry! but you'll make a man of me.'

'Of course we shall,' applauded Macfarlane. 'A man? I tell you, it required a man to back me up the other morning. There are some big, brawling, forty-year-old cowards who would have turned sick at the look of the d----d thing; but not you—you kept your head. I watched you.'

'Well, and why not?' Fettes thus vaunted himself. 'It was no affair of mine. There was nothing to gain on the one side but disturbance, and on

---

[1] Both to temper their nerves and to warm their flesh, they have pocketed a jug of whisky

[2] The largest village in the vicinity of Glencorse Parish Church (1.8 miles away), said to be a stomping ground of Burke and Hare. Nearly as old as the church, the village today has a population of some 16,000, though at the time it stood at a few thousand

[3] The pub – a squat, simple building billed as a lounge – is still serving guests today. The name refers to the many fishing holes in the vicinity which drew tourists and locals alike

[4] He is now thoroughly and irretrievably in Macfarlane's pocket: not only has he paid him blood money, but he has accepted blood money

[5] Satan is well remembered for having tempted Eve with the fruit of Knowledge of Good and Evil saying "For God knows that when you eat from it your eyes will be opened, and you will be like God, knowing good and evil." Likewise, Fettes admires Macfarlane for having bestowed him with wisdom, or – to borrow Macfarlane's pet term – for having made him a man of the world

the other I could count on your gratitude[1], don't you see?' And he slapped his pocket till the gold pieces rang.

Macfarlane somehow felt a certain touch of alarm at these unpleasant words. He may have regretted that he had taught his young companion so successfully[2], but he had no time to interfere, for the other noisily continued in this boastful strain:—

'The great thing is not to be afraid. Now, between you and me, I don't want to hang—that's practical[3]; but for all cant, Macfarlane, I was born with a contempt[4]. Hell, God, Devil, right, wrong, sin, crime, and all the old gallery of curiosities—they may frighten boys, but men of the world[5], like you and me, despise them. Here's to the memory of Gray[6]!'

---

[1] The two men inhabit a world where morality (to use the term liberally) is determined by personal benefit, not concern for others' welfare: a good act is one that advances one social, enhances one's powers over others, or prevents one from getting into trouble. To Fettes, enabling Gray's murder to go undetected is the equivalent of a moral act because it puts Macfarlane in his good graces and furthers his budding career

[2] Indeed. One wonders if Gray was a former pupil of Macfarlane's, because Fettes is only two strains of thought short of becoming a blackmailer (and one threat of blackmail short of popping up on a dissecting table)

[3] Fettes' morality in a word – practical. He does what is good for him regardless of its effects on society, the wellbeing of others, or the toll on his increasingly nonexistent conscience. While some have argued in favor of utilitarian morality ("that which causes the most good and the least pain") or Vulcan morality ("the needs of the many outweigh the needs of the one or the few"), but Fettes' moral code is infantile and Machiavellian simultaneously – a baby who wails with crafty discretion

[4] Fettes' utter disregard for his fellow man – his moral apathy and social contempt, to use his term – are his defining sins. It is not so much his complicity in Grey's murder so much as it is his scorn for humanity (Grey included) that damns him

[5] Ah! And there is that phrase again. Fettes openly espouses the ways of the World (again, being a byword for the ways of hell, villainy, crime, and sin) and offers himself openly to Macfarlane's satanic worldview, verbally owning his corruption like a man swearing an oath of allegiance: Fettes has forever left the company of the Sheep – he is for the Lions

[6] In so toasting, Fettes symbolically condones the murder and ironically – given his wording – cheers his destruction and signs off on his deletion. This will, of course, quite literally come back to haunt Fettes, and – along with his payment to Macfarlane and his acceptance of payment – ensures his spiritual, psychological, and social damnation

It was by this time growing somewhat late. The gig, according to order, was brought round to the door with both lamps brightly shining[1], and the young men had to pay their bill and take the road. They announced that they were bound for Peebles[2], and drove in that direction till they were clear of the last houses of the town; then, extinguishing the lamps, returned upon their course, and followed a by-road toward Glencorse[3]. There was no sound but that of their own passage, and the incessant, strident pouring of the rain. It was pitch dark; here and there a white gate or a white stone in the wall guided them for a short space across the night; but for the most part it was at a foot pace, and almost groping, that they picked their way through that resonant blackness to their solemn and isolated destination. In the sunken woods that traverse the neighbourhood of the burying-ground the last glimmer failed them, and it became necessary to kindle a match and re-illumine one of the lanterns of the gig[4]. Thus, under the dripping trees, and environed by huge and moving shadows, they reached the scene of their unhallowed labours.

They were both experienced in such affairs, and powerful with the spade; and they had scarce been twenty minutes at their task before they were rewarded by a dull rattle on the coffin lid. At the same moment Macfarlane, having hurt his hand upon a stone, flung it carelessly above his head. The grave, in which they now stood almost to the shoulders, was close to the edge of the plateau of the graveyard; and the gig lamp had been propped, the better to illuminate their labours, against a tree, and on the immediate verge of the steep bank descending to the stream. Chance[5] had taken a sure aim with the stone. Then came a clang of broken glass; night fell upon them; sounds alternately dull and ringing announced the bounding of the lantern down the bank, and its occasional collision with the trees. A stone or two, which it had dislodged in its descent, rattled behind it into the profundities of the glen; and then silence, like night, resumed its sway; and they might bend their hearing to its utmost pitch, but naught was to be

---

[1] So-called "gig lamps" were bright, large oil lamps with lenses made of round, thick glass similar to a policeman's bulls-eye lantern

[2] A town almost 30 miles to the south

[3] They are now back-tracking: it is a two mile drive in the direction of Edinburgh, but out of the was though it was, the Fisher's Tryst offered them a necessary rest before their ordeal

[4] One might be mistaken for the lamp of a loitering schoolboy or farmhand, but two lamps bobbing parallel to one another would unquestionably draw attention weaving their way towards the churchyard at night

[5] Fate once more rears its head as we are drawn to wonder whether these events are coincidental, orchestrated by the supernatural, or the dictates of unavoidable destiny

heard except the rain, now marching to the wind, now steadily falling over miles of open country.

They were so nearly at an end of their abhorred task that they judged it wisest to complete it in the dark. The coffin was exhumed and broken open; the body inserted in the dripping sack and carried between them to the gig; one mounted to keep it in its place, and the other, taking the horse by the mouth, groped along by wall and bush until they reached the wider road by the Fisher's Tryst. Here was a faint, diffused radiancy[1], which they hailed like daylight; by that they pushed the horse to a good pace and began to rattle along merrily in the direction of the town.

They had both been wetted to the skin during their operations, and now, as the gig jumped among the deep ruts, the thing that stood propped between them fell now upon one and now upon the other. At every repetition of the horrid contact each instinctively repelled it with the greater haste; and the process, natural although it was, began to tell upon the nerves of the companions. Macfarlane made some ill-favoured jest about the farmer's wife, but it came hollowly from his lips, and was allowed to drop in silence. Still their unnatural burden bumped from side to side; and now the head would be laid, as if in confidence, upon their shoulders, and now the drenching sack-cloth would flap icily about their faces. A creeping chill began to possess the soul of Fettes. He peered at the bundle, and it seemed somehow larger than at first. All over the country-side, and from every degree of distance, the farm dogs accompanied their passage with tragic ululations[2]; and it grew and grew upon his mind that some unnatural miracle had been accomplished[3], that some nameless change had

-----

[1] Perhaps this is not noteworthy, but on a dreary night drenched in sheets of rain and thick with storm clouds, in the middle of the country, I would be wary of any soft pale light without a human source (also keep in mind that the Edinburgh of the early 1800s was illuminated by street lamps in the best parts of town, and these were still only oil, so it is unlikely that light pollution could be the source)

[2] A sobering sign: the wild, synchronized cries of dogs are closely associated with the presence of the supernatural, specifically of a very wicked and unnatural brand – vampires, demons, evil gods and Satan himself. No mere ghost ever inspired a dog to howl unless it was in the same room – the fact that all the local dogs take up the cry suggests that a tremendous and earth-moving action has rent the natural fabric of the universe. And this is not at all meant to be a mere atmospheric ("And then a random dog howled in the distance, and Fettes thought that was kind of spooky on a dark night like this"), but a very clear sign of active danger, akin to walking down the street and noticing that everyone you pass looks behind you warily as if they see some predatory figure

[3] As foreshadowed by the dark humor concerning the body snatchers who disregard the symbolism of the trumpets and scrolls, effectively resurrecting their quarry before the judgment day in violation of divine law, these two

befallen the dead body, and that it was in fear of their unholy burden that the dogs were howling.

'For God's sake,' said he, making a great effort to arrive at speech, 'for God's sake, let's have a light!'

Seemingly Macfarlane was affected in the same direction; for, though he made no reply, he stopped the horse, passed the reins to his companion, got down, and proceeded to kindle the remaining lamp. They had by that time got no farther than the cross-road down to Auchendinny[1]. The rain still poured as though the deluge were returning, and it was no easy matter to make a light in such a world of wet and darkness. When at last the flickering blue flame[2] had been transferred to the wick and began to expand and clarify, and shed a wide circle of misty brightness round the gig, it became possible for the two young men to see each other and the thing they had along with them. The rain had moulded the rough sacking to the outlines of the body underneath; the head was distinct from the trunk, the

---

resurrection men have inadvertently fulfilled the metaphor of their colloquial title: a literal resurrection has transpired – "an unnatural miracle"

[1] If the historical crossroad is anywhere near the current one, then our villains have only driven point seven miles. Auchendinny is now as it was then a very tiny hamlet a mile east of the church. Today the triangular Glencrose Golf Club separates the two areas

[2] This detail, to the average Victorian reader, would have been positively bone-chilling, and removes any doubt that something is amiss in the fabric of the universe as it provides a flashing warning sign of prowling devilry. Blue flame has long been associated with the presence of the supernatural (it was famously employed in *Dracula* in the form of will-o'-the-wisps), whether it be the natural blue-green flicker of swamp gas, or – far more terrifying – the subtle transition of a healthy, yellow candle flame into a chilly blue blaze. While the association of blue fire with swamp gases and phosphorescent decaying matter (when describing the glow on Marley's dead face, Dickens compares it to the sickly glow of a rotten lobster in a dark cellar) makes perfect scientific sense, the candle flame has often been seen as mere dramatics. However, if you consider the confused horror that a man – say one caught in the rain who breaks into a long-deserted house for shelter – would experience when, holding a candle above his head to probe the darkness, he walks into a room filled with air made foul by rotting wood, mold, and the gases of natural decay, and suddenly sees the yellow fire freeze into a blue-green-purple tongue. While it is sensible to reason that the flame is now burning up gases in the stagnant air and producing the same natural fire as a will-o'-the-wisp, our interloper might be justified in identifying the hand of the supernatural in this very unusal, and very creepy transformation

shoulders plainly modelled; something at once spectral and human[1] riveted their eyes upon the ghastly comrade of their drive[2].

For some time Macfarlane stood motionless, holding up the lamp. A nameless dread was swathed, like a wet sheet, about the body, and tightened the white skin upon the face of Fettes; a fear that was meaningless, a horror of what could not be, kept mounting to his brain. Another beat of the watch, and he had spoken. But his comrade forestalled him.

'That is not a woman,' said Macfarlane, in a hushed voice.

'It was a woman when we put her in,' whispered Fettes.

'Hold that lamp,' said the other. 'I must see her face[3].'

---

[1] Gray's manifestation is both natural and supernatural – it is a genuine, physical change brought about by an unearthly, spiritual medium – and it frightens Fettes both naturally and supernaturally, for both his body and his soul are at stake: his body, if the shrouded form should prove physically violent like a vampire or werewolf, and his soul in light of the damnation that Gray's murder has assured, and which his supernatural manifestation (which – all Fettes' protestations aside – is more than enough to prove the existence of an afterlife to the criminals, and thereby hint at eternal punishment for their deeds). In another sense, Gray's appearance draws attention to the way that sin, crime, and wickedness can affect a person both in body and in spirit: bodily in that the pleasures of life – the same that are so dearly won and funded by murder, body-snatching, and social climbing – are dwarfed by fear, paranoia, violence, and guilt, and spiritually in the loss of innocence, peace of mind, and self-respect

[2] Comrade indeed: Stevenson here underscores the earlier sentiment of "today it is me, tomorrow you" by portraying the dead man as a social equal and indeed a companion to the living men, illustrating Dickens' phrase of "fellow passengers to the grave." In spite of all their materialism and educated atheism, Macfarlane and Fettes simply do not seem – until now – to have realized that they are mortal, and Gray is more than happy to inform them of the news

[3] And here it comes around full circle: the motif of staring – of needing to stare – into the face of something for which one is responsible, but which one hopes not to be true. The motif continues to advance the story's central themes: moral culpability, the horror of guilt, coming to terms with the ramifications of one's actions, the vain impossibility of moral denial, the mental dissonance caused by the same denial, and the revulsion of one's own secret sins. Fettes and Macfarlane each feel compelled to view the face of their companion – an unspoken wish to rule out that which they know only too well that they must verify. Like a drunk who returns to the home he dismantled hoping to find the furniture unsmashed and his wife's car and luggage still where it had been the previous morning, the two culprits hope against hope that the figure isn't Gray – READ: THAT THEIR ACTIONS DO NOT HAVE RAMIFICATIONS FOR THEIR FUTURE LIVES, FOR THEIR SOULS – and they are sorely disappointed: it is Gray, and their

And as Fettes took the lamp his companion untied the fastenings of the sack and drew down the cover from the head. The light fell very clear upon the dark, well-moulded features and smooth-shaven cheeks[1] of a too familiar countenance, often beheld in dreams of both of these young men. A wild yell rang up into the night; each leaped from his own side into the roadway: the lamp fell, broke, and was extinguished; and the horse, terrified by this unusual commotion, bounded and went off toward Edinburgh at a gallop, bearing along with it, sole occupant of the gig, the body of the dead and long-dissected Gray[2].

---

crimes – detected or undetected – will haunt their lives, spirits, and happiness until they join Gray in death

[1] A nice touch by Stevenson that increases suspense while holding off on the reveal: this little detail confirms (or should confirm) that the corpse is indeed now a man

[2] Don't be too perplexed, and for God's sake, don't look for a natural explanation. I have known many who are absolutely confused by this ending. Yes, Gray was in fact dissected, no his body (which would now be in pieces scattered amongst students) wasn't buried in that graveyard, yes they did originally get the right grave, yes they did originally get an old woman, and yes that body metamorphosed into Gray supernaturally. Don't overthink it; it's a bogey tale. Gray manifests in the old woman's body to haunt his murderers and remind them of the reckoning that they have coming to them – in this world (especially felt by the anti-social drunk Fettes) and the next (perhaps most especially felt by the outwardly lavish Macfarlane), and to remind them that their outward actions have internal consequences. We have reason to believe that this was not the last time that Gray appeared to his killers (maybe think Jacob Marley showing up in door knockers, Dutch tiles, and the like), since Fettes asks if Macfarlane has (implying that such has been his experience), and Macfarlane balks flusteredly (implying that he has and doesn't want to remember it)

130

"I must see him face to face..." Fettes' demand to address his Mephistophelean tormentor calls to mind the similarly eerie, similarly confrontational phantom in Edgar Allan Poe's "William Wilson." In that case, an immoral man was haunted by his conscience in the form of a persistent Doppelganger, in Stevenson's tale, Fettes must continually face the ramifications of his actions by staring them in the face: first that of poor smothered Jane (he is forced to confront his role as an indirect accessory to her death), then that of black-hearted Grey (accessory becomes enabler), then (after symbolically selling his soul by first paying, then accepting blood money, and finally by solemnizing the murder with a condoning toast) that of Grey's spirit (enabler becomes complicit), then that of Macfarlane (complicit conspirator becomes actualized sinner as Fettes sees decades later that he has lost his soul to Macfarlane and been abandoned by God). This also resembles Victor Frankenstein's obsession with challenging his Creature face to face in the wake of his murders – a character which we have already likened to the involuntary necromancer, Fettes. Like Frankenstein, Fettes' disregard for ethical mores and human decency has resulted in the vitalization of a dead corpse (or at least its supernatural transformation), which comes to represent the inescapable physicality of sin: like Shelley's Creature and Stevenson's Grey, crimes against our common humanity cannot be ignored or expected to fade into the past, for they are pregnant with ramifications which will sooner or later open their eyes and stare us in the face. Grey's weird theophany in the body of a dead widow is hardly a conventional haunting, and if for no other reason, this tale should be venerated for its bizarre imagery and creative supernaturalism. Stevenson is permitted to use such strange and unclassifiable spooks (is it a vampire, zombie, ghost, or hysteria?) because his objective is not to scare the audience (a blood sucker would easily have sufficed), but to make a philosophical statement. He doesn't care how it is that the second body transmuted into the first, all that matters is that Fettes and Macfarlane were shown that no amount of creativity or cleverness can rid a person of their unaccounted sins.

II.

Still unrepentant in his old age (Fettes' purgatorial lifestyle in the limbo of an east coast tavern suggests as much) has prevented him from avoiding Grey's continued hauntings, which he and Macfarlane – in a tantalizingly suggestive move by Stevenson – appear to suffer on a regular basis. Still unwilling to come clean to the authorities or otherwise unweigh his soul, Fettes is cast into the night after coming face to face with his successful Tempter – metaphorically (and perhaps literally: Stevenson strongly implies that Fettes may have died that night) falling from purgatory into Hell. Stevenson's work (Jekyll, Markheim, The Bottle Imp, Thrawn Janet, etc.) is regularly concerned with social hypocrisy, the pitfalls of anti-social rebellion, and the cleansing salvation of integrity, accountability, and public confession. Like Hawthorne's Reverend Dimmesdale (himself a Jekyll forebearer), the characters of Markheim, Jekyll and others are purified through death when they atone for their secret lives with acts of public contrition: Jekyll leaves his confession and slays himself, Markheim abandons his plot and surrenders to the gallows, Keawe sells the bottle imp full well expecting to be damned if it means saving Kokua. Perhaps there is redemption for the misanthropic bar fly as well: if he does go to his death after demanding to peer into Macfarlane's face – an act of confrontation and accountability, since he must come to terms with the fact that it is his silence and his apathy which have allowed the sociopathic Macfarlane to escape the gallows and mellow into old age amongst the highest classes of society – then we might view his death differently, not as a coward being cast into Hell, but as a denizen of purgatory rising up and willingly marching himself to Perdition after the shock of how far his culpability has gone. If Stevenson's supernatural oeuvre had one message to impart, I wonder if it would not be this: hide nothing away if you hope it to remain hidden forever, for hidden things grow, and they bear hideous fruit.

ALTHOUGH commonly classed among Stevenson's best supernatural work – typically listed after "Jekyll," "Snatcher," and "Imp," respectively – "Markheim" is more accurately seen as a little Gothic parable or fable. It is quite straightforward without a terrible amount of nuance or moral discomfort, unlike the chilling webs of "Jekyll" and "Snatcher." Nonetheless, "Markheim" is a crucial chapter in Stevenson's development as a sometimes writer of horror fiction. Taking his cue from Goethe (*Faust*), Washington Irving ("The Devil and Tom Walker," "Golden Dreams"), Charles Dickens ("The Goblins Who Stole a Sexton," *A Christmas Carol*), and Nathaniel Hawthorne ("Young Goodman Brown," *The Scarlet Letter*), Stevenson sets out to write a tale about a man on the threshold of selling his soul, his encounter with a tempting spirit, and his resolution to change and amend his heart at the cost of his personal liberty. This is not the case in some of the aforementioned episodes ("Tom Walker" and "Goodman Brown" being obvious examples), but the theme of a greedy, selfish man meeting Satan at the crossroads of his moral development, being goaded into signing away his soul for material comfort, and coming face to face with the results of that spiritual treason is a common archetype in Western literature, and one which Stevenson both belabors and makes refreshingly original. As such, the story of a murderer who is allowed the opportunity to either escape at the cost of his soul, or to surrender at the cost of his life has quite a different intensity than Goethe's cosmopolitan scholar, Dickens' stingy misers, or Irving's treasure-hungry caricatures. The cost here is greater, and the story is not entirely without its horror. But it is no horror of specters or demons or witches: it is the horror of an otherwise good man who can – if only at first – justify a capital sin.

Markheim
{1884}

"YES," said the dealer, "our windfalls are of various kinds. Some customers are ignorant, and then I touch a dividend on my superior knowledge. Some are dishonest," and here he held up the candle, so that the light fell strongly on his visitor, "and in that case," he continued, "I profit by my virtue."

Markheim had but just entered from the daylight streets, and his eyes had not yet grown familiar with the mingled shine and darkness in the shop. At these pointed words, and before the near presence of the flame, he blinked painfully and looked aside.

The dealer chuckled. "You come to me on Christmas Day," he resumed, "when you know that I am alone in my house, put up my shutters, and make a point of refusing business. Well, you will have to pay for that; you will have to pay for my loss of time, when I should be balancing my books; you will have to pay, besides, for a kind of manner that I remark in you to-day very strongly. I am the essence of discretion, and ask no awkward questions; but when a customer cannot look me in the eye, he has to pay for it." The dealer once more chuckled; and then, changing to his usual business voice, though still with a note of irony, "You can give, as usual, a clear account of how you came into the possession of the object?" he continued. "Still your uncle's cabinet? A remarkable collector, sir!"

And the little pale, round-shouldered dealer stood almost on tip-toe, looking over the top of his gold spectacles, and nodding his head with every mark of disbelief. Markheim returned his gaze with one of infinite pity, and a touch of horror.

"This time," said he, "you are in error. I have not come to sell, but to buy. I have no curios to dispose of; my uncle's cabinet is bare to the wainscot; even were it still intact, I have done well on the Stock Exchange, and should more likely add to it than otherwise, and my errand to-day is simplicity itself. I seek a Christmas present for a lady," he continued, waxing more fluent as he struck into the speech he had prepared; "and certainly I owe you every excuse for thus disturbing you upon so small a matter. But the thing was neglected yesterday; I must produce my little compliment at dinner; and, as you very well know, a rich marriage is not a thing to be neglected."

There followed a pause, during which the dealer seemed to weigh this statement incredulously. The ticking of many clocks among the curious lumber of the shop, and the faint rushing of the cabs in a near thoroughfare, filled up the interval of silence.

"Well, sir," said the dealer, "be it so. You are an old customer after all; and if, as you say, you have the chance of a good marriage, far be it from me to be an obstacle. Here is a nice thing for a lady now," he went on, "this hand-glass--fifteenth century, warranted; comes from a good collection, too; but I reserve the name, in the interests of my customer, who was just like yourself, my dear sir, the nephew and sole heir of a remarkable collector."

The dealer, while he thus ran on in his dry and biting voice, had stooped to take the object from its place; and, as he had done so, a shock had passed through Markheim, a start both of hand and foot, a sudden leap of many tumultuous passions to the face. It passed as swiftly as it came, and left no trace beyond a certain trembling of the hand that now received the glass.

"A glass," he said hoarsely, and then paused, and repeated it more clearly. "A glass? For Christmas? Surely not?"

"And why not?" cried the dealer. "Why not a glass?"

Markheim was looking upon him with an indefinable expression. "You ask me why not?" he said. "Why, look here--look in it--look at yourself! Do you like to see it? No! nor I--nor any man."

The little man had jumped back when Markheim had so suddenly confronted him with the mirror; but now, perceiving there was nothing worse on hand, he chuckled. "Your future lady, sir, must be pretty hard favoured," said he.

"I ask you," said Markheim, "for a Christmas present, and you give me this--this damned reminder of years, and sins and follies--this hand-conscience! Did you mean it? Had you a thought in your mind? Tell me. It will be better for you if you do. Come, tell me about yourself. I hazard a guess now, that you are in secret a very charitable man."

The dealer looked closely at his companion. It was very odd, Markheim did not appear to be laughing; there was something in his face like an eager sparkle of hope, but nothing of mirth.

"What are you driving at?" the dealer asked.

"Not charitable?" returned the other, gloomily. "Not charitable; not pious; not scrupulous; unloving, unbeloved; a hand to get money, a safe to keep it. Is that all? Dear God, man, is that all?"

"I will tell you what it is," began the dealer, with some sharpness, and then broke off again into a chuckle. "But I see this is a love match of yours, and you have been drinking the lady's health."

"Ah!" cried Markheim, with a strange curiosity. "Ah, have you been in love? Tell me about that."

"I," cried the dealer. "I in love! I never had the time, nor have I the time to-day for all this nonsense. Will you take the glass?"

"Where is the hurry?" returned Markheim. "It is very pleasant to stand here talking; and life is so short and insecure that I would not hurry away from any pleasure--no, not even from so mild a one as this. We should rather cling, cling to what little we can get, like a man at a cliff's edge. Every second is a cliff, if you think upon it--a cliff a mile high--high enough, if we fall, to dash us out of every feature of humanity. Hence it is best to talk pleasantly. Let us talk of each other; why should we wear this mask? Let us be confidential. Who knows? we might become friends."

"I have just one word to say to you," said the dealer. "Either make your purchase, or walk out of my shop."

"True, true," said Markheim. "Enough fooling. To business. Show me something else."

The dealer stooped once more, this time to replace the glass upon the shelf, his thin blond hair falling over his eyes as he did so. Markheim moved a little nearer, with one hand in the pocket of his greatcoat; he drew himself up and filled his lungs; at the same time many different emotions were depicted together on his face--terror, horror, and resolve, fascination and a physical repulsion; and through a haggard lift of his upper lip, his teeth looked out.

"This, perhaps, may suit," observed the dealer. And then, as he began to rearise, Markheim bounded from behind upon his victim. The long, skewer-like dagger flashed and fell. The dealer struggled like a hen, striking his temple on the shelf, and then tumbled on the floor in a heap.

Time had some score of small voices in that shop--some stately and slow as was becoming to their great age; others garrulous and hurried. All these told out the seconds in an intricate chorus of tickings. Then the passage of a lad's feet, heavily running on the pavement, broke in upon these smaller voices and startled Markheim into the consciousness of his surroundings. He looked about him awfully. The candle stood on the counter, its flame solemnly wagging in a draught; and by that inconsiderable movement the whole room was filled with noiseless bustle and kept heaving like a sea: the tall shadows nodding, the gross blots of darkness swelling and dwindling as with respiration, the faces of the portraits and the china gods changing and wavering like images in water. The inner door stood ajar, and peered into that leaguer of shadows with a long slit of daylight like a pointing finger.

From these fear-stricken rovings, Markheim's eyes returned to the body of his victim, where it lay, both humped and sprawling, incredibly small and strangely meaner than in life. In these poor, miserly clothes, in that ungainly attitude, the dealer lay like so much sawdust. Markheim had feared to see it, and, lo! it was nothing. And yet, as he gazed, this bundle of old clothes and pool of blood began to find eloquent voices. There it must lie; there was none to work the cunning hinges or direct the miracle of locomotion; there it must lie till it was found. Found! ay, and then? Then would this dead flesh lift up a cry that would ring over England, and fill the world with the echoes of pursuit. Ay, dead or not, this was still the enemy. "Time was that when the brains were out," he thought; and the first word struck into his mind. Time, now that the deed was accomplished-- time, which had closed for the victim, had become instant and momentous for the slayer.

The thought was yet in his mind, when, first one and then another, with every variety of pace and voice--one deep as the bell from a cathedral turret, another ringing on its treble notes the prelude of a waltz,--the clocks began to strike the hour of three in the afternoon.

The sudden outbreak of so many tongues in that dumb chamber staggered him. He began to bestir himself, going to and fro with the candle, beleaguered by moving shadows, and startled to the soul by chance reflections. In many rich mirrors, some of home design, some from Venice or Amsterdam, he saw his face repeated and repeated, as it were an army of spies; his own eyes met and detected him; and the sound of his own steps, lightly as they fell, vexed the surrounding quiet. And still, as he continued to fill his pockets, his mind accused him with a sickening iteration, of the thousand faults of his design. He should have chosen a more quiet hour; he should have prepared an alibi; he should not have used a knife; he should have been more cautious, and only bound and gagged the dealer, and not killed him; he should have been more bold, and killed the servant also; he should have done all things otherwise. Poignant regrets, weary, incessant toiling of the mind to change what was unchangeable, to plan what was now useless, to be the architect of the irrevocable past. Meanwhile, and behind all this activity, brute terrors, like the scurrying of rats in a deserted attic, filled the more remote chambers of his brain with riot; the hand of the constable would fall heavy on his shoulder, and his nerves would jerk like a hooked fish; or he beheld, in galloping defile, the dock, the prison, the gallows, and the black coffin.

Terror of the people in the street sat down before his mind like a besieging army. It was impossible, he thought, but that some rumour of the struggle must have reached their ears and set on edge their curiosity; and now, in all the neighbouring houses, he divined them sitting motionless and with uplifted ear--solitary people, condemned to spend Christmas dwelling alone on memories of the past, and now startingly recalled from that tender exercise; happy family parties struck into silence round the table, the mother still with raised finger--every degree and age and humour, but all, by their own hearths, prying and hearkening and weaving the rope that was to hang him. Sometimes it seemed to him he could not move too softly; the clink of the tall Bohemian goblets rang out loudly like a bell; and alarmed by the bigness of the ticking, he was tempted to stop the clocks. And then, again, with a swift transition of his terrors, the very silence of the place appeared a source of peril, and a thing to strike and freeze the passer-by; and he would step more boldly, and bustle aloud among the contents of the shop, and imitate, with elaborate bravado, the movements of a busy man at ease in his own house.

But he was now so pulled about by different alarms that, while one portion of his mind was still alert and cunning, another trembled on the brink of lunacy. One hallucination in particular took a strong hold on his credulity. The neighbour hearkening with white face beside his window, the passer-by arrested by a horrible surmise on the pavement--these could at worst suspect, they could not know; through the brick walls and shuttered windows only sounds could penetrate. But here, within the house, was he alone? He knew he was; he had watched the servant set forth sweet-hearting, in her poor best, "out for the day" written in every ribbon and smile. Yes, he was alone, of course; and yet, in the bulk of empty house above him, he could surely hear a stir of delicate footing; he was surely conscious, inexplicably conscious of some presence. Ay, surely; to every room and corner of the house his imagination followed it; and now it was a faceless thing, and yet had eyes to see with; and again it was a shadow of himself; and yet again behold the image of the dead dealer, reinspired with cunning and hatred.

At times, with a strong effort, he would glance at the open door which still seemed to repel his eyes. The house was tall, the skylight small and dirty, the day blind with fog; and the light that filtered down to the ground story was exceedingly faint, and showed dimly on the threshold of the shop.

And yet, in that strip of doubtful brightness, did there not hang wavering a shadow?

Suddenly, from the street outside, a very jovial gentleman began to beat with a staff on the shop door, accompanying his blows with shouts and railleries in which the dealer was continually called upon by name. Markheim, smitten into ice, glanced at the dead man. But no! he lay quite still; he was fled away far beyond earshot of these blows and shoutings; he was sunk beneath seas of silence; and his name, which would once have caught his notice above the howling of a storm, had become an empty sound. And presently the jovial gentleman desisted from his knocking and departed.

Here was a broad hint to hurry what remained to be done, to get forth from this accusing neighbourhood, to plunge into a bath of London multitudes, and to reach, on the other side of day, that haven of safety and apparent innocence--his bed. One visitor had come; at any moment another might follow and be more obstinate. To have done the deed, and yet not to reap the profit, would be too abhorrent a failure. The money--that was now Markheim's concern; and as a means to that, the keys.

He glanced over his shoulder at the open door, where the shadow was still lingering and shivering; and with no conscious repugnance of the mind, yet with a tremor of the belly, he drew near the body of his victim. The human character had quite departed. Like a suit half- stuffed with bran, the limbs lay scattered, the trunk doubled, on the floor; and yet the thing repelled him. Although so dingy and inconsiderable to the eye, he feared it might have more significance to the touch. He took the body by the shoulders, and turned it on its back. It was strangely light and supple, and the limbs, as if they had been broken, fell into the oddest postures. The face was robbed of all expression; but it was as pale as wax, and shockingly smeared with blood about one temple. That was, for Markheim, the one displeasing circumstance. It carried him back, upon the instant, to a certain fair-day in a fishers' village: a gray day, a piping wind, a crowd upon the street, the blare of brasses, the booming of drums, the nasal voice of a ballad singer; and a boy going to and fro, buried overhead in the crowd and divided between interest and fear, until, coming out upon the chief place of concourse, he beheld a booth and a great screen with pictures, dismally designed, garishly coloured--Brownrigg with her apprentice, the Mannings with their murdered guest, Weare in the death-grip of Thurtell, and a score besides of famous crimes. The thing was as clear as an illusion He was once again that little boy; he was looking once again, and with the same sense of physical revolt, at these vile pictures; he was still stunned by the thumping of the drums. A bar of that day's music returned upon his memory; and at that, for the first time, a qualm came over him, a breath of nausea, a sudden weakness of the joints, which he must instantly resist and conquer.

He judged it more prudent to confront than to flee from these considerations, looking the more hardily in the dead face, bending his mind to realise the nature and greatness of his crime. So little a while ago that face had moved with every change of sentiment, that pale mouth had spoken, that body had been all on fire with governable energies; and now, and by his act, that piece of life had been arrested, as the horologist, with interjected finger, arrests the beating of the clock. So he reasoned in vain; he could rise to no more remorseful consciousness; the same heart which had shuddered before the painted effigies of crime, looked on its reality unmoved. At best, he felt a gleam of pity for one who had been endowed in vain with all those faculties that can make the world a garden of enchantment, one who had never lived and who was now dead. But of penitence, no, not a tremor.

With that, shaking himself clear of these considerations, he found the keys and advanced toward the open door of the shop. Outside, it had begun to rain smartly, and the sound of the shower upon the roof had banished silence. Like some dripping cavern, the chambers of the house were haunted by an incessant echoing, which filled the ear and mingled with the ticking of the clocks. And, as Markheim approached the door, he seemed to hear, in answer to his own cautious tread, the steps of another foot withdrawing up the stair. The shadow still palpitated loosely on the threshold. He threw a ton's weight of resolve upon his muscles, and drew back the door.

The faint, foggy daylight glimmered dimly on the bare floor and stairs; on the bright suit of armour posted, halbert in hand, upon the landing; and on the dark wood-carvings, and framed pictures that hung against the yellow panels of the wainscot. So loud was the beating of the rain through all the house that, in Markheim's ears, it began to be distinguished into many different sounds. Footsteps and sighs, the tread of regiments marching in the distance, the chink of money in the counting, and the creaking of doors held stealthily ajar, appeared to mingle with the patter of the drops upon the cupola and the gushing of the water in the pipes. The sense that he was not alone grew upon him to the verge of madness. On every side he was haunted and begirt by presences. He heard them moving in the upper chambers; from the shop, he heard the dead man getting to his legs; and as he began with a great effort to mount the stairs, feet fled quietly before him and followed stealthily behind. If he were but deaf, he thought, how tranquilly he would possess his soul! And then again, and hearkening with ever fresh attention, he blessed himself for that unresting sense which held the outposts and stood a trusty sentinel upon his life. His head turned continually on his neck; his eyes, which seemed starting from their orbits, scouted on every side, and on every side were half rewarded as with the tail of something nameless vanishing. The four and twenty steps to the first floor were four and twenty agonies.

On that first story, the doors stood ajar--three of them, like three ambushes, shaking his nerves like the throats of cannon. He could never again, he felt, be sufficiently immured and fortified from men's observing eyes; he longed to be home, girt in by walls, buried among bedclothes, and invisible to all but God. And at that thought he wondered a little, recollecting tales of other murderers and the fear they were said to entertain of heavenly avengers. It was not so, at least, with him. He feared the laws of nature, lest, in their callous and immutable procedure, they should preserve some damning evidence of his crime. He feared tenfold more, with a slavish, superstitious terror, some scission in the continuity of man's experience, some wilful illegality of nature. He played a game of skill, depending on the rules, calculating consequence from cause; and what if nature, as the defeated tyrant overthrew the chess-board, should break the mould of their succession? The like had befallen Napoleon (so writers said) when the winter changed the time of its appearance. The like might befall Markheim: the solid walls might become transparent and reveal his doings like those of bees in a glass hive; the stout planks might yield under his foot like quicksands and detain him in their clutch. Ay, and there were soberer accidents that might destroy him; if, for instance, the house should fall and imprison him beside the body of his victim, or the house next door should fly on fire, and the firemen invade him from all sides. These things he feared; and, in a sense, these things might be called the hands of God reached forth against sin. But about God himself he was at ease; his act was doubtless exceptional, but so were his excuses, which God knew; it was there, and not among men, that he felt sure of justice.

When he had got safe into the drawing-room, and shut the door behind him, he was aware of a respite from alarms. The room was quite dismantled, uncarpeted besides, and strewn with packing-cases and incongruous furniture; several great pier-glasses, in which he beheld himself at various angles, like an actor on a stage; many pictures, framed and unframed, standing, with their faces to the wall; a fine Sheraton sideboard, a cabinet of marquetry, and a great old bed, with tapestry hangings. The windows opened to the floor; but by great good fortune the lower part of the shutters had been closed, and this concealed him from the neighbours. Here, then, Markheim drew in a packing-case before the cabinet, and began to search among the keys. It was a long business, for there were many; and it was irksome, besides; for, after all, there might be nothing in the cabinet, and time was on the wing. But the closeness of the occupation sobered him. With the tail of his eye he saw the door--even glanced at it from time to time directly, like a besieged commander pleased to verify the good estate of his defences. But in truth he was at peace. The rain falling in the street sounded natural and pleasant. Presently, on the other side, the notes of a piano were wakened to the music of a hymn, and the voices of many children took up the air and words. How stately, how comfortable was the melody! How fresh the youthful voices! Markheim gave ear to it smilingly, as he sorted out the keys; and his mind was thronged with answerable ideas and images: church-going children, and the pealing of the high organ; children afield, bathers by the brookside, ramblers on the brambly common, kite-flyers in the windy and cloud-navigated sky; and then, at another cadence of the hymn, back again to church, and the somnolence of summer Sundays, and the high genteel voice of the parson (which he smiled a little to recall) and the painted Jacobean tombs, and the dim lettering of the Ten Commandments in the chancel.

And as he sat thus, at once busy and absent, he was startled to his feet. A flash of ice, a flash of fire, a bursting gush of blood, went over him, and then he stood transfixed and thrilling. A step mounted the stair slowly and steadily, and presently a hand was laid upon the knob, and the lock clicked, and the door opened.

Fear held Markheim in a vice. What to expect he knew not--whether the dead man walking, or the official ministers of human justice, or some chance witness blindly stumbling in to consign him to the gallows. But when a face was thrust into the aperture, glanced round the room, looked at him, nodded and smiled as if in friendly recognition, and then withdrew again, and the door closed behind it, his fear broke loose from his control in a hoarse cry. At the sound of this the visitant returned.

"Did you call me?" he asked, pleasantly, and with that he entered the room and closed the door behind him.

Markheim stood and gazed at him with all his eyes. Perhaps there was a film upon his sight, but the outlines of the new comer seemed to change and waver like those of the idols in the wavering candle-light of the shop; and at times he thought he knew him; and at times he thought he bore a likeness to himself; and always, like a lump of living terror, there lay in his bosom the conviction that this thing was not of the earth and not of God.

And yet the creature had a strange air of the commonplace, as he stood looking on Markheim with a smile; and when he added, "You are looking for the money, I believe?" it was in the tones of everyday politeness.

Markheim made no answer.

"I should warn you," resumed the other, "that the maid has left her sweetheart earlier than usual and will soon be here. If Mr. Markheim be found in this house, I need not describe to him the consequences."

"You know me?" cried the murderer.

The visitor smiled. "You have long been a favourite of mine," he said; "and I have long observed and often sought to help you."

"What are you?" cried Markheim; "the devil?"

"What I may be," returned the other, "cannot affect the service I propose to render you."

"It can," cried Markheim; "it does! Be helped by you? No, never; not by you! You do not know me yet; thank God, you do not know me!"

141

"I know you," replied the visitant, with a sort of kind severity or rather firmness. "I know you to the soul."

"Know me!" cried Markheim. "Who can do so? My life is but a travesty and slander on myself. I have lived to belie my nature. All men do; all men are better than this disguise that grows about and stifles them. You see each dragged away by life, like one whom bravos have seized and muffled in a cloak. If they had their own control--if you could see their faces, they would be altogether different, they would shine out for heroes and saints! I am worse than most; myself is more overlaid; my excuse is known to me and God. But, had I the time, I could disclose myself."

"To me?" inquired the visitant.

"To you before all," returned the murderer. "I supposed you were intelligent. I thought--since you exist--you would prove a reader of the heart. And yet you would propose to judge me by my acts! Think of it--my acts! I was born and I have lived in a land of giants; giants have dragged me by the wrists since I was born out of my mother--the giants of circumstance. And you would judge me by my acts! But can you not look within? Can you not understand that evil is hateful to me? Can you not see within me the clear writing of conscience, never blurred by any wilful sophistry, although too often disregarded? Can you not read me for a thing that surely must be common as humanity-- the unwilling sinner?"

"All this is very feelingly expressed," was the reply, "but it regards me not. These points of consistency are beyond my province, and I care not in the least by what compulsion you may have been dragged away, so as you are but carried in the right direction. But time flies; the servant delays, looking in the faces of the crowd and at the pictures on the hoardings, but still she keeps moving nearer; and remember, it is as if the gallows itself was striding towards you through the Christmas streets! Shall I help you--I, who know all? Shall I tell you where to find the money?"

"For what price?" asked Markheim.

"I offer you the service for a Christmas gift," returned the other.

Markheim could not refrain from smiling with a kind of bitter triumph. "No," said he, "I will take nothing at your hands; if I were dying of thirst, and it was your hand that put the pitcher to my lips, I should find the courage to refuse. It may be credulous, but I will do nothing to commit myself to evil."

"I have no objection to a death-bed repentance," observed the visitant.

"Because you disbelieve their efficacy!" Markheim cried.

"I do not say so," returned the other; "but I look on these things from a different side, and when the life is done my interest falls. The man has lived to serve me, to spread black looks under colour of religion, or to sow tares in the wheat-field, as you do, in a course of weak compliance with desire. Now that he draws so near to his deliverance, he can add but one act of service: to repent, to die smiling, and thus to build up in confidence and hope the more timorous of my surviving followers. I am not so hard a master. Try me; accept my help. Please yourself in life as you have done hitherto; please yourself more amply, spread your elbows at the board; and when the night begins to fall and the curtains to be drawn, I tell you, for your greater comfort, that you will find it even easy to compound your quarrel with your conscience, and to make a truckling peace with God. I came but now from such a death-bed, and the room was full of sincere mourners, listening to the man's last words; and when I looked into that face, which had been set as a flint against mercy, I found it smiling with hope."

"And do you, then, suppose me such a creature?" asked Markheim. "Do you think I have no more generous aspirations than to sin and sin and sin and at last sneak into heaven? My heart rises at the thought. Is this, then, your experience of mankind? or is it because you find me with red hands that you presume such baseness? And is this crime of murder indeed so impious as to dry up the very springs of good?"

"Murder is to me no special category," replied the other. "All sins are murder, even as all life is war. I behold your race, like starving mariners on a raft, plucking crusts out of the hands of famine and feeding on each other's lives. I follow sins beyond the moment of their acting; I find in all that the last consequence is death, and to my eyes, the pretty maid who thwarts her mother with such taking graces on a question of a ball, drips no less visibly with human gore than such a murderer as yourself. Do I say that I follow sins? I follow virtues also. They differ not by the thickness of a nail; they are both scythes for the reaping angel of Death. Evil, for which I live, consists not in action but in character. The bad man is dear to me, not the bad act, whose fruits, if we could follow them far enough down the hurtling cataract of the ages, might yet be found more blessed than those of the rarest virtues. And it is not because you have killed a dealer, but because you are Markheim, that I offer to forward your escape."

"I will lay my heart open to you," answered Markheim. "This crime on which you find me is my last. On my way to it I have learned many lessons; itself is a lesson--a momentous lesson. Hitherto I have been driven with revolt to what I would not; I was a bond-slave to poverty, driven and scourged. There are robust virtues that can stand in these temptations; mine was not so; I had a thirst of pleasure. But to-day, and out of this deed, I pluck both warning and riches--both the power and a fresh resolve to be myself. I become in all things a free actor in the world; I begin to see myself all changed, these hands the agents of good, this heart at peace. Something comes over me out of the past--something of what I have dreamed on Sabbath evenings to the sound of the church organ, of what I forecast when I shed tears over noble books, or talked, an innocent child, with my mother. There lies my life; I have wandered a few years, but now I see once more my city of destination."

143

"You are to use this money on the Stock Exchange, I think?" remarked the visitor; "and there, if I mistake not, you have already lost some thousands?"

"Ah," said Markheim, "but this time I have a sure thing."

"This time, again, you will lose," replied the visitor quietly.

"Ah, but I keep back the half!" cried Markheim.

"That also you will lose," said the other.

The sweat started upon Markheim's brow. "Well then, what matter?" he exclaimed. "Say it be lost, say I am plunged again in poverty, shall one part of me, and that the worse, continue until the end to override the better? Evil and good run strong in me, hailing me both ways. I do not love the one thing; I love all. I can conceive great deeds, renunciations, martyrdoms; and though I be fallen to such a crime as murder, pity is no stranger to my thoughts. I pity the poor; who knows their trials better than myself? I pity and help them. I prize love; I love honest laughter; there is no good thing nor true thing on earth but I love it from my heart. And are my vices only to direct my life, and my virtues to lie without effect, like some passive lumber of the mind? Not so; good, also, is a spring of acts."

But the visitant raised his finger. "For six and thirty years that you have been in this world," said he, "through many changes of fortune and varieties of humour, I have watched you steadily fall. Fifteen years ago you would have started at a theft. Three years back you would have blenched at the name of murder. Is there any crime, is there any cruelty or meanness, from which you still recoil? Five years from now I shall detect you in the fact! Downward, downward, lies your way; nor can anything but death avail to stop you."

"It is true," Markheim said huskily, "I have in some degree complied with evil. But it is so with all; the very saints, in the mere exercise of living, grow less dainty, and take on the tone of their surroundings."

"I will propound to you one simple question," said the other; "and as you answer I shall read to you your moral horoscope. You have grown in many things more lax; possibly you do right to be so; and at any account, it is the same with all men. But granting that, are you in any one particular, however trifling, more difficult to please with your own conduct, or do you go in all things with a looser rein?"

"In any one?" repeated Markheim, with an anguish of consideration. "No," he added, with despair; "in none! I have gone down in all."

"Then," said the visitor, "content yourself with what you are, for you will never change; and the words of your part on this stage are irrevocably written down."

Markheim stood for a long while silent, and, indeed, it was the visitor who first broke the silence. "That being so," he said, "shall I show you the money?"

"And grace?" cried Markheim.

145

"Have you not tried it?" returned the other. "Two or three years ago did I not see you on the platform of revival meetings, and was not your voice the loudest in the hymn?"

"It is true," said Markheim; "and I see clearly what remains for me by way of duty. I thank you for these lessons from my soul; my eyes are opened, and I behold myself at last for what I am."

At this moment, the sharp note of the door-bell rang through the house; and the visitant, as though this were some concerted signal for which he had been waiting, changed at once in his demeanour.

"The maid!" he cried. "She has returned, as I forewarned you, and there is now before you one more difficult passage. Her master, you must say, is ill; you must let her in, with an assured but rather serious countenance; no smiles, no overacting, and I promise you success! Once the girl within, and the door closed, the same dexterity that has already rid you of the dealer will relieve you of this last danger in your path. Thenceforward you have the whole evening--the whole night, if needful--to ransack the treasures of the house and to make good your safety. This is help that comes to you with the mask of danger. Up!" he cried; "up, friend. Your life hangs trembling in the scales; up, and act!"

Markheim steadily regarded his counsellor. "If I be condemned to evil acts," he said, "there is still one door of freedom open: I can cease from action. If my life be an ill thing, I can lay it down. Though I be, as you say truly, at the beck of every small temptation, I can yet, by one decisive gesture, place myself beyond the reach of all. My love of good is damned to barrenness; it may, and let it be! But I have still my hatred of evil; and from that, to your galling disappointment, you shall see that I can draw both energy and courage."

The features of the visitor began to undergo a wonderful and lovely change: they brightened and softened with a tender triumph, and, even as they brightened, faded and dislimned. But Markheim did not pause to watch or understand the transformation. He opened the door and went downstairs very slowly, thinking to himself. His past went soberly before him; he beheld it as it was, ugly and strenuous like a dream, random as chance medley--a scene of defeat. Life, as he thus reviewed it, tempted him no longer; but on the further side he perceived a quiet haven for his bark. He paused in the passage, and looked into the shop, where the candle still burned by the dead body. It was strangely silent. Thoughts of the dealer swarmed into his mind, as he stood gazing. And then the bell once more broke out into impatient clamour.

He confronted the maid upon the threshold with something like a smile.

"You had better go for the police," said he; "I have killed your master."

146

"MARKHEIM" is justifiably called a precursor to "Jekyll," the crown jewel in Stevenson's speculative canon. But the pedigree alone isn't enough to make the grandsire a royal favorite. Charles Dickens' "The Goblins Who Stole a Sexton" is likewise considered the progenitor of his more-renowned *Christmas Carol*, featuring as it does a covetous miser who is captured by supernatural beings on Christmas Eve, forced to watch visions of the past, the present, and the future, and is released into the natural world a changed man. "Markheim" does not have the same relationship with its inspired descendant. It is quintessentially optimistic, if dark, with a sympathetic albeit confused protagonist who is inadvertently (or is he...?) goaded into taking responsibility for his sins in order to avoid a slippery slope of murder and deceit. Indeed, there is good reason to question the motives of the diabolical stranger. Like *Faust's* Mephistopheles, he vigorously tries to convince his prey to surrender to self-indulgence and self-preservation at the cost of his soul, but unlike Mephistopheles, his rhetoric almost seems like reverse psychology. We might even wonder if this devil is a disguise donned by his conscience. Psychologists refer to this as reaction formation: the idea of surrendering himself to the executioner is hateful and terrifying, but his Super-Ego/conscience may be adopting a seemingly comforting persona as a way of gaining the confidence of his rabbity Ego and subversively introducing the idea of surrender through reverse psychology rather than direct suggestion. In fact, comparisons could be drawn between this story and Poe's "William Wilson," in which an amoral man is haunted by his conscience in the form of a glowering Doppelgänger. While Wilson, when cornered by his conscience at the climax, slaughters his leering Super-Ego, realizing only too late that he has killed himself in the act, Markheim – if we accept the premise that the "Devil" really is a minister of repentance – refuses the chance to flee, accepts the spirit's appeal to do penance, and is released by the specter voluntarily. In any case, the trajectory of Markheim is far more optimistic than that of Jekyll or the characters of "The Body Snatcher." In fact, "Markheim" is most useful as a foil to its more popular cousins, showing us how Jekyll and Fettes could have redeemed themselves.

II.

As I noted in the annotations for each story, the solution to their agony – Jekyll's Self-rending schizophrenia and Fettes' purgatorial misery and presumed haunting – is not an easy step, for it ends on the scaffold of a gallows. Both men would, like Markheim, have to offer their lives as a sacrifice to redeem their souls. We might be able to imagine Hyde crumpling to the floor of his cell, fading into Jekyll who then marches with clear eyes and a high head to the noose, or Fettes feeling the sun on his face and the weight lifted from his shoulders just before the trap door releases him to death. The spirit is willing, the saying goes, but the flesh is weak. For

Fettes and Jekyll, the flesh is simply too strong. They have given it far too much leeway in the past – Fettes as a egomaniacal narcissist and Jekyll as a people-pleasing social climber. But Markheim is different, and his example illuminates some of the unclear pathways in the other two stories: as Satan (or his guilt-producing Super-Ego/conscience) likes to remind him, he is not a perfect person. He has been wicked in the past, and only stands to become wickeder as time marches on. But his crimes are genuinely human – relatable, understandable – and his soul is no blacker than an average man with good intentions. He has not yet given himself over to self-worship unlike the egotistical Fettes or the self-conscious Jekyll. And so, his salvation is a matter of self-denial, a habit which – as a poor man – he is not unfamiliar with. One last time, he denies himself the ability to flee for his life, and though he loses *that* in the end, as his cloven-footed conscience will attest, he gains integrity, and that – so Stevenson would have us belief – is worth the heavy cost.

ONE of Stevenson's most shamefully underrated short stories, "Olalla" (pronounced oh-LAY-*uh*), is a masterpiece of erotic horror, one of the most teasingly ambiguous vampire stories in English, and a prefiguration of Jung's analytical theories of the Self. The novelette also represents one of the most successful pastiches of Edgar Allan Poe's metaphysical fiction. Combining elements of "The Fall of the House of Usher," "Berenice," "Morella," "Ligeia," and the poems "Ulalume," "Annabel Lee," "Lenore," and "The Haunted Palace," Olalla is the only story I've ever read which I would confidently say out-Poes Poe. It broods with rich Gothicism: a crumbling castle, wild wastelands, violent storms, a decadent family thinned out by inbreeding and corruption, an unnamed curse, a haunting portrait which demonstrates the similarity between ancestors and descendants, hints of sexual sadism, a sensitive and spiritually precocious young woman with irresistible beauty and large, luminous eyes, paranoid villagers, the struggle between piety and pleasure, the conflict between death and lust, and strong suggestions of vampirism. It is a rich, succulent feast for the Gothically inclined, and for reasons unknown – possibly its weak ending, probably its lush sexuality including homoeroticism and female androgyny – it has remained unappreciated, taking a back seat to *Dracula*, which it outpaces in literary value, and *Carmilla*, which it admirably matches in violent eroticism. Moreover – like "Jekyll and Hyde" – "Olalla" is a masterwork in psychoanalysis presaging Jung's theories of human identity – specifically the concepts of the Anima and Animus. The story is set either in the Napoleonic Peninsular Wars or in the Carlist Civil Wars of the 1830s and '40s (neither war is especially likelier than the other since arguments could be made to support either) and features an unnamed narrator who – like many of Poe's – becomes enamored with the only daughter of a degenerate family wasted to sedated stupidity by centuries of wickedness, inbreeding, and seclusion (cf. the Ushers). But like so many of Poe's heroines, Olalla is *different*: her eyes shine with spiritual intelligence, her heart and mind are strong with philosophy and religion, and her body – to borrow one of the narrator's many lustful expressions, is "perfect." But her brother is a sadistic savant (who appears to have some form of autism) who tortures squirrels and sings in inhuman tones, and her mother is a creature of uncontrolled pleasures – slumbering gluttonously, undisturbed by human intelligence, and drunk on stupefying satisfaction – and what's more, she and her degenerating offspring may be vampires.

Olalla[1]

---

[1] Pronounced oh-*LAH*-yah – the double "L" making the "Y" sound in Spanish – Olalla is the Iberian form of the Greek name Eulalia (you-LAY-lee-uh) and means "well-spoken" or "the girl with the sweet voice." This is the first stop in the Poe

'NOW,' said the doctor, 'my part is done, and, I may say, with some vanity, well done. It remains only to get you out of this cold and poisonous city[1], and to give you two months of a pure air and an easy conscience. The last is your affair[2]. To the first I think I can help you. It fells indeed rather oddly; it was but the other day the Padre came in from the country; and as he and I are old friends, although of contrary professions[3], he applied to me in a matter of distress among some of his parishioners. This was a family--but you are ignorant of Spain, and even the names of our grandees[4] are hardly known to you; suffice it, then, that they were once great people, and are now fallen to the brink of destitution. Nothing now belongs to them but the residencia[5], and certain leagues of desert mountain, in the greater part of which not even a goat could support life. But the house is a fine old place, and stands at a great height among the hills, and most salubriously; and I

---

express (which is to say, the first obvious indication that the tale is a dutiful homage to the American master of the macabre – which it is). Poe frequently named his tales and poems about strange women and their transformations (which, in our collection of Poe's tales I have termed stories of "gender metaphysics") with the woman's name, and these names universally have a fluid, poetic sound, with French/Spanish/Greek/Italian roots. Some of the most obvious: Berenice (bare-UH-nye-see), Morella (in this case typically pronounced in the English manner), Ligeia (lie-GEE-uh), Lenore, Eleonora, Annabel Lee, Ulalume (oo-LAH-loom), and – *wait for it* – Eulalie (oo-la-LEE – and yes, that is the French version of Olalla)

[1] Advice given to Stevenson about his own fading health during the 1880s. He was constantly on the move, seeking a climate that would help his chronic illnesses. Most likely the city referred to is Toledo. This is for three reasons: 1. It has a "cold semi-arid climate" as it is perched in the Montes de Toledo 2. This was the setting of the Poe story "The Pit and the Pendulum" 3. Toledo was a Spanish stronghold, and while it was never captured the way Poe depicts, but several battles were fought in the area, some – such as the Battle of Talavera – including the British allies

[2] The first of several comments that hint at the atrocities of war. The Peninsular War especially was well known for hideous atrocities (on both sides) which were well documented in Goya's wartime paintings and etchings

[3] Again, a caustic indictment of soldiering. The doctor/priest heals bodies and the soldier mangles them. Another fairly disturbing idea is that the profession in question isn't his medical capacity but his spiritual one: the priest saves souls and the soldier's activities are so atrocious that they destroy others' faith. In a sense, the priest is in the employ of God, and the soldier in the employ of Satan

[4] Noble families

[5] Manor house or mansion

had no sooner heard my friend's tale, than I remembered you. I told him I had a wounded officer[1], wounded in the good cause[2], who was now able to make a change; and I proposed that his friends should take you for a lodger. Instantly the Padre's face grew dark, as I had maliciously foreseen it would. It was out of the question, he said. Then let them starve, said I, for I have no sympathy with tatterdemalion[3] pride. There-upon we separated, not very content with one another; but yesterday, to my wonder, the Padre returned and made a submission: the difficulty, he said, he had found upon enquiry to be less than he had feared; or, in other words, these proud people had put their pride in their pocket. I closed with the offer; and, subject to your approval, I have taken rooms for you in the residencia. The air of these

---

[1] This resembles the plot of Poe's "The Oval Portrait," where a wounded man recuperates in a grand mountain home. In that case it was Italy and the wound was suffered at the hands of bandits

[2] As I have previously suggested, this takes place in the Penninsular War (1807 – 1814) during the broader Napoleonic Wars. *"[It] was a military conflict between Napoleon's empire and the allied powers of Spain, Britain and Portugal for control of the Iberian Peninsula during the Napoleonic Wars. The war started when French and Spanish armies invaded and occupied Portugal in 1807, and escalated in 1808 when France turned on Spain, its ally until then. The war on the peninsula lasted until the Sixth Coalition defeated Napoleon in 1814, and is regarded as one of the first wars of national liberation, significant for the emergence of large-scale guerrilla warfare.*

"The Peninsular War overlaps with what the Spanish-speaking world calls the Guerra de la Independencia Española (Spanish War of Independence), which began with the Dos de Mayo Uprising on 2 May 1808 and ended on 17 April 1814. The French occupation destroyed the Spanish administration, which fragmented into quarrelling provincial juntas. In 1810, a reconstituted national government, the Cádiz Cortes—effectively a government-in-exile—fortified itself in Cádiz but could not raise effective armies because it was besieged by 70,000 French troops. British and Portuguese forces eventually secured Portugal, using it as a safe position from which to launch campaigns against the French army and to provide whatever supplies they could get to the Spanish, while the Spanish armies and guerrillas tied down vast numbers of Napoleon's troops. These combined regular and irregular allied forces prevented Napoleon's marshals from subduing the rebellious Spanish provinces by restricting French control of territory and the war continued through years of stalemate." The narrator, though it may be unnecessary to say, is fighting for the "good cause" of Spanish liberty against Napoleon's Grand Armee

[3] Ragged, in a state of disrepair. The idea here is that the family is poor but in denial about their status: a ragged aristocracy that still demands due diligence

mountains will renew your blood[1]; and the quiet in which you will there live is worth all the medicines in the world.'

'Doctor,' said I, 'you have been throughout my good angel, and your advice is a command. But tell me, if you please, something of the family with which I am to reside.'

'I am coming to that,' replied my friend; 'and, indeed, there is a difficulty in the way. These beggars are, as I have said, of very high descent and swollen with the most baseless vanity; they have lived for some generations in a growing isolation, drawing away, on either hand, from the rich who had now become too high for them, and from the poor, whom they still regarded as too low; and even to-day, when poverty forces them to unfasten their door to a guest, they cannot do so without a most ungracious stipulation. You are to remain, they say, a stranger; they will give you attendance, but they refuse from the first the idea of the smallest intimacy[2].'

I will not deny that I was piqued, and perhaps the feeling strengthened my desire to go, for I was confident that I could break down that barrier if I desired. 'There is nothing offensive in such a stipulation,' said I; 'and I even sympathise with the feeling that inspired it.'

'It is true they have never seen you,' returned the doctor politely; 'and if they knew you were the handsomest and the most pleasant man that ever came from England (where I am told that handsome men are common, but pleasant ones not so much so[3]), they would doubtless make you welcome with a better grace. But since you take the thing so well, it matters not. To me, indeed, it seems discourteous. But you will find yourself the gainer. The family will not much tempt you. A mother, a son, and a daughter; an old woman said to be halfwitted, a country lout, and a country girl, who stands very high with her confessor, and is, therefore,' chuckled the physician, 'most likely plain[4]; there is not much in that to attract the fancy of a dashing officer.'

'And yet you say they are high-born,' I objected.

---

[1] The theme of renewed blood is a crucial one

[2] As a Protestant and (presumably) a commoner, the officer would not be seen as a peer to Catholic nobility, and would be expected to mind his business and not put on airs or presume to familiarize with the grandees

[3] The English were stereotyped (especially in Romance countries like Spain, France, and Italy) as being cynical, closed-minded, humorless, and prone to complaints

[4] The assumption here is that a girl who is in good standing with her priest is probably able to do so because she has not been tempted because she is not tempting – a pretty girl would attract male attention and thus distance herself from the confessor in order to indulge in vanity, gossip, and coquettish behavior

'Well, as to that, I should distinguish,' returned the doctor. 'The mother is; not so the children. The mother was the last representative of a princely stock, degenerate both in parts and fortune. Her father was not only poor, he was mad: and the girl ran wild about the residencia till his death. Then, much of the fortune having died with him, and the family being quite extinct, the girl ran wilder than ever, until at last she married, Heaven knows whom, a muleteer[1] some say, others a smuggler; while there are some who uphold there was no marriage at all, and that Felipe and Olalla are bastards[2]. The union, such as it was, was tragically dissolved some years ago; but they live in such seclusion, and the country at that time was in so much disorder, that the precise manner of the man's end is known only to the priest--if even to him.'

'I begin to think I shall have strange experiences,' said I.

'I would not romance[3], if I were you,' replied the doctor; 'you will find, I fear, a very grovelling and commonplace reality. Felipe, for instance, I have seen. And what am I to say? He is very rustic, very cunning, very loutish, and, I should say, an innocent[4]; the others are probably to match. No, no, senor commandante[5], you must seek congenial society among the great sights of our mountains; and in these at least, if you are at all a lover of the works of nature, I promise you will not be disappointed.'

The next day Felipe came for me in a rough country cart, drawn by a mule; and a little before the stroke of noon, after I had said farewell to the doctor, the innkeeper, and different good souls who had befriended me during my sickness, we set forth out of the city by the Eastern gate, and began to ascend into the Sierra. I had been so long a prisoner, since I was left behind for dying after the loss of the convoy[6], that the mere smell of the

---

[1] A mule teamster

[2] Bastards? Probably, and also potentially born out of incest

[3] That is, build it up in his mind as an adventure

[4] A euphemism for mental retardation – literally meaning that he is not responsible for his actions like a toddler who has no concept of sin

[5] A Spanish generalism for a captain or a field officer (our narrator is probably a major or lieutenant colonel)

[6] The word "prisoner" almost certainly refers to his bedridden state rather than an actual prisoner of war situation (since he is celebrated for having supported the "good cause"). We have here also an idea of the situation of his wounding: it sounds as though he was escorting a convoy, possibly bringing food and materials to the garrison at Toledo, when his convoy was attacked and overwhelmed by the French. Managing to escape he was taken to the Padre for medical attention and is only just now overcoming what was almost certainly an infection that led to fever (hence the need to stabilize his entire system, not just a wounded limb)

earth[1] set me smiling. The country through which we went was wild and rocky, partially covered with rough woods, now of the cork-tree, and now of the great Spanish chestnut, and frequently intersected by the beds of mountain torrents. The sun shone, the wind rustled joyously; and we had advanced some miles, and the city had already shrunk into an inconsiderable knoll upon the plain behind us, before my attention began to be diverted to the companion of my drive. To the eye, he seemed but a diminutive, loutish, well-made country lad, such as the doctor had described, mighty quick and active, but devoid of any culture; and this first impression was with most observers final. What began to strike me was his familiar, chattering talk; so strangely inconsistent with the terms on which I was to be received; and partly from his imperfect enunciation, partly from the sprightly incoherence of the matter, so very difficult to follow clearly without an effort of the mind. It is true I had before talked with persons of a similar mental constitution; persons who seemed to live (as he did) by the senses, taken and possessed by the visual object of the moment and unable to discharge their minds of that impression. His seemed to me (as I sat, distantly giving ear) a kind of conversation proper to drivers, who pass much of their time in a great vacancy of the intellect and threading the sights of a familiar country. But this was not the case of Felipe; by his own account, he was a home- keeper; 'I wish I was there now,' he said; and then, spying a tree by the wayside, he broke off to tell me that he had once seen a crow among its branches.

'A crow?' I repeated, struck by the ineptitude of the remark, and thinking I had heard imperfectly.

But by this time he was already filled with a new idea; hearkening with a rapt intentness, his head on one side, his face puckered; and he struck me rudely, to make me hold my peace. Then he smiled and shook his head.

'What did you hear?' I asked.

'O, it is all right,' he said; and began encouraging his mule with cries that echoed unhumanly[2] up the mountain walls.

I looked at him more closely. He was superlatively well-built, light, and lithe and strong; he was well-featured; his yellow eyes[3] were very large, though, perhaps, not very expressive; take him altogether, he was a pleasant-looking lad, and I had no fault to find with him, beyond that he

---

[1] He has been cooped up in a hospital in a city, far from the scent of the outdoors
[2] Whether this is a tale of vampire or of inbreeding or of both, Felipe is certainly cast as an Other – someone on the outskirts of human reasoning and morality. While this may be an unfair portrait of a person with a severe learning disability, it is nonetheless necessary to Stevenson's overall theme of degeneration: how civilization is created through growth, openness, and edification, not through complacency and inertia
[3] Suggestive of wolves and dogs

was of a dusky hue, and inclined to hairyness[1]; two characteristics that I disliked. It was his mind that puzzled, and yet attracted me. The doctor's phrase--an innocent--came back to me; and I was wondering if that were, after all, the true description, when the road began to go down into the narrow and naked chasm of a torrent. The waters thundered tumultuously in the bottom; and the ravine was filled full of the sound, the thin spray, and the claps of wind, that accompanied their descent. The scene was certainly impressive; but the road was in that part very securely walled in; the mule went steadily forward; and I was astonished to perceive the paleness of terror in the face of my companion. The voice of that wild river was inconstant, now sinking lower as if in weariness, now doubling its hoarse tones; momentary freshets seemed to swell its volume, sweeping down the gorge, raving and booming against the barrier walls[2]; and I observed it was at each of these accessions to the clamour, that my driver more particularly winced and blanched. Some thoughts of Scottish superstition and the river Kelpie[3], passed across my mind; I wondered if perchance the like were prevalent in that part of Spain; and turning to Felipe, sought to draw him out.

'What is the matter?' I asked.

'O, I am afraid,' he replied.

'Of what are you afraid?' I returned. 'This seems one of the safest places on this very dangerous road.'

'It makes a noise[4],' he said, with a simplicity of awe that set my doubts at rest.

The lad was but a child in intellect; his mind was like his body, active and swift, but stunted in development; and I began from that time forth to regard him with a measure of pity, and to listen at first with indulgence, and at last even with pleasure, to his disjointed babble.

By about four in the afternoon we had crossed the summit of the mountain line, said farewell to the western sunshine, and began to go down

---

[1] Ditto. The dusky hue comment may be less a racist prejudice against coloring and more an aversion to skin which is made bluish and leaden by poor health and circulation, or poor quality blood (or, say vampirism)

[2] An obvious relationship to "The Merry Men," where the pounding of the surf had a connection to the wrath of God and the presence of corruption

[3] Another link to "Merry Men," where this superstition is mentioned: an insidious mermaid that haunts a lake or river or inlet, who is prone to luring men and women to a drowning death by seducing them in the form of a beautiful youth

[4] "The Fall of the House of Usher" is the chief influence on this story, and Felipe shares many traits with the hypochondriac, self-professying Usher. In this instance, both share the trait of hypersensitivity to sound, a condition that symbolizes a connection to the deep currents of spirituality which most people are numb to

upon the other side, skirting the edge of many ravines and moving through the shadow of dusky woods. There rose upon all sides the voice of falling water, not condensed and formidable as in the gorge of the river, but scattered and sounding gaily and musically from glen to glen. Here, too, the spirits of my driver mended, and he began to sing aloud in a falsetto voice, and with a singular bluntness of musical perception, never true either to melody or key, but wandering at will, and yet somehow with an effect that was natural and pleasing, like that of the of birds[1]. As the dusk increased, I fell more and more under the spell of this artless warbling, listening and waiting for some articulate air[2], and still disappointed; and when at last I asked him what it was he sang--'O,' cried he, 'I am just singing!' Above all, I was taken with a trick he had of unweariedly repeating the same note at little intervals; it was not so monotonous as you would think, or, at least, not disagreeable; and it seemed to breathe a wonderful contentment with what is, such as we love to fancy in the attitude of trees, or the quiescence of a pool[3].

Night had fallen dark before we came out upon a plateau, and drew up a little after, before a certain lump of superior blackness which I could only conjecture to be the residencia. Here, my guide, getting down from the cart, hooted and whistled for a long time in vain; until at last an old peasant man came towards us from somewhere in the surrounding dark, carrying a candle in his hand. By the light of this I was able to perceive a great arched doorway of a Moorish[4] character: it was closed by iron-studded gates, in one of the leaves of which Felipe opened a wicket. The peasant carried off the cart to some out-building; but my guide and I passed through the wicket, which was closed again behind us; and by the glimmer of the candle, passed through a court, up a stone stair, along a section of an open gallery, and up more stairs again, until we came at last to the door of a great and somewhat

---

[1] Like Usher, he too has a gift for making strange but lovely music that extends beyond conventions and is more in line with nature than culture (to borrow Stevenson's simile, he is more like a bird warbling than a tenor singing). Generations of inbreeding and isolation have caused the family to drift further away from the expressions of civilization, and nearer to the instincts of nature

[2] Lacking art or articulation, his singing is the echo of his "innocent" soul rather than a response to or interpretation of cultural ideals

[3] Like nature (trees and pools specifically), Felipe is utterly content: he has no reason to challenge his thinking, stretch himself, or seek out new ideas. Instead, he is utterly content and very happy to remain the way he is. While this might sound romantic in our current culture of "you just gotta be you" mentalities, the narrator is correct in being both enamored and alarmed by the idea of a man who is thoroughly content with resisting any change

[4] The Moors – North African Muslims – occupied parts of Spain until the Reconquista in 1492

bare apartment. This room, which I understood was to be mine, was pierced by three windows, lined with some lustrous wood disposed in panels, and carpeted with the skins of many savage animals. A bright fire burned in the chimney, and shed abroad a changeful flicker; close up to the blaze there was drawn a table, laid for supper; and in the far end a bed stood ready. I was pleased by these preparations, and said so to Felipe; and he, with the same simplicity of disposition that I held already remarked in him, warmly re-echoed my praises. 'A fine room,' he said; 'a very fine room. And fire, too; fire is good; it melts out the pleasure in your bones. And the bed,' he continued, carrying over the candle in that direction--'see what fine sheets-- how soft, how smooth, smooth;' and he passed his hand again and again over their texture, and then laid down his head and rubbed his cheeks among them with a grossness of content that somehow offended me[1]. I took the candle from his hand (for I feared he would set the bed on fire) and walked back to the supper-table, where, perceiving a measure of wine, I poured out a cup and called to him to come and drink of it. He started to his feet at once and ran to me with a strong expression of hope; but when he saw the wine, he visibly shuddered.

'Oh, no,' he said, 'not that; that is for you. I hate it[2].'

'Very well, Senor,' said I; 'then I will drink to your good health, and to the prosperity of your house and family. Speaking of which,' I added, after I had drunk, 'shall I not have the pleasure of laying my salutations in person at the feet of the Senora, your mother?'

But at these words all the childishness passed out of his face, and was succeeded by a look of indescribable cunning and secrecy. He backed away from me at the same time, as though I were an animal about to leap or some dangerous fellow with a weapon, and when he had got near the door, glowered at me sullenly with contracted pupils[3]. 'No,' he said at last, and the next moment was gone noiselessly out of the room; and I heard his footing die away downstairs as light as rainfall, and silence closed over the house.

---

[1] Felipe is utterly invested in contentment – in personal pleasure like a man who eagerly lives in his boyhood room with his parents for as long as he possibly can. The narrator is disturbed by Felipe's catlike rubbing against the sheets and his rhapsody over the fire and food. So fixated is he on material comfort that he is almost wholly material with very little spirit to speak of (that is, morality or curiosity)

[2] Presaging beautifully Dracula's famous refusal to drink the fruit of the grape: "I never drink... wine." Likewise, Felipe's disgust at wine certainly suggests that he prefers a different sort of libation: blood, namely his family's blood, on which the whole clan has glutted itself into a stupor of satisfaction

[3] This protectiveness over his mother is certainly very Norman-Bates-esque, but it also might be a protective impulse towards the handsome young officer, whose blood would be quite a treat to Felipe's mother

After I had supped I drew up the table nearer to the bed and began to prepare for rest; but in the new position of the light, I was struck by a picture on the wall[1]. It represented a woman, still young. To judge by her costume and the mellow unity which reigned over the canvas[2], she had long been dead; to judge by the vivacity of the attitude, the eyes and the features, I might have been beholding in a mirror the image of life. Her figure was very slim and strong, and of a just proportion; red tresses lay like a crown over her brow[3]; her eyes, of a very golden brown, held mine with a look; and her face, which was perfectly shaped, was yet marred by a cruel, sullen, and sensual expression[4]. Something in both face and figure, something exquisitely intangible, like the echo of an echo, suggested the features and bearing of my guide; and I stood awhile, unpleasantly attracted and wondering at the oddity of the resemblance. The common, carnal stock of that race, which had been originally designed for such high dames as the one now looking on me from the canvas, had fallen to baser uses, wearing country clothes, sitting on the shaft and holding the reins of a mule cart, to bring home a lodger. Perhaps an actual link subsisted; perhaps some scruple of the delicate flesh that was once clothed upon with the satin and brocade[5] of the dead lady, now winced at the rude contact of Felipe's frieze.

The first light of the morning shone full upon the portrait, and, as I lay awake, my eyes continued to dwell upon it with growing complacency[6]; its beauty crept about my heart insidiously, silencing my scruples one after another; and while I knew that to love such a woman were to sign and seal

---

[1] The theme of a painting of a long-dead ancestor which reveals either a reincarnation, immortality, or persistence of character in the current generation is a frequent theme in Gothic tales. *Carmilla*, the ultimate female vampire story, by J. S. Le Fanu, was likely the source that Stevenson is borrowing from, wherein an immortal vampire is recognized by her portrait

[2] That is, it has been yellowed uniformly by age

[3] Vampires were historically thought to have red hair (that is, before *Dracula* broke the trend). The same has been thought of Judas and the harlot Mary Magdalene

[4] She appears to be a person of physical indulgence, preferring excesses of feeling and gluttony to moral self-control and self-regulation

[5] Embroidered silk — a popular dress material during the 17th and early 18th centuries

[6] The spell of complacency is apparently contagious, since this brief contact with it is already quenching the narrator's moral courage. And here, too, we see that he is not a mere prude projecting his British shame onto a band of proto-hippies: they are not simply a family of Spanish Thoreaus, living off the land and being content with the rugged life God gave them — they have had their souls withered away until the warmth of human generosity and curiosity have decayed and been blown away

one's own sentence of degeneration, I still knew that, if she were alive, I should love her. Day after day the double knowledge of her wickedness and of my weakness grew clearer. She came to be the heroine of many day-dreams, in which her eyes led on to, and sufficiently rewarded, crimes. She cast a dark shadow on my fancy; and when I was out in the free air of heaven, taking vigorous exercise and healthily renewing the current of my blood, it was often a glad thought to me that my enchantress was safe in the grave, her wand of beauty broken, her lips closed in silence, her philtre[1] spilt. And yet I had a half-lingering terror that she might not be dead after all, but re-arisen in the body of some descendant[2].

Felipe served my meals in my own apartment; and his resemblance to the portrait haunted me[3]. At times it was not; at times, upon some change of attitude or flash of expression, it would leap out upon me like a ghost. It was above all in his ill tempers that the likeness triumphed. He certainly liked me; he was proud of my notice, which he sought to engage by many simple and childlike devices; he loved to sit close before my fire, talking his broken talk or singing his odd, endless, wordless songs[4], and sometimes drawing his hand over my clothes with an affectionate manner of caressing that never failed to cause in me an embarrassment of which I was ashamed[5]. But for all that, he was capable of flashes of causeless anger and fits of sturdy sullenness. At a word of reproof, I have seen him upset the dish of which I was about to eat, and this not surreptitiously, but with defiance; and similarly at a hint of inquisition. I was not unnaturally curious, being in a

---

[1] A love potion

[2] Such is the case in Poe's "Morella," and in a more insidious way in "Ligeia"

[3] Felipe may be easily read as a bisexual or even transsexual man, whose femininity – though not beauty – presents a strange temptation to the narrator

[4] Usher's songs had lyrics ("The Haunted Palace" is the title of the one we are given), but they also had a weird, unnatural quality that exceeded the standards and practices of contemporary musicianship

[5] This is unquestionably a Victorian euphemism for a homosexual feeling – "the love that dare not speak its name." Felipe is both effeminate, and thus an object of sexuality, and doting towards the narrator, and this a subject of sexuality. His doglike devotion bespeaks a sexual submission, but his brazen petting bespeaks an ability to cow the narrator by sexually objectifying him. At any rate, no Victorian reader would look at that and say "ah, he doesn't like being touched; me either" – this is perhaps one of the most obvious ways that a writer in this era could suggest the homoerotic without fear of censorship, and Stevenson flies the flag as high as he can: this moment is riddled with homoerotic tension between the impulsive, unrestrained "innocent" and the beautiful officer. *Carmilla* is also redolent with homoeroticism in the form of the obvious lesbianism (petting, kissing, possessiveness) between the naïve, submissive narrator and the sexually gluttonous, dominating Carmilla

strange place and surrounded by strange people; but at the shadow of a question, he shrank back, lowering and dangerous[1]. Then it was that, for a fraction of a second, this rough lad might have been the brother of the lady in the frame. But these humours were swift to pass; and the resemblance died along with them.

In these first days I saw nothing of any one but Felipe, unless the portrait is to be counted[2]; and since the lad was plainly of weak mind, and had moments of passion, it may be wondered that I bore his dangerous neighbourhood with equanimity. As a matter of fact, it was for some time irksome; but it happened before long that I obtained over him so complete a mastery as set my disquietude at rest[3].

It fell in this way. He was by nature slothful, and much of a vagabond, and yet he kept by the house, and not only waited upon my wants, but laboured every day in the garden or small farm to the south of the residencia. Here he would be joined by the peasant whom I had seen on the night of my arrival, and who dwelt at the far end of the enclosure, about half a mile away, in a rude out-house; but it was plain to me that, of these two, it was Felipe who did most; and though I would sometimes see him throw down his spade and go to sleep among the very plants he had been digging, his constancy and energy were admirable in themselves, and still more so since I was well assured they were foreign to his disposition and the fruit of an ungrateful effort. But while I admired, I wondered what had called forth in a lad so shuttle-witted this enduring sense of duty. How was it sustained? I asked myself, and to what length did it prevail over his instincts? The priest was possibly his inspirer; but the priest came one day to the residencia. I saw him both come and go after an interval of close upon an hour, from a knoll where I was sketching, and all that time Felipe continued to labour undisturbed in the garden.

At last, in a very unworthy spirit, I determined to debauch the lad from his good resolutions, and, way-laying him at the gate, easily pursuaded him to join me in a ramble[4]. It was a fine day, and the woods to which I led him

---

[1] Wolflike and predatory

[2] Indeed, like that personality that it projects through space and time, the portrait seems to have a life of its own

[3] Nervous about his sense of sexual objectification (and the possible threat of outright victimization at Felipe's caressing hands), the narrator remains unsettled until he dominates Felipe, thus removing the threat of sexual subjection. This, however, only helps to encourage a reading of the narrator as being himself bisexual, since he takes a keen delight in physically dominating his male oggler

[4] The narrator takes the role of tempter, luring Felipe from his good intentions and symbolically seducing him (every Victorian knew what it meant when a man convinced a woman to follow him into the woods, especially under false pretenses)

were green and pleasant and sweet-smelling and alive with the hum of insects. Here he discovered himself in a fresh character, mounting up to heights of gaiety that abashed me, and displaying an energy and grace of movement that delighted the eye[1]. He leaped, he ran round me in mere glee; he would stop, and look and listen, and seem to drink in the world like a cordial; and then he would suddenly spring into a tree with one bound, and hang and gambol there like one at home[2]. Little as he said to me, and that of not much import, I have rarely enjoyed more stirring company; the sight of his delight was a continual feast; the speed and accuracy of his movements pleased me to the heart[3]; and I might have been so thoughtlessly unkind as to make a habit of these wants, had not chance prepared a very rude conclusion to my pleasure. By some swiftness or dexterity the lad captured a squirrel in a tree top. He was then some way ahead of me, but I saw him drop to the ground and crouch there, crying aloud for pleasure like a child. The sound stirred my sympathies, it was so fresh and innocent; but as I bettered my pace to draw near, the cry of the squirrel knocked upon my heart. I have heard and seen much of the cruelty of lads, and above all of peasants; but what I now beheld struck me into a passion of anger[4]. I thrust the fellow aside, plucked the poor brute out of his hands, and with swift mercy killed it. Then I turned upon the torturer, spoke to him long out of the heat of my indignation, calling him names at which he seemed to wither[5]; and at length, pointing toward the residencia, bade him begone and

---

[1] Simultaneously abashed and delighted? This combination of shame and pleasure echoes the feelings that the narrator harbored towards the painting (which both chilled and thrilled him) and Felipe's earlier soft petting (which he claims to have disturbed him, but failed to interrupt). The officer seems to be both disgusted by Felipe's lack of restraint, but allured by his sensuality (equally in the antiquated sense – being deeply tied to the senses – and the modern sense – being alluring in a sexual manner)

[2] Felipe is at home in nature for obvious reasons

[3] Watching Felipe play both provides a feast to his eyes and pleasure to his heart. This may be harmless fun, but it sounds like a more sensuous pastime

[4] A truly disturbing scene that Stevenson wisely leaves to the imagination. What on earth did Felipe do with that squirrel? Clearly he maimed it beyond survival and then proceeded to torture it. Cruelty to animals is commonly associated with psychopathy, chiefly in the Macdonald Triad, or homicidal triad, which has identified three traits in children which might forecast a murderous future: bedwetting, fire setting, and animal torture (the triad has, however, been largely debated and is considered debunked by some in the field)

[5] The behavior of a dom putting a submissive in his place: this is not mere anger, this is expressive verbal abuse meant to shame and belittle. The narrator may genuinely be jealous of Felipe's lack of shame or self-awareness, for he certainly delights in instilling those emotions into his amoral friend

leave me, for I chose to walk with men, not with vermin. He fell upon his knees, and, the words coming to him with more cleanness than usual, poured out a stream of the most touching supplications, begging me in mercy to forgive him, to forget what he had done, to look to the future. 'O, I try so hard,' he said. 'O, commandante, bear with Felipe this once; he will never be a brute again!' Thereupon, much more affected than I cared to show, I suffered myself to be persuaded, and at last shook hands with him and made it up. But the squirrel, by way of penance, I made him bury; speaking of the poor thing's beauty, telling him what pains it had suffered, and how base a thing was the abuse of strength[1]. 'See, Felipe,' said I, 'you are strong indeed; but in my hands you are as helpless as that poor thing of the trees. Give me your hand in mine. You cannot remove it[2]. Now suppose that I were cruel like you, and took a pleasure in pain. I only tighten my hold, and see how you suffer.' He screamed aloud, his face stricken ashy and dotted with needle points of sweat; and when I set him free, he fell to the earth and nursed his hand and moaned over it like a baby. But he took the lesson in good part; and whether from that, or from what I had said to him, or the higher notion he now had of my bodily strength[3], his original affection was changed into a dog- like, adoring fidelity[4].

Meanwhile I gained rapidly in health. The residencia stood on the crown of a stony plateau; on every side the mountains hemmed it about; only from the roof, where was a bartizan[5], there might be seen between two peaks, a small segment of plain, blue with extreme distance. The air in these altitudes moved freely and largely; great clouds congregated there, and were broken up by the wind and left in tatters on the hilltops; a hoarse, and yet faint rumbling of torrents rose from all round; and one could there study all the ruder and more ancient characters of nature in something of their

---

[1] This seems to be generated from a class angle: Felipe, as a noble, has never learned the word "no," and has a feeling of superiority over others than has gone unchallenged for generations. The officer is keen to teach him humility in hopes that it might trump his class-based entitlement and arrogance

[2] This is now tremendously suggestive of a BDSM situation ("submit to my will, allow yourself to suffer under my hand")

[3] The commandante certainly relishes his chance to demonstrate his physical superiority. It may be a matter of class consciousness (bitterness towards the superiority that the nobles feel towards him), or it may have a psychosexual motivation complete with an implied rapacious threat ("you thought you could feel me up and get away with it, but see now how if I wanted to, it would be easy for me to totally dominate you")

[4] Once the subject of affection – like a leering, lustful suitor – Felipe is now content to be the submissive to the former object of his awkward affections

[5] A section of turret that extends from the corner of a building, overhanging like a balcony

pristine force. I delighted from the first in the vigorous scenery and changeful weather; nor less in the antique and dilapidated mansion where I dwelt. This was a large oblong, flanked at two opposite corners by bastion-like projections, one of which commanded the door, while both were loopholed[1] for musketry. The lower storey was, besides, naked of windows, so that the building, if garrisoned, could not be carried without artillery[2]. It enclosed an open court planted with pomegranate trees[3]. From this a broad flight of marble stairs ascended to an open gallery, running all round and resting, towards the court, on slender pillars. Thence again, several enclosed stairs led to the upper storeys of the house, which were thus broken up into distinct divisions. The windows, both within and without, were closely shuttered; some of the stone-work in the upper parts had fallen; the roof, in one place, had been wrecked in one of the flurries of wind which were common in these mountains; and the whole house, in the strong, beating sunlight, and standing out above a grove of stunted cork-trees, thickly laden and discoloured with dust, looked like the sleeping palace of the legend. The court, in particular, seemed the very home of slumber. A hoarse cooing of doves haunted about the eaves; the winds were excluded, but when they blew outside, the mountain dust fell here as thick as rain, and veiled the red bloom of the pomegranates[4]; shuttered windows and the closed doors of numerous cellars, and the vacant, arches of the gallery, enclosed it; and all day long the sun made broken profiles on the four sides, and paraded the shadow of the pillars on the gallery floor. At the ground level there was, however, a certain pillared recess, which bore the marks of human habitation. Though it was open in front upon the court, it was yet provided with a chimney, where a wood fire would be always prettily blazing; and the tile floor was littered with the skins of animals.

It was in this place that I first saw my hostess. She had drawn one of the skins forward and sat in the sun, leaning against a pillar. It was her dress that struck me first of all, for it was rich and brightly coloured, and shone out in that dusty courtyard with something of the same relief as the flowers of the pomegranates[5]. At a second look it was her beauty of person that took

---

[1] Having narrow openings or slits that would allow a musket or arrow to leave the castle, while providing very little space for return fire to enter
[2] The walls, therefore, are so strong and impenetrable, that if they were defended by a garrison of soldiers, only stone-crushing cannonfire could defeat them
[3] Ancient symbols of human sexuality and fecundity
[4] This symbolizes the fact that although the castle is the home of lust and unfettered desire, the long years of stasis, inbreeding, and complacency (symbolized by the dull dust) have diluted the power of their particularly sensual lifestyle
[5] She, like a pomegranate, is a symbol of lust and desire incarnated

hold of me. As she sat back--watching me, I thought, though with invisible eyes--and wearing at the same time an expression of almost imbecile good-humour and contentment[1], she showed a perfectness of feature and a quiet nobility of attitude that were beyond a statue's. I took off my hat to her in passing, and her face puckered with suspicion as swiftly and lightly as a pool ruffles in the breeze; but she paid no heed to my courtesy. I went forth on my customary walk a trifle daunted, her idol-like impassivity haunting me; and when I returned, although she was still in much the same posture, I was half surprised to see that she had moved as far as the next pillar, following the sunshine. This time, however, she addressed me with some trivial salutation, civilly enough conceived, and uttered in the same deep-chested, and yet indistinct and lisping tones, that had already baffled the utmost niceness of my hearing from her son. I answered rather at a venture; for not only did I fail to take her meaning with precision, but the sudden disclosure of her eyes disturbed me[2]. They were unusually large, the iris golden like Felipe's, but the pupil at that moment so distended that they seemed almost black[3]; and what affected me was not so much their size as (what was perhaps its consequence) the singular insignificance of their regard. A look more blankly stupid I have never met[4]. My eyes dropped before it even as I spoke, and I went on my way upstairs to my own room, at once baffled and embarrassed. Yet, when I came there and saw the face of the portrait, I was again reminded of the miracle of family descent. My hostess was, indeed, both older and fuller in person; her eyes were of a different colour; her face, besides, was not only free from the ill-significance that offended and attracted me in the painting; it was devoid of either good or bad--a moral blank expressing literally naught. And yet there was a likeness, not so much speaking as immanent, not so much in any particular feature as upon the whole. It should seem, I thought, as if when the master set his signature to

---

[1] Again, the family is stricken with a dull contentment so thorough that they are virtually stupefied by their own brainless passivity

[2] Poe habitually used the eye to symbolize sensitivity and strength of spirit. As a result, his heroines (and Usher) are often usettling because their eyes are large, watery, and unblinking, as if they are pools which allow a glimpse at some unspeakable spiritual depths. This is the case with Ligeia, Morella, and Usher in particular, whose large, luminous orbs hint at a connection to some unconscious power of will or spirit or vision

[3] A common feature in horror movies today, where a supernatural villain's pupils are so dilated that the eyes seem black. This suggests a high state of arousal

[4] They take in everything they see – and this is important – without any discretion or discrimination: everything is the same to them, and nothing piques either interest or alarm. Life is one smooth, unrippled pond of deep contentment, and the affect on others is unsettling in the extreme

that grave canvas, he had not only caught the image of one smiling and false-eyed woman, but stamped the essential quality of a race.

From that day forth, whether I came or went, I was sure to find the Senora seated in the sun against a pillar, or stretched on a rug before the fire[1]; only at times she would shift her station to the top round of the stone staircase, where she lay with the same nonchalance right across my path. In all these days, I never knew her to display the least spark of energy beyond what she expended in brushing and re-brushing her copious copper-coloured hair[2], or in lisping out, in the rich and broken hoarseness of her voice, her customary idle salutations to myself. These, I think, were her two chief pleasures, beyond that of mere quiescence[3]. She seemed always proud of her remarks, as though they had been witticisms: and, indeed, though they were empty enough, like the conversation of many respectable persons, and turned on a very narrow range of subjects, they were never meaningless or incoherent; nay, they had a certain beauty of their own, breathing, as they did, of her entire contentment. Now she would speak of the warmth, in which (like her son) she greatly delighted; now of the flowers of the pomegranate trees[4], and now of the white doves and long-winged swallows that fanned the air of the court. The birds excited her. As they raked the eaves in their swift flight, or skimmed sidelong past her with a rush of wind, she would sometimes stir, and sit a little up, and seem to awaken from her doze of satisfaction. But for the rest of her days she lay luxuriously folded on herself and sunk in sloth and pleasure. Her invincible content at first annoyed me, but I came gradually to find repose in the spectacle, until at last it grew to be my habit to sit down beside her four times in the day, both coming and going, and to talk with her sleepily, I scarce knew of what. I had come to like her dull, almost animal neighbourhood; her beauty and her stupidity soothed and amused me[5]. I began to find a kind of transcendental good sense in her remarks, and her unfathomable good nature moved me to admiration and envy. The liking was returned; she enjoyed my presence half-unconsciously, as a man in deep meditation may enjoy the babbling of a brook[6]. I can scarce say she brightened when I came, for satisfaction was

---

[1] She basks in heat like a lizard or an old dog – both creatures who drink up comfort with a passion for idleness and complacency

[2] Her hair – like the sitter of the haunting portrait – is red, the traditional color of vampires' hair

[3] Latency, dormancy, idleness

[4] More sexual imagery

[5] Just as he was almost immediately lured into content repose by the sight of the ancestral painting, the living descendent of the sitter causes the narrator to feel at peace purely by virtue of her sluggish complacency and mental vacancy

[6] Society is nothing more to her than the prattle of nature. In the same manner that Felipe sings like a bird, she hears little more than the babble of water when

written on her face eternally, as on some foolish statue's; but I was made conscious of her pleasure by some more intimate communication than the sight. And one day, as I set within reach of her on the marble step, she suddenly shot forth one of her hands and patted mine. The thing was done, and she was back in her accustomed attitude, before my mind had received intelligence of the caress; and when I turned to look her in the face I could perceive no answerable sentiment. It was plain she attached no moment to the act, and I blamed myself for my own more uneasy consciousness[1].

The sight and (if I may so call it) the acquaintance of the mother confirmed the view I had already taken of the son. The family blood had been impoverished[2], perhaps by long inbreeding, which I knew to be a common error among the proud and the exclusive[3]. No decline, indeed, was to be traced in the body, which had been handed down unimpaired in shapeliness and strength; and the faces of to-day were struck as sharply from the mint, as the face of two centuries ago that smiled upon me from the portrait. But the intelligence (that more precious heirloom) was degenerate; the treasure of ancestral memory ran low; and it had required the potent, plebeian[4] crossing of a muleteer or mountain contrabandista[5] to raise, what approached hebetude[6] in the mother, into the active oddity of the son. Yet of the two, it was the mother I preferred. Of Felipe, vengeful and placable, full of starts and shyings, inconstant as a hare, I could even conceive as a creature possibly noxious[7]. Of the mother I had no thoughts but those of kindness. And indeed, as spectators are apt ignorantly to take sides, I grew something of a partisan in the enmity which I perceived to

---

the narrator converses with her. This demonstrates that both the family's outputting and intaking sensations are closely linked to nature and far removed from humanity

[1] Especially for a noble, this act would be wrought with suggestive impropriety, but to the donna it is stripped of meaning, like most things. The result is a life secured in unshakable pleasure, but devoid of any genuine sentiments

[2] This is the situation in "The House of Usher" as well: the family has maintained an enclosed, incestuous line of descent that has been starved of genetic variation, resulting in their current self-satisfaction and complete lack of curiosity or aspirations

[3] The royal families of Europe – though now prone to marry non-royals and thus reinvigorate their genetic material – became infamous during the late 19th century for the potency of their inherited ailments (hemophilia being the most famous) as a result of generations of cousins marrying one another

[4] Someone of lower class

[5] Smuggler

[6] The state of being dull and lethargic

[7] Felipe, he fears, might actually pose a danger to others, whereas the donna is relatively harmless (so he thinks)

smoulder between them. True, it seemed mostly on the mother's part. She would sometimes draw in her breath as he came near, and the pupils of her vacant eyes would contract as if with horror or fear. Her emotions, such as they were, were much upon the surface and readily shared; and this latent repulsion occupied my mind, and kept me wondering on what grounds it rested, and whether the son was certainly in fault.

I had been about ten days in the residencia, when there sprang up a high and harsh wind, carrying clouds of dust[1]. It came out of malarious lowlands, and over several snowy sierras. The nerves of those on whom it blew were strung and jangled; their eyes smarted with the dust; their legs ached under the burthen of their body; and the touch of one hand upon another grew to be odious. The wind, besides, came down the gullies of the hills and stormed about the house with a great, hollow buzzing and whistling that was wearisome to the ear and dismally depressing to the mind[2]. It did not so much blow in gusts as with the steady sweep of a waterfall, so that there was no remission of discomfort while it blew. But higher upon the mountain, it was probably of a more variable strength, with accesses of fury; for there came down at times a far-off wailing, infinitely grievous to hear; and at times, on one of the high shelves or terraces, there would start up, and then disperse, a tower of dust, like the smoke of in explosion[3].

I no sooner awoke in bed than I was conscious of the nervous tension and depression of the weather, and the effect grew stronger as the day proceeded. It was in vain that I resisted; in vain that I set forth upon my customary morning's walk; the irrational, unchanging fury of the storm had soon beat down my strength and wrecked my temper; and I returned to the residencia, glowing with dry heat, and foul and gritty with dust. The court had a forlorn appearance; now and then a glimmer of sun fled over it; now and then the wind swooped down upon the pomegranates, and scattered the blossoms[4], and set the window shutters clapping on the wall. In the recess the Senora was pacing to and fro with a flushed countenance and

---

[1] This is called a sirocco – a Mediterranean dust storm of tremendous magnitude that often begins in the Sahara and gusts its way into southern Europe

[2] This calls to mind the fatal storm that terrified Roderick Usher and kept Poe's narrator awake with its preternatural bangings and moanings: a symbolic raging of nature against unnatural behavior (viz. incest)

[3] This is hardly accidental imagery considering Stevenson's religious upbringing. In Exodus, God leads the Israelites out of Egypt in the guise of a pillar of cloud by day and a pillar of fire by night. Stevenson suggests that the raging forces of nature are attempting to lead the family out of their self-enforced exile and into the wider world. They are of course insensitive to its calling

[4] The warnings of nature symbolically take the attraction out of the sexual playland that is the residencia: alluring and tempting, its attractions are nonetheless frail, easily shattered, and quickly lost to time

bright eyes; I thought, too, she was speaking to herself, like one in anger. But when I addressed her with my customary salutation, she only replied by a sharp gesture and continued her walk. The weather had distempered even this impassive creature; and as I went on upstairs I was the less ashamed of my own discomposure.

All day the wind continued; and I sat in my room and made a feint of reading, or walked up and down, and listened to the riot overhead. Night fell, and I had not so much as a candle. I began to long for some society, and stole down to the court. It was now plunged in the blue of the first darkness; but the recess was redly lighted by the fire. The wood had been piled high, and was crowned by a shock of flames, which the draught of the chimney brandished to and fro. In this strong and shaken brightness the Senora continued pacing from wall to wall with disconnected gestures, clasping her hands, stretching forth her arms, throwing back her head as in appeal to heaven[1]. In these disordered movements the beauty and grace of the woman showed more clearly; but there was a light in her eye that struck on me unpleasantly; and when I had looked on awhile in silence, and seemingly unobserved, I turned tail as I had come, and groped my way back again to my own chamber.

By the time Felipe brought my supper and lights, my nerve was utterly gone; and, had the lad been such as I was used to seeing him, I should have kept him (even by force had that been necessary[2]) to take off the edge from my distasteful solitude. But on Felipe, also, the wind had exercised its influence. He had been feverish all day; now that the night had come he was fallen into a low and tremulous humour that reacted on my own. The sight of his scared face, his starts and pallors and sudden harkenings, unstrung me; and when he dropped and broke a dish, I fairly leaped out of my seat.

'I think we are all mad to-day,' said I, affecting to laugh.

'It is the black wind,' he replied dolefully. 'You feel as if you must do something, and you don't know what it is[3].'

I noted the aptness of the description; but, indeed, Felipe had sometimes a strange felicity in rendering into words the sensations of the body. 'And your mother, too,' said I; 'she seems to feel this weather much. Do you not fear she may be unwell?'

He stared at me a little, and then said, 'No,' almost defiantly; and the next moment, carrying his hand to his brow, cried out lamentably on the wind and the noise that made his head go round like a millwheel. 'Who can

---

[1] One might imagine that she is asking for leniency, forgiveness, or peace

[2] The rapacious tone of this muffled threat is truly disturbing since it shows that the narrator – who scolded Felipe on the abuses of power – is not heeding his own advice

[3] That *something*, I would imagine, is to leave the residencia, to change, to adapt, and to experience the wider world

be well?' he cried; and, indeed, I could only echo his question, for I was disturbed enough myself.

I went to bed early, wearied with day-long restlessness, but the poisonous nature of the wind, and its ungodly and unintermittent uproar, would not suffer me to sleep. I lay there and tossed, my nerves and senses on the stretch. At times I would doze, dream horribly, and wake again; and these snatches of oblivion confused me as to time. But it must have been late on in the night, when I was suddenly startled by an outbreak of pitiable and hateful cries. I leaped from my bed, supposing I had dreamed; but the cries still continued to fill the house, cries of pain, I thought, but certainly of rage also, and so savage and discordant that they shocked the heart. It was no illusion; some living thing, some lunatic or some wild animal, was being foully tortured. The thought of Felipe and the squirrel flashed into my mind, and I ran to the door, but it had been locked from the outside; and I might shake it as I pleased, I was a fast prisoner. Still the cries continued. Now they would dwindle down into a moaning that seemed to be articulate, and at these times I made sure they must be human; and again they would break forth and fill the house with ravings worthy of hell. I stood at the door and gave ear to them, till at, last they died away. Long after that, I still lingered and still continued to hear them mingle in fancy with the storming of the wind; and when at last I crept to my bed, it was with a deadly sickness and a blackness of horror on my heart.

It was little wonder if I slept no more. Why had I been locked in? What had passed? Who was the author of these indescribable and shocking cries? A human being? It was inconceivable. A beast? The cries were scarce quite bestial; and what animal, short of a lion or a tiger, could thus shake the solid walls of the residencia? And while I was thus turning over the elements of the mystery, it came into my mind that I had not yet set eyes upon the daughter of the house. What was more probable than that the daughter of the Senora, and the sister of Felipe, should be herself insane? Or, what more likely than that these ignorant and half- witted people should seek to manage an afflicted kinswoman by violence? Here was a solution; and yet when I called to mind the cries (which I never did without a shuddering chill) it seemed altogether insufficient: not even cruelty could wring such cries from madness. But of one thing I was sure: I could not live in a house where such a thing was half conceivable, and not probe the matter home and, if necessary, interfere.

The next day came, the wind had blown itself out, and there was nothing to remind me of the business of the night. Felipe came to my bedside with obvious cheerfulness; as I passed through the court, the Senora was sunning herself with her accustomed immobility; and when I issued from the gateway, I found the whole face of nature austerely smiling, the heavens of a cold blue, and sown with great cloud islands, and the mountain-sides mapped forth into provinces of light and shadow. A short walk restored me to myself, and renewed within me the resolve to plumb this mystery; and when, from the vantage of my knoll, I had seen Felipe pass forth to his labours in the garden, I returned at once to the residencia to put my design in practice. The Senora appeared plunged in slumber; I stood awhile and marked her, but she did not stir; even if my design were indiscreet, I had little to fear from such a guardian; and turning away, I mounted to the gallery and began my exploration of the house.

All morning I went from one door to another, and entered spacious and faded chambers, some rudely shuttered, some receiving their full charge[1] of daylight, all empty and unhomely. It was a rich house, on which Time had breathed his tarnish and dust had scattered disillusion. The spider[2] swung there; the bloated tarantula scampered on the cornices; ants had their crowded highways on the floor of halls of audience; the big and foul fly, that lives on carrion and is often the messenger of death, had set up his nest in the rotten woodwork[3], and buzzed heavily about the rooms. Here and there a stool or two, a couch, a bed, or a great carved chair remained behind, like islets on the bare floors, to testify of man's bygone habitation; and everywhere the walls were set with the portraits of the dead[4]. I could judge, by these decaying effigies, in the house of what a great and what a handsome race I was then wandering. Many of the men wore orders on their

---

[1] An explosive, intrusive metaphor: "full charge" refers to the full measure of gunpowder poured into a musket or cannon to give them lethal power. This is in comparison with a half charge – or a blank – which would be used to fire a salute or a ceremonial discharge without projectiles. Sunlight gushes violently into the residencia

[2] Spiders, tarantula, ants, and carrion flies are all insects that can and often do feed on blood. Spiders and tarantulas liquefy their victims from within and drink the dissolved flesh, and ants and carrion flies are known for swarming over battlefield corpses and feasting greedily on the putrescence of decay – fitting residents for a house with a vampiric curse

[3] The messenger of death makes his home in the residencia. It is nothing if not poignant that this family is so carelessly, nonchalantly welcoming to the messengers of death and decay

[4] Stevenson's prose is rich and delicious throughout this atmospheric tale; the sense that the dead are anchoring the living to a nether-region that prevents them from ascending into the world of men or descending into the depths of hell is overpowering. The dead reign in this house: they have more power, intellect, and will than the living, and like the occupants of the House of Usher, they are prisoners to their home (not IN, but TO), which nurses off of them and prevents them from leaving. If anything is vampiric in this tale it is the residencia which is little more than a tomb for the greedy dead

breasts[1] and had the port of noble offices; the women were all richly attired; the canvases most of them by famous hands. But it was not so much these evidences of greatness that took hold upon my mind, even contrasted, as they were, with the present depopulation and decay of that great house. It was rather the parable of family life that I read in this succession of fair faces and shapely bodies. Never before had I so realised the miracle of the continued race, the creation and recreation, the weaving and changing and handing down of fleshly elements. That a child should be born of its mother, that it should grow and clothe itself (we know not how) with humanity[2], and put on inherited looks, and turn its head with the manner of one ascendant, and offer its hand with the gesture of another, are wonders dulled for us by repetition. But in the singular unity of look, in the common features and common bearing, of all these painted generations on the walls of the residencia, the miracle started out and looked me in the face. And an ancient mirror falling opportunely in my way, I stood and read my own features a long while, tracing out on either hand the filaments of descent and the bonds that knit me with my family.

At last, in the course of these investigations, I opened the door of a chamber that bore the marks of habitation. It was of large proportions and faced to the north, where the mountains were most wildly figured[3]. The embers of a fire smouldered and smoked upon the hearth, to which a chair had been drawn close. And yet the aspect of the chamber was ascetic to the degree of sternness; the chair was uncushioned; the floor and walls were naked[4]; and beyond the books which lay here and there in some confusion, there was no instrument of either work or pleasure. The sight of books in the house of such a family exceedingly amazed me[5]; and I began with a great hurry, and in momentary fear of interruption, to go from one to another and hastily inspect their character. They were of all sorts, devotional, historical, and scientific, but mostly of a great age and in the Latin tongue. Some I could see to bear the marks of constant study; others had been torn across

---

[1] Medals and ribbons that denote knighthood (in Spain the greatest of these is the Order of the Golden Fleece)

[2] One of many references that Stevenson will make to the theory (advanced by Jekyll and Hyde) that the spirit is separate from the body – that the physical flesh is the vessel of the psychological spirit – a concept that Poe reworked constantly in stories where a man becomes obsessed with a woman whose divine spirit is betrayed by its mortal body

[3] The occupant of this room would thus spend most of her time looking at the lofty mountains – traditional symbols of divinity and God

[4] One should expect them to be muffled (both from sound and cold) in tapestries and rugs

[5] Considering their intellectual sloth it is indeed a surprise that they should suffer books to line their walls

and tossed aside as if in petulance or disapproval[1]. Lastly, as I cruised about that empty chamber, I espied some papers written upon with pencil on a table near the window. An unthinking curiosity led me to take one up. It bore a copy of verses, very roughly metred in the original Spanish, and which I may render somewhat thus--

> *Pleasure approached with pain and shame,*
> *Grief with a wreath of lilies came.*
> *Pleasure showed the lovely sun;*
> *Jesu dear, how sweet it shone!*
> *Grief with her worn hand pointed on,*
> *Jesu dear, to thee![2]*

Shame and confusion at once fell on me[3]; and, laying down the paper, I beat an immediate retreat from the apartment. Neither Felipe nor his mother could have read the books nor written these rough but feeling verses. It was plain I had stumbled with sacrilegious feet into the room of the daughter of the house. God knows, my own heart most sharply punished me for my indiscretion. The thought that I had thus secretly pushed my way into the confidence of a girl so strangely situated, and the fear that she might somehow come to hear of it, oppressed me like guilt[4]. I blamed myself besides for my suspicions of the night before; wondered that I should ever have attributed those shocking cries to one of whom I now conceived as of a saint, spectral of mien[5], wasted with maceration[6], bound up in the practices of a mechanical devotion, and dwelling in a great isolation of soul with her incongruous relatives[7]; and as I leaned on the

---

[1] The reader is clearly searching for something – a solution, I might point out, to a particular family problem. Since few reputable modern sources would bother discussing family curses seriously, Olalla must seek help in ancient Latin texts

[2] The verse suggests the following thoughts: Olalla cannot enjoy the vacant, indolent pleasure that consumes her family because she is stricken with shame at their idle lifestyle. She is reminded – by personified Grief – that she will die and that her destiny is to join her family in their curse. Pleasure tries to distract her with comfort, but Grief rallies her in her devotion to her religion, which is the only source of relief that she can experience

[3] These are obviously very personal thoughts, and to read them unasked is a great breech of etiquette

[4] Unlike Felipe and the Senora, Olalla shares passion, remorse, and feeling with the narrator

[5] Look or manner – he expects her to be a gaunt, wasted ascetic (not unlike Madeline Usher)

[6] The softening of flesh with liquid. The narrator refers here to pious crying

[7] He certainly seems preemptively attracted to this girl who is – as he put it – so incongruous to her bizarre, mentally frail relatives

balustrade of the gallery and looked down into the bright close[1] of pomegranates and at the gaily dressed and somnolent woman, who just then stretched herself and delicately licked her lips as in the very sensuality of sloth, my mind swiftly compared the scene with the cold chamber looking northward on the mountains, where the daughter dwelt.

That same afternoon, as I sat upon my knoll, I saw the Padre enter the gates of the residencia. The revelation of the daughter's character had struck home to my fancy, and almost blotted out the horrors of the night before; but at sight of this worthy man the memory revived. I descended, then, from the knoll, and making a circuit among the woods, posted myself by the wayside to await his passage. As soon as he appeared I stepped forth and introduced myself as the lodger of the residencia. He had a very strong, honest countenance, on which it was easy to read the mingled emotions with which he regarded me, as a foreigner, a heretic[2], and yet one who had been wounded for the good cause. Of the family at the residencia he spoke with reserve, and yet with respect. I mentioned that I had not yet seen the daughter, whereupon he remarked that that was as it should be, and looked at me a little askance. Lastly, I plucked up courage to refer to the cries that had disturbed me in the night. He heard me out in silence, and then stopped and partly turned about, as though to mark beyond doubt that he was dismissing me.

'Do you take tobacco powder?' said he, offering his snuff-box; and then, when I had refused, 'I am an old man,' he added, 'and I may be allowed to remind you that you are a guest.'

'I have, then, your authority,' I returned, firmly enough, although I flushed at the implied reproof, 'to let things take their course, and not to interfere?'

He said 'yes,' and with a somewhat uneasy salute turned and left me where I was. But he had done two things: he had set my conscience at rest, and he had awakened my delicacy. I made a great effort, once more dismissed the recollections of the night, and fell once more to brooding on my saintly poetess. At the same time, I could not quite forget that I had been locked in, and that night when Felipe brought me my supper I attacked him warily on both points of interest.

'I never see your sister,' said I casually.

'Oh, no,' said he; 'she is a good, good girl,' and his mind instantly veered to something else.

'Your sister is pious[3], I suppose?' I asked in the next pause.

'Oh!' he cried, joining his hands with extreme fervour, 'a saint; it is she that keeps me up.'

---

[1] A small cluster of trees
[2] Being a Calvinist or – potentially – an atheist, but certainly not a Catholic
[3] A devout religious adherent

'You are very fortunate,' said I, 'for the most of us, I am afraid, and myself among the number, are better at going down.'

'Senor,' said Felipe earnestly, 'I would not say that. You should not tempt your angel. If one goes down, where is he to stop?'

'Why, Felipe,' said I, 'I had no guess you were a preacher, and I may say a good one; but I suppose that is your sister's doing?'

He nodded at me with round eyes.

'Well, then,' I continued, 'she has doubtless reproved you for your sin of cruelty?'

'Twelve times[1]!' he cried; for this was the phrase by which the odd creature expressed the sense of frequency. 'And I told her you had done so-- I remembered that,' he added proudly--'and she was pleased.'

'Then, Felipe,' said I, 'what were those cries that I heard last night? for surely they were cries of some creature in suffering.'

'The wind,' returned Felipe, looking in the fire.

I took his hand in mine, at which, thinking it to be a caress, he smiled with a brightness of pleasure that came near disarming my resolve. But I trod the weakness down. 'The wind,' I repeated; 'and yet I think it was this hand,' holding it up, 'that had first locked me in.' The lad shook visibly, but answered never a word. 'Well,' said I, 'I am a stranger and a guest. It is not my part either to meddle or to judge in your affairs; in these you shall take your sister's counsel, which I cannot doubt to be excellent. But in so far as concerns my own I will be no man's prisoner, and I demand that key.' Half an hour later my door was suddenly thrown open, and the key tossed ringing on the floor.

A day or two after I came in from a walk a little before the point of noon. The Senora was lying lapped in slumber on the threshold of the recess; the pigeons dozed below the eaves like snowdrifts; the house was under a deep spell of noontide quiet; and only a wandering and gentle wind from the mountain stole round the galleries, rustled among the pomegranates, and pleasantly stirred the shadows[2]. Something in the stillness moved me to imitation, and I went very lightly across the court and up the marble staircase. My foot was on the topmost round, when a door opened, and I found myself face to face with Olalla. Surprise transfixed me; her loveliness struck to my heart; she glowed in the deep shadow of the gallery, a gem of colour; her eyes took hold upon mine and clung there, and bound us together like the joining of hands; and the moments we thus stood face to

---

[1] Also the number of apostles, and the number of Israelite tribes – a number seen as symbolic of completion and unity

[2] The symbolism here is of building, brooding love: nestling doves, the stirring of the erotic pomegranate leaves, the slumber of the lusty Senora (whose sleep now allows her to be usurped in beauty by the waking Olalla), and so on

face, drinking each other in, were sacramental and the wedding of souls[1]. I know not how long it was before I awoke out of a deep trance, and, hastily bowing, passed on into the upper stair. She did not move, but followed me with her great, thirsting eyes[2]; and as I passed out of sight it seemed to me as if she paled and faded.

In my own room, I opened the window and looked out, and could not think what change had come upon that austere field of mountains that it should thus sing and shine under the lofty heaven. I had seen her--Olalla! And the stone crags answered, Olalla! and the dumb, unfathomable azure answered, Olalla! The pale saint of my dreams had vanished for ever; and in her place I beheld this maiden on whom God had lavished the richest colours and the most exuberant energies of life, whom he had made active as a deer, slender as a reed, and in whose great eyes he had lighted the torches of the soul. The thrill of her young life, strung like a wild animal's, had entered into me; the force of soul that had looked out from her eyes and

---

[1] The motif of drinking returns, once more in a somewhat vampiric nature – the drinking in of souls – especially with the reference to the sacrament of communion, which is thought by some to be the literal drinking of Christ's blood. Some have noted that the narrator, as much as the family, is a vampire in his own way, needing Olalla's spirit to replenish his own dried up spirituality

[2] There again, the parched motif returns. It is especially suitable that Olalla's eyes – the windows to the soul – are seen as thirsty: her spirit, too, requires replenishment

conquered mine, mantled about my heart and sprang to my lips in singing[1]. She passed through my veins: she was one with me[2].

I will not say that this enthusiasm declined; rather my soul held out in its ecstasy as in a strong castle, and was there besieged by cold and sorrowful considerations. I could not doubt but that I loved her at first sight, and already with a quivering ardour that was strange to my experience. What then was to follow? She was the child of an afflicted house, the Senora's daughter, the sister of Felipe; she bore it even in her beauty. She had the lightness and swiftness of the one, swift as an arrow, light as dew; like the other, she shone on the pale background of the world with the brilliancy of flowers. I could not call by the name of brother that half-witted lad, nor by the name of mother that immovable and lovely thing of flesh, whose silly eyes and perpetual simper now recurred to my mind like something hateful[3]. And if I could not marry, what then? She was helplessly unprotected; her eyes, in that single and long glance which had been all our intercourse[4], had confessed a weakness equal to my own; but in my heart I knew her for the student of the cold northern chamber, and the writer of the sorrowful lines; and this was a knowledge to disarm a brute. To flee was more than I could find courage for; but I registered a vow of unsleeping circumspection.

As I turned from the window, my eyes alighted on the portrait. It had fallen dead, like a candle after sunrise[5]; it followed me with eyes of paint. I knew it to be like, and marvelled at the tenacity of type in that declining race[6]; but the likeness was swallowed up in difference. I remembered how it

---

[1] There is an ambiguity here as to who has the trait of vampirism – Olalla or the narrator – because the narrator seems to draw energy from Olalla's youth and energy just like a vampire who feeds on vital blood

[2] Readers of Dracula will remember how Mina drank the Count's blood and was similarly convinced that he now lived within her. For such a vaguely supernatural tale, there is quite a lot of vampiric imagery to suggest at least a metaphorical if not literal vampirism

[3] As much as he adores – though with dubious rationale – Olalla, he is not willing to become in-laws with her idiotic family, and is concerned that their offspring might inherit her familial curse

[4] The word here means "interaction," but make no mistake, the language he uses to describe this informal eye contact is deeply sexual and implies that they had engaged in spiritual sex (though whether this is a mutual impression is rather doubtful)

[5] Like a candle whose power to shine is made redundant in the rays of the sun, the hypnotic portrait that had initially garnered the narrator's ardor and lust is worthless in the presence of the living original – the lookalike Olalla

[6] In spite of its decadence and degeneration, the family continues to faithfully reproduce its physical beauty from mother to daughter

had seemed to me a thing unapproachable in the life, a creature rather of the painter's craft than of the modesty of nature, and I marvelled at the thought, and exulted in the image of Olalla. Beauty I had seen before, and not been charmed, and I had been often drawn to women, who were not beautiful except to me; but in Olalla all that I desired and had not dared to imagine was united[1].

I did not see her the next day, and my heart ached and my eyes longed for her, as men long for morning[2]. But the day after, when I returned, about my usual hour, she was once more on the gallery, and our looks once more met and embraced. I would have spoken, I would have drawn near to her; but strongly as she plucked at my heart, drawing me like a magnet, something yet more imperious withheld me; and I could only bow and pass by; and she, leaving my salutation unanswered, only followed me with her noble eyes.

I had now her image by rote, and as I conned the traits in memory it seemed as if I read her very heart. She was dressed with something of her mother's coquetry, and love of positive colour. Her robe, which I know she must have made with her own hands, clung about her with a cunning grace. After the fashion of that country, besides, her bodice stood open in the middle, in a long slit, and here, in spite of the poverty of the house, a gold coin, hanging by a ribbon, lay on her brown bosom[3]. These were proofs, had any been needed, of her inborn delight in life and her own loveliness. On the other hand, in her eyes that hung upon mine, I could read depth beyond depth of passion and sadness, lights of poetry and hope, blacknesses of despair, and thoughts that were above the earth[4]. It was a lovely body, but

---

[1] Olalla can be viewed as a sort of anima Doppelganger: the missing female half of the narrator's soul. He is brash, proud, and masculine, she humble, pious, and feminine. Fresh from the ravages of a bloody war, Olalla represents all that he has lost of a more tender, maternal nature, and he is desperate to unite with her as a means of restoring his bifurcated soul

[2] Again, there is a sense that Olalla represents the feminine, maternal nature of the human spirit – morning to the narrator's evening, light to his dark, love to his despair, peace to his war – and he yearns religiously to drink from her offering of wholeness with all the desperation that a vampire lusts after its life-giving prey

[3] There is a virtually undeniable vaginal symbolism here. Olalla's coquettish dress is, as he says, native to her country, but in England it would be scandalously sensual, and the receptive slit of the bodice both invites meditations on the breasts beneath and on the even more indiscreet aperture of the life-producing sexual act

[4] A phenomenally Poe-esque description of the eyes. One wonders that, like "Berenice" where teeth are extracted from a woman in a coma, Poe never wrote a tale about a man who gouged out a woman's bewitching eyes ("The Tell-Tale Heart" ventures into this territory somewhat)

the inmate, the soul, was more than worthy of that lodging. Should I leave this incomparable flower to wither unseen on these rough mountains? Should I despise the great gift offered me in the eloquent silence of her eyes? Here was a soul immured; should I not burst its prison? All side considerations fell off from me; were she the child of Herod[1] I swore I should make her mine; and that very evening I set myself, with a mingled sense of treachery and disgrace, to captivate the brother[2]. Perhaps I read him with more favourable eyes, perhaps the thought of his sister always summoned up the better qualities of that imperfect soul; but he had never seemed to me so amiable, and his very likeness to Olalla, while it annoyed, yet softened me[3].

A third day passed in vain--an empty desert of hours. I would not lose a chance, and loitered all afternoon in the court where (to give myself a countenance) I spoke more than usual with the Senora. God knows it was with a most tender and sincere interest that I now studied her; and even as for Felipe, so now for the mother, I was conscious of a growing warmth of toleration. And yet I wondered. Even while I spoke with her, she would doze off into a little sleep, and presently awake again without embarrassment; and this composure staggered me. And again, as I marked her make infinitesimal changes in her posture, savouring and lingering on the bodily pleasure of the movement, I was driven to wonder at this depth of passive sensuality. She lived in her body; and her consciousness was all sunk into and disseminated through her members, where it luxuriously dwelt[4]. Lastly,

---

[1] Specifically Salome, the girl who danced for her wicked, adulterous father in the New Testament story of John the Baptist. John had accused Herod of incest and adultery (he married his sister-in-law), and was consequently jailed. His step-daughter Salome danced for him (the implications and tradition of the dance, though not described, are that it was erotic in nature), raised his lust, and caused him to promise her anything in the kingdom. After consulting with her mother, who loathed John, Salome asked for the Baptist's head on a platter, which Herod queasily granted. Since then Salome and the Baptist have been seen as symbols of youthful eroticism and aged piety respectively

[2] More homoerotic overtones, as though in order to win over Olalla, the narrator is going to attempt to seduce Felipe and win his devoted adoration. In fact, Stevenson tellingly never tells us what happened in this interview, only that Felipe "softened" him with his girlish beauty and that their interchange was amicable. Though I am typically cautious when reading sexuality into Victorian literature, I think there is a strong suggestion of implied seduction in this passage

[3] There is certainly an element of an androgynous sexuality surrounding the brother and sister who share one another's physical beauty

[4] The Senora is more body than soul. Whereas ghosts and demons are more soul than body, this is a fitting description of the living dead, regardless of their supernatural capabilities: they are living bodies that feed greedily on sustenance

I could not grow accustomed to her eyes. Each time she turned on me these great beautiful and meaningless orbs, wide open to the day, but closed against human inquiry--each time I had occasion to observe the lively changes of her pupils which expanded and contracted in a breath--I know not what it was came over me, I can find no name for the mingled feeling of disappointment, annoyance, and distaste that jarred along my nerves. I tried her on a variety of subjects, equally in vain; and at last led the talk to her daughter. But even there she proved indifferent; said she was pretty, which (as with children) was her highest word of commendation, but was plainly incapable of any higher thought; and when I remarked that Olalla seemed silent, merely yawned in my face and replied that speech was of no great use when you had nothing to say. 'People speak much, very much[1],' she added, looking at me with expanded pupils; and then again yawned and again showed me a mouth that was as dainty as a toy. This time I took the hint, and, leaving her to her repose, went up into my own chamber to sit by the open window, looking on the hills and not beholding them, sunk in lustrous and deep dreams, and hearkening in fancy to the note of a voice that I had never heard.

I awoke on the fifth morning with a brightness of anticipation that seemed to challenge fate. I was sure of myself, light of heart and foot, and resolved to put my love incontinently to the touch of knowledge. It should lie no longer under the bonds of silence, a dumb thing, living by the eye only, like the love of beasts[2]; but should now put on the spirit, and enter upon the joys of the complete human intimacy[3]. I thought of it with wild hopes, like a voyager to El Dorado[4]; into that unknown and lovely country

---

because there is nothing in their spirit that can live off of art or love or religion; they are fully animal a "consciousness [that is] all [sunken] into and disseminated through [their] members, where it luxuriously [dwells]"

[1] She says this almost as if she were an outside observer of "people" – as if she has no relationship with the human race, as one who is more animal than human, more body than soul

[2] This is certainly the way that the narrator views Felipe, who loves him through his manner rather than articulate language

[3] Again, on the surface this is just an expression that means being open with one another intellectually and emotionally, but that doesn't eradicate the fact that the narrator's view of Olalla is virtually just as physical and animalistic as it is spiritual and human

[4] Another fine Poe reference. El Dorado – the subject of Poe's eponymous poem – was a mythical city made of gold somewhere in Latin America. Conquistadors had heard of it and searched wildly for its treasures, but it was of course a groundless legend. The concept still symbolizes hopeless ambitions, and is a fitting reference in regards to Olalla, whom the narrator (like so many of Poe's protagonists) views as a pure soul untainted by physical imperfections, but like

of her soul, I no longer trembled to adventure[1]. Yet when I did indeed encounter her, the same force of passion descended on me and at once submerged my mind; speech seemed to drop away from me like a childish habit; and I but drew near to her as the giddy man draws near to the margin of a gulf. She drew back from me a little as I came; but her eyes did not waver from mine, and these lured me forward. At last, when I was already within reach of her, I stopped. Words were denied me; if I advanced I could but clasp her to my heart in silence; and all that was sane in me, all that was still unconquered, revolted against the thought of such an accost. So we stood for a second, all our life in our eyes, exchanging salvos of attraction and yet each resisting[2]; and then, with a great effort of the will, and conscious at the same time of a sudden bitterness of disappointment, I turned and went away in the same silence.

What power lay upon me that I could not speak? And she, why was she also silent? Why did she draw away before me dumbly, with fascinated eyes? Was this love? or was it a mere brute attraction, mindless and inevitable, like that of the magnet for the steel[3]? We had never spoken, we were wholly strangers: and yet an influence, strong as the grasp of a giant, swept us silently together. On my side, it filled me with impatience; and yet I was sure that she was worthy; I had seen her books, read her verses, and thus, in a sense, divined the soul of my mistress[4]. But on her side, it struck me almost cold. Of me, she knew nothing but my bodily favour[5]; she was drawn to me as stones fall to the earth; the laws that rule the earth

---

Poe's male characters, this man is going to be disappointed when he realizes that Olalla is not an angel, but a flawed mortal who is just as much physical human being as she is spiritual inquirer

[1] I feel as though this is a very polite, Victorian way of saying "your body is a wonderland"

[2] Woooow... This is getting pretty sexually intense. Forgive the drop in professionalism, but this is where – were we in a freshman literature class – someone in the back would say *"bow-chicka-wah-wow."* A genuinely erotic moment for an era where sexuality in literature was expressed solely through suggestion. Well, Stevenson is pounding on the door of suggestion with a battering ram

[3] Again, there is the suggestion that these two characters are halves of a whole human: he, the steel, manly, haughty, violent, and ravenous, she, the magnet, womanly, self-aware, nurturing, maternal, and religious. They are drawn to one another by the desire for completion – a vain and hopeless impulse

[4] Mistress? Before you've ever said "hello"? This spiritual love affair is rapidly drifting into an unhealthy fantasy

[5] His handsomeness

conducted her[1], unconsenting, to my arms; and I drew back at the thought of such a bridal, and began to be jealous for myself. It was not thus that I desired to be loved[2]. And then I began to fall into a great pity for the girl herself[3]. I thought how sharp must be her mortification, that she, the student, the recluse, Felipe's saintly monitress[4], should have thus confessed an overweening weakness for a man with whom she had never exchanged a word. And at the coming of pity, all other thoughts were swallowed up; and I longed only to find and console and reassure her; to tell her how wholly her love was returned on my side, and how her choice, even if blindly made, was not unworthy[5].

The next day it was glorious weather; depth upon depth of blue over-canopied the mountains; the sun shone wide; and the wind in the trees and the many falling torrents in the mountains filled the air with delicate and haunting music. Yet I was prostrated with sadness. My heart wept for the sight of Olalla, as a child weeps for its mother[6]. I sat down on a boulder on the verge of the low cliffs that bound the plateau to the north. Thence I looked down into the wooded valley of a stream, where no foot came. In the mood I was in, it was even touching to behold the place untenanted; it lacked Olalla; and I thought of the delight and glory of a life passed wholly with her in that strong air, and among these rugged and lovely surroundings, at first with a whimpering sentiment, and then again with

---

[1] Yikes! Arrogant much? "Of course she is attracted to me; it's human nature really. Women just flock to me like a stone falls to the ground – something's gotta give"

[2] "Love me for my mind! I'm not just a piece of booty, 'kay"

[3] "I'm just so attractive! I really feel bad for her, having to be around such a handsome guy. Must be tough to resist me, poor thing"

[4] Monitor (Female)

[5] Whoa... "I just wish I could tell her that I'm a real keeper – she has chosen well, even though you are blindly drawn to my good looks. You don't have any choice, of course, but little do you know how good you have it!"

[6] Boom. Here comes Freud with the reality juice (or Jung if you prefer): as much as the narrator acts as though Olalla "needs" him, he needs her even more – not because she is pretty and pious, but because she represents the archetype of the anima that has been wrenched from his soul by war and life. She is a mother figure and as sexual as his feelings might be for her, they are unmistakably Oedipal in their fixation on a beautiful, virginal female figure of purity and care who comes to kiss your boo boos and pet your hair when you're having a good cry. One wonders at his relationship with his own mother (a psychologist might speculate that she died early in his life or was otherwise not attentive, hence his deep-seated vanity, daredevil antics, and desperate desire to impress his hosts, which all bespeak the psychology of a nine year old boy whose mother is either inattentive or unavailable)

such a fiery joy that I seemed to grow in strength and stature, like a Samson[1].

And then suddenly I was aware of Olalla drawing near. She appeared out of a grove of cork-trees, and came straight towards me; and I stood up and waited. She seemed in her walking a creature of such life and fire and lightness as amazed me; yet she came quietly and slowly. Her energy was in the slowness; but for inimitable strength, I felt she would have run, she would have flown to me. Still, as she approached, she kept her eyes lowered to the ground; and when she had drawn quite near, it was without one glance that she addressed me. At the first note of her voice I started. It was for this I had been waiting; this was the last test of my love. And lo, her enunciation was precise and clear, not lisping and incomplete like that of her family; and the voice, though deeper than usual with women[2], was still both youthful and womanly. She spoke in a rich chord; golden contralto strains mingled with hoarseness, as the red threads were mingled with the brown among her tresses[3]. It was not only a voice that spoke to my heart directly; but it spoke to me of her. And yet her words immediately plunged me back upon despair.

'You will go away[4],' she said, 'to-day.'

Her example broke the bonds of my speech; I felt as lightened of a weight, or as if a spell had been dissolved. I know not in what words I answered; but, standing before her on the cliffs, I poured out the whole ardour of my love, telling her that I lived upon the thought of her, slept only

---

[1] A telling reference: Samson was the biblical warrior and strong-man whose strength was supernaturally invested in his never-cut hair. He was seduced by a Mata Hari-esque spy named Delilah who was paid by the Philistines to uncover his weakness. Like Achilles, the weakness was shockingly simple, and after several failed attempts (he would lie, she would test the secret – for instance, he claimed that if he was bound with fresh bowstrings he will be defenseless. She does so during his sleep and hands him over to the Philistines, whom he kills easily) she finally learns the secret, cuts his hair, and has him successfully captured

[2] The androgyny continues – powerful, deep-voiced, and sensual, Olalla – like her effeminate, servile brother – encapsulates both male and female sexuality. This is fitting if we accept the interpretation that she stands for the feminine anima which exists in all mankind regardless of gender: she is not a representation of womanhood, but of the characteristics which are often described as womanly, but which can just as readily exist in a man – compassion, piety, nurturing maternalism, patience, encouragement, and love

[3] Symbolizing the vampiric germ which – while not as predominant as in her auburn-haired mother – are nonetheless a deep part of her personality

[4] Whereas with Felipe the narrator was the dominator, with Olalla he is the submissive: she does not ask or suggest, but commands in her hoarse, deep tone

to dream of her loveliness, and would gladly forswear my country, my language, and my friends, to live for ever by her side[1]. And then, strongly commanding myself, I changed the note; I reassured, I comforted her; I told her I had divined in her a pious and heroic spirit, with which I was worthy to sympathise, and which I longed to share and lighten. 'Nature,' I told her, 'was the voice of God, which men disobey at peril[2]; and if we were thus humbly drawn together, ay, even as by a miracle of love, it must imply a divine fitness in our souls[3]; we must be made,' I said--'made for one another. We should be mad rebels,' I cried out--'mad rebels against God, not to obey this instinct.'

She shook her head. 'You will go to-day,' she repeated, and then with a gesture, and in a sudden, sharp note--'no, not to-day,' she cried, 'to-morrow!'

But at this sign of relenting, power came in upon me in a tide. I stretched out my arms and called upon her name; and she leaped to me and clung to me[4]. The hills rocked about us, the earth quailed[5]; a shock as of a blow went through me and left me blind and dizzy. And the next moment she had thrust me back, broken rudely from my arms, and fled with the speed of a deer among the cork-trees.

I stood and shouted to the mountains; I turned and went back towards the residencia, waltzing upon air. She sent me away, and yet I had but to call upon her name and she came to me. These were but the weaknesses of

---

[1] The prophecy he had made about the painting – that he would forswear everything in his life for a living replication of the woman in the picture – has come true

[2] Very manipulative of him – he uses Olalla's religious piety to tempt her, saying that lust is God's way of bringing people together to marriage, and that if that lust is mutual, it is sinful to resist it

[3] If we accept the premise that lust is God's way of edging people towards marriage, then the narrator is hoping that we will then assume that it implies that the spirits of the two people must be as compatible as their bodies – that lust should follow the suit of spiritual compatibility. A weak argument indeed

[4] This pose – and Olalla's response – will later be mirrored in the finale, when she clings to a giant crucifix. The narrator's outstretched arms and open body imitate the pose of Christ on the cross, and Olalla runs to him as if to salvation

[5] The Bible describes a similar geological aftershock following the death of Christ, and hence the salvation of mankind. Stevenson suggests that Olalla has been saved by her link to the narrator. But she is wrong – Olalla does not represent humanity, whose sins must be forgiven by the sacrifice of an innocent person, she represents the sacrifice

girls, from which even she, the strangest of her sex, was not exempted[1]. Go? Not I, Olalla--O, not I, Olalla, my Olalla! A bird sang near by; and in that season, birds were rare. It bade me be of good cheer. And once more the whole countenance of nature, from the ponderous and stable mountains down to the lightest leaf and the smallest darting fly in the shadow of the groves, began to stir before me and to put on the lineaments of life and wear a face of awful[2] joy. The sunshine struck upon the hills, strong as a hammer on the anvil, and the hills shook; the earth, under that vigorous insulation, yielded up heady scents; the woods smouldered in the blaze. I felt the thrill of travail and delight run through the earth[3]. Something elemental, something rude, violent, and savage, in the love that sang in my heart, was like a key to nature's secrets; and the very stones that rattled under my feet appeared alive and friendly. Olalla! Her touch had quickened, and renewed, and strung me up to the old pitch of concert with the rugged earth, to a swelling of the soul that men learn to forget in their polite assemblies. Love burned in me like rage; tenderness waxed fierce[4]; I hated, I adored, I pitied, I revered her with ecstasy. She seemed the link that bound me in with dead things on the one hand[5], and with our pure and pitying God upon the other[6]: a thing brutal and divine, and akin at once to the innocence and to the unbridled forces of the earth[7].

My head thus reeling, I came into the courtyard of the residencia, and the sight of the mother struck me like a revelation. She sat there, all sloth

---

[1] Even the androgynous Olalla, he supposes, is susceptible to the weakness of womanhood. Today this fellow would be outed on the internet and fired from his job for his opinions

[2] Derived from a sense of awe

[3] These descriptions of seismic power – heady odors rising up, the spine-jolting power of ecstasy, the thrill of savage violence, the thrill of delight – it all bespeaks the flood of feelings and sensations that follow the fallout of an orgasm

[4] Stevenson underscores the inherent duplicity of lust – it is tender but violent, selfless but self-absorbed, worshipful but self-worshipping, devoted but spiteful, kind but cruel, subjectifying but objectifying

[5] Due to the fact that union with her would lead him, inevitably, to drinking in the fatal curse of her family, and either succumb to sloth and degeneration,

[6] Due to Olalla's personal piety. The use of the word "our" helps the argument that, although the Catholics refer to the narrator as "not a Christian," he may be a Calvinist

[7] Olalla is the ultimate Poe-esque heroine – a woman who represents the epitomes of physicality and psychology, materiality and mentality, whose body attracts the adoration of her lover, and whose mind is the source of his deep worship. Like Poe's heroines, she symbolizes humanity's struggle between its transcendental desires and its physical mortality – aspiration vs. degeneration, spirit vs. body, faith vs. lust

and contentment, blinking under the strong sunshine, branded with a passive enjoyment, a creature set quite apart, before whom my ardour fell away like a thing ashamed. I stopped a moment, and, commanding such shaken tones as I was able, said a word or two. She looked at me with her unfathomable kindness; her voice in reply sounded vaguely out of the realm of peace in which she slumbered, and there fell on my mind, for the first time, a sense of respect for one so uniformly innocent and happy, and I passed on in a kind of wonder at myself, that I should be so much disquieted.

On my table there lay a piece of the same yellow paper I had seen in the north room; it was written on with pencil in the same hand, Olalla's hand, and I picked it up with a sudden sinking of alarm, and read, 'If you have any kindness for Olalla, if you have any chivalry for a creature sorely wrought, go from here to-day; in pity, in honour, for the sake of Him who died[1], I supplicate that you shall go.' I looked at this awhile in mere stupidity, then I began to awaken to a weariness and horror of life; the sunshine darkened outside on the bare hills, and I began to shake like a man in terror. The vacancy thus suddenly opened in my life unmanned[2] me like a physical void. It was not my heart, it was not my happiness, it was life itself that was involved. I could not lose her. I said so, and stood repeating it. And then, like one in a dream, I moved to the window, put forth my hand to open the casement[3], and thrust it through the pane. The blood spurted from my wrist; and with an instantaneous quietude and command of myself, I pressed my thumb on the little leaping fountain, and reflected what to do. In that empty room there was nothing to my purpose[4]; I felt, besides, that I required assistance. There shot into my mind a hope that Olalla herself might be my helper, and I turned and went down stairs, still keeping my thumb upon the wound.

There was no sign of either Olalla or Felipe, and I addressed myself to the recess, whither the Senora had now drawn quite back and sat dozing close before the fire[5], for no degree of heat appeared too much for her[6].

---

[1] Christ. The specific reference to His death underscores the suffering of the cross, and the sacrifice of His life, something which Olalla – who is sacrificing happiness for the salvation of her family – relates with

[2] A Victorian term referencing a loss of composure and emotional control. To be unmanned is to be shaken from your resolve to "keep calm and carry on"

[3] A window that opens out from hinges on one side like a door

[4] That is, nothing to bind the gushing wound

[5] As those who have actually been gathered around a wood fire will relate, it quickly becomes too hot and the best place to be is within a few meters of the flames, but not much closer

[6] While some people will feel the restlessness of indulgence after a while – start to feel lazy, start to get twitchy, start to feel guilty for sitting around all day – the

'Pardon me,' said I, 'if I disturb you, but I must apply to you for help.'

She looked up sleepily and asked me what it was, and with the very words I thought she drew in her breath with a widening of the nostrils and seemed to come suddenly and fully alive[1].

'I have cut myself,' I said, 'and rather badly. See!' And I held out my two hands from which the blood was oozing and dripping.

Her great eyes opened wide, the pupils shrank into points; a veil seemed to fall from her face, and leave it sharply expressive and yet inscrutable[2]. And as I still stood, marvelling a little at her disturbance, she came swiftly up to me, and stooped and caught me by the hand; and the next moment my hand was at her mouth, and she had bitten me to the bone[3]. The pang of the bite, the sudden spurting of blood, and the monstrous horror of the act, flashed through me all in one, and I beat her back; and she sprang at me again and again, with bestial cries, cries that I recognised, such cries as had awakened me on the night of the high wind[4]. Her strength was like that of madness; mine was rapidly ebbing with the loss of blood; my mind besides was whirling with the abhorrent strangeness of the onslaught, and I was already forced against the wall, when Olalla ran betwixt us, and Felipe, following at a bound, pinned down his mother on the floor.

A trance-like weakness fell upon me; I saw, heard, and felt, but I was incapable of movement. I heard the struggle roll to and fro upon the floor, the yells of that catamount[5] ringing up to Heaven as she strove to reach me. I felt Olalla clasp me in her arms, her hair falling on my face, and, with the strength of a man, raise and half drag, half carry me upstairs into my own room, where she cast me down upon the bed[6]. Then I saw her hasten

---

Senora relishes it so much that even to the point of pain — being lightly seared by the fire — she has no censor to tell her "okay, that's enough; time to get up and do something"

[1] The smell of blood has awakened her from her hibernation. Starved of variation, she is desperate to binge on fresh life

[2] This deep sloth has prevented the narrator from seeing the monster behind the laziness, and now the veil is removed and what can be seen is hideous

[3] This sudden act of monstrosity is absolutely chilling, especially if one remembers that she has the teeth of a human being, and considers the shocking force and violence it would take to "bite to the bone of a human wrist. Her teeth must be very sharp, and her jaws mercilessly strong

[4] It was not Felipe torturing an animal, or Olalla wailing, that he heard the night he was locked in, but the Senora feeding — feeding on some poor human's blood

[5] A cougar. Literally a wild cat from the mountain — an apt term for the Senora

[6] This is just another instance of Olalla's androgyny — her hoarse, manly voice and her powerful strength (carrying a well-built soldier up a staircase and throwing him on a bed like a bridegroom depositing his bride onto their honeymoon bed) contrast beautifully with her spiritual feminity

to the door and lock it, and stand an instant listening to the savage cries that shook the residencia. And then, swift and light as a thought, she was again beside me, binding up my hand, laying it in her bosom, moaning and mourning over it with dove-like sounds. They were not words that came to her, they were sounds more beautiful than speech, infinitely touching, infinitely tender[1]; and yet as I lay there, a thought stung to my heart, a thought wounded me like a sword, a thought, like a worm in a flower, profaned the holiness of my love. Yes, they were beautiful sounds, and they were inspired by human tenderness; but was their beauty human[2]?

All day I lay there. For a long time the cries of that nameless female thing, as she struggled with her half-witted whelp, resounded through the house, and pierced me with despairing sorrow and disgust. They were the death-cry of my love; my love was murdered; was not only dead, but an offence to me; and yet, think as I pleased, feel as I must, it still swelled within me like a storm of sweetness, and my heart melted at her looks and touch. This horror that had sprung out, this doubt upon Olalla[3], this savage and bestial strain that ran not only through the whole behaviour of her family, but found a place in the very foundations and story of our love-- though it appalled, though it shocked and sickened me, was yet not of power to break the knot of my infatuation.

When the cries had ceased, there came a scraping at the door, by which I knew Felipe was without[4]; and Olalla went and spoke to him--I know not what. With that exception, she stayed close beside me, now kneeling by my bed and fervently praying, now sitting with her eyes upon mine. So then, for these six hours I drank in her beauty, and silently perused the story in her face. I saw the golden coin hover on her breaths; I saw her eyes darken and brighten, and still speak no language but that of an unfathomable kindness; I saw the faultless face, and, through the robe, the lines of the faultless body[5]. Night came at last, and in the growing darkness of the chamber, the

---

[1] Like the twittering Felipe, Olalla appears to speak a birdlike language that indicates their hereditary closeness to the animal kingdom

[2] He suddenly realizes that Olalla, too, has the genetic animalism, and is tainted possibly to the point of inheriting her mother's madness and her brother's stupidity

[3] Until now he had thought that she was untouched by the distortion – that their biggest threat was the possibility of carrying the traits over to their children – but now he realizes that if he succeeds in seducing Olalla, he will be the next muleteer who sires her children and disappears

[4] Like a dog. While the mother is like a queen bee or a sluggish bear, Felipe is like a hyperactive, sometimes offensive, but dearly devoted sporting dog

[5] Wow... Stevenson is really pulling no punches with this uncommonly erotic bit of Victorian fiction. Aside from the sexuality indowed in the phrase, it also

sight of her slowly melted; but even then the touch of her smooth hand lingered in mine and talked with me. To lie thus in deadly weakness and drink in the traits of the beloved, is to reawake to love from whatever shock of disillusion. I reasoned with myself; and I shut my eyes on horrors, and again I was very bold to accept the worst. What mattered it, if that imperious sentiment survived; if her eyes still beckoned and attached me; if now, even as before, every fibre of my dull body yearned and turned to her? Late on in the night some strength revived in me, and I spoke:--

'Olalla,' I said, 'nothing matters; I ask nothing; I am content; I love you.'

She knelt down awhile and prayed, and I devoutly respected her devotions. The moon had begun to shine in upon one side of each of the three windows, and make a misty clearness in the room, by which I saw her indistinctly. When she rearose she made the sign of the cross.

'It is for me to speak,' she said, 'and for you to listen. I know; you can but guess. I prayed, how I prayed for you to leave this place. I begged it of you, and I know you would have granted me even this; or if not, O let me think so!'

'I love you,' I said.

'And yet you have lived in the world,' she said; after a pause, 'you are a man and wise; and I am but a child. Forgive me, if I seem to teach, who am as ignorant as the trees of the mountain[1]; but those who learn much do but skim the face of knowledge; they seize the laws, they conceive the dignity of the design--the horror of the living fact fades from their memory[2]. It is we who sit at home with evil who remember, I think, and are warned and pity. Go, rather, go now, and keep me in mind. So I shall have a life in the cherished places of your memory: a life as much my own, as that which I lead in this body.'

'I love you,' I said once more; and reaching out my weak hand, took hers, and carried it to my lips, and kissed it. Nor did she resist, but winced a little; and I could see her look upon me with a frown that was not unkindly, only sad and baffled. And then it seemed she made a call upon her resolution; plucked my hand towards her, herself at the same time leaning somewhat forward, and laid it on the beating of her heart. 'There,' she cried, 'you feel the very footfall of my life. It only moves for you; it is yours. But is it even mine? It is mine indeed to offer you, as I might take the coin from my neck, as I might break a live branch from a tree, and give it you. And yet not mine!

----

reminds us that the family are physically pure but mentally rotten. Like Hyde they represent the animal nature of man

[1] She falsely suggests that narrator – who is psycho-sexually root-bound – is wiser than her, but also interestingly relates to nature: like Felipe, she feels more related to the natural world than the human realm

[2] In other words, our narrator is not thinking with – pardon the expression – the right head. He is letting desire cloud discretion

I dwell, or I think I dwell (if I exist at all), somewhere apart, an impotent prisoner, and carried about and deafened by a mob that I disown[1]. This capsule, such as throbs against the sides of animals, knows you at a touch for its master; ay, it loves you![2] But my soul, does my soul? I think not; I know not, fearing to ask. Yet when you spoke to me your words were of the soul; it is of the soul that you ask--it is only from the soul that you would take me.'

'Olalla,' I said, 'the soul and the body are one[3], and mostly so in love. What the body chooses, the soul loves; where the body clings, the soul cleaves; body for body, soul to soul, they come together at God's signal; and the lower part (if we can call aught low) is only the footstool and foundation of the highest[4].'

'Have you,' she said, 'seen the portraits in the house of my fathers? Have you looked at my mother or at Felipe? Have your eyes never rested on that picture that hangs by your bed? She who sat for it died ages ago; and she did evil in her life. But, look-again: there is my hand to the least line, there are my eyes and my hair. What is mine, then, and what am I? If not a curve in this poor body of mine (which you love, and for the sake of which you dotingly dream that you love me) not a gesture that I can frame, not a tone of my voice, not any look from my eyes, no, not even now when I speak to him I love, but has belonged to others? Others, ages dead, have wooed other men with my eyes; other men have heard the pleading of the same voice

---

[1] She is governed by a hereditary destiny, but she struggles to resist its pull. This summons suggestions of Calvinist theology and simultaneously challenges it with the concept of free will struggling against predestination

[2] Her heart – also her emotions and lusts. Her animal nature desires union with the narrator (and, psychoanalytically, with her anima), but her spiritual nature repulses the hunger

[3] Olalla – and Jekyll – firmly disagree. Throughout this story Stevenson paints the body and soul as separate elements which can effect one another, but which can also run parallel to each other, un-touching and untouched

[4] Beautiful sermonizing that definitely has a Calvinist flavor and includes several biblical allusions – probably borrowed from Stevenson's parson grandfather and his own childhood ambition to be a powerfully spoken minister

that now sounds in your ears[1]. The hands of the dead are in my bosom[2]; they move me, they pluck me, they guide me[3]; I am a puppet at their command; and I but reinform[4] features and attributes that have long been laid aside from evil in the quiet of the grave[5]. Is it me you love, friend? or the race that made me?[6] The girl who does not know and cannot answer for the least portion of herself[7]? or the stream of which she is a transitory eddy, the tree of which she is the passing fruit? The race[8] exists; it is old, it is ever young, it

---

[1] A haunting, beautiful, and nonetheless disturbing sentence that deftly combines the eroticism of Eros (lust) and the revulsion of Thanatos (death). Olalla warns the narrator – as he shall learn from the peasant – that Olalla's genes have been used as bait to lure many indiscreet men to ruin and damnation, and that her soul – the thing that makes her "her" – is different from her face, that her face is the disguise of a demon, and has as much to do with who she is as an individual as the jewelry she has inherited

[2] The fact that she says "hands" – sensual agents of feeling – rather than "hearts" has an erotic feeling which is nonetheless darkened by the image of decayed fingers groping her breasts. Olalla attempts – as well as she can – to send a message: that a life of passion with her is also a life of necrophilia – she is already claimed by the dead, and although she is young and nubile, her marriage bed is a corpse's casket

[3] Mixtures of spiritual predestination and genetic inheritance – the power of a wicked family and the power of that family's genetics combine for a natural/supernatural two punch which seals Olalla's fate and that of any potential lover

[4] Re-embody, re-infuse, re-habitate

[5] Her family's sins are inherited, regenerating in the heart of each new offspring, and thereby remaining immortal until someone – like Olalla is attempting to do – puts aside the desires of their flesh and allows the race to age and die un-regenerated

[6] Olalla wisely intuits that the narrator is attracted to her – in a rather vampiric way – not because of who she is, but because of what she represents. As the anima to his animus, Olalla's congress offers the narrator a chance at personal reconciliation and wholeness which have been stunted by repression. He yearns to unite with this feminine Other as a means of curing his bifurcated self-identity (which is all the more obvious considering his latent bisexuality), but Olalla challenges him to look within himself rather than at her for a means of self-healing and self discovery. Emotionally and sexually root-bound, it is questionable whether he learns to release himself from the invisible residencia of his heart (where his own psychosexual identity has grown degenerate, stagnant, and feeble)

[7] Hard-core Calvinist theology coming from a devout Catholic

[8] Here she means the "race" of her family, but the phrase also doubles as a code for human nature – original sin

carries its eternal destiny in its bosom[1]; upon it, like waves upon the sea, individual succeeds to individual, mocked with a semblance of self- control, but they are nothing[2]. We speak of the soul, but the soul is in the race[3].'

'You fret against the common law,' I said. 'You rebel against the voice of God, which he has made so winning to convince, so imperious to command. Hear it, and how it speaks between us![4] Your hand clings to mine, your heart leaps at my touch, the unknown elements of which we are compounded awake and run together at a look[5]; the clay of the earth remembers its independent life and yearns to join us[6]; we are drawn together as the stars are turned about in space, or as the tides ebb and flow, by things older and greater than we ourselves[7].'

'Alas!' she said, 'what can I say to you? My fathers, eight hundred years ago, ruled all this province: they were wise, great, cunning, and cruel; they were a picked race of the Spanish; their flags led in war; the king called them his cousin; the people, when the rope was slung for them or when they returned and found their hovels smoking, blasphemed their name.

---

[1] More predestination rhetoric that Stevenson well knew in his Calvinist upbringing

[2] A highly cynical yet highly beautiful description of humanity – having the false assurance of uniqueness while being nothing more than another twist of the same element, and one which will shortly melt in death and revive in a new form, but always made of the same material with the same strengths and weaknesses

[3] Olalla argues that the aspirations of the human spirit are grafted into their inherited weaknesses which are passed down from age to age, and is inseparable from its destiny

[4] She believes that they instinctively know that this is a bad idea and that they should obey instinct (spirit) rather than impulse (flesh)

[5] Symbolizing the natural magnetism between the anima and the animus, the two characters are hopelessly lured towards one another due to the dynamic resonance of their beings – like the poles of magnets. But Olalla warns that this is the attraction of the flesh, not the spirit, and that wisdom must prevail over animalistic lust and metaphysical attraction

[6] A reference to the Bible story of Adam, the first man, who has made out of clay and then breathed into life by the breath of God. Olalla suggests that their baser nature – the clay they come from – is leading them into temptation, but the divine breath that animates them should lead them away from their animal instincts towards their higher calling

[7] What a beautiful line – it suggests the Nature that flows through the human essence and towards which Olalla's family is drawn and identifies. Lovecraft surely resonated with the idea when he read this, with its suggestion of infinite, incomprehensible cosmic forces which dictate human destinies. Really lovely writing

Presently a change began. Man has risen; if he has sprung from the brutes[1], he can descend again to the same level[2]. The breath of weariness blew on their humanity and the cords relaxed; they began to go down; their minds fell on sleep, their passions awoke in gusts, heady and senseless like the wind in the gutters of the mountains; beauty was still handed down, but no longer the guiding wit nor the human heart[3]; the seed passed on, it was wrapped in flesh, the flesh covered the bones, but they were the bones and the flesh of brutes, and their mind was as the mind of flies. I speak to you as I dare; but you have seen for yourself how the wheel has gone backward with my doomed race. I stand, as it were, upon a little rising ground in this desperate descent[4], and see both before and behind, both what we have lost and to what we are condemned to go farther downward. And shall I--I that dwell apart in the house of the dead, my body, loathing its ways--shall I repeat the spell[5]? Shall I bind another spirit, reluctant as my own, into this bewitched and tempest-broken tenement that I now suffer in? Shall I hand down this cursed vessel of humanity, charge it with fresh life as with fresh poison[6], and dash it, like a fire, in the faces of posterity? But my vow has been given; the race shall cease from off the earth. At this hour my brother is making ready; his foot will soon be on the stair; and you will go with him and pass out of my sight for ever. Think of me sometimes as one to whom the lesson of life was very harshly told, but who heard it with courage; as

---

[1] An atypical assertion of Darwinian evolution from a devout Catholic. Of course, the setting predates Darwin, and the reference may be more towards the idea that antediluvian mankind was vicious and animalistic before the Great Flood, but Stevenson is also a sloppy plot writer, and I'm inclined to imagine that Olalla is referencing the same evolutionary theories that led to Hyde's characterization as "ape-like" and "troglodytic"

[2] Stevenson asserts that it is only through challenges, hard work, self-improvement, and desire that mankind prevents itself from descending back to our pre-evolved state – that our progress is not like building a tower that perpetually rises, but like maintaining a house which must have rotten materials removed and replaced to prevent decay

[3] Stevenson argues in favor of the idea that the body is the vessel of the soul: the fleshy vehicle is passed down from generation to generation, untouched, but the spirit is devolved and rotten, growing sicker with each epoch, so that ultimately the shell is clean and pretty but the soul is black and volatile

[4] Olalla suggests that she is a rare, but impermanent break from the downward degeneration of her race – that she is sane enough to understand the past and foresee the future – but that she is a rare variation that will probably not be replicated in the future

[5] Produce children who will carry on the degeneration to another century

[6] As yet, she is the last link in the chain, and her death will put her curse to rest, but if she has children, then the poison is freshly spread

one who loved you indeed, but who hated herself so deeply that her love was hateful to her; as one who sent you away and yet would have longed to keep you for ever; who had no dearer hope than to forget you, and no greater fear than to be forgotten.'

She had drawn towards the door as she spoke, her rich voice sounding softer and farther away; and with the last word she was gone, and I lay alone in the moonlit chamber. What I might have done had not I lain bound by my extreme weakness, I know not; but as it was there fell upon me a great and blank despair. It was not long before there shone in at the door the ruddy glimmer of a lantern, and Felipe coming, charged me without a word upon his shoulders, and carried me down to the great gate, where the cart was waiting. In the moonlight the hills stood out sharply, as if they were of cardboard; on the glimmering surface of the plateau, and from among the low trees which swung together and sparkled in the wind, the great black cube of the residencia stood out bulkily, its mass only broken by three dimly lighted windows in the northern front above the gate. They were Olalla's windows, and as the cart jolted onwards I kept my eyes fixed upon them till, where the road dipped into a valley, they were lost to my view forever. Felipe walked in silence beside the shafts, but from time to time he would cheek the mule and seem to look back upon me; and at length drew quite near and laid his hand upon my head. There was such kindness in the touch, and such a simplicity, as of the brutes, that tears broke from me like the bursting of an artery[1].

'Felipe,' I said, 'take me where they will ask no questions.'

He said never a word, but he turned his mule about, end for end, retraced some part of the way we had gone, and, striking into another path, led me to the mountain village, which was, as we say in Scotland[2], the kirkton[3] of that thinly peopled district. Some broken memories dwell in my mind of the day breaking over the plain, of the cart stopping, of arms that helped me down, of a bare room into which I was carried, and of a swoon that fell upon me like sleep.

---

[1] More blood imagery. Blood represents life and humanity, hence the family are starved of it – literally in the sense that they are inbred and have no deviation in the content of their genetic makeup, or "family blood." Tears – something foreign to the Senora – are as humanizing and spiritual as the blood that pulses through his own arteries, and are used as a symbol of his humanness in contrast to the Senora's cold, emotional lethargy

[2] Throughout the story there are hints that the narrator is Scottish in spite of his description as English (they are two different things, to readers who think that the word describes residents of the U.K. The correct collective term for these nationals is "British")

[3] Chruch-town – a town that hosts the church in a rural district. A county seat would be the American equivalent to this Scottish term

The next day and the days following the old priest was often at my side with his snuff-box and prayer book, and after a while, when I began to pick up strength, he told me that I was now on a fair way to recovery, and must as soon as possible hurry my departure; whereupon, without naming any reason, he took snuff and looked at me sideways. I did not affect ignorance; I knew he must have seen Olalla. 'Sir,' said I, 'you know that I do not ask in wantonness[1]. What of that family?'

He said they were very unfortunate; that it seemed a declining race, and that they were very poor and had been much neglected.

'But she has not,' I said. 'Thanks, doubtless, to yourself, she is instructed and wise beyond the use[2] of women.'

'Yes,' he said; 'the Senorita is well-informed. But the family has been neglected.'

'The mother?' I queried.

'Yes, the mother too,' said the Padre, taking snuff. 'But Felipe is a well-intentioned lad.'

'The mother is odd[3]?' I asked.

'Very odd,' replied the priest.

'I think, sir, we beat about the bush,' said I. 'You must know more of my affairs than you allow. You must know my curiosity to be justified on many grounds. Will you not be frank with me?'

'My son,' said the old gentleman, 'I will be very frank with you on matters within my competence; on those of which I know nothing it does not require much discretion to be silent. I will not fence with you, I take your meaning perfectly; and what can I say, but that we are all in God's hands, and that His ways are not as our ways? I have even advised with my superiors in the church, but they, too, were dumb[4]. It is a great mystery.'

'Is she mad?' I asked.

'I will answer you according to my belief. She is not,' returned the Padre, 'or she was not. When she was young--God help me, I fear I neglected that wild lamb--she was surely sane; and yet, although it did not run to such heights, the same strain was already notable; it had been so before her in her father, ay, and before him, and this inclined me, perhaps, to think too lightly of it. But these things go on growing, not only in the individual but in the race.'

---

[1] With an immoral intent

[2] The regular tendency – she is better educated than most women. Although a sexist element could be read into his surprise, it is nonetheless a realistic reaction to so well-read a woman in early 19th century Spain, and Olalla is genuinely a phenomenon for her time

[3] Meaning mentally afflicted – not just "weird"

[4] Silent on the matter

'When she was young,' I began, and my voice failed me for a moment, and it was only with a great effort that I was able to add, 'was she like Olalla?'

'Now God forbid!' exclaimed the Padre. 'God forbid that any man should think so slightingly[1] of my favourite penitent[2]. No, no; the Senorita (but for her beauty, which I wish most honestly she had less of) has not a hair's resemblance to what her mother was at the same age. I could not bear to have you think so; though, Heaven knows, it were, perhaps, better that you should[3].'

At this, I raised myself in bed, and opened my heart to the old man; telling him of our love and of her decision, owning my own horrors, my own passing fancies, but telling him that these were at an end; and with something more than a purely formal submission, appealing to his judgment.

He heard me very patiently and without surprise; and when I had done, he sat for some time silent. Then he began: 'The church,' and instantly broke off again to apologise. 'I had forgotten, my child, that you were not a Christian[4],' said he. 'And indeed, upon a point so highly unusual, even the church can scarce be said to have decided. But would you have my opinion? The Senorita is, in a matter of this kind, the best judge; I would accept her judgment.'

On the back of that he went away, nor was he thenceforward so assiduous[5] in his visits; indeed, even when I began to get about again, he plainly feared and deprecated my society[6], not as in distaste but much as a man might be disposed to flee from the riddling sphynx[7]. The villagers, too, avoided me; they were unwilling to be my guides upon the mountain. I thought they looked at me askance, and I made sure that the more superstitious crossed themselves on my approach. At first I set this down to

---

[1] Have such a demeaning opinion of

[2] A Catholic who regularly confesses and attends Mass

[3] Because it would drive him away – the fear that Olalla is genetically doomed to develop the Senora's lethargic madness

[4] Again, the narrator is hinted at being a Calvinist, otherwise he shares Stevenson's atheism

[5] In the future he was never as attentive as he was on this particular visit

[6] "Disliked my company"

[7] The sphynx asked questions that led men to death (to pass by it without being killed, one must correctly answer its enigmatic riddles), in the same way that the narrator's curiosity is opening up boxes that the priest would rather leave closed for the sake of his conscience, sanity, and peace

my heretical opinions[1]; but it began at length to dawn upon me that if I was thus redoubted[2] it was because I had stayed at the residencia. All men despise the savage notions[3] of such peasantry; and yet I was conscious of a chill shadow that seemed to fall and dwell upon my love. It did not conquer, but I may not deify that it restrained my ardour.

Some miles westward of the village there was a gap in the sierra[4], from which the eye plunged direct upon the residencia; and thither it became my daily habit to repair. A wood crowned the summit; and just where the pathway issued from its fringes, it was overhung by a considerable shelf of rock, and that, in its turn, was surmounted by a crucifix of the size of life and more than usually painful in design[5]. This was my perch; thence, day after day, I looked down upon the plateau, and the great old house, and could see Felipe, no bigger than a fly, going to and fro about the garden. Sometimes mists would draw across the view, and be broken up again by mountain winds; sometimes the plain slumbered below me in unbroken sunshine; it would sometimes be all blotted out by rain[6]. This distant post, these interrupted sights of the place where my life had been so strangely changed, suited the indecision of my humour. I passed whole days there, debating with myself the various elements of our position; now leaning to the suggestions of love, now giving an ear to prudence, and in the end halting irresolute between the two.

One day, as I was sitting on my rock, there came by that way a somewhat gaunt peasant wrapped in a mantle[7]. He was a stranger, and plainly did not know me even by repute; for, instead of keeping the other side, he drew near and sat down beside me, and we had soon fallen in talk. Among other things he told me he had been a muleteer, and in former years had much frequented these mountains; later on, he had followed the army with his

---

[1] His Calvinism (or potentially his atheism – it isn't made abundantly clear whether he is one or the other; either were considered "un-Christian" by 19th century Spanish Catholics)

[2] Resisted, kept at arm's length

[3] That is, their brutal superstitions which can unfairly tarnish a reputation (for instance – germane to this story – that a redhead could be shunned as a vampire for no more rational reason than their hair color)

[4] The mountains

[5] It is large enough to actually crucify a man on, and is painstakingly detailed in its ornamentation

[6] The residencia is lost amongst nature, and – more importantly – so too are its inmates. They wander aimlessly without ambition, thought, or will, and are pushed around by nature like animals living in the fields or birds nesting in the trees: they make no changes in their habits and are at the mercy of nature's whims (just as their minds are at the mercy of nature's whims)

[7] A garment like a cloak that wraps around the body for warmth

mules, had realised a competence[1], and was now living retired with his family.

'Do you know that house?' I inquired, at last, pointing to the residencia, for I readily wearied of any talk that kept me from the thought of Olalla.

He looked at me darkly and crossed himself[2].

'Too well,' he said, 'it was there that one of my comrades sold himself to Satan[3]; the Virgin shield us from temptations! He has paid the price; he is now burning in the reddest place in Hell!'

A fear came upon me; I could answer nothing; and presently the man resumed, as if to himself: 'Yes,' he said, 'O yes, I know it. I have passed its doors. There was snow upon the pass, the wind was driving it; sure enough there was death that night upon the mountains, but there was worse beside the hearth. I took him by the arm, Senor, and dragged him to the gate; I conjured him, by all he loved and respected, to go forth with me[4]; I went on my knees before him in the snow; and I could see he was moved by my entreaty. And just then she came out on the gallery, and called him by his name; and he turned, and there was she standing with a lamp in her hand and smiling on him to come back. I cried out aloud to God, and threw my arms about him, but he put me by, and left me alone. He had made his choice; God help us. I would pray for him, but to what end? there are sins that not even the Pope can loose[5].'

'And your friend,' I asked, 'what became of him?'

'Nay, God knows,' said the muleteer. 'If all be true that we hear, his end was like his sin, a thing to raise the hair.'

'Do you mean that he was killed?' I asked.

'Sure enough, he was killed,' returned the man. 'But how? Ay, how? But these are things that it is sin to speak of.'

'The people of that house . . . ' I began.

But he interrupted me with a savage outburst. 'The people?' he cried. 'What people? There are neither men nor women in that house of Satan's! What? have you lived here so long, and never heard?' And here he put his mouth to my ear and whispered, as if even the fowls of the mountain might have over-heard and been stricken with horror.

---

[1] Had been given a pension, probably from the army for services rendered

[2] A habit eagerly demonstrated by Stoker in *Dracula* and Blackwood in *The Willows,* crossing oneself is seen by some Catholics as a means of warding off bad luck, inviting the protection of God, and defending against the evil eye

[3] The muleteer who sired Olalla with the Senora

[4] Like the narrator, the muleteer was willing to abandon everything he "loved and respected" – one imagines a wife back home, the laws of the Church, and his own reputation – for the company of such a woman

[5] Forgive, break of their power

What he told me was not true, nor was it even original; being, indeed, but a new edition, vamped up again by village ignorance and superstition, of stories nearly as ancient as the race of man. It was rather the application that appalled me. In the old days, he said, the church would have burned out that nest of basilisks[1]; but the arm of the church was now shortened[2]; his friend Miguel had been unpunished by the hands of men, and left to the more awful judgment of an offended God. This was wrong; but it should be so no more. The Padre was sunk in age; he was even bewitched himself; but the eyes of his flock were now awake to their own danger; and some day--ay, and before long--the smoke of that house should go up to heaven[3].

He left me filled with horror and fear. Which way to turn I knew not; whether first to warn the Padre, or to carry my ill-news direct to the threatened inhabitants of the residencia. Fate was to decide for me; for, while I was still hesitating, I beheld the veiled figure of a woman drawing near to me up the pathway. No veil could deceive my penetration[4]; by every line and every movement I recognised Olalla; and keeping hidden behind a corner of the rock, I suffered her[5] to gain the summit. Then I came forward. She knew me and paused, but did not speak; I, too, remained silent; and we continued for some time to gaze upon each other with a passionate sadness.

'I thought you had gone,' she said at length. 'It is all that you can do for me--to go. It is all I ever asked of you. And you still stay. But do you know, that every day heaps up the peril of death, not only on your head, but on ours? A report has gone about the mountain; it is thought you love me, and the people will not suffer it[6].'

I saw she was already informed of her danger, and I rejoiced at it. 'Olalla,' I said, 'I am ready to go this day, this very hour, but not alone.'

She stepped aside and knelt down before the crucifix to pray, and I stood by and looked now at her and now at the object of her adoration, now at the

---

[1] A legendary repitile – half rooster half serpent – said to be a prince of all lizards and serpents, with breath that killed and a glance that stopped the heart. A word that could be used interchangeably with "demons" or "vipers"

[2] In other words, they could not drag them to the Inquisition to be tried for witchcraft

[3] So apparently the villagers are planning to attack and burn the residencia in the near future. It is with such an air of coming doom that Stevenson begins to close this story. The threat, however, as the narrator's concern suggests, is very real and not hyperbole

[4] Ability to see

[5] Allowed

[6] Threatened with the possibility that the family line might continue (if the narrator were to marry and breed with Olalla), the peasantry are at the point of revolt and are threatening violence against the family and the narrator himself – should he follow through on his attraction

living figure of the penitent, and now at the ghastly, daubed countenance[1], the painted wounds, and the projected ribs[2] of the image. The silence was only broken by the wailing of some large birds[3] that circled sidelong, as if in surprise or alarm, about the summit of the hills. Presently Olalla rose again, turned towards me, raised her veil, and, still leaning with one hand on the shaft of the crucifix[4], looked upon me with a pale and sorrowful countenance.

'I have laid my hand upon the cross,' she said. 'The Padre says you are no Christian; but look up for a moment with my eyes, and behold the face of the Man of Sorrows[5]. We are all such as He was--the inheritors of sin[6]; we must all bear and expiate[7] a past which was not ours[8]; there is in all of us-- ay, even in me--a sparkle of the divine[9]. Like Him, we must endure for a little while, until morning returns bringing peace. Suffer me to pass on upon

---

[1] Of the Christ figure on the cross – his face is accordingly mutilated by thorns and whiplashes and daubed in blood

[2] Some Catholic crucifixes can be overwhelmingly gruesome, and while I take this to mean that the ribcage is jutting out due to the angle of the chest, Stevenson may literally be describing a crucifix where the figure's ribs are broken and the bones are protruding from the torn flesh

[3] There is a sad parallelism here, where we are reminded of Felipe, whose songs were birdlike

[4] Forming an unbreakable connection between Olalla the sensual woman and the moral-driven faith that is her only connection to peace of mind (and the ultimate salvation of her family: that she refuse to procreate and let her family line die with her)

[5] Isaiah 53:3 describes what many interpret as the Messiah to be a man of sorrows, despised and hated: "He was despised and rejected by mankind, a man of suffering, and familiar with pain. Like one from whom people hide their faces he was despised, and we held him in low esteem"

[6] Christ has also been called the Son of Adam since he is considered to have been both fully human and fully God, and – as a son of Adam – he inherited the legacy of sin that all humans are considered to have inherited, however, as a Son of God, he was sinless, and paid for the sins of man with His life

[7] Pay for – make amends for

[8] Like Christ who suffered and died to ameliorate the sins of man, Olalla is suffering to pay off the sins of her family, and like Christ she suffers alone

[9] Unlike her family members who relish their animal nature, Olalla clings to her divinity – her human spirit with its aspirations, nobler inclinations, and good will – and focuses all of her energy on preserving her soul and redeeming her family – something she could not accomplish with the narrator's carnal desires in her life

my way alone[1]; it is thus that I shall be least lonely, counting for my friend Him who is the friend of all the distressed; it is thus that I shall be the most happy, having taken my farewell of earthly happiness, and willingly accepted sorrow for my portion.'

I looked at the face of the crucifix, and, though I was no friend to images[2], and despised that imitative and grimacing art of which it was a rude example, some sense of what the thing implied was carried home to my intelligence. The face looked down upon me with a painful and deadly contraction; but the rays of a glory[3] encircled it, and reminded me that the sacrifice was voluntary[4]. It stood there, crowning the rock, as it still stands on so many highway sides, vainly preaching to passers-by[5], an emblem of sad and noble truths; that pleasure is not an end, but an accident; that pain is the choice of the magnanimous; that it is best to suffer all things and do well. [6]I turned and went down the mountain in silence; and when I looked back for the last time before the wood closed about my path, I saw Olalla still leaning on the crucifix[7].

---

[1] Suggestive of Christ's Via Dolorosa, or the "Way of Suffering" – his walk to the crucifixion site. She is on a Way of Suffering herself, and like Christ, she must walk alone

[2] That is, to religious icons – venerated by Catholics and loathed by Calvinists. This could just as much a result of Calvinism as atheism (again, although we cannot be sure, there are suggestions that the narrator had a Calvinist upbringing, and may or may not still be a Calvinist)

[3] A supernatural shining, often called a halo (though depicted as a gold ring, a halo is really meant to be a globe of light encapsulating and emanating from the head of a holy person)

[4] That is, that Christ chose to die – He was not forced to. Likewise, Olalla is choosing to suffer alone – she is not being forced to

[5] In the same way, Olalla preaches vainly to the narrator, a passerby. Perhaps after this last encounter her words struck home, but throughout the story Olalla has not been able to truly reason with her star-struck suitor. Like the crucifix, Olalla is a visual symbol of suffering – a lesson to those who cross her path on the virtues of sacrifice, the pains of life, and the promise of redemption

[6] A lovely bit of philosophy that cuts down the Senora's lifestyle as being vain and pointless – pleasure, Stevenson bemoans, is an accident, a freak of circumstance, not a guaranteed fact of existence, and suffering is far too often the more common denominator of human life, so those that bear suffering well are more blessed and venerable than those that wallow in their unmerited contentment

[7] Almost a part of it, herself, Olalla clings to the symbol of divine suffering, merging her identity with that of the crucified savior. To a passerby she would appear to be as much a symbol of divine suffering as the crucifix itself

"OLALLA" demonstrates a level of theatrical control for which Stevenson deserves far more credit for than he has gotten. The scene – told in third-person – where the Senora seduces the muleteer from her doorway, luring him to an undescribed death would have been shown in full color by Bram Stoker. But Stevenson restrains himself. He also prevents us from fully understanding either the nature of the family's sins (which certainly include witchcraft or Satanism and some form of supernatural or ritualistic vampirism) or the character of their curse. They are called basilisks – a form of Satanic dragon – and are suggested to consume human blood if not flesh. Possibly vampires, possibly werewolves (many sources cite it as such, especially considering Felipe's doglike characterization and the Senora's sleepy-old-bitch-like behavior), possibly witches, possibly (and Stevenson so artfully offers this natural solution) nothing more than a band of mentally degenerated inbreds with passionate psychosis and violent tendencies; but whatever their nature, the danger is never explicated, and wisely so. The story has several elements that merit individual attention: its sexuality, its psychology, its vampirism, and its philosophy.

II.

Regarding its sexuality, "Olalla" is perhaps the most erotic piece of mainstream prose that I have read from the Victorian era. Other than banned erotica and black-market smut, nothing comes closer to describing orgasms, masturbation, homoerotic lust, or sadomasochism than the preceding story. It is lush with descriptions of physical desire and the emotions that surround it, in particular the way that two people can – without touching or even speaking – make love with their eyes. There is, of course, also the very notable element of homoeroticism and queering that occurs here as in other previous examples of the vampire genre (Coleridge's unfinished "Christabel" and Le Fanu's masterful *Carmilla* being exemplars). The relationship between the narrator and Felipe is very difficult to explain away as the "writing of a different age." The way that he enjoys watching the "beautiful" boy (which "delighted [his] eye"), the powerful emotions that surround his domination of the lad, the undescribed private encounter between the two where the narrator tries to pleasure his friend into letting him court Olalla, and the way that Felipe at first objectifies the narrator by petting him sensually, filling him with "an embarrassment for which I was ashamed," are just a few of the most notable homoerotic elements in their relationship, which ultimately ends in a BDSM power dynamic. Felipe, though male, is coded as very feminine: natural, limber, sensuous, unrestrained, impulsive, lusty, flirtatious, reveling in submissive, obsessed with approval, and devoted to his master's pleasure. Olalla, too, and her mother have gender-bending characterizations. Both lean towards androgyny, but Olalla especially, with her deep voice, sturdy hands, manly body strength, and (for its time) masculine syllabus of education (philosophy, metaphysics, and religion). Her mother, too, is sexually aggressive – rapacious even – violent, and powerful when she is not drunk on contentment. The encounters between the two main characters are virtually orgasmic, with eloquent descriptions of physical and emotional lust and language which unquestionably describes symbolic intercourse. The reason for the dynamic sexual magnetism between the two segues neatly into the next major theme: psychoanalytical symbolism.

III.

Like "Jekyll and Hyde," which is founded in the proto-Freudian interplay between the Id, Ego, and Super-Ego, the powerful affinity between the androgynous Olalla and her bisexual suitor suggests Jung's theory of the anima (female social identity) and the animus (male social identity). According to Jung, neither is wholly male or female, in fact they are more like the yin and yang – leaning in one direction, but asexual and genderless. A man whose anima is dissociated from his Ego (viz., a macho who represses his inborn femininity) will have tendencies towards violence, machismo, and sexual overcompensation. The narrator – a shell-shocked atheist who finds the need to dominate and oppress the carefree, sexually ambiguous Felipe (*armchair psychology session*: he is doing to Felipe what others have done to him because he is afraid of the feelings that Felipe rises in him, either directly or vicariously) – allows little femininity into his life before Olalla enters in. She represents his lost anima – the female side of his Ego which has been beaten down by society, war, and religion – and he is so magnetized by her because reconciliation with her has seismic implications for his psycho-spiritual health.

IV.

This leads nicely into our third major theme, vampirism, because as many commentators have agreed, the vampires in this story are not just members of Olalla's family. The narrator himself – with all of his blood-heavy language – is a psycho-spiritual vampire who feeds off of Olalla (a representation of the feminine energy that he has been starved of) and desires her more as an object to possess and feed from than as an equal partner (Olalla notes this keenly in her eloquent rebuff of his attention: "is it me that you love, friend, or the race that made me?"). Vampires symbolically feed off of that which they have removed themselves from – life, love, goodness, socialization – and the bellicose, domineering, atheistic narrator hopes to gorge himself on the peaceful, nurturing, pious Olalla, just as her mother – equally starved – feeds (literally and metaphorically) on the vigorous, powerful, and passionate.

V.

And now we transition from this thought into our final framing concept: the philosophical meaning of "Olalla." Like so many of Stevenson's tales, it has a theological center: Olalla chooses to suffer in isolation in order to redeem her family's sins by forgoing the option of living a normal human life and denying her human desires. In this way she is a Christ-figure, underscored rather heavily by the final scene of her clinging to the crucifix just as she clings to the identity of "The Man of Sorrows." Like Christ, she denies herself a normal life, isolates herself from society, and thereby hopes to end the curse (cf. the Fall of Man) that plagues her family (by not procreating and thus renewing the cycle of degeneration). Her mother and Felipe languish in self-pleasure. Their sin is both spiritual and intellectual: they do not challenge their stupefying contentment, but rather bathe in it: their minds, souls, and bodies meet no conflicting forces, and are thus allowed to remain the same, generation after generation, melting with each birth into a less evolved race: the fleshy vehicle is passed down from generation to generation, untouched, but the spirit is devolved and rotten, growing sicker with each epoch, so that ultimately the shell is clean and pretty but the soul is black and volatile. Stevenson asserts that it is only through challenges, hard work, self-improvement, and desire that mankind prevents itself from descending back to our pre-evolved state – that our progress is not like building a tower that perpetually rises, but like maintaining a house which must have rotten materials removed and replaced to prevent decay. Ultimately, Olalla acts as a crucifix herself to the narrator, teaching him by her example to broaden himself, deny his lusts, sacrifice his comforts, and open his heart to broader horizons. Emotionally and sexually root-bound, it is questionable whether he learns to release himself from the invisible residencia of his heart (where his own psychosexual identity has grown degenerate, stagnant, and feeble), or if Olalla – like the crucifix on which she casts her identity as suffering savior – is "vainly preaching to [a passer-by], an emblem of sad and noble truths."

EVEN outside of supernatural fiction circles, "The Bottle Imp" is one of Stevenson's most famous short stories. Analogous in reputation to Jacobs' "The Monkey's Paw," Irving's "The Devil and Tom Walker," Bierce's "Occurrence at Owl Creek Bridge," London's "To Build a Fire," and O. Henry's "The Gift of the Magi," it is renowned for its plot twists, irony, tension, drama, romance, and mystery. Like "Monkey's Paw," "Tom Walker," and "Owl Creek Bridge," the horror derives most strictly from the terrifying maxim "be careful what you wish for," from the fear that our greed may harm or alienate us from those we love, and from the deep pathos we experience for the characters and their seemingly impossible attempt to escape their destiny to be separated by damnation. There is certain cosmic wink to be seen in this story which suggests that the diabolical luck of Napoleon and Alexander the Great might be capable of trickling down to aimless drunks and daydreaming islanders – as if the power with which we invest the great figures of history is little more impressive than hand-me-down clothes or second-hand cars with astronomical mileage. The profundity of human awe and might has been so whittled down throughout the ages that it now sits in the hands of the poor and humble – only a few drops of which are left to infuse their souls with that immortal grandiosity. And yet, by sipping from the goblet of power there comes a dark responsibility, for by passing it down the line, you ensure that the last drop – a drop of poison – will damn a mortal soul. The weight that crushes Keawe during the story is not just the fear of his own damnation, nor the horror at Kokua's self-sacrifice, but a spiritual horror at his participation in a system of power which is built on the premise of participating in the misery of others – power is purchased, and has for centuries been purchased, with the understanding that someone at the end of the line must pay the penalty for the misrule of the mighty. It is a form of trickledown economics, yet the last drop of the trickle is not enough to quench the tongue of the man in hell.

The Bottle Imp
{1891}

Note.—Any student of that very unliterary product, the English drama of the early part of the century, will here recognise the name and the root idea of a piece once rendered popular by the redoubtable O. Smith. The root idea is there and identical, and yet I hope I have made it a new thing. And the fact that the tale has been designed and written for a Polynesian audience may lend it some extraneous interest nearer home.—R. L. S.

THERE was a man of the Island of Hawaii, whom I shall call Keawe; for the truth is, he still lives, and his name must be kept secret; but the place of his birth was not far from Honaunau, where the bones of Keawe the Great lie hidden in a cave. This man was poor, brave, and active; he could read and write like a schoolmaster; he was a first-rate mariner besides, sailed for some time in the island steamers, and steered a whaleboat on the Hamakua coast. At length it came in Keawe's mind to have a sight of the great world and foreign cities, and he shipped on a vessel bound to San Francisco.

This is a fine town, with a fine harbour, and rich people uncountable; and, in particular, there is one hill which is covered with palaces. Upon this hill Keawe was one day taking a walk with his pocket full of money, viewing the great houses upon either hand with pleasure, "What fine houses these are!" he was thinking, "and how happy must those people be who dwell in them, and take no care for the morrow!" The thought was in his mind when he came abreast of a house that was smaller than some others, but all finished and beautified like a toy; the steps of that house shone like silver, and the borders of the garden bloomed like garlands, and the windows were bright like diamond; and Keawe stopped and wondered at the excellence of all he saw. So stopping, he was aware of a man that looked forth upon him through a window so clear that Keawe could see him as you see a fish in a pool upon the reef. The man was elderly, with a bald head and a black beard; and his face was heavy with sorrow, and he bitterly sighed. And the truth of it is, that as Keawe looked in upon the man, and the man looked out upon Keawe, each envied the other.

All of a sudden, the man smiled and nodded, and beckoned Keawe to enter, and met him at the door of the house.

"This is a fine house of mine," said the man, and bitterly sighed. "Would you not care to view the chambers?"

So he led Keawe all over it, from the cellar to the roof, and there was nothing there that was not perfect of its kind, and Keawe was astonished.

"Truly," said Keawe, "this is a beautiful house; if I lived in the like of it, I should be laughing all day long. How comes it, then, that you should be sighing?"

"There is no reason," said the man, "why you should not have a house in all points similar to this, and finer, if you wish. You have some money, I suppose?"

"I have fifty dollars," said Keawe; "but a house like this will cost more than fifty dollars."

The man made a computation. "I am sorry you have no more," said he, "for it may raise you trouble in the future; but it shall be yours at fifty dollars."

"The house?" asked Keawe.

"No, not the house," replied the man; "but the bottle. For, I must tell you, although I appear to you so rich and fortunate, all my fortune, and this house itself and its garden, came out of a bottle not much bigger than a pint. This is it."

And he opened a lockfast place, and took out a round-bellied bottle with a long neck; the glass of it was white like milk, with changing rainbow colours in the grain. Withinsides something obscurely moved, like a shadow and a fire.

"This is the bottle," said the man; and, when Keawe laughed, "You do not believe me?" he added. "Try, then, for yourself. See if you can break it."

So Keawe took the bottle up and dashed it on the floor till he was weary; but it jumped on the floor like a child's ball, and was not injured.

"This is a strange thing," said Keawe. "For by the touch of it, as well as by the look, the bottle should be of glass."

"Of glass it is," replied the man, sighing more heavily than ever; "but the glass of it was tempered in the flames of hell. An imp lives in it, and that is the shadow we behold there moving: or so I suppose. If any man buy this bottle the imp is at his command; all that he desires—love, fame, money, houses like this house, ay, or a city like this city—all are his at the word uttered. Napoleon had this bottle, and by it he grew to be the king of the world; but he sold it at the last, and fell. Captain Cook had this bottle, and by it he found his way to so many islands; but he, too, sold it, and was slain upon Hawaii. For, once it is sold, the power goes and the protection; and unless a man remain content with what he has, ill will befall him."

"And yet you talk of selling it yourself?" Keawe said.

"I have all I wish, and I am growing elderly," replied the man. "There is one thing the imp cannot do—he cannot prolong life; and, it would not be fair to conceal from you, there is a drawback to the bottle; for if a man die before he sells it, he must burn in hell forever."

"To be sure, that is a drawback and no mistake," cried Keawe. "I would not meddle with the thing. I can do without a house, thank God; but there is one thing I could not be doing with one particle, and that is to be damned."

"Dear me, you must not run away with things," returned the man. "All you have to do is to use the power of the imp in moderation, and then sell it to someone else, as I do to you, and finish your life in comfort."

"Well, I observe two things," said Keawe. "All the time you keep sighing like a maid in love, that is one; and, for the other, you sell this bottle very cheap."

"I have told you already why I sigh," said the man. "It is because I fear my health is breaking up; and, as you said yourself, to die and go to the devil is a pity for anyone. As for why I sell so cheap, I must explain to you there is a peculiarity about the bottle. Long ago, when the devil brought it first upon earth, it was extremely expensive, and was sold first of all to Prester John for many millions of dollars; but it cannot be sold at all, unless sold at a loss. If you sell it for as much as you paid for it, back it comes to you again like a homing pigeon. It follows that the price has kept falling in these centuries, and the bottle is now remarkably cheap. I bought it myself from one of my great neighbours on this hill, and the price I paid was only ninety dollars. I could sell it for as high as eighty-nine dollars and ninety-nine cents, but not a penny dearer, or back the thing must come to me. Now, about this there are two bothers. First, when you offer a bottle so singular for eighty odd dollars, people suppose you to be jesting. And second—but there is no hurry about that—and I need not go into it. Only remember it must be coined money that you sell it for."

"How am I to know that this is all true?" asked Keawe.

"Some of it you can try at once," replied the man. "Give me your fifty dollars, take the bottle, and wish your fifty dollars back into your pocket. If that does not happen, I pledge you my honour I will cry off the bargain and restore your money."

"You are not deceiving me?" said Keawe.

The man bound himself with a great oath.

"Well, I will risk that much," said Keawe, "for that can do no harm." And he paid over his money to the man, and the man handed him the bottle.

"Imp of the bottle," said Keawe, "I want my fifty dollars back." And sure enough he had scarce said the word before his pocket was as heavy as ever.

"To be sure this is a wonderful bottle," said Keawe.

"And now good-morning to you, my fine fellow, and the devil go with you for me!" said the man.

"Hold on," said Keawe, "I don't want any more of this fun. Here, take your bottle back."

"You have bought it for less than I paid for it," replied the man, rubbing his hands. "It is yours now; and, for my part, I am only concerned to see the back of you." And with that he rang for his Chinese servant, and had Keawe shown out of the house.

Now, when Keawe was in the street, with the bottle under his arm, he began to think. "If all is true about this bottle, I may have made a losing bargain," thinks he. "But perhaps the man was only fooling me." The first thing he did was to count his money; the sum was exact—forty-nine dollars American money, and one Chili piece. "That looks like the truth," said Keawe. "Now I will try another part."

The streets in that part of the city were as clean as a ship's decks, and though it was noon, there were no passengers. Keawe set the bottle in the gutter and walked away. Twice he looked back, and there was the milky, round-bellied bottle where he left it. A third time he looked back, and turned a corner; but he had scarce done so, when something knocked upon his elbow, and behold! it was the long neck sticking up; and as for the round belly, it was jammed into the pocket of his pilot-coat.

"And that looks like the truth," said Keawe.

The next thing he did was to buy a cork-screw in a shop, and go apart into a secret place in the fields. And there he tried to draw the cork, but as often as he put the screw in, out it came again, and the cork as whole as ever.

"This is some new sort of cork," said Keawe, and all at once he began to shake and sweat, for he was afraid of that bottle.

On his way back to the port-side, he saw a shop where a man sold shells and clubs from the wild islands, old heathen deities, old coined money, pictures from China and Japan, and all manner of things that sailors bring in their sea-chests. And here he had an idea. So he went in and offered the bottle for a hundred dollars. The man of the shop laughed at him at the first, and offered him five; but, indeed, it was a curious bottle—such glass was never blown in any human glassworks, so prettily the colours shone under the milky white, and so strangely the shadow hovered in the midst; so, after he had disputed awhile after the manner of his kind, the shop-man gave Keawe sixty silver dollars for the thing, and set it on a shelf in the midst of his window.

"Now," said Keawe, "I have sold that for sixty which I bought for fifty— or, to say truth, a little less, because one of my dollars was from Chili. Now I shall know the truth upon another point."

So he went back on board his ship, and, when he opened his chest, there was the bottle, and had come more quickly than himself. Now Keawe had a mate on board whose name was Lopaka.

"What ails you?" said Lopaka, "that you stare in your chest?"

They were alone in the ship's forecastle, and Keawe bound him to secrecy, and told all.

"This is a very strange affair," said Lopaka; "and I fear you will be in trouble about this bottle. But there is one point very clear—that you are sure of the trouble, and you had better have the profit in the bargain. Make up your mind what you want with it; give the order, and if it is done as you desire, I will buy the bottle myself; for I have an idea of my own to get a schooner, and go trading through the islands."

"That is not my idea," said Keawe; "but to have a beautiful house and garden on the Kona Coast, where I was born, the sun shining in at the door, flowers in the garden, glass in the windows, pictures on the walls, and toys and fine carpets on the tables, for all the world like the house I was in this day—only a storey higher, and with balconies all about like the King's palace; and to live there without care and make merry with my friends and relatives."

"Well," said Lopaka, "let us carry it back with us to Hawaii; and if all comes true, as you suppose, I will buy the bottle, as I said, and ask a schooner."

Upon that they were agreed, and it was not long before the ship returned to Honolulu, carrying Keawe and Lopaka, and the bottle. They were scarce come ashore when they met a friend upon the beach, who began at once to condole with Keawe.

"I do not know what I am to be condoled about," said Keawe.

"Is it possible you have not heard," said the friend, "your uncle—that good old man—is dead, and your cousin—that beautiful boy—was drowned at sea?"

Keawe was filled with sorrow, and, beginning to weep and to lament, he forgot about the bottle. But Lopaka was thinking to himself, and presently, when Keawe's grief was a little abated, "I have been thinking," said Lopaka. "Had not your uncle lands in Hawaii, in the district of Kau?"

"No," said Keawe, "not in Kau; they are on the mountain-side—a little way south of Hookena."

"These lands will now be yours?" asked Lopaka.

"And so they will," says Keawe, and began again to lament for his relatives.

"No," said Lopaka, "do not lament at present. I have a thought in my mind. How if this should be the doing of the bottle? For here is the place ready for your house."

"If this be so," cried Keawe, "it is a very ill way to serve me by killing my relatives. But it may be, indeed; for it was in just such a station that I saw the house with my mind's eye."

"The house, however, is not yet built," said Lopaka.

"No, nor like to be!" said Keawe; "for though my uncle has some coffee and ava and bananas, it will not be more than will keep me in comfort; and the rest of that land is the black lava."

"Let us go to the lawyer," said Lopaka; "I have still this idea in my mind."

Now, when they came to the lawyer's, it appeared Keawe's uncle had grown monstrous rich in the last days, and there was a fund of money.

"And here is the money for the house!" cried Lopaka.

"If you are thinking of a new house," said the lawyer, "here is the card of a new architect, of whom they tell me great things."

"Better and better!" cried Lopaka. "Here is all made plain for us. Let us continue to obey orders."

So they went to the architect, and he had drawings of houses on his table.

"You want something out of the way," said the architect. "How do you like this?" and he handed a drawing to Keawe.

Now, when Keawe set eyes on the drawing, he cried out aloud, for it was the picture of his thought exactly drawn.

"I am in for this house," thought he. "Little as I like the way it comes to me, I am in for it now, and I may as well take the good along with the evil."

So he told the architect all that he wished, and how he would have that house furnished, and about the pictures on the wall and the knick-knacks on the tables; and he asked the man plainly for how much he would undertake the whole affair.

The architect put many questions, and took his pen and made a computation; and when he had done he named the very sum that Keawe had inherited.

Lopaka and Keawe looked at one another and nodded.

"It is quite clear," thought Keawe, "that I am to have this house, whether or no. It comes from the devil, and I fear I will get little good by that; and of one thing I am sure, I will make no more wishes as long as I have this bottle. But with the house I am saddled, and I may as well take the good along with the evil."

So he made his terms with the architect, and they signed a paper; and Keawe and Lopaka took ship again and sailed to Australia; for it was concluded between them they should not interfere at all, but leave the architect and the bottle imp to build and to adorn that house at their own pleasure.

The voyage was a good voyage, only all the time Keawe was holding in his breath, for he had sworn he would utter no more wishes, and take no more favours from the devil. The time was up when they got back. The architect told them that the house was ready, and Keawe and Lopaka took a passage in the *Hall*, and went down Kona way to view the house, and see if all had been done fitly according to the thought that was in Keawe's mind.

Now the house stood on the mountain side, visible to ships. Above, the forest ran up into the clouds of rain; below, the black lava fell in cliffs, where the kings of old lay buried. A garden bloomed about that house with every hue of flowers; and there was an orchard of papaia on the one hand and an orchard of breadfruit on the other, and right in front, toward the sea, a ship's mast had been rigged up and bore a flag. As for the house, it was three storeys high, with great chambers and broad balconies on each. The windows were of glass, so excellent that it was as clear as water and as bright as day. All manner of furniture adorned the chambers. Pictures hung upon the wall in golden frames: pictures of ships, and men fighting, and of the most beautiful women, and of singular places; nowhere in the world are there pictures of so bright a colour as those Keawe found hanging in his house. As for the knick-knacks, they were extraordinary fine; chiming clocks and musical boxes, little men with nodding heads, books filled with pictures, weapons of price from all quarters of the world, and the most elegant puzzles to entertain the leisure of a solitary man. And as no one would care to live in such chambers, only to walk through and view them, the balconies were made so broad that a whole town might have lived upon them in delight; and Keawe knew not which to prefer, whether the back porch, where you got the land breeze, and looked upon the orchards and the flowers, or the front balcony, where you could drink the wind of the sea, and look down the steep wall of the mountain and see the *Hall* going by once a week or so between Hookena and the hills of Pele, or the schooners plying up the coast for wood and ava and bananas.

When they had viewed all, Keawe and Lopaka sat on the porch.

"Well," asked Lopaka, "is it all as you designed?"

"Words cannot utter it," said Keawe. "It is better than I dreamed, and I am sick with satisfaction."

"There is but one thing to consider," said Lopaka; "all this may be quite natural, and the bottle imp have nothing whatever to say to it. If I were to buy the bottle, and got no schooner after all, I should have put my hand in the fire for nothing. I gave you my word, I know; but yet I think you would not grudge me one more proof."

"I have sworn I would take no more favours," said Keawe. "I have gone already deep enough."

"This is no favour I am thinking of," replied Lopaka. "It is only to see the imp himself. There is nothing to be gained by that, and so nothing to be ashamed of; and yet, if I once saw him, I should be sure of the whole matter. So indulge me so far, and let me see the imp; and, after that, here is the money in my hand, and I will buy it."

"There is only one thing I am afraid of," said Keawe. "The imp may be very ugly to view; and if you once set eyes upon him you might be very undesirous of the bottle."

"I am a man of my word," said Lopaka. "And here is the money betwixt us."

"Very well," replied Keawe. "I have a curiosity myself. So come, let us have one look at you, Mr. Imp."

Now as soon as that was said, the imp looked out of the bottle, and in again, swift as a lizard; and there sat Keawe and Lopaka turned to stone. The night had quite come, before either found a thought to say or voice to say it with; and then Lopaka pushed the money over and took the bottle.

"I am a man of my word," said he, "and had need to be so, or I would not touch this bottle with my foot. Well, I shall get my schooner and a dollar or two for my pocket; and then I will be rid of this devil as fast as I can. For to tell you the plain truth, the look of him has cast me down."

"Lopaka," said Keawe, "do not you think any worse of me than you can help; I know it is night, and the roads bad, and the pass by the tombs an ill place to go by so late, but I declare since I have seen that little face, I cannot eat or sleep or pray till it is gone from me. I will give you a lantern and a basket to put the bottle in, and any picture or fine thing in all my house that takes your fancy;—and be gone at once, and go sleep at Hookena with Nahinu."

"Keawe," said Lopaka, "many a man would take this ill; above all, when I am doing you a turn so friendly, as to keep my word and buy the bottle; and for that matter, the night and the dark, and the way by the tombs, must be all tenfold more dangerous to a man with such a sin upon his conscience, and such a bottle under his arm. But for my part, I am so extremely terrified myself, I have not the heart to blame you. Here I go then; and I pray God you may be happy in your house, and I fortunate with my schooner, and both get to heaven in the end in spite of the devil and his bottle."

So Lopaka went down the mountain; and Keawe stood in his front balcony, and listened to the clink of the horse's shoes, and watched the lantern go shining down the path, and along the cliff of caves where the old dead are buried; and all the time he trembled and clasped his hands, and prayed for his friend, and gave glory to God that he himself was escaped out of that trouble.

But the next day came very brightly, and that new house of his was so delightful to behold that he forgot his terrors. One day followed another, and Keawe dwelt there in perpetual joy. He had his place on the back porch; it was there he ate and lived, and read the stories in the Honolulu newspapers; but when anyone came by they would go in and view the chambers and the pictures. And the fame of the house went far and wide; it was called *Ka-Hale Nui*—the Great House—in all Kona; and sometimes the Bright House, for Keawe kept a Chinaman, who was all day dusting and furbishing; and the glass, and the gilt, and the fine stuffs, and the pictures, shone as bright as the morning. As for Keawe himself, he could not walk in the chambers without singing, his heart was so enlarged; and when ships sailed by upon the sea, he would fly his colours on the mast.

So time went by, until one day Keawe went upon a visit as far as Kailua to certain of his friends. There he was well feasted; and left as soon as he could the next morning, and rode hard, for he was impatient to behold his beautiful house; and, besides, the night then coming on was the night in which the dead of old days go abroad in the sides of Kona; and having already meddled with the devil, he was the more chary of meeting with the dead. A little beyond Honaunau, looking far ahead, he was aware of a woman bathing in the edge of the sea; and she seemed a well-grown girl, but he thought no more of it. Then he saw her white shift flutter as she put it on, and then her red holoku; and by the time he came abreast of her she was done with her toilet, and had come up from the sea, and stood by the track-side in her red holoku, and she was all freshened with the bath, and her eyes shone and were kind. Now Keawe no sooner beheld her than he drew rein.

"I thought I knew everyone in this country," said he. "How comes it that I do not know you?"

"I am Kokua, daughter of Kiano," said the girl, "and I have just returned from Oahu. Who are you?"

"I will tell you who I am in a little," said Keawe, dismounting from his horse, "but not now. For I have a thought in my mind, and if you knew who I was, you might have heard of me, and would not give me a true answer. But tell me, first of all, one thing: Are you married?"

At this Kokua laughed out aloud. "It is you who ask questions," she said. "Are you married yourself?"

"Indeed, Kokua, I am not," replied Keawe, "and never thought to be until this hour. But here is the plain truth. I have met you here at the roadside, and I saw your eyes, which are like the stars, and my heart went to you as swift as a bird. And so now, if you want none of me, say so, and I will go on to my own place; but if you think me no worse than any other young man, say so, too, and I will turn aside to your father's for the night, and to-morrow I will talk with the good man."

Kokua said never a word, but she looked at the sea and laughed.

"Kokua," said Keawe, "if you say nothing, I will take that for the good answer; so let us be stepping to your father's door."

She went on ahead of him, still without speech; only sometimes she glanced back and glanced away again, and she kept the strings of her hat in her mouth.

Now, when they had come to the door, Kiano came out on his verandah, and cried out and welcomed Keawe by name. At that the girl looked over, for the fame of the great house had come to her ears; and, to be sure, it was a great temptation. All that evening they were very merry together; and the girl was as bold as brass under the eyes of her parents, and made a mock of Keawe, for she had a quick wit. The next day he had a word with Kiano, and found the girl alone.

"Kokua," said he, "you made a mock of me all the evening; and it is still time to bid me go. I would not tell you who I was, because I have so fine a house, and I feared you would think too much of that house and too little of the man that loves you. Now you know all, and if you wish to have seen the last of me, say so at once."

"No," said Kokua; but this time she did not laugh, nor did Keawe ask for more.

This was the wooing of Keawe; things had gone quickly; but so an arrow goes, and the ball of a rifle swifter still, and yet both may strike the target. Things had gone fast, but they had gone far also, and the thought of Keawe rang in the maiden's head; she heard his voice in the breach of the surf upon the lava, and for this young man that she had seen but twice she would have left father and mother and her native islands. As for Keawe himself, his horse flew up the path of the mountain under the cliff of tombs, and the sound of the hoofs, and the sound of Keawe singing to himself for pleasure, echoed in the caverns of the dead. He came to the Bright House, and still he was singing. He sat and ate in the broad balcony, and the Chinaman wondered at his master, to hear how he sang between the mouthfuls. The sun went down into the sea, and the night came; and Keawe walked the balconies by lamplight, high on the mountains, and the voice of his singing startled men on ships.

"Here am I now upon my high place," he said to himself. "Life may be no better; this is the mountain top; and all shelves about me toward the worse. For the first time I will light up the chambers, and bathe in my fine bath

217

with the hot water and the cold, and sleep alone in the bed of my bridal chamber."

So the Chinaman had word, and he must rise from sleep and light the furnaces; and as he wrought below, beside the boilers, he heard his master singing and rejoicing above him in the lighted chambers. When the water began to be hot the Chinaman cried to his master; and Keawe went into the bathroom; and the Chinaman heard him sing as he filled the marble basin; and heard him sing, and the singing broken, as he undressed; until of a sudden, the song ceased. The Chinaman listened, and listened; he called up the house to Keawe to ask if all were well, and Keawe answered him "Yes," and bade him go to bed; but there was no more singing in the Bright House; and all night long, the Chinaman heard his master's feet go round and round the balconies without repose.

Now the truth of it was this: as Keawe undressed for his bath, he spied upon his flesh a patch like a patch of lichen on a rock, and it was then that he stopped singing. For he knew the likeness of that patch, and knew that he was fallen in the Chinese Evil.

Now, it is a sad thing for any man to fall into this sickness. And it would be a sad thing for anyone to leave a house so beautiful and so commodious, and depart from all his friends to the north coast of Molokai between the mighty cliff and the sea-breakers. But what was that to the case of the man Keawe, he who had met his love but yesterday, and won her but that morning, and now saw all his hopes break, in a moment, like a piece of glass?

Awhile he sat upon the edge of the bath; then sprang, with a cry, and ran outside; and to and fro, to and fro, along the balcony, like one despairing.

"Very willingly could I leave Hawaii, the home of my fathers," Keawe was thinking. "Very lightly could I leave my house, the high-placed, the many-windowed, here upon the mountains. Very bravely could I go to Molokai, to Kalaupapa by the cliffs, to live with the smitten and to sleep there, far from my fathers. But what wrong have I done, what sin lies upon my soul, that I should have encountered Kokua coming cool from the sea-water in the evening? Kokua, the soul ensnarer! Kokua, the light of my life! Her may I never wed, her may I look upon no longer, her may I no more handle with my loving hand; and it is for this, it is for you, O Kokua! that I pour my lamentations!"

Now you are to observe what sort of a man Keawe was, for he might have dwelt there in the Bright House for years, and no one been the wiser of his sickness; but he reckoned nothing of that, if he must lose Kokua. And again, he might have wed Kokua even as he was; and so many would have done, because they have the souls of pigs; but Keawe loved the maid manfully, and he would do her no hurt and bring her in no danger.

A little beyond the midst of the night, there came in his mind the recollection of that bottle. He went round to the back porch, and called to memory the day when the devil had looked forth; and at the thought ice ran in his veins.

"A dreadful thing is the bottle," thought Keawe, "and dreadful is the imp, and it is a dreadful thing to risk the flames of hell. But what other hope have I to cure my sickness or to wed Kokua? What!" he thought, "would I beard the devil once, only to get me a house, and not face him again to win Kokua?"

Thereupon he called to mind it was the next day the *Hall* went by on her return to Honolulu. "There must I go first," he thought, "and see Lopaka. For the best hope that I have now is to find that same bottle I was so pleased to be rid of."

Never a wink could he sleep; the food stuck in his throat; but he sent a letter to Kiano, and about the time when the steamer would be coming, rode down beside the cliff of the tombs. It rained; his horse went heavily; he looked up at the black mouths of the caves, and he envied the dead that slept there and were done with trouble; and called to mind how he had galloped by the day before, and was astonished. So he came down to Hookena, and there was all the country gathered for the steamer as usual. In the shed before the store they sat and jested and passed the news; but there was no matter of speech in Keawe's bosom, and he sat in their midst and looked without on the rain falling on the houses, and the surf beating among the rocks, and the sighs arose in his throat.

"Keawe of the Bright House is out of spirits," said one to another. Indeed, and so he was, and little wonder.

Then the *Hall* came, and the whaleboat carried him on board. The after-part of the ship was full of Haoles who had been to visit the volcano, as their custom is; and the midst was crowded with Kanakas, and the forepart with wild bulls from Hilo and horses from Kau; but Keawe sat apart from all in his sorrow, and watched for the house of Kiano. There it sat, low upon the shore in the black rocks, and shaded by the cocoa palms, and there by the door was a red holoku, no greater than a fly, and going to and fro with a fly's busyness. "Ah, queen of my heart," he cried, "I'll venture my dear soul to win you!"

Soon after, darkness fell, and the cabins were lit up, and the Haoles sat and played at the cards and drank whiskey as their custom is; but Keawe walked the deck all night; and all the next day, as they steamed under the lee of Maui or of Molokai, he was still pacing to and fro like a wild animal in a menagerie.

Towards evening they passed Diamond Head, and came to the pier of Honolulu. Keawe stepped out among the crowd and began to ask for Lopaka. It seemed he had become the owner of a schooner—none better in the islands—and was gone upon an adventure as far as Pola-Pola or Kahiki; so there was no help to be looked for from Lopaka. Keawe called to mind a friend of his, a lawyer in the town (I must not tell his name), and inquired of him. They said he was grown suddenly rich, and had a fine new house upon Waikiki shore; and this put a thought in Keawe's head, and he called a hack and drove to the lawyer's house.

The house was all brand new, and the trees in the garden no greater than walking-sticks, and the lawyer, when he came, had the air of a man well pleased.

"What can I do to serve you?" said the lawyer.

"You are a friend of Lopaka's," replied Keawe, "and Lopaka purchased from me a certain piece of goods that I thought you might enable me to trace."

The lawyer's face became very dark. "I do not profess to misunderstand you, Mr. Keawe," said he, "though this is an ugly business to be stirring in. You may be sure I know nothing, but yet I have a guess, and if you would apply in a certain quarter I think you might have news."

And he named the name of a man, which, again, I had better not repeat. So it was for days, and Keawe went from one to another, finding everywhere new clothes and carriages, and fine new houses and men everywhere in great contentment, although, to be sure, when he hinted at his business their faces would cloud over.

"No doubt I am upon the track," thought Keawe. "These new clothes and carriages are all the gifts of the little imp, and these glad faces are the faces of men who have taken their profit and got rid of the accursed thing in safety. When I see pale cheeks and hear sighing, I shall know that I am near the bottle."

So it befell at last that he was recommended to a Haole in Beritania Street. When he came to the door, about the hour of the evening meal, there were the usual marks of the new house, and the young garden, and the electric light shining in the windows; but when the owner came, a shock of hope and fear ran through Keawe; for here was a young man, white as a corpse, and black about the eyes, the hair shedding from his head, and such a look in his countenance as a man may have when he is waiting for the gallows.

"Here it is, to be sure," thought Keawe, and so with this man he noways veiled his errand. "I am come to buy the bottle," said he.

At the word, the young Haole of Beritania Street reeled against the wall.

"The bottle!" he gasped. "To buy the bottle!" Then he seemed to choke, and seizing Keawe by the arm carried him into a room and poured out wine in two glasses.

"Here is my respects," said Keawe, who had been much about with Haoles in his time. "Yes," he added, "I am come to buy the bottle. What is the price by now?"

At that word the young man let his glass slip through his fingers, and looked upon Keawe like a ghost.

"The price," says he; "the price! You do not know the price?"

"It is for that I am asking you," returned Keawe. "But why are you so much concerned? Is there anything wrong about the price?"

"It has dropped a great deal in value since your time, Mr. Keawe," said the young man stammering.

"Well, well, I shall have the less to pay for it," says Keawe. "How much did it cost you?"

The young man was as white as a sheet. "Two cents," said he.

"What?" cried Keawe, "two cents? Why, then, you can only sell it for one. And he who buys it—" The words died upon Keawe's tongue; he who bought it could never sell it again, the bottle and the bottle imp must abide with him until he died, and when he died must carry him to the red end of hell.

The young man of Beritania Street fell upon his knees. "For God's sake buy it!" he cried. "You can have all my fortune in the bargain. I was mad when I bought it at that price. I had embezzled money at my store; I was lost else; I must have gone to jail."

"Poor creature," said Keawe, "you would risk your soul upon so desperate an adventure, and to avoid the proper punishment of your own disgrace; and you think I could hesitate with love in front of me. Give me the bottle, and the change which I make sure you have all ready. Here is a five-cent piece."

It was as Keawe supposed; the young man had the change ready in a drawer; the bottle changed hands, and Keawe's fingers were no sooner clasped upon the stalk than he had breathed his wish to be a clean man. And, sure enough, when he got home to his room, and stripped himself before a glass, his flesh was whole like an infant's. And here was the strange thing: he had no sooner seen this miracle, than his mind was changed within him, and he cared naught for the Chinese Evil, and little enough for Kokua; and had but the one thought, that here he was bound to the bottle imp for time and for eternity, and had no better hope but to be a cinder for ever in the flames of hell. Away ahead of him he saw them blaze with his mind's eye, and his soul shrank, and darkness fell upon the light.

When Keawe came to himself a little, he was aware it was the night when the band played at the hotel. Thither he went, because he feared to be alone; and there, among happy faces, walked to and fro, and heard the tunes go up and down, and saw Berger beat the measure, and all the while he heard the flames crackle, and saw the red fire burning in the bottomless pit. Of a sudden the band played *Hiki-ao-ao*; that was a song that he had sung with Kokua, and at the strain courage returned to him.

"It is done now," he thought, "and once more let me take the good along with the evil."

So it befell that he returned to Hawaii by the first steamer, and as soon as it could be managed he was wedded to Kokua, and carried her up the mountain side to the Bright House.

221

Now it was so with these two, that when they were together, Keawe's heart was stilled; but so soon as he was alone he fell into a brooding horror, and heard the flames crackle, and saw the red fire burn in the bottomless pit. The girl, indeed, had come to him wholly; her heart leapt in her side at sight of him, her hand clung to his; and she was so fashioned from the hair upon her head to the nails upon her toes that none could see her without joy. She was pleasant in her nature. She had the good word always. Full of song she was, and went to and fro in the Bright House, the brightest thing in its three storeys, carolling like the birds. And Keawe beheld and heard her with delight, and then must shrink upon one side, and weep and groan to think upon the price that he had paid for her; and then he must dry his eyes, and wash his face, and go and sit with her on the broad balconies, joining in her songs, and, with a sick spirit, answering her smiles.

There came a day when her feet began to be heavy and her songs more rare; and now it was not Keawe only that would weep apart, but each would sunder from the other and sit in opposite balconies with the whole width of the Bright House betwixt. Keawe was so sunk in his despair, he scarce observed the change, and was only glad he had more hours to sit alone and brood upon his destiny, and was not so frequently condemned to pull a smiling face on a sick heart. But one day, coming softly through the house, he heard the sound of a child sobbing, and there was Kokua rolling her face upon the balcony floor, and weeping like the lost.

"You do well to weep in this house, Kokua," he said. "And yet I would give the head off my body that you (at least) might have been happy."

"Happy!" she cried. "Keawe, when you lived alone in your Bright House, you were the word of the island for a happy man; laughter and song were in your mouth, and your face was as bright as the sunrise. Then you wedded poor Kokua; and the good God knows what is amiss in her—but from that day you have not smiled. Oh!" she cried, "what ails me? I thought I was pretty, and I knew I loved him. What ails me that I throw this cloud upon my husband?"

"Poor Kokua," said Keawe. He sat down by her side, and sought to take her hand; but that she plucked away. "Poor Kokua," he said, again. "My poor child—my pretty. And I had thought all this while to spare you! Well, you shall know all. Then, at least, you will pity poor Keawe; then you will understand how much he loved you in the past—that he dared hell for your possession—and how much he loves you still (the poor condemned one), that he can yet call up a smile when he beholds you."

With that, he told her all, even from the beginning.

"You have done this for me?" she cried "Ah, well, then what do I care!"— and she clasped and wept upon him.

"Ah, child!" said Keawe, "and yet, when I consider of the fire of hell, I care a good deal!"

"Never tell me," said she; "no man can be lost because he loved Kokua, and no other fault. I tell you, Keawe, I shall save you with these hands, or perish in your company. What! you loved me, and gave your soul, and you think I will not die to save you in return?"

"Ah, my dear! you might die a hundred times, and what difference would that make?" he cried, "except to leave me lonely till the time comes of my damnation?"

"You know nothing," said she. "I was educated in a school in Honolulu; I am no common girl. And I tell you, I shall save my lover. What is this you say about a cent? But all the world is not American. In England they have a piece they call a farthing, which is about half a cent. Ah! sorrow!" she cried, "that makes it scarcely better, for the buyer must be lost, and we shall find none so brave as my Keawe! But, then, there is France; they have a small coin there which they call a centime, and these go five to the cent or thereabout. We could not do better. Come, Keawe, let us go to the French islands; let us go to Tahiti, as fast as ships can bear us. There we have four centimes, three centimes, two centimes, one centime; four possible sales to come and go on; and two of us to push the bargain. Come, my Keawe! kiss me, and banish care. Kokua will defend you."

"Gift of God!" he cried. "I cannot think that God will punish me for desiring aught so good! Be it as you will, then; take me where you please: I put my life and my salvation in your hands."

Early the next day Kokua was about her preparations. She took Keawe's chest that he went with sailoring; and first she put the bottle in a corner; and then packed it with the richest of their clothes and the bravest of the knick-knacks in the house. "For," said she, "we must seem to be rich folks, or who will believe in the bottle?" All the time of her preparation she was as gay as a bird; only when she looked upon Keawe, the tears would spring in her eye, and she must run and kiss him. As for Keawe, a weight was off his soul; now that he had his secret shared, and some hope in front of him, he seemed like a new man, his feet went lightly on the earth, and his breath was good to him again. Yet was terror still at his elbow; and ever and again, as the wind blows out a taper, hope died in him, and he saw the flames toss and the red fire burn in hell.

It was given out in the country they were gone pleasuring to the States, which was thought a strange thing, and yet not so strange as the truth, if any could have guessed it. So they went to Honolulu in the *Hall*, and thence in the *Umatilla* to San Francisco with a crowd of Haoles, and at San Francisco took their passage by the mail brigantine, the *Tropic Bird*, for Papeete, the chief place of the French in the south islands. Thither they came, after a pleasant voyage, on a fair day of the Trade Wind, and saw the reef with the surf breaking, and Motuiti with its palms, and the schooner riding within-side, and the white houses of the town low down along the shore among green trees, and overhead the mountains and the clouds of Tahiti, the wise island.

It was judged the most wise to hire a house, which they did accordingly, opposite the British Consul's, to make a great parade of money, and themselves conspicuous with carriages and horses. This it was very easy to do, so long as they had the bottle in their possession; for Kokua was more bold than Keawe, and, whenever she had a mind, called on the imp for twenty or a hundred dollars. At this rate they soon grew to be remarked in the town; and the strangers from Hawaii, their riding and their driving, the fine holokus and the rich lace of Kokua, became the matter of much talk.

They got on well after the first with the Tahitian language, which is indeed like to the Hawaiian, with a change of certain letters; and as soon as they had any freedom of speech, began to push the bottle. You are to consider it was not an easy subject to introduce; it was not easy to persuade people you were in earnest, when you offered to sell them for four centimes the spring of health and riches inexhaustible. It was necessary besides to explain the dangers of the bottle; and either people disbelieved the whole thing and laughed, or they thought the more of the darker part, became overcast with gravity, and drew away from Keawe and Kokua, as from persons who had dealings with the devil. So far from gaining ground, these two began to find they were avoided in the town; the children ran away from them screaming, a thing intolerable to Kokua; Catholics crossed themselves as they went by; and all persons began with one accord to disengage themselves from their advances.

Depression fell upon their spirits. They would sit at night in their new house, after a day's weariness, and not exchange one word, or the silence would be broken by Kokua bursting suddenly into sobs. Sometimes they would pray together; sometimes they would have the bottle out upon the floor, and sit all evening watching how the shadow hovered in the midst. At such times they would be afraid to go to rest. It was long ere slumber came to them, and, if either dozed off, it would be to wake and find the other silently weeping in the dark, or, perhaps, to wake alone, the other having fled from the house and the neighbourhood of that bottle, to pace under the bananas in the little garden, or to wander on the beach by moonlight.

One night it was so when Kokua awoke. Keawe was gone. She felt in the bed and his place was cold. Then fear fell upon her, and she sat up in bed. A little moonshine filtered through the shutters. The room was bright, and she could spy the bottle on the floor. Outside it blew high, the great trees of the avenue cried aloud, and the fallen leaves rattled in the verandah. In the midst of this Kokua was aware of another sound; whether of a beast or of a man she could scarce tell, but it was as sad as death, and cut her to the soul. Softly she arose, set the door ajar, and looked forth into the moonlit yard. There, under the bananas, lay Keawe, his mouth in the dust, and as he lay he moaned.

224

It was Kokua's first thought to run forward and console him; her second potently withheld her. Keawe had borne himself before his wife like a brave man; it became her little in the hour of weakness to intrude upon his shame. With the thought she drew back into the house.

"Heaven!" she thought, "how careless have I been—how weak! It is he, not I, that stands in this eternal peril; it was he, not I, that took the curse upon his soul. It is for my sake, and for the love of a creature of so little worth and such poor help, that he now beholds so close to him the flames of hell—ay, and smells the smoke of it, lying without there in the wind and moonlight. Am I so dull of spirit that never till now I have surmised my duty, or have I seen it before and turned aside? But now, at least, I take up my soul in both the hands of my affection; now I say farewell to the white steps of heaven and the waiting faces of my friends. A love for a love, and let mine be equalled with Keawe's! A soul for a soul, and be it mine to perish!"

She was a deft woman with her hands, and was soon apparelled. She took in her hands the change—the precious centimes they kept ever at their side; for this coin is little used, and they had made provision at a Government office. When she was forth in the avenue clouds came on the wind, and the moon was blackened. The town slept, and she knew not whither to turn till she heard one coughing in the shadow of the trees.

"Old man," said Kokua, "what do you here abroad in the cold night?"

The old man could scarce express himself for coughing, but she made out that he was old and poor, and a stranger in the island.

"Will you do me a service?" said Kokua. "As one stranger to another, and as an old man to a young woman, will you help a daughter of Hawaii?"

"Ah," said the old man. "So you are the witch from the eight islands, and even my old soul you seek to entangle. But I have heard of you, and defy your wickedness."

"Sit down here," said Kokua, "and let me tell you a tale." And she told him the story of Keawe from the beginning to the end.

"And now," said she, "I am his wife, whom he bought with his soul's welfare. And what should I do? If I went to him myself and offered to buy it, he would refuse. But if you go, he will sell it eagerly; I will await you here; you will buy it for four centimes, and I will buy it again for three. And the Lord strengthen a poor girl!"

"If you meant falsely," said the old man, "I think God would strike you dead."

"He would!" cried Kokua. "Be sure he would. I could not be so treacherous—God would not suffer it."

"Give me the four centimes and await me here," said the old man.

Now, when Kokua stood alone in the street, her spirit died. The wind roared in the trees, and it seemed to her the rushing of the flames of hell; the shadows tossed in the light of the street lamp, and they seemed to her the snatching hands of evil ones. If she had had the strength, she must have

225

run away, and if she had had the breath she must have screamed aloud; but, in truth, she could do neither, and stood and trembled in the avenue, like an affrighted child.

Then she saw the old man returning, and he had the bottle in his hand.

"I have done your bidding," said he. "I left your husband weeping like a child; to-night he will sleep easy." And he held the bottle forth.

"Before you give it me," Kokua panted, "take the good with the evil—ask to be delivered from your cough."

"I am an old man," replied the other, "and too near the gate of the grave to take a favour from the devil. But what is this? Why do you not take the bottle? Do you hesitate?"

"Not hesitate!" cried Kokua. "I am only weak. Give me a moment. It is my hand resists, my flesh shrinks back from the accursed thing. One moment only!"

The old man looked upon Kokua kindly. "Poor child!" said he, "you fear; your soul misgives you. Well, let me keep it. I am old, and can never more be happy in this world, and as for the next—"

"Give it me!" gasped Kokua. "There is your money. Do you think I am so base as that? Give me the bottle."

"God bless you, child," said the old man.

Kokua concealed the bottle under her holoku, said farewell to the old man, and walked off along the avenue, she cared not whither. For all roads were now the same to her, and led equally to hell. Sometimes she walked, and sometimes ran; sometimes she screamed out loud in the night, and sometimes lay by the wayside in the dust and wept. All that she had heard of hell came back to her; she saw the flames blaze, and she smelt the smoke, and her flesh withered on the coals.

Near day she came to her mind again, and returned to the house. It was even as the old man said—Keawe slumbered like a child. Kokua stood and gazed upon his face.

"Now, my husband," said she, "it is your turn to sleep. When you wake it will be your turn to sing and laugh. But for poor Kokua, alas! that meant no evil—for poor Kokua no more sleep, no more singing, no more delight, whether in earth or heaven."

With that she lay down in the bed by his side, and her misery was so extreme that she fell in a deep slumber instantly.

Late in the morning her husband woke her and gave her the good news. It seemed he was silly with delight, for he paid no heed to her distress, ill though she dissembled it. The words stuck in her mouth, it mattered not; Keawe did the speaking. She ate not a bite, but who was to observe it? for Keawe cleared the dish. Kokua saw and heard him, like some strange thing in a dream; there were times when she forgot or doubted, and put her hands to her brow; to know herself doomed and hear her husband babble, seemed so monstrous.

All the while Keawe was eating and talking, and planning the time of their return, and thanking her for saving him, and fondling her, and calling her the true helper after all. He laughed at the old man that was fool enough to buy that bottle.

"A worthy old man he seemed," Keawe said. "But no one can judge by appearances. For why did the old reprobate require the bottle?"

"My husband," said Kokua, humbly, "his purpose may have been good."

Keawe laughed like an angry man.

"Fiddle-de-dee!" cried Keawe. "An old rogue, I tell you; and an old ass to boot. For the bottle was hard enough to sell at four centimes; and at three it will be quite impossible. The margin is not broad enough, the thing begins to smell of scorching—brrr!" said he, and shuddered. "It is true I bought it myself at a cent, when I knew not there were smaller coins. I was a fool for my pains; there will never be found another: and whoever has that bottle now will carry it to the pit."

"O my husband!" said Kokua. "Is it not a terrible thing to save oneself by the eternal ruin of another? It seems to me I could not laugh. I would be humbled. I would be filled with melancholy. I would pray for the poor holder."

Then Keawe, because he felt the truth of what she said, grew the more angry. "Heighty-teighty!" cried he. "You may be filled with melancholy if you please. It is not the mind of a good wife. If you thought at all of me, you would sit shamed."

Thereupon he went out, and Kokua was alone.

What chance had she to sell that bottle at two centimes? None, she perceived. And if she had any, here was her husband hurrying her away to a country where there was nothing lower than a cent. And here—on the morrow of her sacrifice—was her husband leaving her and blaming her.

She would not even try to profit by what time she had, but sat in the house, and now had the bottle out and viewed it with unutterable fear, and now, with loathing, hid it out of sight.

By-and-by, Keawe came back, and would have her take a drive.

"My husband, I am ill," she said. "I am out of heart. Excuse me, I can take no pleasure."

Then was Keawe more wroth than ever. With her, because he thought she was brooding over the case of the old man; and with himself, because he thought she was right, and was ashamed to be so happy.

"This is your truth," cried he, "and this your affection! Your husband is just saved from eternal ruin, which he encountered for the love of you—and you can take no pleasure! Kokua, you have a disloyal heart."

He went forth again furious, and wandered in the town all day. He met friends, and drank with them; they hired a carriage and drove into the country, and there drank again. All the time Keawe was ill at ease, because he was taking this pastime while his wife was sad, and because he knew in his heart that she was more right than he; and the knowledge made him drink the deeper.

Now there was an old brutal Haole drinking with him, one that had been a boatswain of a whaler, a runaway, a digger in gold mines, a convict in prisons. He had a low mind and a foul mouth; he loved to drink and to see others drunken; and he pressed the glass upon Keawe. Soon there was no more money in the company.

"Here, you!" says the boatswain, "you are rich, you have been always saying. You have a bottle or some foolishness."

"Yes," says Keawe, "I am rich; I will go back and get some money from my wife, who keeps it."

"That's a bad idea, mate," said the boatswain. "Never you trust a petticoat with dollars. They're all as false as water; you keep an eye on her."

Now, this word struck in Keawe's mind; for he was muddled with what he had been drinking.

"I should not wonder but she was false, indeed," thought he. "Why else should she be so cast down at my release? But I will show her I am not the man to be fooled. I will catch her in the act."

Accordingly, when they were back in town, Keawe bade the boatswain wait for him at the corner, by the old calaboose, and went forward up the avenue alone to the door of his house. The night had come again; there was a light within, but never a sound; and Keawe crept about the corner, opened the back door softly, and looked in.

There was Kokua on the floor, the lamp at her side; before her was a milk-white bottle, with a round belly and a long neck; and as she viewed it, Kokua wrung her hands.

A long time Keawe stood and looked in the doorway. At first he was struck stupid; and then fear fell upon him that the bargain had been made amiss, and the bottle had come back to him as it came at San Francisco; and at that his knees were loosened, and the fumes of the wine departed from his head like mists off a river in the morning. And then he had another thought; and it was a strange one, that made his cheeks to burn.

"I must make sure of this," thought he.

So he closed the door, and went softly round the corner again, and then came noisily in, as though he were but now returned. And, lo! by the time he opened the front door no bottle was to be seen; and Kokua sat in a chair and started up like one awakened out of sleep.

"I have been drinking all day and making merry," said Keawe. "I have been with good companions, and now I only come back for money, and return to drink and carouse with them again."

Both his face and voice were as stern as judgment, but Kokua was too troubled to observe.

"You do well to use your own, my husband," said she, and her words trembled.

"O, I do well in all things," said Keawe, and he went straight to the chest and took out money. But he looked besides in the corner where they kept the bottle, and there was no bottle there.

At that the chest heaved upon the floor like a sea-billow, and the house span about him like a wreath of smoke, for he saw he was lost now, and there was no escape. "It is what I feared," he thought. "It is she who has bought it."

And then he came to himself a little and rose up; but the sweat streamed on his face as thick as the rain and as cold as the well-water.

"Kokua," said he, "I said to you to-day what ill became me. Now I return to carouse with my jolly companions," and at that he laughed a little quietly. "I will take more pleasure in the cup if you forgive me."

She clasped his knees in a moment; she kissed his knees with flowing tears.

"O," she cried, "I asked but a kind word!"

"Let us never one think hardly of the other," said Keawe, and was gone out of the house.

Now, the money that Keawe had taken was only some of that store of centime pieces they had laid in at their arrival. It was very sure he had no mind to be drinking. His wife had given her soul for him, now he must give his for hers; no other thought was in the world with him.

At the corner, by the old calaboose, there was the boatswain waiting.

"My wife has the bottle," said Keawe, "and, unless you help me to recover it, there can be no more money and no more liquor to-night."

"You do not mean to say you are serious about that bottle?" cried the boatswain.

"There is the lamp," said Keawe. "Do I look as if I was jesting?"

"That is so," said the boatswain. "You look as serious as a ghost."

"Well, then," said Keawe, "here are two centimes; you must go to my wife in the house, and offer her these for the bottle, which (if I am not much mistaken) she will give you instantly. Bring it to me here, and I will buy it back from you for one; for that is the law with this bottle, that it still must be sold for a less sum. But whatever you do, never breathe a word to her that you have come from me."

"Mate, I wonder are you making a fool of me?" asked the boatswain.

"It will do you no harm if I am," returned Keawe.

"That is so, mate," said the boatswain.

"And if you doubt me," added Keawe, "you can try. As soon as you are clear of the house, wish to have your pocket full of money, or a bottle of the best rum, or what you please, and you will see the virtue of the thing."

"Very well, Kanaka," says the boatswain. "I will try; but if you are having your fun out of me, I will take my fun out of you with a belaying pin."

So the whaler-man went off up the avenue; and Keawe stood and waited. It was near the same spot where Kokua had waited the night before; but

Keawe was more resolved, and never faltered in his purpose; only his soul was bitter with despair.

It seemed a long time he had to wait before he heard a voice singing in the darkness of the avenue. He knew the voice to be the boatswain's; but it was strange how drunken it appeared upon a sudden.

Next, the man himself came stumbling into the light of the lamp. He had the devil's bottle buttoned in his coat; another bottle was in his hand; and even as he came in view he raised it to his mouth and drank.

"You have it," said Keawe. "I see that."

"Hands off!" cried the boatswain, jumping back. "Take a step near me, and I'll smash your mouth. You thought you could make a cat's-paw of me, did you?"

"What do you mean?" cried Keawe.

"Mean?" cried the boatswain. "This is a pretty good bottle, this is; that's what I mean. How I got it for two centimes I can't make out; but I'm sure you shan't have it for one."

"You mean you won't sell?" gasped Keawe.

"No, *sir*!" cried the boatswain. "But I'll give you a drink of the rum, if you like."

"I tell you," said Keawe, "the man who has that bottle goes to hell."

"I reckon I'm going anyway," returned the sailor; "and this bottle's the best thing to go with I've struck yet. No, sir!" he cried again, "this is my bottle now, and you can go and fish for another."

"Can this be true?" Keawe cried. "For your own sake, I beseech you, sell it me!"

"I don't value any of your talk," replied the boatswain. "You thought I was a flat; now you see I'm not; and there's an end. If you won't have a swallow of the rum, I'll have one myself. Here's your health, and good-night to you!"

So off he went down the avenue towards town, and there goes the bottle out of the story.

But Keawe ran to Kokua light as the wind; and great was their joy that night; and great, since then, has been the peace of all their days in the Bright House.

"THE Bottle Imp's" power to horrify, touch, and alarm is due to its emotional accessibility. Human beings of all stripes have been in stomach-churning moments where they would gladly surrender almost anything to escape the agony of a hopeless situation: foreclosure, repossession, bankruptcy... a failed exam, a stolen vehicle, a burned down house... divorce, cancer, adultery... the loss of a parent or child (*ahem...* "The Monkey's Paw"), or inescapable poverty (*ahem...* "The Devil and Tom Walker"). We have all experienced periods of savage desperation where the loss of our souls might be tempting if the trade could mollify our misery. This is why the "Deal With the Devil" narrative is so popular: Midas' touch gave him unfathomable wealth but made him a pariah; Achilles was granted superhuman might but with a proviso; Adam and Eve traded innocence for wisdom, as did knowledge-hungry Faust; Dorian Gray, Narcissus, and Adonis paid dearly for their beauty; Paganini, Tartini, Tommy Johnson, and Robert Johnson were all rumored to have purchased their musical acumen with their souls; Rumpelstiltskin, Jack O'Lantern, and The Little Mermaid flippantly make deals with diabolical characters only to suffer when it's time to pay up. The legend floats throughout literature and folklore – in all parts of the world. It resonates with our internal understanding that "wouldn't it be great if all of this could just magically go away" cannot be a simple purchase. A shift in fate demands an equal return, and the devil will have his due. Stevenson's story transcends the typical thematic concerns of a supernatural tale – loneliness, hubris, egotism, and comeuppance – and pores more specifically over the horror of *love*. Keawe would not have been nearly so tempted to sell his soul without his love for Kokua, nor would Kokua have ever dreamed of sacrificing her soul in such a bizarre trade – to take the place of a sinner in hell in spite of her innocence – without the powerhouse of love motivating her. Like "The Gift of the Magi," Stevenson's fable examines the sacrifices of love, how they are sometimes ironic (ironically, for instance, Kokua takes Keawe's place in hell which only serves to send him to hell-on-earth when he learns of her sacrifice, making him more miserable than ever), and how they are often sadly beautiful. Stevenson departs from his norm with this tale: unlike Jekyll (who is too status conscious to repent), Fettes (who is too cynical to repent), or Markheim (who repents but still pays with his life), Keawe is afforded a get-out-of-jail-free card in the form of the irreverent mariner who takes his place in Hell. But the escape is razor thin, and the message – while not as devastating as that which the now-childless Whites receive in "The Monkey's Paw" – is resoundingly clear: be careful what you wish for, and be happy with what you have.

REPRESSED by Stevenson at his wife's insistance, "The Waif Woman" – published posthumously (and only after Mrs. Stevenson's death) is an adaptation of a ghost story told in chapters 50-55 of the Icelandic *Erybyggja Saga*. The story certainly *is* scandalous, even by Stevenson's standards, and presents perhaps his most brutal indictment of material greed yet. The setting is Iceland at the turn of the first Millennium, circa 999 C.E., the date when Christianity was formally introduced to the Viking settlements on that desolate island. In 1892 The *Erybyggja Saga* (pronounced: AIR-*pik*-uh) was translated into English and proved influential to many British writers, including J. R. R. Tolkein, C. S. Lewis, and M. R. James. The cycle followed the culture of Western Iceland in the first decade of its Christianization, and largely concerned itself with the shift from paganism to Catholic orthodoxy. The comingling of pagan folklore with Christian theology proved tremendously appealing to Stevenson who both respected and resented Christian morality and was both drawn to and wary of secular humanism, and the nonchalant materialism that he associated with many of his fellow atheists. The plot is essentially unchanged, largely concerning itself with the fatal greed of an Icelandic woman who befriends an exiled Hebridean noblewoman in hopes of being gifted her unparalleled finery. The tale is, nonetheless, Stevenson's: he packed the long sequence of Gothic hauntings and grisly revenants of the original saga into the restricted space of a short story (he omits such details as bloody rain, drowned sailors appearing at their funeral and drying their clothes on the fire, the deaths of eighteen members of the protagonist's household, a parade of decomposing phantoms who pile their moldering clothes in the house, and the liberal use of holy water to ward off evil), but adds an original ending that is both grimmer and more horrific than the original Norse story. One of Stevenson's very last works, it is the last of many underlinings of his dearly treasured moral belief that greed and materialism – even in the absence of a Christian worldview – are wicked impulses which sour the soul and lead to unparalleled loss and misery.

The Waif Woman
{1893}

THIS is a tale of Iceland, the isle of stories, and of a thing that befell in the year of the coming there of Christianity.

In the spring of that year a ship sailed from the South Isles to traffic, and fell becalmed inside Snowfellness. The winds had speeded her; she was the first comer of the year; and the fishers drew alongside to hear the news of the south, and eager folk put out in boats to see the merchandise and make prices. From the doors of the hall on Frodis Water, the house folk saw the ship becalmed and the boats about her, coming and going; and the merchants from the ship could see the smoke go up and the men and women trooping to their meals in the hall.

The goodman of that house was called Finnward Keelfarer, and his wife Aud the Light-Minded; and they had a son Eyolf, a likely boy, and a daughter Asdis, a slip of a maid. Finnward was well-to-do in his affairs, he kept open house and had good friends. But Aud his wife was not so much considered: her mind was set on trifles, on bright clothing, and the admiration of men, and the envy of women; and it was thought she was not always so circumspect in her bearing as she might have been, but nothing to hurt.

On the evening of the second day men came to the house from sea. They told of the merchandise in the ship, which was well enough and to be had at easy rates, and of a waif woman that sailed in her, no one could tell why, and had chests of clothes beyond comparison, fine coloured stuffs, finely woven, the best that ever came into that island, and gewgaws for a queen. At the hearing of that Aud's eyes began to glisten. She went early to bed; and the day was not yet red before she was on the beach, had a boat launched, and was pulling to the shi By the way she looked closely at all boats, but there was no woman in any; and at that she was better pleased, for she had no fear of the men.

When they came to the ship, boats were there already, and the merchants and the shore folk sat and jested and chaffered in the stern. But in the fore part of the ship, the woman sat alone, and looked before her sourly at the sea. They called her Thorgunna. She was as tall as a man and high in flesh, a buxom wife to look at. Her hair was of the dark red, time had not changed it. Her face was dark, the cheeks full, and the brow smooth. Some of the merchants told that she was sixty years of age and others laughed and said she was but forty; but they spoke of her in whispers, for they seemed to think that she was ill to deal with and not more than ordinary canny.

Aud went to where she sat and made her welcome to Iceland. Thorgunna did the honours of the ship. So for a while they carried it on, praising and watching each other, in the way of women. But Aud was a little vessel to contain a great longing, and presently the cry of her heart came out of her.

"The folk say," says she, "you have the finest women's things that ever came to Iceland?" and as she spoke her eyes grew big.

"It would be strange if I had not," quoth Thorgunna. "Queens have no finer."

So Aud begged that she might see them.

Thorgunna looked on her askance. "Truly," said she, "the things are for no use but to be shown." So she fetched a chest and opened it. Here was a cloak of the rare scarlet laid upon with silver, beautiful beyond belief; hard by was a silver brooch of basket work that was wrought as fine as any shell and was as broad as the face of the full moon; and Aud saw the clothes lying folded in the chest, of all the colours of the day, and fire, and precious gems; and her heart burned with envy. So, because she had so huge a mind to buy, she began to make light of the merchandise.

"They are good enough things," says she, "though I have better in my chest at home. It is a good enough cloak, and I am in need of a new cloak." At that she fingered the scarlet, and the touch of the fine stuff went to her mind like singing. "Come," says she, "if it were only for your civility in showing it, what will you have for your cloak?"

"Woman," said Thorgunna, "I am no merchant." And she closed the chest and locked it, like one angry.

Then Aud fell to protesting and caressing her. That was Aud's practice; for she thought if she hugged and kissed a person none could say her nay. Next she went to flattery, said she knew the things were too noble for the like of her—they were made for a stately, beautiful woman like Thorgunna; and at that she kissed her again, and Thorgunna seemed a little pleased. And now Aud pled poverty and begged for the cloak in a gift; and now she vaunted the wealth of her goodman and offered ounces and ounces of fine silver, the price of three men's lives. Thorgunna smiled, but it was a grim smile, and still she shook her head. At last Aud wrought herself into extremity and wept.

"I would give my soul for it," she cried.

"Fool!" said Thorgunna. "But there have been fools before you!" And a little after, she said this: "Let us be done with beseeching. The things are mine. I was a fool to show you them; but where is their use, unless we show them? Mine they are and mine they shall be till I die. I have paid for them dear enough," said she.

Aud saw it was of no avail; so she dried her tears, and asked Thorgunna about her voyage, and made believe to listen while she plotted in her little mind. "Thorgunna," she asked presently, "do you count kin with any folk in Iceland?"

"I count kin with none," replied Thorgunna. "My kin is of the greatest, but I have not been always lucky, so I say the less."

"So that you have no house to pass the time in till the ship return?" cries Aud. "Dear Thorgunna, you must come and live with us. My goodman is rich, his hand and his house are open, and I will cherish you like a daughter."

At that Thorgunna smiled on the one side; but her soul laughed within her at the woman's shallowness. "I will pay her for that word daughter," she thought, and she smiled again.

"I will live with you gladly," says she, "for your house has a good name, and I have seen the smoke of your kitchen from the ship. But one thing you shall understand. I make no presents, I give nothing where I go—not a rag and not an ounce. Where I stay, I work for my upkeep; and as I am strong as a man and hardy as an ox, they that have had the keeping of me were the better pleased."

It was a hard job for Aud to keep her countenance, for she was like to have wept. And yet she felt it would be unseemly to eat her invitation; and like a shallow woman and one that had always led her husband by the nose, she told herself she would find some means to cajole Thorgunna and come by her purpose after all. So she put a good face on the thing, had Thorgunna into the boat, her and her two great chests, and brought her home with her to the hall by the beach.

All the way in she made much of the wife; and when they were arrived gave her a locked bed-place in the hall, where was a bed, a table, and a stool, and space for the two chests.

"This shall be yours while you stay here," said Aud. And she attended on her guest.

Now Thorgunna opened the second chest and took out her bedding—sheets of English linen, the like of it never seen, a cover of quilted silk, and curtains of purple wrought with silver. At the sight of these Aud was like one distracted, greed blinded her mind; the cry rose strong in her throat, it must out.

"What will you sell your bedding for?" she cried, and her cheeks were hot.

Thorgunna looked upon her with a dusky countenance. "Truly you are a courteous hostess," said she, "but I will not sleep on straw for your amusement."

At that Aud's two ears grew hot as her cheeks; and she took Thorgunna at her word; and left her from that time in peace.

The woman was as good as her spoken word. Inside the house and out she wrought like three, and all that she put her hand to was well done. When she milked, the cows yielded beyond custom; when she made hay, it was always dry weather; when she took her turn at the cooking, the folk licked their spoons. Her manners when she pleased were outside imitation, like one that had sat with kings in their high buildings. It seemed she was pious too, and the day never passed but she was in the church there praying. The rest was not so well. She was of few words, and never one about her kin and fortunes. Gloom sat on her brow, and she was ill to cross. Behind her back they gave her the name of the Waif Woman or the Wind Wife; to her face it must always be Thorgunna. And if any of the young men called her mother, she would speak no more that day, but sit apart in the hall and mutter with her lips.

"This is a queer piece of goods that we have gotten," says Finnward Keelfarer, "I wish we get no harm by her! But the good wife's pleasure must be done," said he, which was his common word.

236

When she was at work, Thorgunna wore the rudest of plain clothes, though ever clean as a cat; but at night in the hall she was more dainty, for she loved to be admired. No doubt she made herself look well, and many thought she was a comely woman still, and to those she was always favourable and full of pleasant speech. But the more that some pleased her, it was thought by good judges that they pleased Aud the less.

When midsummer was past, a company of young men upon a journey came to the house by Frodis Water. That was always a great day for Aud, when there were gallants at table; and what made this day the greater, Alf of the Fells was in the company, and she thought Alf fancied her. So be sure Aud wore her best. But when Thorgunna came from the bed-place, she was arrayed like any queen and the broad brooch was in her bosom. All night in the hall these women strove with each other; and the little maid, Asdis, looked on, and was ashamed and knew not why. But Thorgunna pleased beyond all; she told of strange things that had befallen in the world; when she pleased she had the cue to laughter; she sang, and her voice was full and her songs new in that island; and whenever she turned, the eyes shone in her face and the brooch glittered at her bosom. So that the young men forgot the word of the merchants as to the woman's age, and their looks followed her all night.

Aud was sick with envy. Sleep fled her; her husband slept, but she sat upright beside him in the bed, and gnawed her fingers. Now she began to hate Thorgunna, and the glittering of the great brooch stood before her in the dark. "Sure," she thought, "it must be the glamour of that brooch! She is not so fair as I; she is as old as the dead in the hillside; and as for her wit and her songs, it is little I think of them!" Up she got at that, took a light from the embers, and came to her guest's bed-place. The door was locked, but Aud had a master-key and could go in. Inside, the chests were open, and in the top of one the light of her taper shone upon the glittering of the brooch. As a dog snatches food she snatched it, and turned to the bed. Thorgunna lay on her side; it was to be thought she slept, but she talked the while to herself, and her lips moved. It seemed her years returned to her in slumber, for her face was grey and her brow knotted; and the open eyes of her stared in the eyes of Aud. The heart of the foolish woman died in her bosom; but her greed was the stronger, and she fled with that which she had stolen.

When she was back in bed, the word of Thorgunna came to her mind, that these things were for no use but to be shown. Here she had the brooch and the shame of it, and might not wear it. So all night she quaked with the fear of discovery, and wept tears of rage that she should have sinned in vain. Day came, and Aud must rise; but she went about the house like a crazy woman. She saw the eyes of Asdis rest on her strangely, and at that she beat the maid. She scolded the house folk, and, by her way of it, nothing was done aright. First she was loving to her husband and made much of him,

thinking to be on his good side when trouble came. Then she took a better
way, picked a feud with him, and railed on the poor man till his ears rang,
so that he might be in the wrong beforehand. The brooch she hid without,
in the side of a hayrick. All this while Thorgunna lay in the bed-place,
which was not her way, for by custom she was early astir. At last she came
forth, and there was that in her face that made all the house look one at the
other and the heart of Aud to be straitened. Never a word the guest spoke,
not a bite she swallowed, and they saw the strong shudderings take and
shake her in her place. Yet a little, and still without speech, back she went
into her bad-place, and the door was shut.

"That is a sick wife," said Finnward, "Her weird has come on her."

And at that the heart of Aud was lifted up with hope.

All day Thorgunna lay on her bed, and the next day sent for Finnward.

"Finnward Keelfarer," said she, "my trouble is come upon me, and I am
at the end of my days."

He made the customary talk.

"I have had my good things; now my hour is come; and let suffice," quoth
she. "I did not send for you to hear your prating."

Finnward knew not what to answer, for he saw her soul was dark.

"I sent for you on needful matters," she began again. "I die here—I!--in
this black house, in a bleak island, far from all decency and proper ways of
man; and now my treasure must be left. Small pleasure have I had of it, and
leave it with the less!" cried she.

"Good woman, as the saying is, needs must," says Finnward, for he was
nettled with that speech.

"For that I called you," quoth Thorgunna. "In these two chests are much
wealth and things greatly to be desired. I wish my body to be laid in
Skalaholt in the new church, where I trust to hear the mass-priests singing
over my head so long as time endures. To that church I will you to give
what is sufficient, leaving your conscience judge of it. My scarlet cloak with
the silver, I will to that poor fool your wife. She longed for it so bitterly, I
may not even now deny her. Give her the brooch as well. I warn you of her;
I was such as she, only wiser; I warn you, the ground she stands upon is
water, and whoso trusts her leans on rottenness. I hate her and I pity her.
When she comes to lie where I lie—" There she broke off. "The rest of my
goods I leave to your black-eyed maid, young Asdis, for her slim body and
clean mind. Only the things of my bed, you shall see burned."

"It is well," said Finnward.

"It may be well," quoth she, "if you obey. My life has been a wonder to
all and a fear to many. While I lived none thwarted me and prospered. See
to it that none thwart me after I am dead. It stands upon your safety."

"It stands upon my honour," quoth Finnward, "and I have the name of an
honourable man."

"You have the name of a weak one," says Thorgunna. "Look to it, look to it, Finnward. Your house shall rue it else."

"The rooftree of my house is my word," said Finnward.

"And that is a true saying," says the woman. "See to it, then. The speech of Thorgunna is ended."

With that she turned her face against the wall and Finnward left her.

The same night, in the small hours of the clock, Thorgunna passed. It was a wild night for summer, and the wind sang about the eaves and clouds covered the moon, when the dark woman wended. From that day to this no man has learned her story or her people's name; but be sure the one was stormy and the other great. She had come to that isle, a waif woman, on a ship; thence she flitted, and no more remained of her but her heavy chests and her big body.

In the morning the house women streaked and dressed the corpse. Then came Finnward, and carried the sheets and curtains from the house, and caused build a fire upon the sands. But Aud had an eye on her man's doings.

"And what is this that you are at?" said she.

So he told her.

"Burn the good sheets!" she cried. "And where would I be with my two hands? No, troth," said Aud, "not so long as your wife is above ground!"

"Good wife," said Finnward, "this is beyond your province. Here is my word pledged and the woman dead I pledged it to. So much the more am I bound. Let me be doing as I must, goodwife."

"Tilly-valley!" says she, "and a fiddlestick's end, goodman! You may know well about fishing and be good at shearing sheep for what I know; but you are little of a judge of damask sheets. And the best word I can say is just this," she says, laying hold of one end of the goods, "that if ye are made up to burn the plenishing, you must burn your wife along with it."

"I trust it will not go so hard," says Finnward, "and I beg you not to speak so loud and let the house folk hear you."

"Let them speak low that are ashamed!" cries Aud. "I speak only in reason."

"You are to consider that the woman died in my house," says Finnward, "and this was her last behest. In truth, goodwife, if I were to fail, it is a thing that would stick long in my throat, and would give us an ill name with the neighbours."

"And you are to consider," says she, "that I am your true wife and worth all the witches ever burnt, and loving her old husband"—here she put her arms about his neck. "And you are to consider that what you wish to do is to destroy fine stuff, such as we have no means of replacing; and that she bade you do it singly to spite me, for I sought to buy this bedding from her while she was alive at her own price; and that she hated me because I was young and handsome."

"That is a true word that she hated you, for she said so herself before she wended," says Finnward.

"So that here is an old faggot that hated me, and she dead as a bucket," says Aud; "and here is a young wife that loves you dear, and is alive forby"—and at that she kissed him—"and the point is, which are you to do the will of?"

The man's weakness caught him hard, and he faltered. "I fear some hurt will come of it," said he.

There she cut in, and bade the lads tread out the fire, and the lasses roll the bed-stuff up and carry it within.

"My dear," says he, "my honour—this is against my honour."

But she took his arm under hers, and caressed his hand, and kissed his knuckles, and led him down the bay. "Bubble-bubble-bubble!" says she, imitating him like a baby, though she was none so young. "Bubble-bubble, and a silly old man! We must bury the troll wife, and here is trouble enough, and a vengeance! Horses will sweat for it before she comes to Skalaholt; 'tis my belief she was a man in a woman's habit. And so now, have done, good man, and let us get her waked and buried, which is more than she deserves, or her old duds are like to pay for. And when that is ended, we can consult upon the rest."

So Finnward was but too well pleased to put it off.

The next day they set forth early for Skalaholt across the heaths. It was heavy weather, and grey overhead; the horses sweated and neighed, and the men went silent, for it was nowhere in their minds that the dead wife was canny. Only Aud talked by the way, like a silly sea-gull piping on a cliff, and the rest held their peace. The sun went down before they were across Whitewater; and the black night fell on them this side of Netherness. At Netherness they beat upon the door. The goodman was not abed nor any of his folk, but sat in the hall talking; and to them Finnward made clear his business.

"I will never deny you a roof," said the goodman of Netherness. "But I have no food ready, and if you cannot be doing without meat, you must e'en fare farther."

They laid the body in a shed, made fast their horses, and came into the house, and the door was closed again. So there they sat about the lights, and there was little said, for they were none so well pleased with their reception. Presently, in the place where the food was kept, began a clattering of dishes; and it fell to a bondman of the house to go and see what made the clatter. He was no sooner gone than he was back again; and told it was a big, buxom woman, high in flesh and naked as she was born, setting meats upon a dresser. Finnward grew pale as the dawn; he got to his feet, and the rest rose with him, and all the party of the funeral came to the buttery-door. And the dead Thorgunna took no heed of their coming, but went on setting forth meats, and seemed to talk with herself as she did so; and she was naked to the buff.

Great fear fell upon them; the marrow of their back grew cold. Not one word they spoke, neither good nor bad; but back into the hall, and down upon their bended knees, and to their prayers.

"Now, in the name of God, what ails you?" cried the goodman of Netherness.

And when they had told him, shame fell upon him for his churlishness.

"The dead wife reproves me," said the honest man.

And he blessed himself and his house, and caused spread the tables, and they all ate of the meats that the dead wife laid out.

This was the first walking of Thorgunna, and it is thought by good judges it would have been the last as well, if men had been more wise.

The next day they came to Skalaholt, and there was the body buried, and the next after they set out for home. Finnward's heart was heavy, and his mind divided. He feared the dead wife and the living; he feared dishonour and he feared dispeace; and his will was like a sea-gull in the wind. Now he cleared his throat and made as if to speak; and at that Aud cocked her eye and looked at the goodman mocking, and his voice died unborn. At the last, shame gave him courage.

"Aud," said he, "yon was a most uncanny thing at Netherness."

"No doubt," said Aud.

"I have never had it in my mind," said he, "that yon woman was the thing she should be."

"I dare say not," said Aud. "I never thought so either."

"It stands beyond question she was more than canny," says Finnward, shaking his head. "No manner of doubt but what she was ancient of mind."

"She was getting pretty old in body, too," says Aud.

"Wife," says he, "it comes in upon me strongly this is no kind of woman to disobey; above all, being dead and her walking. I think, wife, we must even do as she commanded."

"Now what is ever your word?" says she, riding up close and setting her hand upon his shoulder. "'The goodwife's pleasure must be done'; is not that my Finnward?"

"The good God knows I grudge you nothing," cried Finnward. "But my blood runs cold upon this business. Worse will come of it!" he cried, "worse will flow from it!"

"What is this todo?" cries Aud. "Here is an old brimstone hag that should have been stoned with stones, and hated me besides. Vainly she tried to frighten me when she was living; shall she frighten me now when she is dead and rotten? I trow not. Think shame to your beard, goodman! Are these a man's shoes I see you shaking in, when your wife rides by your bridle-hand, as bold as nails?"

"Ay, ay," quoth Finnward. "But there goes a byword in the country:

Little wit, little fear."

At this Aud began to be concerned, for he was usually easier to lead. So now she tried the other method on the man.

"Is that your word?" cried she. "I kiss the hands of ye! If I have not wit enough, I can rid you of my company. Wit is it he seeks?" she cried. "The old broomstick that we buried yesterday had wit for you."

So she rode on ahead and looked not the road that he was on.

Poor Finnward followed on his horse, but the light of the day was gone out, for his wife was like his life to him. He went six miles and was true to his heart; but the seventh was not half through when he rode up to her.

"Is it to be the goodwife's pleasure?" she asked.

"Aud, you shall have your way," says he; "God grant there come no ill of it!"

So she made much of him, and his heart was comforted.

When they came to the house, Aud had the two chests to her own bed-place, and gloated all night on what she found. Finnward looked on, and trouble darkened his mind.

"Wife," says he at last, "you will not forget these things belong to Asdis?"

At that she barked upon him like a dog.

"Am I a thief?" she cried. "The brat shall have them in her turn when she grows up. Would you have me give her them now to turn her minx's head with?"

So the weak man went his way out of the house in sorrow and fell to his affairs. Those that wrought with him that day observed that now he would labour and toil like a man furious, and now would sit and stare like one stupid; for in truth he judged the business would end ill.

For a while there was no more done and no more said. Aud cherished her treasures by herself, and none was the wiser except Finnward. Only the cloak she sometimes wore, for that was hers by the will of the dead wife; but the others she let lie, because she knew she had them foully, and she feared Finnward somewhat and Thorgunna much.

At last husband and wife were bound to bed one night, and he was the first stripped and got in. "What sheets are these?" he screamed, as his legs touched them, for these were smooth as water, but the sheets of Iceland were like sacking.

"Clean sheets, I suppose," says Aud, but her hand quavered as she wound her hair.

"Woman!" cried Finnward, "these are the bed-sheets of Thorgunna—these are the sheets she died in! do not lie to me!"

At that Aud turned and looked at him. "Well?" says she, "they have been washed."

Finnward lay down again in the bed between Thorgunna's sheets, and groaned; never a word more he said, for now he knew he was a coward and a man dishonoured. Presently his wife came beside him, and they lay still, but neither slept.

It might be twelve in the night when Aud felt Finnward shudder so strong that the bed shook.

"What ails you?" said she.

"I know not," he said. "It is a chill like the chill of death. My soul is sick with it." His voice fell low. "It was so Thorgunna sickened," said he. And he arose and walked in the hall in the dark till it came morning.

Early in the morning he went forth to the sea-fishing with four lads. Aud was troubled at heart and watched him from the door, and even as he went down the beach she saw him shaken with Thorgunna's shudder. It was a rough day, the sea was wild, the boat laboured exceedingly, and it may be that Finnward's mind was troubled with his sickness. Certain it is that they struck, and their boat was burst, upon a skerry under Snowfellness. The four lads were spilled into the sea, and the sea broke and buried them, but Finnward was cast upon the skerry, and clambered up, and sat there all day long: God knows his thoughts. The sun was half-way down, when a shepherd went by on the cliffs about his business, and spied a man in the midst of the breach of the loud seas, upon a pinnacle of reef. He hailed him, and the man turned and hailed again. There was in that cove so great a clashing of the seas and so shrill a cry of sea-fowl that the herd might hear the voice and nor the words. But the name Thorgunna came to him, and he saw the face of Finnward Keelfarer like the face of an old man. Lively ran the herd to Finnward's house; and when his tale was told there, Eyolf the boy was lively to out a boat and hasten to his father's aid. By the strength of hands they drove the keel against the seas, and with skill and courage Eyolf won upon the skerry and climbed up, There sat his father dead; and this was the first vengeance of Thorgunna against broken faith.

It was a sore job to get the corpse on board, and a sorer yet to bring it home before the rolling seas. But the lad Eyolf was a lad of promise, and the lads that pulled for him were sturdy men. So the break-faith's body was got home, and waked, and buried on the hill. Aud was a good widow and wept much, for she liked Finnward well enough. Yet a bird sang in her ears that now she might marry a young man. Little fear that she might have her choice of them, she thought, with all Thorgunna's fine things; and her heart was cheered.

Now, when the corpse was laid in the hill, Asdis came where Aud sat solitary in hall, and stood by her awhile without speech.

"Well, child?" says Aud; and again "Well?" and then "Keep us holy, if you have anything to say, out with it!"

So the maid came so much nearer, "Mother," says she, "I wish you would not wear these things that were Thorgunna's."

"Aha," cries Aud. "This is what it is? You begin early, brat! And who has been poisoning your mind? Your fool of a father, I suppose." And then she stopped and went all scarlet. "Who told you they were yours?" she asked again, taking it all the higher for her stumble. "When you are grown, then you shall have your share and not a day before. These things are not for babies."

The child looked at her and was amazed. "I do not wish them," she said. "I wish they might be burned."

"Upon my word, what next?" cried Aud. "And why should they be burned?"

"I know my father tried to burn these things," said Asdis, "and he named Thorgunna's name upon the skerry ere he died. And, O mother, I doubt they have brought ill luck."

But the more Aud was terrified, the more she would make light of it.

Then the girl put her hand upon her mother's. "I fear they are ill come by," said she.

The blood sprang in Aud's face. "And who made you a judge upon your mother that bore you?" cried she.

"Kinswoman," said Asdis, looking down, "I saw you with the brooch."

"What do you mean? When? Where did you see me?" cried the mother.

"Here in the hall," said Asdis, looking on the floor, "the night you stole it."

At that Aud let out a cry. Then she heaved up her hand to strike the child. "You little spy!" she cried. Then she covered her face, and wept, and rocked herself. "What can you know?" she cried. "How can you understand, that are a baby, not so long weaned? He could—your father could, the dear good man, dead and gone! He could understand and pity, he was good to me. Now he has left me alone with heartless children! Asdis," she cried, "have you no nature in your blood? You do not know what I have done and suffered for them. I have done—oh, and I could have done anything! And there is your father dead. And after all, you ask me not to use them? No woman in Iceland has the like. And you wish me to destroy them? Not if the dead should rise!" she cried. "No, no," and she stopped her ears, "not if the dead should rise, and let that end it!"

So she ran into her bed-place, and clapped at the door, and left the child amazed.

But for all Aud spoke with so much passion, it was noticed that for long she left the things unused. Only she would be locked somewhere daily in her bed-place, where she pored on them and secretly wore them for her pleasure.

Now winter was at hand; the days grew short and the nights long; and under the golden face of morning the isle would stand silver with frost. Word came from Holyfell to Frodis Water of a company of young men upon a journey; that night they supped at Holyfell, the next it would be at Frodis Water; and Alf of the Fells was there, and Thongbrand Ketilson, and Hall the Fair. Aud went early to her bed-place, and there she pored upon these fineries till her heart was melted with self-love. There was a kirtle of a mingled colour, and the blue shot into the green, and the green lightened from the blue, as the colours play in the ocean between deeps and shallows: she thought she could endure to live no longer and not wear it. There was a bracelet of an ell long, wrought like a serpent and with fiery jewels for the eyes; she saw it shine on her white arm and her head grew dizzy with desire. "Ah!" she thought, "never were fine lendings better met with a fair wearer." And she closed her eyelids, and she thought she saw herself among the company and the men's eyes go after her admiring. With that she considered that she must soon marry one of them and wondered which; and she thought Alf was perhaps the best, or Hall the Fair, but was not certain, and then she remembered Finnward Keelfarer in his cairn upon the hill, and was concerned. "Well, he was a good husband to me," she thought, "and I was a good wife to him. But that is an old song now." So she turned again to handling the stuffs and jewels. At last she got to bed in the smooth sheets, and lay, and fancied how she would look, and admired herself, and saw others admire her, and told herself stories, till her heart grew warm and she chuckled to herself between the sheets. So she shook awhile with laughter; and then the mirth abated but not the shaking; and a grue took hold upon her flesh, and the cold of the grave upon her belly, and the terror of death upon her soul. With that a voice was in her ear: "It was so Thorgunna sickened." Thrice in the night the chill and the terror took her, and thrice it passed away; and when she rose on the morrow, death had breathed upon her countenance.

She saw the house folk and her children gaze upon her; well she knew why! She knew her day was come, and the last of her days, and her last hour was at her back; and it was so in her soul that she scarce minded. All was lost, all was past mending, she would carry on until she fell. So she went as usual, and hurried the feast for the young men, and railed upon her house folk, but her feet stumbled,
and her voice was strange in her own ears, and the eyes of the folk fled before her. At times, too, the chill took her and the fear along with it; and she must sit down, and the teeth beat together in her head, and the stool tottered on the floor. At these times, she thought she was passing, and the

voice of Thorgunna sounded in her ear: "The things are for no use but to be shown," it said. "Aud, Aud, have you shown them once? No, not once!"

And at the sting of the thought her courage and strength would revive, and she would rise again and move about her business.

Now the hour drew near, and Aud went to her bed-place, and did on the bravest of her finery, and came forth to greet her guests. Was never woman in Iceland robed as she was. The words of greeting were yet between her lips, when the shuddering fell upon her strong as labour, and a horror as deep as hell. Her face was changed amidst her finery, and the faces of her guests were changed as they beheld her: fear puckered their brows, fear drew back their feet; and she took her doom from the looks of them, and fled to her bed-place. There she flung herself on the wife's coverlet, and turned her face against the wall.

That was the end of all the words of Aud; and in the small hours on the clock her spirit wended. Asdis had come to and fro, seeing if she might help, where was no help possible of man or woman. It was light in the bed-place when the maid returned, for a taper stood upon a chest. There lay Aud in her fine clothes, and there by her side on the bed the big dead wife Thorgunna squatted on her hams. No sound was heard, but it seemed by the movement of her mouth as if Thorgunna sang, and she waved her arms as if to singing.

"God be good to us!" cried Asdis, "she is dead."

"Dead," said the dead wife.

"Is the weird passed?" cried Asdis.

"When the sin is done the weird is dreed," said Thorgunna, and with that she was not.

But the next day Eyolf and Asdis caused build a fire on the shore betwixt tide-marks. There they burned the bed-clothes, and the clothes, and the jewels, and the very boards of the waif woman's chests; and when the tide returned it washed away their ashes. So the weird of Thorgunna was lifted from the house on Frodis Water.

IT is a pity that Fanny Stevenson was so repulsed by "The Waif Woman," because it is truly one of her husband's great supernatural tales, combining elements of "Thrawn Janet" and "The Body Snatcher" – specifically the ideas of a witchy-woman returning as a revenant and of an unethical parasite being hounded by the ghost of one from whom they have leeched ill-gotten gain. As he neared the end of his life, Stevenson's confidence in his literary abilities was nearly shot, and although at one point he angrily chided his publisher for not including the admittedly out of place "Waif Woman" in the South Seas themed *Island Nights' Entertainment*, he dropped his defense for the story when his wife criticized it for reasons which were never

247

clarified, though there is speculation that she considered it a weak plagiarism. The unattractive portrayal of a materialistic wife doesn't seem to line up with Fanny Stevenson, at any rate, who was content to live a bohemian lifestyle, but the protest that she raised nearly obliterated the tale from history until its rescue in 1914. Regardless of its very clear status as an adaptation of a folktale (Howard Pyle did no worse with his *Merry Adventures of Robin Hood* nor the Grimms with their fairy tales), the story has a uniquely Stevesonian ending. In the *original*, the covetous wife (named Thurid, not Aud) comes to her senses after losing eighteen members of her household, and has the bedclothes buried and anointed with holy water to end the haunting. But Stevenson is not so forgiving: he closes his tale with the toadlike Thurgonna squatting over the stricken body of Aud, passing a word of warning onto the as-yet virtuous daughter: learn from your mother; she did not get a second chance, and if you follow in her green-eyed ways, you too might lose everything dear to you. It is also worth noting, as we close this book, a theme which Thurgonna reiterates throughout the tale: wealth is so often only worth looking at – it is not practical or useful or caring or relatable or huggable or kissable or warm or tender or comforting or tangible or kind or patient or fleeting or even precious. A silver broach is good just for pulling out of a drawer, turning it over, and folding it back up in linen. A husband, however old or unattractive, is far more precious than silver. A soul that resonates with other souls is far dearer than damask sheets. Wealth, Stevenson continues to thump on his humanist pulpit as he approached death, is pointless. It leads to distraction, self-absorption, and loss. In the end, Aud is not haunted by a vengeful queen, but by the specter of her own naked mortality. It is noteworthy, is it not, that Thurgonna has the very unusual feature of being a nude ghost? While this may allude to the threat of her timeless sexuality, which – in spite of her age – seems to allure the village men, Stevenson does not work very hard to highlight the attractiveness of his disrobed ghost. Instead, he uses this stitchless specter to remind Aud that – as the saying goes – "you can't take it with you." Scratch away at material happiness – claw and bite and struggle if you must – but at the end of your life, you may find yourself dying alone, stricken by the horror of what you have lost for the sake of petty baubles, and what you have gained at such a steep price.

STRANGE CASE OF

Dr. Jekyll and Mr. Hyde

{1886}

WHAT YOU SHOULD KNOW BEFORE READING:
STRANGE CASE of DR JEKYLL & MR HYDE

I was six years old when I walked into a bookstore in Holland, Michigan with my family and met Dr. Jekyll for the first time. We had recently watched *The Great Mouse Detective* and I saw the unmistakable archetypes of villainy and goodness emblazoned on an inexpensive hardback edition of Robert Louis Stevenson's most famous horror story: here, to the right, was the hero – handsome with his steely eyes and brown sideburns, analyzing a test tube that to me symbolized detective work and wisdom, neatly attired in a high collar and a warm, brown frock – and there, to the left, was the unquestionable evildoer – wearing the top hat and satin cloak, and wielding the silver-headed cane that I somehow instinctively associated with decadent aristocracy, his animalistic teeth were set viciously, his face was corded and dark, and his eyes bulged madly from beneath the rim of his hat. In the background of the hero glowed the warmth of a Victorian parlor. In the background of the villain shone the silhouette of a moonlit cityscape. So the story was clear to me, and in my childish way I explained the tale: here was the brilliant detective – dashing, intellectual, and openhearted – examining the evidence that would lead him to capturing the debased enemy – a wealthy degenerate, possibly insane, certainly cruel. But my mom patiently pulled down the book. I was close, she said, but wrong: they were the same person.

The revelation went through me like a shock of electricity. Without having read the story, only primed by the cover, I was stupefied to learn the truth of one of Western literature's most enduring parables. And it haunts me to this day. That man is not one, but two (or as Jekyll noted, presaging Jung, manifold), that goodness can conceal wickedness, that goodness could willingly give birth to wickedness. Why would a good man want to be bad? I think that even at the early age, I instinctively understood: sometimes it's nice to be bad – sometimes getting away with what is wrong is attractive. And even though I hated the very sight of him – the clenched fist and teeth, the peering white eye, the wild tangle of black hair – I secretly understood the attraction in his existence, and that secret understanding shamed me and brought wonder to my mind.

Of course, the book whose cover had stunned my embryonic mind was Robert Louis Stevenson's horror masterpiece, *Strange Case of Dr Jekyll and Mr Hyde* (there is no article "The" in the title, and the doctor's name should be pronounced JEE-*kull*, like "fecal," and *was* until the 1941 Spencer Tracy film popularized the erroneous "JZEH-*kull*" pronunciation). The story of the tale's genesis is famous, and frequently repeated in introductions for its sheer dramatism. Louis was sleeping fitfully, as he regularly did, but his wife, Fanny (a strong-headed woman from my native Indiana) elbowed him back into consciousness when the tossing escalated into the shouts of a night terror. Dazed and shocked, he turned to her with a look of admonishment. In his thick, Edinburgh brogue he hissed: "Why did you wake me? I was dreaming a fine bogey tale..." He had been dreaming of man's duality, and there in the mists of his unconscious, a tall, handsome man had drunk a potion, and now there stood his transformed body: dwarfish, dusky, and vile. Stevenson had much reason to brood over this topic: as a resident of Edinburgh he was well aware of the stories of Burke and Hare, and of Deacon Brodie, especially.

Burke and Hare were two thugs – or as Jekyll would say, bravos – who found a loophole in their poverty-stricken lives when they sold the body of a lodger to representatives of the esteemed surgeon, Dr. Robert Knox, for roughly $1,200 in modern currency. The first body died in a kosher manner, but the subsequent 16 corpses were victims of foul play, and no one questioned why these two shady louts were so capable of feeding Knox the bodies he needed. When the news broke that Dr. Knox was turning a blind eye to serial murder, the scandal in Edinburgh society was seismic. Hare became Crown evidence, Burke was hanged, and Knox – once reputable if eccentric – became an abhorred pariah. At the time of the nightmare, Stevenson had been working on "Markheim," which had springboarded off of a play he had attempted on the life of Deacon William Brodie. Brodie was an 18th century gentleman who moonlighted as a burglar. A cabinet-maker and carpenter, Brodie rose rapidly to the executive post of the tradesman guild of Edinburgh – Deacon, or president – and at the peak of his career even sat on the city council. He hobnobbed with the gentry, even meeting Scotland's national poet, Robert Burns, and one the confidence of Edinburgh's richest and most esteemed citizens. It was with this trust that he began a campaign of crime: doing odd repairs on the homes of his friends and professional clients, Brodie acquainted himself with their security devices. As a cabinet maker, he was also part-locksmith, and would often be asked to fix doors and office drawers that needed repair. He used these opportunities to make wax impressions of the keys, which he would later use to create copies. With the cash and valuables that he stole, Brodie was able to afford a second life of gambling, multiple families in different cities, and fencing stolen goods. Eventually he even commanded a little band of thieves who followed his bidding and assisted his crimes. After an armed attack on a tax office failed, Brodie realized that his net had gone too wide, and attempted to claim a pardon from the government, but to no avail. He was arrested in Holland en route to the United States. The fallout of his unmasking was earthshaking, and he became something of a folk figure (certainly not a folk *hero*) to the Scottish in the same way that Billy the Kid, Al Capone, and Lizzy Borden have fascinated Americans with their duplicitous villainy. Burke and Hare were transformed into his second most notable bogey tale, "The Body Snatcher," and Deacon Brodie found life in Dr. Henry Jekyll.

The foundation of Stevenson's tale, however, was more philosophical than historical: his family's Calvinism. Calvinism rears its head in so many of Stevenson's stories, but Jekyll's struggle to have fun on the side is particularly suggestive of Calvinist social mores. Let's begin by discussing the theological basis of the faith, and then look at how Calvinism was so often practiced. The basic concept behind the faith that had made such an impact on Stevenson's childhood was the idea that God chooses, or predestines those who will be saved, called the Elect. He also chooses who will be damned, all before birth and time. Nothing can be done to change this destiny: a man born damned can give to the poor, spent whole hours in pious prayer, and devote his life to Christ, without altering his infernal destination. Likewise, one of the Elect can spend his life whoring, killing, thieving, and corrupting, but due to the holy seal on his head, he will be saved. The basic element behind all of this is a belief in the absolute power of God; unlike Catholics who saw the Pope, saints, and confessors as having been apportioned divine power, or even Anglicans who acknowledge the Archbishop of Canterbury, or Lutherans who celebrate the lives of the saints, Calvinists saw all power in God's hands – even the power to receive salvation. In Christianity, there is a potent struggle between two major concepts: "salvation by grace" (which implies that salvation is a gift freely given without any expectations) and "faith without works is dead" (which argues – from the same phrase used in James – that salvation is free, but faith cannot be real without the evidence of good deeds, or that you don't have to be good to be a Christian, but that a real Christian will naturally tend towards goodness). Calvinism falls sharply on these concepts, and while it looks harshly on those who do good things hoping that God will let them into heaven (violation: salvation by grace), it also deals roughly with those who do not do visible good deeds (violation: faith sans works).

The resultant society is a group of people who pretend to be humble (you can't tout your deeds or be proud of them; this implies you are not Elect) but are in fact desperate to be seen doing good deeds to squash any gossip that they are not among the Elect. To avoid being judged or considered un-elected by the members of their church, Calvinists would work strenuously to cultivate a good public image (think Jekyll), to make their neighbors think that the good behavior signaled a natural member of the Elect. This was less in order to spread goodness (after all, good works meant nothing in and of themselves; they were but a SYMPTOM of election), and more to avoid gossip or suggestions that they were not among the Elect. But behind closed doors, actions did not matter and whatever wickedness had been pent up during the daytime could be unleashed (think Hyde). Calvinists believed that there was no good in man, so wickedness was expected and as long as a person was a churchgoing member of the Elect, no amount of evil could be privately mourned: it was just the human condition and there was no use restraining it (except in public to avoid gossip). Stevenson loathed this hypocrisy, and it stained his entire oeuvre with themes of secrecy, doubt, two-faced-ness, and shame. When we consider also the fact that his nanny, Cummy – a brutally strict Calvinist – alternatively read him the Bible (complete with bedside sermons about damnation and hell) and told him folk stories of ghosts, body snatchers, and goblins, it is easy to see the connection between Stevenson's religious upbringing and tales of terror.

After his dream, Stevenson worked feverishly on creating a text out of the vision. Stricken with a very literal fever, bedridden from a hemorrhage, and buzzing with the cocaine that he used to push down the agony of the affliction, he blazed through three days of white-hot scribbling before reading the story to his wife. Fanny was his editor, sounding board, and muse, and she listened carefully to the story while her husband rambled, mopping sweat from his flushed skin and coughing into his hand. While the others in the room were thrilled with the story, Fanny seemed unmoved. She took the manuscript in hand, writing notes of critique in the margins. Leaving it for him to read, she explained that her husband had been too heavy handed: what could be a powerful allegory had been over dramatized into a cheap fright story. As Sir Graham Balfour relates, in the original draft, Jekyll had been more of a Deacon Brodie: "bad all through," using Hyde "only for the sake of disguise." Stevenson was livid. He raged his way upstairs and avoided the household. This lasted for a brief time, however, and he called her into his room, pointing proudly to the fireplace. To her horror, she realized that he had burned the manuscript. He had taken her notes to heart, and – in fear that he would try to revise what he considered a disaster – had destroyed it. He started fresh again that day. Inflamed with cocaine, Stevenson underwent a frantic rewrite, completing the new novella in just three days. In just six days he had written the same story twice over – a phenomenal rate of work. Fanny recalled the vitality that the mission seemed to stir in him, bringing him out of his solemn sickness into a frenzy of creative power. He polished the text up over the next four weeks, and it saw daylight on 6 January 1886, when it became an international sensation.

WEREWOLF FOLKLORE AND HISTORICAL MODELS.

In his groundbreaking review of the horror genre, Stephen King divided the horror story into five possible prototypes, with five definitive exemplars. The archetypes were The Nameless Thing (*Frankenstein*), The Vampire (*Dracula*), The Ghost (*The Turn of the Screw*), The Bad Place (*The Haunting of Hill House*), and the Werewolf (*Dr Jekyll and Mr Hyde*). Purists may take umbrage with the suggestion that Hyde is a werewolf, and may blame Frederic March's makeup for giving the impression that Hyde (only described as having a disturbing expression, corded and hairy hands, dwarfish stature, and an ape-like personality) is some kind of literal monster with fangs and a snout. While this complaint has its grounds, Jungian myth theorists would unquestionably consider the transformation to have its roots in the werewolf legend. So while Stoker may be seen as the godfather of the literary vampire, Shelley the parent of the literary monster, and Conan Doyle (*Lot No. 249, The Ring of Thoth*) may be viewed as sire to the literary mummy, Stevenson has a debatable claim to the literary werewolf.

As with my commentary on the vampire folklore that led to *Dracula*, I think that in this book it would be fitting to discuss the werewolf mythology that led to Hyde – and what exactly it all means. The shapeshifting man – the civilized person who is capable of concealing their passions – is more dangerous than a madman. A madman is obvious, unchanging, and easily tracked, but a shapeshifter is subtle, cunning, and disguised. The concept of hidden character – repressed, denied, or covered up – has been a fascinating and terrifying part of the human narrative since men began to murder one another and deny their guilt. They didn't rage until they were captured, they butchered, then they concealed, then they walked away and reentered the village, unchanged. Werewolf stories have saturated our global folklore long before stories were printed, bound, and sold. *Beauty and the Beast, Little Red Riding Hood,* and *Bluebeard* each concern a man whose nature, whether wicked or good, is concealed.

In Greek mythology Herodotus wrote of the Nueri, a tribe of shapeshifters who changed into wolves for a span of several days each year. Lycaon gave his name to lycanthropy (or werewolf-ism) when he tricked Zeus into eating his own offspring (a ploy borrowed in Shakespeare's infamously brutal *Titus Andronicus*) and was turned into a wolf as punishment. Ovid described werewolves lurking through the Arcadian woodlands, and Virgil and Pliny the Elder both recorded stories of lycanthropes. Vikings described Berserkers – or bear-shirted men – and Ulfhednar – or wolf-shirted men: warriors who wore animal skins into battle and adopted the personality of the fiends they wore, transforming into bears, wolves, and wild cats (and giving us the phrase "to go berserk"). Werewolves became a very real concern to Europeans in the Middle Ages, where werewolf trials were as spectacular and dramatic as those for witchcraft. Unlike the witchcraft craze, however, many of the suspected werewolves were genuine serial killers and cannibals (Peter Stumpp, for instance, was a German farmer who murdered and cannibalized 18 people, calling himself "an insatiable bloodsucker") but the supernatural link was popularized to explain away the unthinkable as the work of Satan. In her *Bisclavret* (c. 1200), Marie de France depicted a werewolf (a shapeshifting courtier who was betrayed by his wife, trapped by the King's hunting party, pitied, and made a member of the royal hunting pack), and *The Tale of Igor's Campaign* depicted the historical Belarusian Prince Usiaslau of Polatsk (rumored to have superhuman strength and speed) as a werewolf ("as prince, he ruled towns; but at night he prowled in the guise of a wolf"). Slavic and Russian folklore offered the legends of the vlkodlak and the vourdalak – crosses between werewolves, vampires, and revenants: shapeshifting, cannibalistic corpses.

WEREWOLF LITERATURE IN VICTORIAN BRITAIN.

Some of the first werewolf literature to make an impact on the printed page were folktales repeated in larger works of fiction to conjure atmosphere. Such is the case of Captain Marryat's Gothic novel *The Phantom Ship* (1839) which features the popular anecdote, "The White Wolf of the Harz Mountains" – a story about a Satanic female werewolf who attacks her stepchildren and eats rotting flesh like a ghoul. In 1847 – presumably trying to build on the momentum of the popular *Varney the Vampire* melodramas – G. W. M. Reynolds published *Wagner the Wehr-Wolf*, a Jekyll and Hyde prototype that follows the devolution of a good natured man who enters into a pact with Satan to become a werewolf for a year and a half in return for youth and affluence. Over the course of his journeys (in the company of fellow soul-exchanger, Dr. Faust), he kills, maims, and cannibalizes human beings that he encounters in manners that recall the death of Carew.

By the time that supernatural fiction was entering into its heyday (approximately 1864 – 1934), werewolves – or suggestions thereof – were becoming common tropes. Arthur Machen's *The Great God Pan* features a proto-Lovecraftian female werewolf who seduces men and terrifies them into suicide by revealing her otherworldly nature. Sir Arthur Conan Doyle wrote a similar story called "John Barrington Cowles" which hosts another erotic female lead who is equal parts dominatrix, sadist, vampire, hypnotist, and werewolf. Her unfortunate suitor, Cowles, calls her a "wehr-wolf" and compares her to the child-eating fiend in "The White Wolf of the Harz Mountains," but her ultimate nature – like the shapeshifter in *The Great God Pan* – is left unclear. His "A Pastoral Horror," the story of a mannerly pastor who is, by night, a pickaxe wielding psychopath, is cited as a psychological werewolf story, and contains obvious links to *Jekyll and Hyde*. Rudyard Kipling's famous "Mark of the Beast" concerns a werewolf curse which slowly and horrifically changes a man into a beast after he desecrates a Hindu shrine, and Ambrose Bierce's "Eyes of the Panther" tells the story of a woman who is afraid that she carries hereditary insanity, when in fact she seems to be an offspring of her mother's violent rape by a panther (which is suggested to be her mother's husband, who had left to go hunting, but returned as a were-cat).

Jekyll and Hyde represent the same essential concerns that all good werewolf stories do: that virtue can be faked, that wickedness can be concealed, and that enemies may walk, undetected, beside us every day. Werewolves have become metaphors for the far less romantic realities of our society: rapists, serial murderers, domestic abusers, child molesters, and all variety of other sequestered violators of our mores and standards. There is overall a sexual potency to the myth of the werewolf, and it is interesting that during the Victorian era most werewolves were women (suggesting the hidden lusts and appetites that men feared to acknowledge), but ever since

World War One, most werewolves have been exclusively male (suggesting the wildness of male violence – of war, rape, and murder – which the horrors of the Great War exposed, and which suddenly made female libidos seem the least of our race's worries). The myth continues to organize a conversation around our anxieties about the animals that prowl around us, work with us, and sleep beside us, and it is for this reason that Dr Jekyll and Mr Hyde, and the whole gamut of werewolf literature – from Herodotus to Kipling – continue to fascinate and disturb us.

CHARACTER ANALYSES.

DR. HENRY JEKYLL

Henry Jekyll has sadly been much maligned by pop culture. Rather than the figure of pathos modelled after Greek tragedies which Stevenson intended him to be (less Dorian Gray and more Oedipus Rex), he has been used to represent a subversive sexual predator and treated as a metaphor for sexual deviancy and violence – all this despite Stevenson's well-controlled decision not to portray either Jekyll's appetites or Hyde's crimes (with three exceptions). In private letters Stevenson does acknowledge that he feels that Jekyll's struggle was with "sexuality," but in the book all we know is that his weaknesses were indiscretions – specifically "undignified" – without any further details. So the whore-with-a-heart-of-gold that Jekyll rapes and keeps locked in Hyde's sex dungeon? Purely an invention of film makers. Jekyll represents so much more than sexual depravity: he represents human weakness and desperation in a way that should conjure nothing but sympathy and pity. Jekyll was raised with a tremendously strong Super-Ego – the internalized parent, or moral center of the unconscious – and found himself ashamed of behaviors and appetites that, as he put it, other respectable men would glibly brag about. In other words, his "sins" were so inoffensive that most people in high society would laugh them off, but to him (and, based on two telling references, to his father) they were inexcusable. Jekyll wants to be liked and admired, but he also wants to enjoy life – not like a decadent sociopath, but like a regular guy. And this is all Jekyll wants – to be a regular guy. So he summons Hyde to siphon off his desire for unmonitored fun. That Hyde overwhelms both his Super-Ego and his executive Ego is not only an oversight, it is a great human tragedy. Here is a man who simply desires relaxation and self-contentment – to be and like himself for who he is – but instead of coming out of the closet (either as a manner of speaking or as we mean it in the euphemism), he continues to Hyde himself away from his friends. Jekyll is terrified of disapproval (Freudians would again blame his influential father—or at least the father that Jekyll has enthroned in his head), and has kept Hyde repressed for half a century. When he escapes, he is fed by an unmet hunger, not – as in Stevenson's original manuscript – by a lifetime of hypocrisy. Jekyll is not a secret sinner pining over a solution that would allow him to wickedly sin as much as he wants during the night and live comfortably during the day (although this IS Hyde's M.O.); he is an overly-repressed man whose starved Id comes charging out of its cage, leaving carnage in its wake. Jekyll doesn't even die with Hyde: his spirit departs their body eight days before Hyde kills himself, surrendering to the powerful lusts of an under-serviced animal nature which – had it been given more liberty to taste and enjoy life – may not have been such a brutal usurper.

MR. EDWARD HYDE

Like Jekyll, Hyde is the subject of much misunderstanding – again largely due to film adaptations. Hyde may be a sexual deviant, but not necessarily. We know of three wicked deeds of his: trampling a girl, bludgeoning Carew (who may have been soliciting him for sex), and beating a prostitute/matchgirl. Films depict Hyde as very obviously misshapen, usually physically imposing, with brazen rudeness, a prostitute sex-slave at hand, and a flair for foppish togs. This is almost entirely wrong: Hyde is inexplicably disturbing to view, though those who have seen him blame his expression and aura, not a physical deformity. What we know of his physique is that he is dwarfish and slight ("troglodytic" is one of my favorite words in the novel), that he has ape-ish moods, a strange, lunging walk, and small hands with dusky skin, thick hair, and muscular flesh. We also know that – hardly a dandy (silk top-hat, opera cape, sparkling rings, and Oscar Wilde-esque striped trousers and fey ascots are *de rigueur* for film adaptations) – Hyde is dressed plainly in expensive materials. We might imagine a man in a black frock coat with a Homburg hat and a black tie. To me, this is far more disturbing to imagine than the easily broadcasted Jack-the-Ripper crossover outfit (who, by the way, was also probably dressed plainly). Hyde's height is his most telling trait, and it is a pity that this has almost never been depicted accurately. He actually seems to have the appearance of a teenager (Utterson calls him "Master" – an address used for males under the age of nineteen – and refers to him as a protégée, also implying that he could live on Jekyll's legacy for many decades). Hyde has this appearance because his growth has been stunted – spiritually speaking – and it shows in his physical appearance.

Hyde is also not a brute, but a coward. Tremendously polite to Utterson (especially under the circumstances), he is also pandering to Lanyon, and sugar-lipped to his would-be lynch mob (most cinematic Hydes have a "fuck you all" attitude, even when faced with brutality). But the real Hyde is – as Jekyll notes – propelled by two chief emotions: fear and hate. He is animalistic, an Id which never fully developed and is thus stunted and devolved. In fact, there is a great deal of Darwinism in Stevenson's regular references to apes and monkeys when describing young Hyde. Frederic March's makeup showed this literally (he was chimp-like in appearance and devolved as the film progressed), but Stevenson only implies that his behavior and moods had simian qualities. Like an animal, though, Hyde is not motivated by deep emotions, but by self-preservation and egoism. He is almost like a toddler with terrifying muscularity, and his demise is actually cause for pity rather than disgust: for eight days he madly paces his prison cell, weeping "like a woman" and calling on God. Hyde is not the vicious beast we so often picture, but a pathetic egotist made dangerous by self-involvement and pitiable by spiritual idiocy. Hyde grows stronger as Jekyll invests more and more of his Ego into Hyde, robbing the Super-Ego of the executive Self which should be evenly spread between the animalistic Id and the puritanical Super-Ego.

The switch that most terrifies Jekyll happens when he is in a park, mulling over one of his forays as Hyde (and debatably masturbating in public over the memory). Hyde springs into his skin unbidden and without the potion. This brings up Stevenson's great metaphysical argument (repeated in "Olalla") that mankind is truly four parts: a fleshy vessel – the mortal organ of humanity – a spiritual nature (the Super-Ego), a gluttonous nature (the Id), and consciousness (the Ego) which struggle for dominance. The mostly spiritual man is a saint, the gluttonous one a sinner, the fleshly one an imbecile, and the purely conscious one a ghost. Hyde pushes the Super-Ego out, killing Jekyll (whose consciousness is tied up in it), and finds himself trapped in the stunted, hairy, dwarfish fleshly vessel of young Master Edward Hyde.

John Gabriel Utterson
Utterson is the consummate Victorian man of honor – not particularly clubbable, certainly not the man about town that his cousin is, dry, curmudgeonly, and irascible, but beloved by his many friends. What makes Utterson so likeable in spite of his cantankerous ways is his indefatigable loyalty. Utterson has a taste for pathos: like Horatio in *Hamlet* or the chorus in a Greek tragedy, he is intimately involved in the lives of ruined men, undaunted by scandal, and stubbornly loyal. Utterson's comfort with imperfection makes him a perfect observer of Jekyll's implosion: he is not judgmental or gossipy, and is typically unattracted to the melodrama of scandal, and yet he is deeply disturbed by Jekyll's alliance with the young Master Hyde, and his dreams are haunted by visions and speculations of what might be happening behind the battered lab door. Unimaginative Utterson is tormented by dreams, unromantic Utterson is driven to heroically intercede, uncorrupted Utterson is reminded of his youthful sins, uninvolved Utterson becomes a bonafide busy body. This is how strong Hyde's shadow over Jekyll is, and while Utterson's character may say more about Hyde than Utterson himself, he is still a dynamic, rich character, terribly maligned by his exclusion from most film adaptations. The power of Utterson's personality is his dogged loyalty, his stubborn integrity, and his

imperviousness to scandal; he is not ashamed of wayward friends, but he keeps his own weaknesses in check; he does not shun the corrupted, but he suppresses (not represses) his own temptations by accepting them and rechanneling them (he "mortifies" a gluttonous taste for rich wines by drinking cheap gin). Utterson is the perfect, grounded observer to watch the drama unfold in a relatively impartial manner. Like the steadfast Horatio or the unwavering Greek chorus, Utterson follows Jekyll in his steady degeneration and is present at his pitiable end... *"And flights of angels sing thee to thy rest."*

DR. HASTIE LANYON

Lanyon represents the conservative wing of the scientific establishment – a symbol of emotionally constipated, intellectually timid, morally repressed Victorian manhood. Grounded, hard-nosed, and practical, he loathes Jekyll's speculative nature, preferring accepted facts and ideas to possibilities and imagination. Lanyon is a consummate Victorian, and a model Darwinian (in my illustration I couldn't even help but to suggest a similarity between the two) whose materialism – the belief only in that which can be observed and measured – cements in him a deep-founded trust in his senses: he can sense who is good, see who is bad, and note who belongs and who doesn't. Adaptations often bring a class element into Lanyon's personality, in that he thinks that gentlemen are good, working men corruptible, and criminals hopelessly debased. However, Lanyon harbors a secret taste for curiosity – an unwillingness to let things remain unseen – and this is what Hyde uses to lure him into witnessing the transformation. What breaks Lanyon's mind and body isn't the shock of what Jekyll has hidden from him, but the implications of what is hidden within himself. Having seen (thus validating it with his senses) the virtually seamless transition of the debased villain Hyde into the unsuspected socialite Jekyll, Lanyon is wasted by the realization that there is more to heaven and earth than can be measured by the senses – that he is not in control of his own soul, that he cannot fully comprehend the world around him, and that he cannot firmly define his own identity. Lanyon's death – symbolic of what Stevenson predicted to be the inevitable demise of rigid Victorian manhood with its jingoistic machismo and puritanical morality – is due to a loss of control, both of his understanding of the universe at large, and of himself as a complex (rather than black and white) *"polity of multifarious, incongruous and independent denizens."*

SIR DANVERS CAREW, MP

A beautiful white-haired gentleman with "pretty manners" who is beaten to death after accosting Hyde. Often recast as a potential father-in-law (thanks again to the Sullivan stage play plot), Sir Danvers is hardly as fleshed out as the disapproving father figure whose death is an Oedipal triumph for Hyde.

In fact, Carew may actually be much less of a moral tower and more of a Jekyll himself. What we do know of him suggests something may be off: he is wandering alone at night – very late – without identifying papers, carrying a letter for Utterson, and prettily approaching Hyde. Even in his confession, Jekyll never discusses the conversation (which many have interpreted as asking for directions), leading me – and Leonard Wolf, Gwen Hyman, and Francesco Billari, among others – to suspect that Carew was either soliciting Hyde as homosexual hookup, or asking directions to a neighborhood where such things happened. Wolf in particular suggests that Carew's death may have been literal gay-bashing summoned from the homophobic "fear and rage" that constitute Hyde. There has been some suggestion that maybe Hyde was even blackmailing Carew (he had visited the maid's master before – why? Perhaps he has run into these men on his nightly maneuvers and uses the information to blackmail them) and became suspicious that he was on his way to confess to Utterson (hence the letter) and expose Hyde. In any case, the upstanding knight and member of Parliament seems to have secret appetites like Jekyll, and has paid for them with his life.

RICHARD ENFIELD

Like Carew, Enfield appears to be a man with secrets. He also takes strolls late at night in neighborhoods where gentlemen aren't given to walking at late hours. Returning home from "some place at the end of the world" – often interpreted as a brothel, a drag burlesque, or some kind of decadent gentlemen's club – Enfield encounters Hyde after he has trampled a little girl, and leads the lynch mob that bullies him into blackmail at the risk of his life. Enfield, a confirmed "man about town," is even more clearly given to his vices than Carew, but has little pretense (unlike Carew and Jekyll) of being a reputable man. He is well known for his tastes, and he and Utterson respect of code of tolerance and silence whereby they understand one another's differences – the dry, dusty lawyer and the wild, punchy playboy – something which Jekyll and Hyde are unable to do for one another. His disgust towards Hyde is suggestive because of his wanton ways: had a prim and proper Victorian patriarch felt similarly towards the man, we would hardly be surprised, but when a tolerant, laissez-faire, man-about-town like Enfield must stifle the instinctive urge to kill him... well, that is certainly meaningful.

MR. POOLE

So much of *Jekyll and Hyde* is a social commentary on class and society, and Poole, like Lanyon, represents a relic of a fading age. A sturdy, loyal manservant of the Jeeves cast (and caste), Poole is brave and unflinching, personally moral, but willing to turn a blind eye to his master's sins as a courtesy of his class. Eventually, however, it is Poole's hand at the axe which breaks its way into Jekyll's secret. It is as if Stevenson is warning Victorian

Britain that a hypocritical society can lord itself over the lower classes for only so long before they will have to take moral ownership of their civilization – and at that point it might be too late for the corrupt decadents they had so long suffered to rule them.

POPULAR CRITICAL INTERPRETATIONS: EIGHT LITERARY ANALYSES.

Like Frankenstein and Dracula, Jekyll and Hyde has been plucked apart by thousands of critics since it appeared on the scene. Critics use a particular pattern of study to derive a cohesion vision of the meaning of a text, or the way that it could be read. Throughout the text I will elaborate on my own personal interpretation in the notes (for the record, I identify heavily with Freudian, Jungian/Mythic, New Historical, and Marxist schools), but I would like to briefly discuss some of the most popular interpretations of this book. There are many other lenses (Postcolonial, New Historical, Postmodern, Deconstructive, Formalist, and Poststructural are just a few that I don't include here), but below are those that I consider the most notable.

FREUDIAN / PSYCHOANALYSIS. Freudian readings of Jekyll and Hyde are some of the most popular. They interpret Jekyll as the Ego of his personality – the executive center – his conscience as the Freudian Super-Ego (the internalized parent), and Hyde as the Id – animal lusts, impulses, and hatred (what Stevenson boils down to "fear and hate"). Jekyll tries to suppress his powerful, shame-causing Super-Ego (implanted by society and – it would seem – his father), and thus releases his Id, Hyde. As the Id, Hyde reacts impulsively, rages causelessly, and is consumed by paranoia and self-love. Hyde is dwarflike from decades of repression, and could be interpreted as being roughly 17 years old in appearance. Freudians would interpret this as warning of the dangers of repression and latency, and see Jekyll's self-destruction as a parable against the mismanagement of the Unconscious forces that drive the Ego. Jekyll's house (like those of Usher and Norman Bates) also presents a near-perfect metaphor for the Unconscious, wherein the Super-Ego guards the public front, the Ego dwells in the top, and the Id is released through the private backway. Sexuality, of course, is often read into the text (see: Queer Theory), and although Carew is not Jekyll's future father-in-law, most films cast him as a conservative mainstay of paternal Victorianism, making his murder an Oedipal response from the sexually frustrated Jekyll who resents this father-figure as the sole obstacle to sexual fulfilment (brilliantly depicted in the 1931 film).

JUNGIAN / ARCHETYPE THEORY / MYTHIC. Jungian psychoanalytical treatments look at the novel both for a model of Jung's Subconscious, and for the mythic archetypes that Carl G. Jung saw populating the Collective Conscious of mankind. Jekyll himself makes the very Jungian claim that mankind is not one, nor even two, but a bustling city of personalities. Jungians will see Hyde as an expression of Jekyll's Shadow (the Jungian Id – the dark side of human desire and passion), and will view Jekyll's metaphorical psychosis as the result of an unintegrated Shadow: Jung believed that neuroses developed when the disparate parts of the human psyche were not properly socialized with one another: the macho who represses his feminine side (anima) becomes fixated on masculinity and chronically overcompensates. Likewise Jekyll tries to divide his good and bad side when in reality he should reconcile them (like Yin and Yang, which are distinct but related and carry the capacity of the other within themselves), ideally through analytical therapy. Myth theorists will be drawn to the story as an archetype, tracing it through the folklore of werewolves (otherwise good citizens who secretly harbor an asocial nature), and will locate the archetypes that Stevenson enlists: The Questing Hero (Utterson), The Martyr (Carew), The Threshold (the closet), The Tower (the lab with its overlooking windows), The Crossroads (the no-going-back moment), The Tempter (Hyde-to-Lanyon), The Dreamer (pre-Hyde Jekyll), Battle-of-Good-and-Evil, Death and Rebirth, Initiation, and "These are things man was not meant to know," among others.

STRUCTURALISM. Structrualism is a branch of linguistics, and while it typically is focused on language, it also attempts to take apart the structural mechanics of a story – the way the characters and settings interact with one another like pieces in an engine. They would be most interested by the duality of Jekyll-to-Hyde, Utterson-to-Lanyon, Poole-to-the landlady, the front door –to- the backdoor, the trampled girl (starts the story) –to- the slapped prostitute (ends the story), and the general momentum of the plot – exposition, problem developments, quest, peaks and troughs, climax, and denouement. A structuralist would be particularly intrigued by the circularity of the plot (it begins and ends with similar motifs), and the dichotomies that link so many of the characters. This critical approach is more interested in plot mechanics than social commentary and is related to Formalism (i.e., discussing the science of good writing).

FEMINISM. Feminist critics are concerned with the ways that literature demonstrates the way that gender, sexuality, and power interplay, either as a means of oppressing the disenfranchised or as means for the powerless to subvert and undermine the networks of power (the earliest feminist critics were focused on female subjects, but today they are more interested in power dynamics of all kinds, including racial, sexual, and religious minorities, overlapping with the Marxist, Postcolonial, and Queer schools). Feminist critics might interpret Jekyll and Hyde as a critique of the patriarchal society that has repressed Jekyll, tempting him to draw out his violent tendencies. A feminist reading of the novel would consider Hyde's rampages to be the expression of suppressed passions which are twisted and distorted by the demands of the upper-class, white, male patriarchy. They may also view that moral domination (refusing Jekyll the ability to indulge in harmless but undignified indulgences) as a ploy to regulate subversive behavior and ideas as a means of maintaining power over social minorities.

GENDER THEORY / QUEER THEORY. Gender theorists and queer theorists explore the ways that characters in a text handle issues of gender (socialized sexuality) and sex (physical sexuality). Queer Theory specifically focuses on Otherness in sexuality – not limited to but including homosexuality, fetishes, polygamy, and sexual deviancy. Jekyll and Hyde is almost always shown in film as a metaphor for the repressed temptations of heterosexual lust (rape – never mentioned by Stevenson – is almost ubiquitous with Hyde), but if any sexual appetite lurks in the text, it is the "love that dare not speak its name": Victorian homosexuality. All of the main characters are middle-aged, never-been-married, homosocial male bachelors who spend most of their time either roaming the streets or drinking together. Utterson has visions of Hyde lingering over Jekyll's sleeping form without a servant present. He also wonders if seeing Hyde's face might explain Jekyll's inability to kick his habit (perhaps, he wonders, he might be remarkably beautiful), and suggests to Poole that Jekyll may have caught syphilis. Sir Danvers Carew, also, is not a father-in-law slain in an Oedipal rage (as the movies almost universally depict), but a lovely man with queer mannerisms who Hyde slays after being accosted. Jekyll never describes their conversation other than to call it "pathetic," leading some to speculate that Carew was soliciting Hyde and that his death is an example of gay bashing. Queer theorists have often seen Jekyll's harmless-but-undignified desires (and his wish to explore them while keeping them a secret) as suggesting the mental dissonance of a closeted man. Stevenson described Jekyll's sins as "sexual" in letters (though going into no further detail), and Gender theorists have long been fascinated by what many interpret to be a novel that depicts the struggles of single Victorian men to pass as straight while still indulging their sexually deviant appetites – homosexual or otherwise.

MARXISM. Beginning with the economic criticism of Karl Marx, Marxist theorists study the ways that social classes struggle over financial, social, and political power. Marxists would likely be drawn to Jekyll's wealth and that of his peers as a corrupting influence. Jekyll leaves his posh house to live as Hyde in working class Soho, enjoying the social freedoms of the poor while clinging to the financial power of the rich. Marxists would critique Victorian society for hoarding power from the poor and condemning them for their morals while secretly envying them. By sharing his wealth instead of clinging to high society, Jekyll would have been less conflicted by his desire to enjoy lower class social morals and his desire to hold onto his public esteem. Marxists would also find interest in Poole, the working class servant who must ultimately subvert his master's orders, breaking into his aristocratic secrets through force – a revolutionary act of agency.

CHRISTIAN ALLEGORY. Unsurprisingly considering Stevenson's background, it is easy to read Jekyll and Hyde as a Christian allegory for the struggle between good and evil, and – regardless of specific religious affiliation – this continues to be the popular interpretation of the novel. Hyde can be viewed as either Satan or personal temptation. By trying to subvert the will of God – not unlike his literary kinsman, Victor Frankenstein – Henry Jekyll relies on his own power to resist temptation, inviting sin into his life. Rather than attempting to reconcile the good with the bad, he attempts to separate them – tantamount to Satan's great sin of trying to be like God. Like Eve, Jekyll is enamored with the idea of truly knowing what it is to be good and to be evil, and this is his downfall. Rather than relying on the gift of God's grace, Jekyll tries to become fully good, but in a twist that draws heavily from Calvinist theology, Jekyll finds that his evil side is naturally stronger and we never even meet his good side. Still the most prevalent reading of the story (although usually without references to a Christian God), this interpretation essentially views the novel as a study in good versus evil, the power of evil to overwhelm good (when given enough freedom), the hubris of mankind, the dangers of moral laxity (and of giving in to temptations – even to a slight degree), and the fundamental dichotomy of mankind (and the universe) as consisting of two warring parts: Good and Evil, God and Satan, spirit and flesh.

ADDICTION ALLEGORY. As anyone who has read Dr Jekyll and Mr Hyde will know, there are times when the language used effortlessly suggests the struggle of addiction. Jekyll uses his potion to give vent to repressed passions inside of him, and attempts to keep this socially unacceptable side of his personality roped off from his friends and colleagues – his hope is that he can have his proverbial cake and eat it, too. But as the Alcoholics Anonymous adage goes, "first the man takes the drink, then the drink takes the drink, then the drink takes the man." Like a person addicted to alcohol, narcotics, or pain killers, Jekyll's indulgence begins as a means to express a dark part of his soul, but that shadow rapidly begins to overtake his personality. Like an addict, he hides his addiction from friends, he increases his use overtime (from experimental to regular usage), he finds that he must continually increase the dosage, that he was mistaken in the common belief that he was in control of his addiction (that he could "stop whenever [he] wants to"), and that at some point he goes from trying to give voice to a small part of himself to desperately trying to keep that once small part from dominating the whole. Also like most addicts, Jekyll experiences depression, avoids friends, lets his social and professional life suffer, and experiences a huge shift in personality. For Stevenson who used cocaine and alcohol to soothe stomach pains and insomnia, the language of addiction came quite authentically.

One of the best versions of the story – perhaps only trumped by March – the silent *John Barrymore* adaptation is notable for several ways that it influenced the future of Jekyll & Hyde productions. In a coincidental way it began a trend of cranking out adaptations roughly every ten years (the first American version was done in 1912, this in 1920, and notable adaptations followed in 1931, 1941, 1951, 1971, 1981, 1990, 2002, and 2013). In a more serious manner, Barrymore's version cemented what would become the popular understanding of the Jekyll myth by enlisting the plot of the 1887 stage play adaptation by Thomas Russell Sullivan and elements of *The Picture of Dorian Gray*. The resultant plot will be familiar: Utterson is the name of a minor character and is otherwise erased; Jekyll is a young and dashing romantic and a confirmed heterosexual; he is engaged to a society lady – the archetypal virgin; he is attracted to a loose woman – the archetypal whore with a heart of gold; Carew becomes his fiancée's disapproving, conservative father (making the murder highly Oedipal). In this adaptation, Carew (who also doubles as the Lanyon and Enfield figures) is a cynical macho who actually tempts Jekyll by mocking his goodness ("no man could be as good as he looks") and chiding him for wasting his youth when he could be sowing his wild oats ("The only way to get rid of temptation is to yield to it"), making the film a rather progressive critique of upper-class cynicism. After adapting the persona of Hyde as an experiment in oat-sowing, Jekyll becomes estranged from his fiancée, shacking up with a dance hall wench and spending his nights engrossed in opium, gin, and brothels. In the climax, Carew witnesses the transformation and is murdered shortly thereafter, and Jekyll commits suicide just in time to prevent Hyde from raping his distraught fiancée. The film is an absolute masterwork – acted splendidly, photographed lushly, directed bravely. The transformation and makeup are perhaps the most accurate ever done, and the acting and direction are far ahead of their time, tremendously compelling, and artistic in every sense of the word.

In many ways, *Frederic March's* Academy Award-winning 1931 film is the unquestionable masterpiece of the Jekyll & Hyde tradition. A pre-code movie, it wriggles with daring sexuality, grey ethics, and moral authenticity. The four greatest features of this expressionist tour de force are its lush, chiaroscuro photography, its brilliant, cutting-edge direction by Rouben Mamoulian (including a mesmerizing opening sequence shot from Jekyll's P.O.V.), March's emotionally grueling Academy Award winning acting, and make-up that rivals the stunning work of Jack Pierce (*Frankenstein, The Mummy, The Wolf Man*). The film certainly has a maturity about it – emotionally and artistically – that most versions lack, and few ever come close to. Ripe with sexuality, Jekyll's downfall is explained as that of one who "loved not too wisely but too well": repressing his romantic passions for his fiancée, Jekyll is enflamed by the sexually available whore Ivy Pearson (in a bawdy role that will shock those unused to pre-code cinema), and the egotistical Hyde essentially keeps her as a sex slave. She runs to Jekyll (for whom she developed a licentious attraction) for help, but when he transforms into Hyde (and each time the makeup devolves a little more, until his last, most troglodytic transformation – a dripping, goony chimp) he reveals the truth to Ivy before strangling her. Jekyll's transformation is thoroughly believable, and what's more – unlike many adaptations – it is rich with pathos. His desires are innocent enough, his ambition understandable, and his suffering relatable. We don't relish Hyde's defeat – like the weeping Poole, we despair in Jekyll's loss. Much like the equally ingenious *Picture of Dorian Gray*, March's version is a masterpiece of American expressionism, pregnant with atmosphere, blessed with ingenious acting, and dominated by a steady directorial vision and photography and effects that secure it legacy as a classic.

After Barrymore and March, few adaptations made a splash with critics, though several were notable. The **Spencer Tracy** version (1941) is a disaster, but left a legacy that merits discussion. Miscast, mis-shot, and mis-acted, we have the lantern jawed American Tracy failing to convince us that he is a British aristocrat. Brutish, heavy-limbed, and big-boned, with his Midwestern accent and mannerisms, he is the last person who should have been selected as Jekyll. Ingrid Bergman is equally bizarre as a Cockney barmaid (not, I repeat, *not* a prostitute – thank you, Code), and only Donald Crisp – in one of the best performances of Carew – stands out as perfectly suited to his role as the sneering, British father-in-law. Hyde's makeup was decidedly minimalist (thicker hair, some eye makeup, and a hint at a widows peak are about it), and visitors to the set often joked "who is he now, Jekyll or Hyde?" The fantasy sequence during the transformation is hatefully bizarre: the fiancée and mistress are ridden like horses, and at one point Bergman's head is drawn out of a champagne bottle like a cork. But this is also the version that changed Jekyll's pronunciation from JEE-*kull* to JZEH-*kull* (a literary annoyance nearly as keen as Karloff's inadvertent christening Frankenstein's Creature with his patronymic), and it also transformed Barrymore and March's nuanced performances into a moral melodrama. Incidentally, Paramount destroyed almost every copy of March's film in a bid to prevent competition with their new movie, and the film was barely saved from destruction, and after its disastrous reviews, March thanked his friend Tracy – tongue in cheek of course – for "the biggest boost to his career."

In 1971 – after a string of lackluster, made-for-TV-movies and campy spin-offs, **Christopher Lee** revived the story in *I, Monster*, a revisionist film which recast Jekyll as a Freudian psychoanalyst and is notable for reintroducing Utterson, played deftly by Peter Cushing. Lee's acting is the salvation of this film, which would otherwise have been another formulaic sex-and-blood Hammer production. Unlike Tracy, Lee exudes aristocratic atmosphere, and (also unlike Tracy) can convincingly transform into his depraved alter-ego with only a few dabs of makeup, conveying the rest – with a Barrymore-esque flair – through posture, expression, and carriage. The film is lush with Freudian symbolism, suggestion, and sexuality – implying much while showing little (one transformation is shown in silhouette – sheer discipline on the director's part). Cushing and Lee play off one another beautifully, and the revisionist direction leaves us with a stark, psychologically smart rendition that harkens to the power of March's portrayal and Mamoulian's dreary vision.

Following a few notable if tawdry adaptations – **Michael Caine** as a disgusting Elephant Man who rapes his sister-in-law (1990), **Anthony Perkins** as a thoroughly psychotic Hyde / Jack the Ripper (1989), and **David Hemmings** as a shaggy Neanderthal (1981) – **John Malkovich** took up the cape and top-hat in *Mary Reilly*. The 1996 film was an adaptation of the revisionist novel by Valerie Martin and starred an awkward Julia Roberts as the eponymous main character, Jekyll's Irish maidservant. In spite of a lack of genuine chemistry, the odd choice of Roberts (presumably based on the strength of her similar role in *Pretty Woman*), and the hideous box office reports and lackluster critical response, the film is actually rather well done. Malkovich plays Jekyll authentically as a middle aged man – weak, timid, and deeply repressed – while the sexually potent Hyde is slick, seductive, and powerful. The dreary setting, stark photography, and character studies make it a compelling and impossible to miss submission to the growing catalog of Jekyll & Hyde films. Roger Ebert – who was nonetheless underwhelmed by the overall product – accurately identified the movie's power: "[It] is in some ways more faithful to the spirit of Robert Lewis Stevenson's original story than any of the earlier films based on it, because it's true to the underlying horror. This film is not about makeup or special effects, or Hyde turning into the Wolf Man. It's about a powerless young woman who feels sympathy for one side of a man's nature, and horror of the other... [It] is a dark, sad, frightening, gloomy story... " Sexually electric, psychologically brooding, emotionally tolling, it is certainly weak, like its Jekyll, but unquestionably compelling, like its Hyde.

In 2002 **John Hannah** – whose Edinburgh brogue and Stevenson lookalike features match the source convincingly – offered one of the most psychologically tortured renditions in a dreary and gore-splashed TV movie. Realism is the theme of this adaptation, which offers only subtle hints at science fiction or the supernatural. Hannah (I can't overstate how much he looks and sounds like Stevenson must have) is experimenting with what appears to be opium, and Hyde – who is only differentiated by his pimp coat, March-esque claw footed cane, and a tall beaver hat – is brought about by a combination of narcotics, drug-induced psychosis, and fugue states.

This Jekyll isn't transformed – he is high, and as cheap as this might sound, the effect is refreshingly believable. This adaptation is shocking and compelling, being equal parts *Dorian Gray*, Jack the Ripper, Sweeney Todd (a blackmailing servant boy is modelled on Todd's lad, Toby), *The Prince and the Pauper*, *Mary Reilly* (in the form of Jekyll's fawning, compliant, Catholic maidservant), and Fight Club, this adaptation is highly ambitious, but ultimately suffers from an unnecessarily grim plot (which oddly enough seems founded in Catholic theology) wherein Hyde butchers his lackey, sadistically date rapes Jekyll's fiancée (twice), bludgeons the social reformer, Carew, and needlessly slays the single redemptive figure in the film. Gore flows like summer rain. One fascinating element here is the choice to make the contrite Carew father to both the posh fiancée (whose vicious date rape early in the film essentially silences her) and the Mary Reilly character who is born to Carew's favorite prostitute. The two sisters offer the theme of duplicity another level of depth, making a very vocal social argument (much like the socially conscious, repentant Carew, a reforming progressive). Utterson is also notably present, though an unimportant character used only as a framing device. Hannah's performance is psychologically brutal, sometimes difficult to watch, and drenched in pathos. Although it is at times too ambitious, relies on too much gore, has too many subplots, and is afflicted with a needlessly dreary ending, the film remains one of my favorite adaptations if only for its earnestness, social message, and psychological realism.

The final adaptation that we will consider was a British miniseries produced by the BBC and written by Steven Moffat. Fans of *Sherlock* will recognize Moffat's Moriarty in the impish, black humored Hyde (right down to the Ulster accent), so splendidly played by **James Nesbitt**. Like Moriarty, Hyde is a villain that we love to hate, but with an emphasis on love. This Hyde is animalistic but also instinctively protective of those he cares for (yes, cares for). Something of a paranormal/psychological thriller in the vein of *The X-Files*, *Jekyll* follows the world-weary every man, Tom Jackman, the balding descendent of Dr Henry Jekyll (depicted as a Scot, his name pronounced JEE-*kull*), who has inherited Hyde in his genes. Like Hannah and Lee, Nesbitt's Hyde is tremendously minimalistic (sporting thicker, blacker hair and black contact lenses, but otherwise relying on brilliant facial acting), and his potency is infectious. Set in modern London, we are sucked into the drama as soon as we meet Jackman restrained in a dingy basement where he appears to be possessed by the psychopathic Hyde. Ultimately, this adaptation traces the motives of the historical Jekyll (here *Mary Reilly* once again proves the power of its influence – yes, there is a gold-hearted-maid subplot), while Jackman battles covert government programs, tries to protect his beautiful wife and little boy, and learns about the mysterious, primal emotions which motivate his alter-ego. The series – six episodes long – is not quite an adaptation (though we do meet the good

Doctor Jekyll), but invests the story with a fresh perspective, lush visuals, and outstanding acting. Other than Gina Bellman's miscast role as Jackman's wife (she doesn't seem to know where she is or why, and is a tad too model-like to be believable in this role), and a sluggish third act, the series is a brilliant revision.

DR JEKYLL'S CONTINUED ATTRACTION

I would like to end this exploration of Stevenson's horror masterpiece with a few thoughts on its consistent durability. From literary circles to the stage to the screen to the vernacular, Dr Jekyll and his menacing double have become just as impossible to avoid as Frankenstein's Creature and Count Dracula. The concept of the duplicitous scientist has made its way into cartoons (Bugs Bunny, for instance), comedies (*The Nutty Professor*, et al), children's movies (*The Pagemaster*), PBS programming (*Wishbone*), and the understandably welcoming arms of camp (*Victor/Victoria*). The reason, I suppose, that the story continues to fascinate is because – as much as we want to be third-party viewers and as much as we want to judge and condemn Jekyll – we identify with the good doctor's desire to give vent to his "undignified" appetites. There is something tremendously human and relatable about wishing that we could express our indiscreet impulses without hurting those we love or losing the esteem of our friends. For some that is the obvious metaphor, sexual liberation, but for others it falls more along Jekyll's description: the odd tastes, strange interests, bizarre habits, and unspoken wishes that we lock away from our friends and family in order to preserve their good will.

Some of those impulses are malignant – like gambling addictions, alcoholism, or pornography – but others (perhaps like Jekyll's) are less "wicked": a hobby that your coworkers would ridicule (LARPing, perhaps, reenacting, collecting cookie jars, or DJing on weekends), a passion for a career that your family disapproves of, a fanatic taste for burlesque theater or karaoke, or – particularly germane to our society today – closeted homosexuality or transsexuality. The desire to be authentic without being rejected, to taste happiness without feeling disapproval, to have integrity without having to sacrifice the respect, admiration, or love of family, friends, and coworkers. We all harbor secret wishes or tastes that are sometimes awkward to reveal – sometimes excruciating. Yet Jekyll attempts to have it both ways without experiencing the pang of social rejection: as he puts it, others "have before hired bravos to transact their crimes, while their own person and reputation sat under shelter. I was the first that ever did so for his pleasures." And this is the so-often overlooked tragedy of Jekyll – one exacerbated by unfair and inaccurate cinematic interpretations: Jekyll didn't create Hyde to get away with rape and murder, he created Hyde to slip away – if momentarily – from the scrutiny of society (if you will excuse the sappy expression, to dance like no one is watching). He wanted to be himself for once, but his bid for liberation only led to a greater captivity than ever, and herein is the lesson that Stevenson wants to impart: not to give it up, all those hidden dreams and secret passions, but to live authentically. Utterson and Enfield represent the form of non-judgmental integrity that could have saved Jekyll, had he opted to live humbly, self-deprecatingly, and without concern for others' opinions.

In today's society the need to deeply feel and understand Jekyll's dilemma is greater than ever. Social media has made the façade that weighed Jekyll down even larger and heavier. We all host carefully manicured Jekylls on Facebook, Twitter, LinkedIn, Google+, Instagram, Snapchat, and more. Jekylls desperate to be seen, to be approved, to be condoned. And yet the Hyde rages against this social fakery. In the year that I write this, several people committed suicide after an adultery website called Ashley Madison was hacked and information released. These poor victims of a duplicitous society reminded me of Carew – a good man with a secret vice, who were punished far more cruelly by a vicious stranger than their own families ever would. Technology has made it easier than ever to cultivate Hydes even as we polish and position our Jekylls. On Facebook we are happy – vacationing obscenely, hugging constantly, cuddling with our perfect babies – while at night we are discontent, hyper-comparative, annoyed with the disparity in image and feeling. We hemorrhage money to maintain an image, obsessively document every moment in order to invite commentary and acknowledgement, and then get out of bed in the middle of the night, creep downstairs, and live a different life from the one we are so desperate to have approved and acknowledged. In today's society, more than ever, there is a desperate need to understand Jekyll's downfall and Stevenson's message: stop caring about the demands of your social circle and simply live a happy life. Do the things you enjoy and do them fully, involve your family and friends in your passions, be open about your interests, be genuine in all parts of your life. If you don't want to go, stay in. If you do want to go, speak up. A life lived between duty and desire is one torn in opposite directions. A life lived in existential compromise – the life of a wine-loving, gin-drinking Utterson – is one which can tend to the tastes of the heart but preserve the fabric of our family.

M. Grant Kellermeyer
Fort Wayne, Hallowe'en 2015

Strange¹ Case of Dr Jekyll² and Mr Hyde³
{1886}

Story of the Door

MR. Utterson[4] the lawyer was a man of a rugged countenance that was never lighted by a smile; cold, scanty and embarrassed in discourse; backward in sentiment; lean, long, dusty, dreary and yet somehow lovable[5]. At friendly meetings, and when the wine was to his taste, something eminently human beaconed from his eye; something indeed which never found its way into his

---

[1] To the surprise of most readers – and to the horror of many grammar sticklers – the title of Stevenson's story begins without an article, in spite of most publishers' tendency to print the book as *The* Strange Case of Dr Jekyll and Mr Hyde

[2] Pronounced JEE-*kull* (rhymes with "fecal") until 1941 (*1941!!!* It has only been known in its corrupted version since World War II, but the damage has been irreparable ever since the Spencer Tracy film adaptation chose to rhyme the name with "heckle"). The name has been alternatively traced to the French invaders of 1099 and the Danish invaders of Viking times, with such fitting meanings as "he who battles" and "generous man"

[3] The name also has a Danish route, meaning a harbor, haven, or hiding place – apropos considering Hyde's utility as the fortified hiding place of Jekyll's libidinal aggressions

[4] Critics have noted a significance in Utterson's name: while some point to "utter" in the sense of "speaking out" or "calling attention to" – in the context that he tracks and decries Hyde – others have seen him as an everyman – an *utter* son of Man, a premium example of a complex, well-rounded human who is neither the repressed dreamer that Jekyll is, nor the idealistic Victorian that Lanyon is, nor the impulsive hedonist that Hyde is. Utterson is utterly human, if curmudgeonly and somewhat misanthropic. Nonetheless, he is flawed and aware of his flaws: whereas Jekyll's flaws are compartmentalized (and thus schizophrenic), Utterson's are a part of his life that he has no choice but to accept, and does so sensibly and stoically. Also important to note, Utterson is a Scottish name, and his grumpy, antisocial personality seems in line with stereotypes of Edinburgh intellectuals: practical to a fault, unsentimental, and emotionally stingy. Thus Stevenson – through Utterson – infuses his "fine bogey tale" with a flavor of its native Scotch-ness

[5] An utter-man indeed: Utterson's lack of warmth and sentiment prepare him to be the objective, unbiased lens of this libelous biography, allowing us to trust his observations and project onto his essentially blank personality. Utterson is something of a cynic, unlike Jekyll and Lanyon who are subjects to ambition and idealism, and his dark, misanthropic worldview is receptive to the shocking narrative of Jekyll's hideous hypocrisies

talk, but which spoke not only in these silent symbols of the after-dinner face, but more often and loudly in the acts of his life[1]. He was austere with himself; drank gin when he was alone, to mortify a taste for vintages[2]; and though he enjoyed the theatre, had not crossed the doors of one for twenty years[3]. But he had an approved[4] tolerance for others; sometimes wondering, almost with envy, at the high pressure of spirits involved in their misdeeds; and in any extremity inclined to help rather than to reprove[5]. "I incline to Cain's heresy[6]," he used to say quaintly: "I let my brother go to the devil in his own way." In this character, it was frequently his fortune to be the last reputable acquaintance and the last good influence in the lives of downgoing men. And

---

[1] Unlike Jekyll, Utterson is sincere (if relatively unpleasant) in that he expresses himself in behavior and actions rather than in language and rhetoric

[2] Utterson is something of a masochist – and this may be a gross understatement. In order to balance his snobbish taste in wine, he privately indulges in the (at the time) lower-class spirit of choice, one which William Hogarth chose to signifying the dregs of human society in his *Beer Lane / Gin Alley* prints, and one which was deeply associated with alcoholism, which Utterson may in fact suffer from. But while he consciously explores himself, checking and balancing his pride with humility and his virtue with vice, essentially allowing his many archetypes to cohabitate in a sustainable cycle of competition, Jekyll lets his two chief archetypes have their own houses, where they run unchecked: virtue growing weak without humility and vice growing titanic without shame

[3] Utterson acknowledges but does not indulge his tastes (the "theatre" he refers to is not the cultural edification that we think of today: at the time theatre might be analogous to action movies and soppy rom-coms – an undiscerning indulgence frequented by fops, cads, and daydreamers). While Jekyll would deny this weakness, and Hyde would surrender wholly to it, Utterson openly admits his affinity but simply doesn't make it out – probably more from practical inconvenience than self-control

[4] That is, "proven," "renowned"

[5] Some might locate Utterson on the autism spectrum, and his wondrous, detached, curiousness about his fellow man certainly smacks of Asperger's Syndrome. At any rate he is an observer of mankind who is fascinated by vice, motives, and human psychology in a pre-Freudian era where his interest in moral failure was truly ahead of its time

[6] The heresy in question refers to Cain's unfeeling quip after having slain his brother Abel: "am I my brother's keeper?" Utterson uses this callous sentiment to argue in favor of a lasses-faire approach to mankind – staying out of others' affairs and allowing them to self-destruct unimpeded. This policy will, of course, become increasingly less important to him as he tracks Hyde with building interest

to such as these, so long as they came about his chambers, he never marked a shade of change in his demeanour[1].

No doubt the feat was easy to Mr. Utterson; for he was undemonstrative at the best, and even his friendship seemed to be founded in a similar catholicity[2] of good-nature. It is the mark of a modest man to accept his friendly circle ready-made from the hands of opportunity; and that was the lawyer's way. His friends were those of his own blood or those whom he had known the longest; his affections, like ivy, were the growth of time, they implied no aptness in the object[3]. Hence, no doubt the bond that united him to Mr. Richard Enfield, his distant kinsman, the well-known man about town[4]. It was a nut to crack for many, what these two could see in each other, or what subject they could find in common. It was reported by those who encountered them in their Sunday walks, that they said nothing, looked singularly dull and would hail with obvious relief the appearance of a friend. For all that, the two men put the greatest store by these excursions, counted them the chief jewel of each week, and not only set aside occasions of pleasure, but even resisted the calls of business, that they might enjoy them uninterrupted[5].

---

[1] Utterson acts as a judicial Ego to Jekyll's Super-Ego and Hyde's Id, coexisting with noble and ignoble men alike. He neither rejects ruined men nor joins in their self-destruction, but like a vulture or an undertaker, he finds some personal profit from accepting the company that most members of respectable society rebuke. In all cases – prosperity and ruin, virtue and vice – Utterson is there to offer his nonjudgmental company. Utterson consistently treads the no-man's land between Jekyll and Hyde as an undiscriminating noncombatant, and is perfectly placed for his role as emissary between the two

[2] Liberality of sentiment, generosity

[3] Which is to say, many of his friends were underserving of the title, but stayed so due to history or blood. This is the first of several implications that Enfield is a cad

[4] There is a strong sexual implication in this euphemism, suggesting that Enfield is known for straying into certain neighborhoods and certain establishments at certain times of night which have led to his becoming infamous. Today the term denotes a socialite who is well-known in hot spots and clubs, but in Victorian Britain the phrase was much more nefarious

[5] In spite of the awkwardness of their relationship – the dusty, unemotional curmudgeon and the spritely, indulgent playboy – Utterson embraces his relative, and the two brazenly accept each other's existence in their respective lives. This is yet another example of Utterson's metaphorical self-actualization: he accepts all parts of himself, rejecting none and denying nothing. Rather than spurn or even avoid a relative who is no doubt a social liability (read: psychological denial), Utterson not only keeps company with him, but does so

It chanced on one of these rambles that their way led them down a by-street in a busy quarter of London[1]. The street was small and what is called quiet[2], but it drove a thriving trade on the weekdays. The inhabitants were all doing well, it seemed and all emulously hoping to do better still, and laying out the surplus of their grains in coquetry; so that the shop fronts stood along that thoroughfare with an air of invitation, like rows of smiling saleswomen. Even on Sunday, when it veiled its more florid charms and lay comparatively empty of passage, the street shone out in contrast to its dingy neighbourhood, like a fire in a forest; and with its freshly painted shutters, well-polished brasses, and general cleanliness and gaiety of note, instantly caught and pleased the eye of the passenger[3].

Two doors from one corner, on the left hand going east the line was broken by the entry of a court; and just at that point a certain sinister block of building thrust forward its gable on the street. It was two storeys high; showed no window, nothing but a door on the lower storey and a blind forehead of discoloured wall on the upper; and bore in every feature, the marks of prolonged and sordid negligence[4]. The door, which was equipped

---

regularly and publically. Utterson has no skeletons in his closet because he brings them out and rattles around town with them

[1] Much commentary has been made about how Stevenson's "London" is unquestionably Edinburgh, based on the description of the winding neighborhoods which can blur easily from fashionable to red light districts in the space of a few strides. Edinburgh, unlike London, was filled with narrow, winding streets that had little rhyme or reason. Crammed, unclean, and claustrophobic, it had a decidedly "old" feeling about it that the modern avenues of London lacked, even in its poorest districts

[2] One of many times that characters will comment on something being "called" one thing, rather than openly saying that it "is" that thing. Jekyll, for instance is said to do that which is "called good," emphasizing the subjective nature of a man's character

[3] Like Jekyll, who shines from its midst as a beacon of reputability in spite of living in a neighborhood encroached upon by slummy streets and prostitution. However, there is an emphasis here on how things are presented versus how they are – shutters are painted pleasing colors and brasses are polished well, but they are not inherently attractive without the work required to keep up appearances

[4] As in Poe's "House of Usher," Hawthorne's "House of Seven Gables," and Stoker's *Dracula*, the exterior of an abode is typically considered to symbolize the moral or psychological condition of its occupant. Jekyll is a compartmentalized soul, and his house demonstrates this neatly: his public side is well tended to and cultivated, but his thought life has long been abandoned to degeneration – not due to evilness, mind you, but to repression and denial. His private self has been stunted (as Hyde's stature suggests), and the exterior of the half of his home

with neither bell nor knocker, was blistered and distained[1]. Tramps slouched into the recess and struck matches on the panels; children kept shop upon the steps; the schoolboy had tried his knife on the mouldings[2]; and for close on a generation, no one had appeared to drive away these random visitors or to repair their ravages[3].

Mr. Enfield and the lawyer were on the other side of the by-street; but when they came abreast of the entry, the former lifted up his cane and pointed.

"Did you ever remark that door?" he asked; and when his companion had replied in the affirmative. "It is connected in my mind," added he, "with a very odd story."

"Indeed?" said Mr. Utterson, with a slight change of voice, "and what was that?"

"Well, it was this way," returned Mr. Enfield: "I was coming home from some place at the end of the world[4], about three o'clock[5] of a black winter morning, and my way lay through a part of town where there was literally nothing to be seen but lamps. Street after street and all the folks asleep— street after street, all lighted up as if for a procession and all as empty as a church[6]—till at last I got into that state of mind when a man listens and listens and begins to long for the sight of a policeman[7]. All at once, I saw two

---

which shelters that portion of his personality suggests much. The "blind forehead" detail especially seems to imply a man without a conscience or foresight

[1] It has no means of external communication because it has been used for letting something OUT not letting others IN. Hyde's door – and his half of the house – are used for self soothing and indulgence and therefore have no social use, unlike the door that welcomes dinner guests and grateful patients

[2] To make a cut in order to see just how keen a blade is after sharpening

[3] Close on a generation – or roughly the fifty-some years of Jekyll's existence

[4] I would guess a brothel. "From the end of the world" suggests a place far removed from the good things of society, like a location where a visitor might risk fall off of the globe and into dark space or hell itself. At any rate, Enfield is clear that it is not a "good" place or one that is well-known in polite society

[5] Not at all a respectable time for a gentleman to be wandering home through a seedy neighborhood

[6] It is as though there is a moral play about to be performed (and indeed there is)

[7] Other than the issue of safety, the sight of a policeman would suggest the reinforced existence of law and order – a reminder that there are ramifications to wicked behavior. Enfield's anxiety reminds me of Sartre's comment that a man standing at a cliff edge is filled with horror because he understands that – if he wanted to – at any moment he could make the choice to jump, regardless of whether or not he was suicidal. Like Sartre, Enfield might be anxious because he is aware of his willfulness, and longs to see a policeman because it would prevent

figures: one a little man who was stumping along[1] eastward at a good walk, and the other a girl of maybe eight or ten who was running as hard as she was able down a cross street. Well, sir, the two ran into one another naturally enough at the corner; and then came the horrible part of the thing; for the man trampled calmly over the child's body and left her screaming on the ground[2]. It sounds nothing to hear, but it was hellish to see. It wasn't like a man; it was like some damned Juggernaut[3]. I gave a few halloa[4], took to my heels, collared my gentleman, and brought him back to where there was already quite a group about the screaming child. He was perfectly cool and made no resistance, but gave me one look, so ugly that it brought out the sweat on me like running. The people who had turned out were the girl's own family; and pretty soon, the doctor, for whom she had been sent put in his appearance[5]. Well, the child was not much the worse, more frightened, according to the Sawbones[6]; and there you might have supposed would be an end to it. But there was one curious circumstance. I had taken a loathing to my gentleman at first sight. So had the child's family, which was only natural. But the doctor's case was what struck me. He was the usual cut and dry apothecary[7], of no particular age and colour, with a strong Edinburgh accent and about as emotional as a bagpipe[8]. Well, sir, he was like the rest of us; every time he looked at my prisoner, I saw that Sawbones turn sick and white

---

him from committing a crime – without the presence of law and authority, this lonely London street has the potential to become the island in *Lord of the Flies*

[1] Not a very human gerund. "Stumping" implies animalism or deformity – the behavior of a bear or crocodile, not a man

[2] Stevenson was known for his love of children, and the fact that Hyde's first victim is a child is a particularly keen indictment of his character coming from Stevenson

[3] A massive sixteen wheeled carriage dragged by fifty men. The enormous train was pulled by devotees of the Indian god Vishnu, and was known to be difficult to stop once set in motion, and responsible for crushing those unfortunate enough to cross its path

[4] Hunting cries shouted when the prey has been sighted

[5] Due to the absence of a mother in this party, many have interpreted the girl's trip to the doctor as being an errand for an ailing mother who needed medicine. Stevenson never clarifies

[6] A derogatory term for a rustic doctor or a medical jack-of-all-trades. The term comes from a battlefield surgeon's most important task: amputation

[7] General practitioner, no just a pharmacist as the term is used today

[8] Further reinforcing the inescapably Scottish mood of this story, with its Edinburgh-esque setting and Calvinistic morality

with desire to kill him[1]. I knew what was in his mind, just as he knew what was in mine; and killing being out of the question, we did the next best. We told the man we could and would make such a scandal out of this as should make his name stink from one end of London to the other. If he had any friends or any credit, we undertook that he should lose them[2]. And all the time, as we were pitching it in red hot, we were keeping the women off him as best we could for they were as wild as harpies. I never saw a circle of such hateful faces; and there was the man in the middle, with a kind of black sneering coolness—frightened too, I could see that—but carrying it off, sir, really like Satan[3]. 'If you choose to make capital out of this accident[4],' said he, 'I am naturally helpless. No gentleman but wishes to avoid a scene[5],' says he. 'Name your figure.' Well, we screwed him up to a hundred pounds[6] for the child's family; he would have clearly liked to stick out; but there was something about the lot of us that meant mischief, and at last he struck[7]. The next thing was to get the money; and where do you think he carried us but to that place with the door?—whipped out a key, went in, and presently came back with the matter of ten pounds in gold and a cheque for the balance on Coutts's[8], drawn payable to bearer and signed with a name that I can't mention, though it's one of the points of my story, but it was a name at least

---

[1] This emotion is very telling. Pariahs, or those that brazenly disregard moral codes, in hunter-gatherer tribes are often killed on the spot. Those who offend the mores of the tribe so horrify and disgust their fellows that they are summarily put to death out of instinctual hatred. Hyde represents the antithesis of the Victorian ethos, and his captors must restrain an instinctive urge to put him to death because of the threat he poses to their moral code as a brazen rule breaker. This would not be the case were he to show shame or even annoyance, but his unapologetic indifference rises Enfield's gorge and inspires a primeavel instinct to slay the nonconformist

[2] Hyde's fashionable dress make this assumption possible. He is not – as some depict him – dressed in tatters or foppish campiness, but in elegant eveningwear, and is – as Enfield says – clearly a social gentleman

[3] Hyde, like Satan, rebels against moral conventions, spitting in the face of community values as a strict individualist

[4] Hyde suggests that they are unfairly blaming him for an accident, and that they are mere blackmailers

[5] Also unlike some depictions, Hyde is not a saucy Cockney, but a well-spoken gentleman who negotiates his release with cool articulation

[6] Roughly £9,300 or $14,000 in 2015 currency

[7] Which is to say, he clearly wanted to drive down the price, but the group seemed so intent on violence that he was probably afraid of being lynched on the spot. Hyde truly inspires the worst in people, even when that is a reaction against him

[8] A fashionable London bank

very well known and often printed[1]. The figure was stiff; but the signature was good for more than that if it was only genuine[2]. I took the liberty of pointing out to my gentleman that the whole business looked apocryphal[3], and that a man does not, in real life, walk into a cellar door at four in the morning and come out with another man's cheque for close upon a hundred pounds. But he was quite easy and sneering. 'Set your mind at rest,' says he, 'I will stay with you till the banks open[4] and cash the cheque myself.' So we all set off, the doctor, and the child's father, and our friend and myself, and passed the rest of the night in my chambers; and next day, when we had breakfasted[5], went in a body to the bank. I gave in the cheque myself, and said I had every reason to believe it was a forgery. Not a bit of it. The cheque was genuine."

"Tut-tut," said Mr. Utterson.

"I see you feel as I do," said Mr. Enfield. "Yes, it's a bad story. For my man was a fellow that nobody could have to do with, a really damnable man; and the person that drew the cheque is the very pink of the proprieties[6], celebrated too, and (what makes it worse) one of your fellows who do what they call good[7]. Black mail I suppose; an honest man paying through the nose for some of the capers of his youth[8]. Black Mail House is what I call the place with the door, in consequence. Though even that, you know, is far from explaining all," he added, and with the words fell into a vein of musing.

From this he was recalled by Mr. Utterson asking rather suddenly: "And you don't know if the drawer of the cheque lives there?"

---

[1] That is, printed in the society section of the newspapers and in professional journals – a famous person

[2] The amount of money is very high, but for the wealthy Henry Jekyll it would mean very little

[3] Fake, forged. It would be like nabbing a mugger in New York City who pays for his harassment with a check signed by Conan O'Brien – highly suspicious if not downright ludicrous

[4] Bank hours ran from 9 AM to 3:30 PM

[5] Leonard Wolfnotes – with much delight – just how horribly awkward this must have been: a lynchmob drags their victim to Enfield's parlor where they twiddle their thumbs for six hours, including a big family breakfast. Wolfjokes that the conversation at the breakfast table must have been very peculiar ("Pass the crumpits, you dirty bugger, and do you require any butter for your scone, damn your eyes?")

[6] An exemplar of something; the

[7] "What they call good." Enfield may be saying this to disparage do-goodery as being self-gratifying and hypocritical, or he may be saying it as one who openly does no good: as a playboy and bon vivant, he may be very comfortable admitting that good deeds are fairly alien to him

[8] Jekyll will later admit to harboring some "capers." The reference, opaque as it is, is to sexual indiscretions – something that would be keen on Enfield's radar

"A likely place, isn't it?" returned Mr. Enfield. "But I happen to have noticed his address; he lives in some square or other[1]."

"And you never asked about the—place with the door?" said Mr. Utterson.

"No, sir: I had a delicacy," was the reply. "I feel very strongly about putting questions; it partakes too much of the style of the day of judgment. You start a question, and it's like starting a stone. You sit quietly on the top of a hill; and away the stone goes, starting others; and presently some bland old bird (the last you would have thought of) is knocked on the head in his own back garden and the family have to change their name[2]. No sir, I make it a rule of mine: the more it looks like Queer Street, the less I ask."

"A very good rule, too," said the lawyer.

"But I have studied the place for myself," continued Mr. Enfield. "It seems scarcely a house. There is no other door, and nobody goes in or out of that one but, once in a great while, the gentleman of my adventure. There are three windows looking on the court on the first floor; none below; the windows are always shut but they're clean. And then there is a chimney which is generally smoking; so somebody must live there. And yet it's not so sure; for the buildings are so packed together about the court, that it's hard to say where one ends and another begins."

The pair walked on again for a while in silence; and then "Enfield," said Mr. Utterson, "that's a good rule of yours[3]."

"Yes, I think it is," returned Enfield.

"But for all that," continued the lawyer, "there's one point I want to ask: I want to ask the name of that man who walked over the child."

"Well," said Mr. Enfield, "I can't see what harm it would do. It was a man of the name of Hyde."

"Hm," said Mr. Utterson. "What sort of a man is he to see?"

"He is not easy to describe. There is something wrong with his appearance; something displeasing, something down-right detestable[4]. I

---

[1] Indeed – right around the corner if they chose to making a right turn on the next street. The implication is that Jekyll lives in a posh street like Berkeley Square

[2] A prophetic concern. Like Utterson, Enfield harbors a "live and let live" philosophy which shuns judgment of his neighbors' sin. The metaphor that Enfield conjures was a genuine concern in the Victorian era: too much prying into suppressed indiscretions might accidentally result in the ruin of good men, often – as he says – the last you would expect: harmless old men who were guilty of a few indiscretions in their youth. The reference to name-changing is also not without precedent, and often was brought about by legal scandals (Oscar Wilde's for instance) or suicide

[3] Enfield's own adherence to that rule has already been keenly described

[4] Stevenson goes out of his way to avoid describing Hyde's physical appearance. Though we can't know for sure, it may have been that Fanny Stevenson's dislike

never saw a man I so disliked, and yet I scarce know why. He must be deformed somewhere; he gives a strong feeling of deformity, although I couldn't specify the point. He's an extraordinary looking man, and yet I really can name nothing out of the way. No, sir; I can make no hand of it; I can't describe him. And it's not want of memory; for I declare I can see him this moment."

Mr. Utterson again walked some way in silence and obviously under a weight of consideration. "You are sure he used a key?" he inquired at last.

"My dear sir..." began Enfield, surprised out of himself[1].

"Yes, I know," said Utterson; "I know it must seem strange. The fact is, if I do not ask you the name of the other party, it is because I know it already. You see, Richard, your tale has gone home[2]. If you have been inexact in any point you had better correct it."

"I think you might have warned me," returned the other with a touch of sullenness. "But I have been pedantically exact, as you call it. The fellow had a key; and what's more, he has it still. I saw him use it not a week ago."

Mr. Utterson sighed deeply but said never a word; and the young man presently resumed. "Here is another lesson to say nothing," said he. "I am ashamed of my long tongue[3]. Let us make a bargain never to refer to this again."

"With all my heart," said the lawyer. "I shake hands on that, Richard."

Search for Mr Hyde

---

of his first draft was due to a monstrous rather than vague description of his physique. The original illustrator, too, opted to keep Hyde's face always hidden. The result – which is mercifully evocative unlike the many hirsuite depictions in film (March's being one of the worst, though the makeup was truly brilliant, and the *League of Extraordinary Gentlemen* being so bad that I prefer not to go into detail) – is one which is less melodramatic and more psychological. Hyde is not a monster, and while the transformation is physical, too, his deformity is more about his character than about a werewolf transformation

[1] Utterson's uncharacteristically nosy attitude shocks his nephew, who thinks he may be prying into these matters for nefarious reasons, viz. blackmail

[2] A fencing term meaning a direct hit. He might also have set "your tale has cut me to the core," or "has resonated with me"

[3] A parable that illustrates the pair's mutually regarded laisses-faire philosophy of "let sleeping dogs lie." Both walk away from the encounter more certain than ever that no good can come from gossip, and that the best life is that which permits the stones one passes to remain un-turned-over. While Stevenson's Calvinist background encouraged prying, judging, and gossip, he was nauseated by it, sure of the dire consequences that prying can have

That evening Mr. Utterson came home to his bachelor[1] house in sombre spirits and sat down to dinner without relish. It was his custom of a Sunday, when this meal was over, to sit close by the fire, a volume of some dry divinity[2] on his reading desk, until the clock of the neighbouring church rang out the hour of twelve, when he would go soberly and gratefully to bed. On this night however, as soon as the cloth was taken away, he took up a candle and went into his business room. There he opened his safe, took from the most private part of it a document endorsed on the envelope as Dr. Jekyll's Will and sat down with a clouded brow to study its contents. The will was holograph[3], for Mr. Utterson though he took charge of it now that it was made, had refused to lend the least assistance in the making of it; it provided not only that, in case of the decease of Henry Jekyll, M.D., D.C.L., L.L.D., F.R.S., etc.[4], all his possessions were to pass into the hands of his "friend and benefactor[5] Edward Hyde," but that in case of Dr. Jekyll's "disappearance or unexplained absence for any period exceeding three calendar months[6]," the said Edward Hyde should step into the said Henry Jekyll's shoes without further delay and free from any burthen or obligation beyond the payment of a few small sums to the members of the doctor's household. This document had long been the

---

[1] All of the principle characters in this story are middle-aged, confirmed old bachelors. Homoerotic readings of the text are understandably common, but the principle sense here is one of boys who have grown into men and never come to terms with their adulthood – rebels who resist the societal pressure to marry and have a family. Utterson, Enfield, Lanyon, and Jekyll each tread on the environs of society, a dangerous frontier that offers independence and seclusion, but that seclusion results in vulnerability and at least two of these characters will fall prey to the predatory spirits that haunt this Neverland

[2] Presumably of a Calvinist vein. Utterson, like the Uiniversity-of-Edinburgh-esque intellectuals Lanyon and Jekyll, has a very Scottish character, and this grumpy, wine-loving, divinity-reading, laissez-faire old curmudgeon smacks strongly of a man who – like Stevenson – has been raised in a Covenanter family, who has abandoned his faith, but finds an odd attraction to it nonetheless. Unlike Jekyll, Utterson is thoroughly self-integrated, and his dour Calvinist side sups alongside his worldly wine-afficianado side

[3] Written in the hand of the author – not a copy

[4] Medical Doctor, Doctor of Civil Law, Doctor of Laws, Fellow of the Royal Society of London for Improving Natural Knowledge (viz. science)

[5] Benefactor is an interesting term here, since Jekyll is rich. Hyde is not his financial benefactor, as the term is most typically used, but his psychological benefactor – so Jekyll thinks – in that he theoretically wicks away Jekyll's baser self and renders him, theoretically, a better human being

[6] Leonard Wolfnotes that this is a legal impossibility since – for a will cannot be enforced until its subject is legally dead, not disappeared, and without a body this process can take many years, often a decade at least

lawyer's eyesore. It offended him both as a lawyer and as a lover of the sane and customary sides of life, to whom the fanciful was the immodest[1]. And hitherto it was his ignorance of Mr. Hyde that had swelled his indignation; now, by a sudden turn, it was his knowledge. It was already bad enough when the name was but a name of which he could learn no more. It was worse when it began to be clothed upon with detestable attributes; and out of the shifting, insubstantial mists that had so long baffled his eye, there leaped up the sudden, definite presentment of a fiend[2].

"I thought it was madness," he said, as he replaced the obnoxious paper in the safe, "and now I begin to fear it is disgrace[3]."

With that he blew out his candle, put on a greatcoat, and set forth in the direction of Cavendish Square[4], that citadel[5] of medicine, where his friend, the great Dr. Lanyon, had his house and received his crowding patients. "If anyone knows, it will be Lanyon," he had thought.

The solemn butler knew and welcomed him; he was subjected to no stage of delay, but ushered direct from the door to the dining-room where Dr. Lanyon sat alone over his wine. This was a hearty, healthy, dapper, red-faced gentleman[6], with a shock of hair prematurely white[7], and a boisterous and decided manner. At sight of Mr. Utterson, he sprang up from his chair and welcomed him with both hands. The geniality, as was the way of the man, was somewhat theatrical to the eye; but it reposed on genuine feeling. For these two were old friends, old mates both at school and college, both

---

[1] Utterson is, pardon the pun, utterly even keeled. Unlike the idealistic Lanyon or the speculative Jekyll, he survives this story because of his moderation and cynicism

[2] Without even meeting him, Utterson's impression of Hyde is not that of a normal rogue, but as something inhuman and diabolical. Such is the power of Hyde's revolting aura that it is communicated even in third person

[3] At first he thought the will was an irresponsible whim of eccentricity, but now – like Enfield – he fears blackmail

[4] A fashionable district known for its eighteenth century apartments and prestige – a neighborhood where many of London's most reputable physicians held their offices (incidentally, it is not far from John H. Watson's lodgings at Baker Street)

[5] Lanyon represents the solid, Darwinian scientific establishment of Victorian Britain, and could be seen as the commandant of this citadel which defends the values and mores of the main stream. Utterson represents intellectual moderation, Jekyll intellectual progressiveness, and Lanyon intellectual conservatism. That he is morally assassinated by Hyde is one of the great unnerving events of the book

[6] Red-faced from a taste for rich wines. Something he shares with Utterson

[7] A symbol of wisdom, and a badge of his office as the guardian of the scientific establishment

thorough respectors of themselves and of each other, and what does not always follow, men who thoroughly enjoyed each other's company.

After a little rambling talk, the lawyer led up to the subject which so disagreeably preoccupied his mind.

"I suppose, Lanyon," said he, "you and I must be the two oldest friends that Henry Jekyll has?"

"I wish the friends were younger," chuckled Dr. Lanyon. "But I suppose we are. And what of that? I see little of him now."

"Indeed?" said Utterson. "I thought you had a bond of common interest."

"We had," was the reply. "But it is more than ten years since Henry Jekyll became too fanciful for me. He began to go wrong, wrong in mind; and though of course I continue to take an interest in him for old sake's sake[1], as they say, I see and I have seen devilish little of the man. Such unscientific balderdash," added the doctor, flushing suddenly purple, "would have estranged Damon and Pythias[2]."

This little spirit of temper was somewhat of a relief to Mr. Utterson. "They have only differed on some point of science," he thought; and being a man of no scientific passions (except in the matter of conveyancing), he even added: "It is nothing worse than that!" He gave his friend a few seconds to recover his composure, and then approached the question he had come to put. "Did you ever come across a protege of his—one Hyde?" he asked.

"Hyde?" repeated Lanyon. "No. Never heard of him. Since my time[3]."

That was the amount of information that the lawyer carried back with him to the great, dark bed[4] on which he tossed to and fro, until the small hours of the morning began to grow large. It was a night of little ease to his toiling mind, toiling in mere darkness and beseiged by questions.

---

[1] Or, as Stevenson was surely thinking – for this is the English translation of the famous Scots phrase – *for auld lang syne*. Just one more distinctively Scottish taste in this very Scottish story

[2] "In Greek historiography, Damon and Pythias (or Phintias) is a legend surrounding the Pythagorean ideal of friendship. Pythias is accused and charged of creating a plot against the tyrannical Dionysius I of Syracuse. Pythias makes a request of Dionysius that he be allowed to settle his affairs on the condition that he leaves his friend, Damon as a hostage, therefore if Pythias doesn't return, Damon would be executed. Eventually, Pythias returns to face execution to the amazement of Dionysius, who because of the sincere trust and love of their friendship then let both Damon and Pythias go free"

[3] A sad comment – "since our friendship ended" is what he alludes to

[4] Literally Utterson may have a bed with dark sheets, but I think it more likely that Stevenson poetically alludes to Utterson's unconscious – a dim, misty realm of fears and anxieties that a man might leave during the day, but which nonetheless exists, and upon which he must abide during the lonely hours of the night

Six o'clock[1] struck on the bells of the church that was so conveniently near to Mr. Utterson's dwelling, and still he was digging at the problem. Hitherto it had touched him on the intellectual side alone; but now his imagination also was engaged[2], or rather enslaved; and as he lay and tossed in the gross darkness of the night and the curtained room, Mr. Enfield's tale went by before his mind in a scroll of lighted pictures[3]. He would be aware of the great field of lamps of a nocturnal city; then of the figure of a man walking swiftly; then of a child running from the doctor's; and then these met, and that human Juggernaut trod the child down and passed on regardless of her screams. Or else he would see a room in a rich house, where his friend lay asleep, dreaming and smiling at his dreams; and then the door of that room would be opened, the curtains of the bed plucked apart[4], the sleeper recalled, and lo! there would stand by his side a figure to whom power was given, and even at that dead hour, he must rise and do its bidding. The figure in these two phases haunted the lawyer all night; and if at any time he dozed over, it was but to see it glide more stealthily through sleeping houses, or move the more swiftly and still the more swiftly, even to dizziness, through wider labyrinths of lamplighted city, and at every street corner crush a child and leave her screaming. And still the figure had no face by which he might know it; even in his dreams, it had no face, or one that baffled him and melted before his eyes; and thus it was that there sprang up and grew apace in the lawyer's mind a singularly strong, almost an inordinate, curiosity to behold the features of the real Mr. Hyde[5]. If he could but once set eyes on him, he thought the mystery would lighten and perhaps roll altogether away, as was

---

[1] Still quite dark in October, especially in smog-choked London

[2] And this from a man who has admittedly very little imagination to engage

[3] The description, which sounds to us like a movie – most like a silent film – is a reference to a magic lantern show

[4] A suggestively homoerotic scene, both for Utterson who daydreams about Jekyll smiling dreamily in his sleep, and for Hyde whose intrusion into Jekyll's bedroom is far more intimate than it sounds: typically a midnight guest would wake knock or ring the staff awake, who would then knock on the master's door to alert him (the door remaining closed), after which the master would likely don a dressing gown and slippers and meet the guest in the parlor. For Hyde to sneak into the bedroom, pull back the curtains, and arouse his victim alone in the intimacy of his bed has very serious connotations to the attentive Victorian reader

[5] The curiosity and need to see Hyde's face is not unlike Jekyll's curiosity and need to create Hyde: both men are drawn to Hyde as a representation of something that is so foreign to them, so juxtaposed to their worldviews, mores, and values, that he becomes something of a guilty pleasure: to look on the face of unapologetic evil might be a cathartic experience for someone like the unadventurous, unassuming Utterson

the habit of mysterious things when well examined. He might see a reason for his friend's strange preference[1] or bondage[2] (call it which you please) and even for the startling clause of the will. At least it would be a face worth seeing: the face of a man who was without bowels of mercy: a face which had but to show itself to raise up, in the mind of the unimpressionable Enfield, a spirit of enduring hatred.

From that time forward, Mr. Utterson began to haunt the door in the by-street of shops. In the morning before office hours, at noon when business was plenty, and time scarce, at night under the face of the fogged city moon, by all lights and at all hours of solitude or concourse, the lawyer was to be found on his chosen post.

"If he be Mr. Hyde," he had thought, "I shall be Mr. Seek[3]."

And at last his patience was rewarded. It was a fine dry night; frost in the air; the streets as clean as a ballroom floor; the lamps, unshaken by any wind, drawing a regular pattern of light and shadow. By ten o'clock, when the shops were closed the by-street was very solitary and, in spite of the low growl of London from all round, very silent. Small sounds carried far; domestic sounds out of the houses were clearly audible on either side of the roadway; and the rumour of the approach of any passenger preceded him by a long time[4]. Mr. Utterson had been some minutes at his post, when he was aware of an odd light footstep[5] drawing near. In the course of his nightly patrols, he had long grown accustomed to the quaint effect with which the footfalls of a single person, while he is still a great way off, suddenly spring out distinct from the vast hum and clatter of the city. Yet his attention had never before been so sharply and decisively arrested; and it was with a strong, superstitious prevision of success that he withdrew into the entry of the court.

---

[1] "Strange preference" might be a mere choice of words, but it might also further illustrate Utterson's concern that Hyde is Jekyll's lover, since he imagines that looking at him might help explain his odd proclivity for Hyde – does he imagine that the man might be uncommonly beautiful, and that at least the sight of a phenomenally handsome man might explain Jekyll's temptation?

[2] Indeed! Little does he know how accurate this sentiment is, since Jekyll's association with Hyde is caused both by a preference and (increasingly as time passes) a bondage

[3] An apt description of the two: Hyde is the embodiment of repression – the schism of a man who wants to indulge his Id but deny its existence – while Utterson (whose very name suggests a man who speaks his mind) is all that he appears to be, shabby, dour, and unromantic; he is seeks after reality while Hyde attempts to bypass it

[4] That is, the echo of distant footsteps

[5] Two things to note: first, that the step is odd, which suggests a lopping, animal-like gait, and second that it is light, unlike the heavy, violent stomping of most movie Hydes. Indeed, this Hyde is no burly brute, but a wisp of a man

The steps drew swiftly nearer, and swelled out suddenly louder as they turned the end of the street. The lawyer, looking forth from the entry, could soon see what manner of man he had to deal with. He was small and very plainly dressed[1] and the look of him, even at that distance, went somehow strongly against the watcher's inclination[2]. But he made straight for the door, crossing the roadway to save time; and as he came, he drew a key from his pocket like one approaching home.

Mr. Utterson stepped out and touched him on the shoulder as he passed. "Mr. Hyde, I think?"

Mr. Hyde shrank back with a hissing intake of the breath[3]. But his fear was only momentary; and though he did not look the lawyer in the face, he answered coolly enough: "That is my name. What do you want?"

"I see you are going in," returned the lawyer. "I am an old friend of Dr. Jekyll's—Mr. Utterson of Gaunt Street—you must have heard of my name; and meeting you so conveniently, I thought you might admit me."

"You will not find Dr. Jekyll; he is from home," replied Mr. Hyde, blowing in the key. And then suddenly, but still without looking up, "How did you know me?" he asked.

"On your side," said Mr. Utterson "will you do me a favour?"

"With pleasure," replied the other. "What shall it be[4]?"

"Will you let me see your face?" asked the lawyer.

---

[1] Sorry, no glossy top hat, oversized foppish bowtie, or billowing satin cape. Hyde is dressed in luxuriant materials, but they are unassuming and fail to attract attention the way that movies typically render him in the cast of a Jack-the-Ripper-esque, decadent aristocrat

[2] Wolfnotes that Stevenson avoids pointing out any distinct deformities, because decent people who observe Hyde, even from a distance are instinctively inclined to sense his degeneration

[3] The sound a snake makes, an animal linked to the Tempter, Satan. A purposeful choice of words

[4] Hyde's continued civility is truly chilling. Again, he is not a Cockney gorilla, but a slim, mannerly toff – one that might explode into hysterical violence unexpectedly

Mr. Hyde appeared to hesitate, and then, as if upon some sudden reflection, fronted about with an air of defiance[1]; and the pair stared at each other pretty fixedly for a few seconds. "Now I shall know you again," said Mr. Utterson. "It may be useful."

"Yes," returned Mr. Hyde, "It is as well we have met[2]; and apropos, you should have my address." And he gave a number of a street in Soho[3].

"Good God!" thought Mr. Utterson, "can he, too, have been thinking of the will[4]?" But he kept his feelings to himself and only grunted in acknowledgment of the address.

"And now," said the other, "how did you know me?"

"By description," was the reply.

"Whose description?"

"We have common friends," said Mr. Utterson.

"Common friends," echoed Mr. Hyde, a little hoarsely. "Who are they?"

"Jekyll, for instance," said the lawyer.

"He never told you," cried Mr. Hyde, with a flush of anger. "I did not think you would have lied[5]."

"Come," said Mr. Utterson, "that is not fitting language[6]."

The other snarled aloud into a savage laugh[7]; and the next moment, with extraordinary quickness, he had unlocked the door and disappeared into the house.

The lawyer stood awhile when Mr. Hyde had left him, the picture of disquietude. Then he began slowly to mount the street, pausing every step or two and putting his hand to his brow like a man in mental perplexity. The problem he was thus debating as he walked, was one of a class that is rarely solved. Mr. Hyde was pale and dwarfish[8], he gave an impression of deformity

---

[1] Almost as if he takes delight in revealing the full import of his wickedness — "You want to see me, eh? Fine — look upon me and see evil"

[2] Hyde instinctively senses his nemesis in Utterson, and like the Joker who can at times show professional respect for Batman, indulges his obviously distrustful request in order that they might be able to combat each other on a later date

[3] A slummy neighborhood

[4] If Hyde expects to make use of the will in the future, it is probably beneficial that he cultivate a working relationship with Jekyll's attorney ahead of time

[5] Revealing something which Utterson apparently takes for granted or misinterprets: Hyde knows Utterson

[6] It is indeed a lie, but to charge a gentleman of lying was just as serious an offense

[7] To Hyde the concept of appropriate social behavior is a hilarious joke

[8] Hyde's most detailed physical descriptions paint him as stunted, misshapen, and vestigial. The idea that he is pale and dwarfish suggests someone who has not fully developed or been allowed into society. Indeed, Jekyll's Id has not been permitted to be integrated into his conscious self, and as a result — like a child

without any nameable malformation, he had a displeasing smile[1], he had borne himself to the lawyer with a sort of murderous mixture of timidity and boldness[2], and he spoke with a husky, whispering and somewhat broken voice[3]; all these were points against him, but not all of these together could explain the hitherto unknown disgust, loathing and fear with which Mr. Utterson regarded him. "There must be something else," said the perplexed gentleman. "There is something more, if I could find a name for it. God bless me, the man seems hardly human! Something troglodytic[4], shall we say? or can it be the old story of Dr. Fell[5]? or is it the mere radiance of a foul soul that thus transpires through, and transfigures, its clay continent[6]? The last, I think; for, O my poor old Harry Jekyll, if ever I read Satan's signature upon a face, it is on that of your new friend."

Round the corner from the by-street, there was a square of ancient, handsome houses, now for the most part decayed from their high estate and let in flats and chambers to all sorts and conditions of men; map-engravers, architects, shady lawyers and the agents of obscure enterprises. One house, however, second from the corner, was still occupied entire; and at the door of this, which wore a great air of wealth and comfort, though it was now

---

locked in a cramped cell and hidden from sunlight – Hyde is physically malformed and pale from a life of confinement

[1] One which suggests an unhinged mind, or one which delights in all the wrong things

[2] Like a petulant child, Hyde is both shy and brazen, both easily cowed and easily enraged. In a child the result is a raving, sullen brat. In a man the result is a raving, sullen sociopath

[3] We might reasonably speculate that Hyde actually has Jekyll's voice and is attempting to disguise it

[4] A caveman. This is one of many suggestions that Hyde represents an unevolved man – or one which has devolved – a fascinating concept during the peak of the Darwinian scientific revolution

[5] An old nursery rhyme about an indescribable dislike for the eponymous worthy. Thomas Brown, the founder of the Oxford University Press, was – as a student – expelled briefly by Dr Fell, dean of Christchurch, and wrote the famous Suessian verse which somewhat recalls "Green Eggs and Ham":

> I do not love thee, Dr Fell
> The reason why I cannot tell
> But this I know, I know full well
> I do not love thee, Dr Fell

[6] A wonderfully evocative idea: perhaps Hyde has nothing physically wrong about his appearance, but his revolting soul radiates through and transforms his flesh

plunged in darkness except for the fanlight[1], Mr. Utterson stopped and knocked. A well-dressed, elderly servant opened the door.

"Is Dr. Jekyll at home, Poole?" asked the lawyer.

"I will see, Mr. Utterson," said Poole, admitting the visitor, as he spoke, into a large, low-roofed, comfortable hall paved with flags, warmed (after the fashion of a country house[2]) by a bright, open fire, and furnished with costly cabinets of oak. "Will you wait here by the fire, sir? or shall I give you a light in the dining-room?"

"Here, thank you," said the lawyer, and he drew near and leaned on the tall fender[3]. This hall, in which he was now left alone, was a pet fancy of his friend the doctor's; and Utterson himself was wont to speak of it as the pleasantest room in London[4]. But tonight there was a shudder in his blood; the face of Hyde sat heavy on his memory; he felt (what was rare with him) a nausea and distaste of life; and in the gloom of his spirits, he seemed to read a menace in the flickering of the firelight on the polished cabinets and the uneasy starting of the shadow on the roof. He was ashamed of his relief, when Poole presently returned to announce that Dr. Jekyll was gone out.

"I saw Mr. Hyde go in by the old dissecting room[5], Poole," he said. "Is that right, when Dr. Jekyll is from home?"

"Quite right, Mr. Utterson, sir," replied the servant. "Mr. Hyde has a key."

"Your master seems to repose a great deal of trust in that young man[6], Poole," resumed the other musingly.

"Yes, sir, he does indeed," said Poole. "We have all orders to obey him."

"I do not think I ever met Mr. Hyde?[7]" asked Utterson.

"O, dear no, sir. He never dines here," replied the butler. "Indeed we see very little of him on this side of the house; he mostly comes and goes by the laboratory."

"Well, good-night, Poole."

---

[1] The half-circle window – or transom – on top of the door. These usually are broken up into panes which radiate from the center like sunrays or the ribs of a lady's fan (hence the name)

[2] As opposed to the small coal grates of most city houses

[3] A metal screen that prevents sparks from popping out of the hearth

[4] Symbolic of course of Jekyll, whose manner is (or has been) among the pleasantest in London

[5] Jekyll's house is L-shaped, with the old door leading to the laboratory at toe of the L and the front door being at its top

[6] Previously termed a protégée, Hyde is now definitively referred to as being younger (apparently by a sizable degree) in appearance to the other main characters who are in their fifties. This is fitting since he is the embodiment of Jekyll's underdeveloped and unmatured libido

[7] Another lie, though Utterson is specifically enquiring as to whether Hyde is a regular dinner guest at Jekyll's

"Good-night, Mr. Utterson."

And the lawyer set out homeward with a very heavy heart. "Poor Harry Jekyll," he thought, "my mind misgives me he is in deep waters! He was wild when he was young; a long while ago to be sure; but in the law of God, there is no statute of limitations[1]. Ay, it must be that; the ghost of some old sin, the cancer of some concealed disgrace: punishment coming, *pede claudo*[2], years after memory has forgotten and self-love condoned the fault." And the lawyer, scared by the thought, brooded awhile on his own past, groping in all the corners of memory, least by chance some Jack-in-the-Box of an old iniquity should leap to light there. His past was fairly blameless; few men could read the rolls of their life with less apprehension; yet he was humbled to the dust by the many ill things he had done, and raised up again into a sober and fearful gratitude by the many he had come so near to doing yet avoided[3]. And then by a return on his former subject, he conceived a spark of hope. "This Master Hyde[4], if he were studied," thought he, "must have secrets of his own; black secrets, by the look of him; secrets compared to which poor Jekyll's worst would be like sunshine[5]. Things cannot continue as they are. It turns

---

[1] Jekyll will confirm this in his confession. Though the sins are never fully described, they certainly appear to be sexual in nature

[2] Latin: literally "with a limping foot," this is an abbreviation of the phrase "pede poena claudo," or "punishment comes with a limping foot," meaning that one's sins will eventually catch up with them even if there are at first no consequences

[3] A wonderful moment where even the "dry as dust" Utterson is "humbled to the dust" by his own personal sins. We have a strong sense of Stevenson's philosophy that "all have sinned and fallen short of the glory of God," something which Calvinists (on paper) tended to ignore. They believed that the Elect – those chosen by God to be saved – might even be incapable of sin. But Utterson, probably the tamest, most bland character in Victorian literature, is sent into an introspective spiral of self-inspection as he ponders Jekyll's own checkered past. It is pointless to meditate on what Utterson's sins were, but his language and descriptions of just-barely-avoided indiscretions imply – like Jekyll – that Utterson has had some sexual scandals in his past, and barely avoided others. It is in any case a lovely and unexpected passage where the morality shifts from the suspicious Jekyll to the unassuming Utterson. This bit of introspection and fear of scandal is really quite moving and anxiety-producing, and it gives us a glimpse into the state of Utterson's mind, and possibly into the origins of his laissez-faire policy on gossip and scandal

[4] Hyde may be terribly young, in fact – much less the heavily mutton-chopped thug with discolored teeth, curling eyebrow hair, and paw-like hands, and more of a pimply, croaky-voiced teenager. The address "Master" is an honorific given to boys under the age of eighteen in Britain

[5] The implication is that Utterson finds hope in the concept of counter-blackmailing Hyde if he is indeed currently blackmailing Jekyll

me cold to think of this creature stealing like a thief to Harry's bedside; poor Harry, what a wakening[1]! And the danger of it; for if this Hyde suspects the existence of the will, he may grow impatient to inherit. Ay, I must put my shoulders to the wheel—if Jekyll will but let me," he added, "if Jekyll will only let me." For once more he saw before his mind's eye, as clear as transparency, the strange clauses of the will.

Dr Jekyll Was Quite At Ease

A fortnight later, by excellent good fortune, the doctor gave one of his pleasant dinners[2] to some five or six old cronies, all intelligent, reputable men and all judges of good wine[3]; and Mr. Utterson so contrived that he remained behind after the others had departed. This was no new arrangement, but a thing that had befallen many scores of times. Where Utterson was liked, he was liked well[4]. Hosts loved to detain the dry lawyer, when the light-hearted and loose-tongued had already their foot on the threshold; they liked to sit a while in his unobtrusive company, practising for solitude, sobering their minds in the man's rich silence after the expense and strain of gaiety. To this rule, Dr. Jekyll was no exception; and as he now sat on the opposite side of the fire—a large, well-made, smooth-faced man of fifty[5], with something of a

---

[1] Utterson repeats this striking vision of Jekyll waking to Hyde leering at him through the bed curtains. Wolfremarks on the similarity this scene has to Fuseli's infamous painting, *The Nightmare*, where a phallic, goblin horse appears jutting its face through vaginal bed curtains while a grotesque gnome squats oppressively on the breast of a terrified woman. He also notes that Utterson's obsession with this bedside scene makes us wonder once again whether Hyde's 'black secrets,' as well as Jekyll's do not also include homosexuality"

[2] Jekyll is clearly in the habit of throwing lavish dinner parties for close friends – a very social chap whose hospitality is at odds with Hyde's loner ways (recall especially how Hyde's voice croaked with confusion at the suggestion that he and Utterson shared friends)

[3] And none have brought their wives. This is, then, probably a klatch of old bachelors, all of whom relish their independence, solitude, and detachment from society's expectations

[4] As befits a self-possessed, transparent man, Utterson has a divisive personality and probably attracts a good deal of disdain from those who don't appreciate his dusty personality, disregard for scandal, and un-sensational character

[5] Film versions love to cast Jekyll as an intellectual heart-throb – a dashing romantic lead in the prime of life. Unconventional, radical, and hot-blooded, he is prone to be a dreamy John Barrymore, a young Spencer Tracy, or a lantern-jawed Adam Baldwin. In fact, Jekyll is past middle life

stylish cast perhaps, but every mark of capacity and kindness[1]—you could see by his looks that he cherished for Mr. Utterson a sincere and warm affection.

"I have been wanting to speak to you, Jekyll," began the latter. "You know that will of yours?"

A close observer might have gathered that the topic was distasteful[2]; but the doctor carried it off gaily. "My poor Utterson," said he, "you are unfortunate in such a client. I never saw a man so distressed as you were by my will; unless it were that hide-bound[3] pedant, Lanyon, at what he called my scientific heresies. O, I know he's a good fellow—you needn't frown—an excellent fellow, and I always mean to see more of him; but a hide-bound pedant for all that; an ignorant, blatant pedant. I was never more disappointed in any man than Lanyon."

"You know I never approved of it," pursued Utterson, ruthlessly disregarding the fresh topic.

"My will? Yes, certainly, I know that," said the doctor, a trifle sharply. "You have told me so."

"Well, I tell you so again," continued the lawyer. "I have been learning something of young Hyde."

The large handsome face of Dr. Jekyll grew pale to the very lips, and there came a blackness about his eyes. "I do not care to hear more," said he. "This is a matter I thought we had agreed to drop."

"What I heard was abominable," said Utterson.

"It can make no change. You do not understand my position," returned the doctor, with a certain incoherency of manner. "I am painfully situated, Utterson; my position is a very strange—a very strange one. It is one of those affairs that cannot be mended by talking."

---

[1] Unlike the dwarfish Hyde, Jekyll's body fills space warmly and announces his presence

[2] The real Hyde – the Hyde within Jekyll, not the one compartmentalized in the dwarfish body – bridles noticeably at the topic, but Jekyll is an expert hypocrite, and represses his annoyance

[3] Just reading that sentence gives me the chills. Jekyll mocks Lanyon for supposing that humans are bound by their hides – the philosophy that biology is destiny. He seems to slip here in this joking, letting us know that he thinks that mankind can transcend beyond the flesh they are born in. What he doesn't know is that in the months to come he will become himself Hyde-bound – trapped in the hide of his unleashed libido. Both Lanyon and Jekyll appear to be right: we can become something other than what we are, but one or the other – our socialization or our will – will eventually dominate the whole, and return will become impossible

"Jekyll," said Utterson, "you know me: I am a man to be trusted. Make a clean breast of this in confidence; and I make no doubt I can get you out of it[1]."

"My good Utterson," said the doctor, "this is very good of you, this is downright good of you, and I cannot find words to thank you in. I believe you fully; I would trust you before any man alive, ay, before myself, if I could make the choice; but indeed it isn't what you fancy; it is not as bad as that; and just to put your good heart at rest, I will tell you one thing: the moment I choose, I can be rid of Mr. Hyde[2]. I give you my hand upon that; and I thank you again and again; and I will just add one little word, Utterson, that I'm sure you'll take in good part: this is a private matter, and I beg of you to let it sleep."

Utterson reflected a little, looking in the fire.

"I have no doubt you are perfectly right," he said at last, getting to his feet.

"Well, but since we have touched upon this business, and for the last time I hope," continued the doctor, "there is one point I should like you to understand. I have really a very great interest in poor Hyde[3]. I know you have seen him; he told me so; and I fear he was rude. But I do sincerely take a great, a very great interest in that young man; and if I am taken away, Utterson, I wish you to promise me that you will bear with him and get his rights for him. I think you would, if you knew all; and it would be a weight off my mind if you would promise."

"I can't pretend that I shall ever like him," said the lawyer.

---

[1] Utterson cuts to the throat: "if you are being blackmailed tell me about it; I can be trusted with your secret and together we can fight against Hyde"

[2] This invites some lovely analogies with dependency problems – drugs and alcohol, etc. – which are depicted in Jekyll's hubris with remarkable accuracy. Though the tale is not a parable about cocaine use or alcoholism, it eagerly suggests the psychology of an addict. Jekyll falsely assumes himself to be in control of his situation, when in fact he is embodying the famous Alcoholics Anonymous adage: "Firs the man takes the drink, then the drink takes the drink, then the drink takes the man." Few proverbs exist that more concisely explain the plot of *Jekyll and Hyde*

[3] Jekyll views Hyde as the most authentic version of himself – the child within, as it were – and thus looks at the diminutive outcast with self-pity and tenderness. We all harbor a scared but selfish child within us, and were we able to manifest that vulnerable (and typically traumatized) self, our feelings towards it would likely be sympathetic, parental, and protective. Of course, like so many plots in horror films and literature, that thing which we attempt to protect from the world so often becomes the thing which we eventually require protecting from

"I don't ask that," pleaded Jekyll, laying his hand upon the other's arm; "I only ask for justice; I only ask you to help him for my sake, when I am no longer here[1]."

Utterson heaved an irrepressible sigh. "Well," said he, "I promise."

The Carew Murder Case

Nearly a year later, in the month of October, 18—, London was startled by a crime of singular ferocity and rendered all the more notable by the high position of the victim. The details were few and startling. A maid servant living alone[2] in a house not far from the river, had gone upstairs to bed about eleven. Although a fog rolled over the city in the small hours[3], the early part of the night was cloudless, and the lane, which the maid's window overlooked, was brilliantly lit by the full moon. It seems she was romantically given, for she sat down upon her box[4], which stood immediately under the window, and fell into a dream of musing. Never (she used to say, with streaming tears, when she narrated that experience), never had she felt more at peace with all men or thought more kindly of the world. And as she so sat she became aware of an aged beautiful gentleman with white hair, drawing near along the lane; and advancing to meet him, another and very small gentleman, to whom at first she paid less attention. When they had come within speech (which was just under the maid's eyes) the older man bowed and accosted the other with a very pretty manner of politeness. It did not seem as if the subject of his address were of great importance; indeed, from his pointing, it some times appeared as if he were only inquiring his way; but the moon shone on his face as he spoke, and the girl was pleased to watch it, it seemed to breathe such an innocent and old-world kindnessof disposition, yet with something high too, as of a well-founded self-content[5]. Presently her eye wandered to the other, and she was surprised to recognise in him a

---

[1] Considering the age difference in the men (thirty years or more), this comment might not be as nefarious as it first sounds, since Hyde should outlive Jekyll by many decades, but it still disturbs Utterson

[2] That is, she has no bedfellows, as was typical of maids to houses with large staffs. Instead, while the family sleep in their rooms (and any manservant in his), she is left in a room by herself

[3] Smog, more accurately

[4] A chest that carried her valuables, linens, and toiletries

[5] Like Utterson, Carew seems to exude a sense of homely self-contentment. He is not arrogant like Lanyon or bitter and ambitious like Jekyll, and it may be a mixture of hatred of Utterson and jealousy of the satisfied old man that drives Hyde to bludgeon him

certain Mr. Hyde, who had once visited her master and for whom she had conceived a dislike[1]. He had in his hand a heavy cane[2], with which he was trifling; but he answered never a word, and seemed to listen with an ill-contained impatience. And then all of a sudden he broke out in a great flame of anger, stamping with his foot, brandishing the cane, and carrying on (as the maid described it) like a madman. The old gentleman took a step back, with the air of one very much surprised and a trifle hurt; and at that Mr. Hyde broke out of all bounds and clubbed him to the earth. And next moment, with ape-like fury[3], he was trampling his victim under foot and hailing down a storm of blows, under which the bones were audibly shattered and the body jumped upon the roadway. At the horror of these sights and sounds, the maid fainted.

It was two o'clock when she came to herself and called for the police. The murderer was gone long ago; but there lay his victim in the middle of the lane, incredibly mangled[4]. The stick with which the deed had been done, although it was of some rare and very tough and heavy wood, had broken in the middle under the stress of this insensate cruelty; and one splintered half had rolled in the neighbouring gutter—the other, without doubt, had been carried away by the murderer. A purse and gold watch were found upon the victim: but no cards or papers[5], except a sealed and stamped envelope, which

---

[1] We never learn who the master is, but there is a distinct sense here that Hyde might actually be – as Utterson suspects – a blackmailer. Some even have suggested that he is blackmailing Carew and murders him because he suspects that the old man is about to enlist Utterson (hence the letter) in putting Hyde behind bars

[2] Stevenson himself owned a cane made of solid steel – it was thin and attractive looking, but when picked up was surprisingly heavy – that he bragged was the "finest weapon a man could carry" should he find himself "in a tight place" where he fancied "nothing [could] equal it" as a bludgeon

[3] The first of several references that lend Hyde a simian cast. He continues to strike people as monkey-like in appearance and behavior, something that would be understood in the atmosphere surrounding Darwin's celebrated theory of evolution to suggest that Hyde represents the under-evolved primate that still dwells in homo sapiens. Films (March's especially) love to play up the ape-like descriptives given to the little man, in spite of the fact that none of these terms are used to describe his face or hair, but rather his carriage and mannerisms

[4] The murder sounds extremely gruesome considering that no blade was used: Carew's body is beaten to hamburger only with the power of the cane-head and Hyde's stomping heels, and yet the result is more than bruising and broken skin: it is carnage

[5] Wolfand other commentators have noted that as lovely an old toff as Carew may be, his actions bespeak something fairly sinister. Wolfe: "Everything about Sir Danvers Carew is suspicious. He is out late at night. He accosts a stranger. He

he had been probably carrying to the post, and which bore the name and address of Mr. Utterson[1].

This was brought to the lawyer the next morning, before he was out of bed; and he had no sooner seen it and been told the circumstances, than he shot out a solemn lip. "I shall say nothing till I have seen the body," said he; "this may be very serious[2]. Have the kindness to wait while I dress." And with the same grave countenance he hurried through his breakfast and drove to the police station, whither the body had been carried. As soon as he came into the cell, he nodded.

"Yes," said he, "I recognise him. I am sorry to say that this is Sir Danvers Carew."

"Good God, sir," exclaimed the officer, "is it possible?" And the next moment his eye lighted up with professional ambition. "This will make a deal of noise," he said. "And perhaps you can help us to the man[3]." And he briefly narrated what the maid had seen, and showed the broken stick.

Mr. Utterson had already quailed at the name of Hyde; but when the stick was laid before him, he could doubt no longer; broken and battered as it was, he recognized it for one that he had himself presented many years before to Henry Jekyll[4].

---

carries a watch and a purse full of money but no immediate way to identify him." There has been a considerable amount of discussion in critical readings of this text that Carew may have been soliciting Hyde for prostitution. Others see Hyde as a homophobe, and have interpreted the attack as being brought on by Carew's queer mannerisms: beautiful to look at, perhaps overly polite ("a very pretty manner of politeness"), and very possibly asking directions to a part of town known for gay rendezvous, Carew sets off Hyde's radar and is beaten to death in a manner all too familiar to us today – a very literal gay-bashing that bespeaks the brutal, masculinist rage latent in the ethos of the Victorian era

[1] It is note-worthy that all of the major characters – even Carew – chose at some point to bring Utterson into their confidence. He inspires sympathy and trust because of his philosophy of Cain. We never learn the letter's contents, though it is not difficult to imagine – considering the rampant speculation of blackmail that perfumes the text with such a stench – that he was contacting the lawyer out of fear of being blackmailed

[2] Of course the incident is serious; Utterson implies that it may be more than an act of random violence, but indicative of a psychopathic behavior which may propagate into serial murder

[3] The killer

[4] There is a form of perverse poetry in Hyde's use of Utterson's present in this way: it literally symbolizes the broken trust between Jekyll and Utterson, it shows disdain for the gift-giver (even a craven killer wouldn't break a treasured gift in the act of murder), and it indicts – even teases – Utterson, whose mission to stop Hyde has gone no where in the last year. It has a distinctly comic book vibe about

"Is this Mr. Hyde a person of small stature?" he inquired.

"Particularly small and particularly wicked-looking, is what the maid calls him," said the officer.

Mr. Utterson reflected; and then, raising his head, "If you will come with me in my cab," he said, "I think I can take you to his house."

It was by this time about nine in the morning, and the first fog of the season. A great chocolate-coloured pall lowered over heaven, but the wind was continually charging and routing these embattled vapours; so that as the cab crawled from street to street, Mr. Utterson beheld a marvelous number of degrees and hues of twilight; for here it would be dark like the back-end of evening; and there would be a glow of a rich, lurid brown, like the light of some strange conflagration[1]; and here, for a moment, the fog would be quite broken up, and a haggard shaft of daylight would glance in between the swirling wreaths. The dismal quarter of Soho seen under these changing glimpses, with its muddy ways, and slatternly passengers, and its lamps, which had never been extinguished or had been kindled afresh to combat this mournful reinvasion of darkness, seemed, in the lawyer's eyes, like a district of some city in a nightmare. The thoughts of his mind, besides, were of the gloomiest dye; and when he glanced at the companion of his drive, he was conscious of some touch of that terror of the law and the law's officers, which may at times assail the most honest[2].

As the cab drew up before the address indicated, the fog lifted a little and showed him a dingy street, a gin palace, a low French eating house, a shop for the retail of penny numbers and twopenny salads, many ragged children huddled in the doorways, and many women of many different nationalities passing out, key in hand, to have a morning glass[3]; and the next moment the fog settled down again upon that part, as brown as umber, and cut him off

---

it: the villain taunts the hero by pointing out their inability to prevent a particularly personal tragedy

[1] The imagery of a fire – of something being destroyed by the consuming heat of a growing power – are certainly poignant in regards to Jekyll's loss of power of Hyde

[2] Another intriguing suggestion of the universality of guilt and sin: Utterson experiences a twinge of terror of policemen, even when he is in their company as an ally. Perhaps – and I heartily recommend this theory – Utterson's sense of unease comes from Hyde's successfully communicated indictment: he is to blame for Carew's death as much as anyone because he has ceased his inquiries and his philosophy of Cain has come full circle, for Carew's blood – like Abel's – now cries from the earth for justice

[3] Of gin, at the time a particularly low-class beverage (one which, you may recall, Utterson enjoys) made from grain alcohol, seasoned with juniper berries and other botanicals to give it the characteristic taste

from his blackguardly surroundings. This was the home of Henry Jekyll's favourite[1]; of a man who was heir to a quarter of a million sterling[2].

An ivory-faced and silvery-haired old woman opened the door. She had an evil face, smoothed by hypocrisy[3]: but her manners were excellent. Yes, she said, this was Mr. Hyde's, but he was not at home; he had been in that night very late, but he had gone away again in less than an hour; there was nothing strange in that; his habits were very irregular, and he was often absent; for instance, it was nearly two months since she had seen him till yesterday.

"Very well, then, we wish to see his rooms," said the lawyer; and when the woman began to declare it was impossible, "I had better tell you who this person is," he added. "This is Inspector Newcomen of Scotland Yard."

A flash of odious joy[4] appeared upon the woman's face. "Ah!" said she, "he is in trouble! What has he done?"

Mr. Utterson and the inspector exchanged glances. "He don't seem a very popular character," observed the latter. "And now, my good woman, just let me and this gentleman have a look about us."

In the whole extent of the house, which but for the old woman remained otherwise empty, Mr. Hyde had only used a couple of rooms; but these were furnished with luxury and good taste[5]. A closet was filled with wine; the plate was of silver, the napery elegant; a good picture[6] hung upon the walls, a gift (as Utterson supposed) from Henry Jekyll, who was much of a connoisseur; and the carpets were of many plies and agreeable in colour[7]. At this moment, however, the rooms bore every mark of having been recently and hurriedly

---

[1] A sexually suggestive term that hints that Hyde is a kept man, or a secret lover who is paid on the side to keep out of the public eye

[2] Hyde would stand to inherit roughly $3.5 million or £2.3 million at 2015 rates

[3] Being a hypocrite – easily able to behave in whatever manner best suits her needs – the woman's face is unwrinkled by the stresses of integrity

[4] Odious in that – so long as she thought that they were friends of Hyde's, she kept up the ruse that they were on good terms, but that as soon as she realizes that Hyde is in trouble, she drops the mask. This is no simple transition from polite conversation to a sigh of repressed relief – we might imagine a revoltingly gushy woman with stilted manners and affectations suddenly plummeting to revolting squeals of childish glee

[5] Jekyll's style, we might imagine. It is somewhat poetic that, like Hyde's door into Jekyll's rooms, Hyde's personal apartment is outwardly decrepit and inwardly luxuriant

[6] An expensive painting in fashionable taste

[7] Carpets – or rugs – were symbols of status and wealth in the time before carpeting became commonplace. The wealthier a person was, the more he could afford to have, often piling two or three on top of each other to make the floor plush and soft

ransacked; clothes lay about the floor, with their pockets inside out; lock-fast drawers stood open[1]; and on the hearth there lay a pile of grey ashes, as though many papers had been burned. From these embers the inspector disinterred the butt end of a green cheque book, which had resisted the action of the fire; the other half of the stick was found behind the door; and as this clinched his suspicions, the officer declared himself delighted. A visit to the bank, where several thousand pounds were found to be lying to the murderer's credit, completed his gratification.

"You may depend upon it, sir," he told Mr. Utterson: "I have him in my hand. He must have lost his head, or he never would have left the stick or, above all, burned the cheque book. Why, money's life to the man. We have nothing to do but wait for him at the bank, and get out the handbills[2]."

This last, however, was not so easy of accomplishment; for Mr. Hyde had numbered few familiars—even the master of the servant maid had only seen him twice; his family could nowhere be traced; he had never been photographed; and the few who could describe him differed widely[3], as common observers will. Only on one point were they agreed; and that was the haunting sense of unexpressed deformity with which the fugitive impressed his beholders.

Incident of the Letter

It was late in the afternoon, when Mr. Utterson found his way to Dr. Jekyll's door, where he was at once admitted by Poole, and carried down by the kitchen offices and across a yard which had once been a garden, to the building which was indifferently known as the laboratory or dissecting rooms. The doctor had bought the house from the heirs of a celebrated surgeon; and his own tastes being rather chemical than anatomical, had changed the destination[4] of the block at the bottom of the garden. It was the first time that the lawyer had been received in that part of his friend's quarters; and he eyed the dingy, windowless structure with curiosity, and gazed round with a distasteful sense of strangeness as he crossed the theatre,

---

[1] Popular among medical men, lock-fast cabinets automatically locked when closed, allowing for expensive medicines to be quickly gathered and the door secured without having to bother with one's keys twice

[2] Wanted posters

[3] Although Stevenson politely suggests that this is the nature of eyewitnesses, we might also wonder if the issue is not really that pure evil might be seen differently by each person who projects their own fears and sins onto him: to one man Hyde might seem gluttonous and lazy, to another rapacious and libidinous, and to another sly and treacherous

[4] Purpose. He has changed it from an operating room to a chemical laboratory

once crowded with eager students and now lying gaunt and silent, the tables laden with chemical apparatus, the floor strewn with crates and littered with packing straw, and the light falling dimly through the foggy cupola[1]. At the further end, a flight of stairs mounted to a door covered with red baize[2]; and through this, Mr. Utterson was at last received into the doctor's cabinet[3]. It was a large room fitted round with glass presses[4], furnished, among other things, with a cheval-glass[5] and a business table, and looking out upon the court by three dusty windows barred with iron. The fire burned in the grate; a lamp was set lighted on the chimney shelf, for even in the houses the fog began to lie thickly; and there, close up to the warmth, sat Dr. Jekyll, looking deathly sick. He did not rise to meet his visitor[6], but held out a cold hand and bade him welcome in a changed voice.

"And now," said Mr. Utterson, as soon as Poole had left them, "you have heard the news?"

The doctor shuddered. "They were crying it in the square[7]," he said. "I heard them in my dining-room."

"One word," said the lawyer. "Carew was my client, but so are you, and I want to know what I am doing. You have not been mad enough to hide this fellow?"

"Utterson, I swear to God," cried the doctor, "I swear to God I will never set eyes on him again. I bind my honour to you that I am done with him in this world[8]. It is all at an end. And indeed he does not want my help; you do not know him as I do; he is safe, he is quite safe; mark my words, he will never more be heard of."

The lawyer listened gloomily; he did not like his friend's feverish manner. "You seem pretty sure of him," said he; "and for your sake, I hope you may be right. If it came to a trial, your name might appear."

"I am quite sure of him," replied Jekyll; "I have grounds for certainty that I cannot share with any one. But there is one thing on which you may advise me. I have—I have received a letter; and I am at a loss whether I should show

---

[1] A small, windowed tower on the top of a roof, used to let in air and light, and oftentimes equipped with a bell or a clock face

[2] Wool drapery

[3] A closed-off office

[4] A glass-press is a Scots term (again, the Scottish feeling of the novel spreads) for a recessed, built-in cupboard for holding glassware, in this case one might imagine an alcove lined with shelves that hold medical and chemical gear

[5] Full length mirror that pivots on posts

[6] Exceptionally rude to the point of gross eccentricity

[7] Newsboys calling out the headlines

[8] In the next, however, Jekyll seems to sense that he will have to account to God for his "relationship" with Hyde

it to the police. I should like to leave it in your hands, Utterson; you would judge wisely, I am sure; I have so great a trust in you."

"You fear, I suppose, that it might lead to his detection?" asked the lawyer.

"No," said the other. "I cannot say that I care what becomes of Hyde; I am quite done with him. I was thinking of my own character, which this hateful business has rather exposed."

Utterson ruminated awhile; he was surprised at his friend's selfishness, and yet relieved by it. "Well," said he, at last, "let me see the letter."

The letter was written in an odd, upright hand and signed "Edward Hyde": and it signified, briefly enough, that the writer's benefactor, Dr. Jekyll, whom he had long so unworthily repaid for a thousand generosities, need labour under no alarm for his safety, as he had means of escape on which he placed a sure dependence. The lawyer liked this letter well enough; it put a better colour on the intimacy than he had looked for; and he blamed himself for some of his past suspicions.

"Have you the envelope?" he asked.

"I burned it," replied Jekyll, "before I thought what I was about. But it bore no postmark. The note was handed in."

"Shall I keep this and sleep upon it?" asked Utterson.

"I wish you to judge for me entirely," was the reply. "I have lost confidence in myself."

"Well, I shall consider," returned the lawyer. "And now one word more: it was Hyde who dictated the terms in your will about that disappearance?"

The doctor seemed seized with a qualm of faintness; he shut his mouth tight and nodded.

"I knew it," said Utterson. "He meant to murder you. You had a fine escape."

"I have had what is far more to the purpose," returned the doctor solemnly: "I have had a lesson—O God, Utterson, what a lesson I have had!" And he covered his face for a moment with his hands.

On his way out, the lawyer stopped and had a word or two with Poole. "By the bye," said he, "there was a letter handed in to-day: what was the messenger like?" But Poole was positive nothing had come except by post; "and only circulars by that," he added.

This news sent off the visitor with his fears renewed. Plainly the letter had come by the laboratory door; possibly, indeed, it had been written in the cabinet; and if that were so, it must be differently judged, and handled with the more caution[1]. The newsboys, as he went, were crying themselves hoarse along the footways: "Special edition. Shocking murder of an M.P.[2]." That was the funeral oration of one friend and client; and he could not help a certain

---

[1] Because Hyde would seem to be involved in the matter if Jekyll has written it himself – perhaps blackmailing him into doing it

[2] Member of Parliament. Carew was a political as well as social eminence

apprehension lest the good name of another should be sucked down in the eddy of the scandal. It was, at least, a ticklish decision that he had to make; and self-reliant as he was by habit, he began to cherish a longing for advice. It was not to be had directly; but perhaps, he thought, it might be fished for.

Presently after, he sat on one side of his own hearth, with Mr. Guest, his head clerk, upon the other, and midway between, at a nicely calculated distance from the fire, a bottle of a particular old wine that had long dwelt unsunned in the foundations of his house[1]. The fog still slept on the wing above the drowned city, where the lamps glimmered like carbuncles[2]; and through the muffle and smother of these fallen clouds, the procession of the town's life was still rolling in through the great arteries with a sound as of a mighty wind. But the room was gay with firelight. In the bottle the acids were long ago resolved; the imperial dye[3] had softened with time, as the colour grows richer in stained windows; and the glow of hot autumn afternoons on hillside vineyards, was ready to be set free and to disperse the fogs of London. Insensibly the lawyer melted. There was no man from whom he kept fewer secrets than Mr. Guest[4]; and he was not always sure that he kept as many as he meant. Guest had often been on business to the doctor's; he knew Poole; he could scarce have failed to hear of Mr. Hyde's familiarity about the house; he might draw conclusions: was it not as well, then, that he should see a letter which put that mystery to right? and above all since Guest, being a great student and critic of handwriting, would consider the step natural and obliging? The clerk, besides, was a man of counsel; he could scarce read so strange a document without dropping a remark; and by that remark Mr. Utterson might shape his future course.

"This is a sad business about Sir Danvers," he said.

"Yes, sir, indeed. It has elicited a great deal of public feeling," returned Guest. "The man, of course, was mad."

"I should like to hear your views on that," replied Utterson. "I have a document here in his handwriting; it is between ourselves, for I scarce know what to do about it; it is an ugly business at the best. But there it is; quite in your way[5]: a murderer's autograph."

Guest's eyes brightened, and he sat down at once and studied it with passion. "No sir," he said: "not mad; but it is an odd hand."

---

[1] A comment that aids in symbolizing Utterson's transition from a "live and let live" philosophy to his attitude of snooping into long neglected and ignored affairs – searching in the hidden shadows of secrecy for the vintage of truth

[2] Lamps continue to serve as symbols for probing into secret affairs – the light of truth cutting through the fogs of hypocrisy

[3] The purple hue of the wine has gradually mellowed and brightened with time as the acids balanced out

[4] Mr Guest, then, is Utterson's Utterson

[5] Something that will certainly interest you; right up your alley

"And by all accounts a very odd writer," added the lawyer.

Just then the servant entered with a note.

"Is that from Dr. Jekyll, sir?" inquired the clerk. "I thought I knew the writing. Anything private, Mr. Utterson?"

"Only an invitation to dinner. Why? Do you want to see it?"

"One moment. I thank you, sir;" and the clerk laid the two sheets of paper alongside and sedulously compared their contents. "Thank you, sir," he said at last, returning both; "it's a very interesting autograph."

There was a pause, during which Mr. Utterson struggled with himself. "Why did you compare them, Guest?" he inquired suddenly.

"Well, sir," returned the clerk, "there's a rather singular resemblance; the two hands are in many points identical: only differently sloped."

"Rather quaint[1]," said Utterson.

"It is, as you say, rather quaint," returned Guest.

"I wouldn't speak of this note, you know," said the master.

"No, sir," said the clerk. "I understand."

But no sooner was Mr. Utterson alone that night, than he locked the note into his safe, where it reposed from that time forward. "What!" he thought. "Henry Jekyll forge for a murderer!" And his blood ran cold in his veins.

Incident of Dr Lanyon

Time ran on; thousands of pounds were offered in reward, for the death of Sir Danvers was resented as a public injury; but Mr. Hyde had disappeared out of the ken[2] of the police as though he had never existed. Much of his past was unearthed, indeed, and all disreputable: tales came out of the man's cruelty, at once so callous and violent[3]; of his vile life, of his strange associates, of the hatred that seemed to have surrounded his career; but of his present whereabouts, not a whisper. From the time he had left the house in Soho on the morning of the murder, he was simply blotted out; and gradually, as time drew on, Mr. Utterson began to recover from the hotness of his alarm, and to grow more at quiet with himself. The death of Sir Danvers was, to his way of thinking, more than paid for by the disappearance of Mr. Hyde. Now that that evil influence had been withdrawn, a new life began for Dr. Jekyll. He came

---

[1] Here the meaning of the word "quaint" is "cleverly done." Both men are pretending (for Guest, as a keen student of handwritten, obviously understands the situation) that a forger has attempted to copy Jekyll's hand and merely failed in one respect

[2] Understanding, observation – "out from under the nose"

[3] Apparently – although there is no reason to suspect any more murders than Carew's – Hyde has been guilty of much more violence than that of the trampled girl and bludgeoned M.P.

out of his seclusion, renewed relations with his friends, became once more their familiar guest and entertainer; and whilst he had always been known for charities, he was now no less distinguished for religion[1]. He was busy, he was much in the open air, he did good; his face seemed to open and brighten, as if with an inward consciousness of service; and for more than two months, the doctor was at peace.

On the 8th of January Utterson had dined at the doctor's with a small party; Lanyon had been there; and the face of the host had looked from one to the other as in the old days when the trio were inseparable friends. On the 12th, and again on the 14th, the door was shut against the lawyer. "The doctor was confined to the house," Poole said, "and saw no one." On the 15th, he tried again, and was again refused; and having now been used for the last two months to see his friend almost daily, he found this return of solitude to weigh upon his spirits. The fifth night he had in Guest to dine with him; and the sixth he betook himself to Dr. Lanyon's.

There at least he was not denied admittance; but when he came in, he was shocked at the change which had taken place in the doctor's appearance. He had his death-warrant written legibly upon his face. The rosy man had grown pale; his flesh had fallen away; he was visibly balder and older; and yet it was not so much these tokens of a swift physical decay that arrested the lawyer's notice, as a look in the eye and quality of manner that seemed to testify to some deep-seated terror of the mind. It was unlikely that the doctor should fear death; and yet that was what Utterson was tempted to suspect. "Yes," he thought; "he is a doctor, he must know his own state and that his days are counted; and the knowledge is more than he can bear." And yet when Utterson remarked on his ill-looks, it was with an air of great firmness that Lanyon declared himself a doomed man.

"I have had a shock," he said, "and I shall never recover. It is a question of weeks. Well, life has been pleasant; I liked it; yes, sir, I used to like it. I sometimes think if we knew all, we should be more glad to get away."

"Jekyll is ill, too," observed Utterson. "Have you seen him?"

But Lanyon's face changed, and he held up a trembling hand. "I wish to see or hear no more of Dr. Jekyll," he said in a loud, unsteady voice. "I am quite done with that person; and I beg that you will spare me any allusion to one whom I regard as dead."

---

[1] Popular culture likes to draw the distinction between Jekyll and Hyde as that between good and evil, but – as Jekyll himself later testifies – Jekyll is a mixture of the two and Hyde is pure wickedness. Jekyll is a great and respected man, but the only clue we have to his "goodness" is in this paragraph where he is said to become even more deeply involved in charities and churchgoing, something that any popular socialite of high repute would already be engaged in. More than the "good side" of man, Jekyll represents the "fashionable side"

"Tut-tut[1]," said Mr. Utterson; and then after a considerable pause, "Can't I do anything?" he inquired. "We are three very old friends, Lanyon; we shall not live to make others."

"Nothing can be done," returned Lanyon; "ask himself."

"He will not see me," said the lawyer.

"I am not surprised at that," was the reply. "Some day, Utterson, after I am dead, you may perhaps come to learn the right and wrong of this[2]. I cannot tell you. And in the meantime, if you can sit and talk with me of other things, for God's sake, stay and do so; but if you cannot keep clear of this accursed topic, then in God's name, go, for I cannot bear it."

As soon as he got home, Utterson sat down and wrote to Jekyll, complaining of his exclusion from the house, and asking the cause of this unhappy break with Lanyon; and the next day brought him a long answer, often very pathetically worded, and sometimes darkly mysterious in drift. The quarrel with Lanyon was incurable. "I do not blame our old friend," Jekyll wrote, "but I share his view that we must never meet. I mean from henceforth to lead a life of extreme seclusion; you must not be surprised, nor must you doubt my friendship, if my door is often shut even to you. You must suffer me to go my own dark way. I have brought on myself a punishment and a danger that I cannot name. If I am the chief of sinners, I am the chief of sufferers also[3]. I could not think that this earth contained a place for sufferings and terrors so unmanning; and you can do but one thing, Utterson, to lighten this destiny, and that is to respect my silence." Utterson was amazed; the dark influence of Hyde had been withdrawn, the doctor had returned to his old tasks and amities; a week ago, the prospect had smiled with every promise of a cheerful and an honoured age; and now in a moment, friendship, and peace of mind, and the whole tenor of his life were wrecked. So great and unprepared a change pointed to madness; but in view of Lanyon's manner and words, there must lie for it[4] some deeper ground.

A week afterwards Dr. Lanyon took to his bed, and in something less than a fortnight[5] he was dead. The night after the funeral, at which he had been sadly affected, Utterson locked the door of his business room, and sitting there by the light of a melancholy candle, drew out and set before him an

---

[1] "Here now!" "Come on, now!" "Is that any way to be?"

[2] Lanyon, ever the conventional representative of the conservative establishment is still deeply struck by the duality of Jekyll's sins against God and man. Rather than discussing the "right and wrong" in humanity itself, as Jekyll does, Lanyon is struck by the wrong in Jekyll as a complete person – it is Jekyll, not Hyde, whom Lanyon loathes – it is he, not Hyde, that is wicked and detestable

[3] This phrase comes from the prayerbook of the Church of Scotland – another Scotch flavor to this secretly Edinburghian tale

[4] To be behind it, to cause

[5] Two weeks

envelope addressed by the hand and sealed with the seal of his dead friend. "PRIVATE: for the hands of G. J. Utterson ALONE, and in case of his predecease[1] to be destroyed unread," so it was emphatically superscribed; and the lawyer dreaded to behold the contents. "I have buried one friend to-day," he thought: "what if this should cost me another[2]?" And then he condemned the fear as a disloyalty, and broke the seal. Within there was another enclosure, likewise sealed, and marked upon the cover as "not to be opened till the death or disappearance[3] of Dr. Henry Jekyll." Utterson could not trust his eyes. Yes, it was disappearance; here again, as in the mad will which he had long ago restored to its author, here again were the idea of a disappearance and the name of Henry Jekyll bracketted. But in the will, that idea had sprung from the sinister suggestion of the man Hyde; it was set there with a purpose all too plain and horrible. Written by the hand of Lanyon, what should it mean? A great curiosity came on the trustee, to disregard the prohibition and dive at once to the bottom of these mysteries; but professional honour and faith to his dead friend were stringent obligations; and the packet slept in the inmost corner of his private safe.

It is one thing to mortify[4] curiosity, another to conquer it; and it may be doubted if, from that day forth, Utterson desired the society of his surviving friend with the same eagerness. He thought of him kindly; but his thoughts were disquieted and fearful. He went to call indeed; but he was perhaps relieved to be denied admittance; perhaps, in his heart, he preferred to speak with Poole upon the doorstep and surrounded by the air and sounds of the open city, rather than to be admitted into that house of voluntary bondage[5], and to sit and speak with its inscrutable recluse. Poole had, indeed, no very pleasant news to communicate. The doctor, it appeared, now more than ever confined himself to the cabinet over the laboratory, where he would sometimes even sleep; he was out of spirits, he had grown very silent, he did not read; it seemed as if he had something on his mind. Utterson became so used to the unvarying character of these reports, that he fell off little by little in the frequency of his visits.

---

[1] Were Utterson to die first, the letter should be destroyed. Though Lanyon naturally does not expect this to occur, being as he is on death's door, he nonetheless is tremendously serious about the secrecy that must surround the letter

[2] Without being told, he already suspects that the contents might regard Jekyll, and correctly supposes that knowing them could easily result in the end of his friendship with Jekyll

[3] A chilling possibility. Lanyon must suppose that if Hyde takes over Jekyll, there is no longer a need to shelter him, since the former will now be a public threat

[4] Stall, freeze

[5] He imagines that the voluntarily bondage is between Jekyll and Hyde, and he is right, but the nature of the bondage still alludes him since he imagines blackmail

It chanced on Sunday, when Mr. Utterson was on his usual walk with Mr. Enfield, that their way lay once again through the by-street; and that when they came in front of the door, both stopped to gaze on it.

"Well," said Enfield, "that story's at an end at least. We shall never see more of Mr. Hyde."

"I hope not," said Utterson. "Did I ever tell you that I once saw him, and shared your feeling of repulsion?"

"It was impossible to do the one without the other," returned Enfield. "And by the way, what an ass you must have thought me, not to know that this was a back way to Dr. Jekyll's! It was partly your own fault that I found it out¹, even when I did."

"So you found it out, did you?" said Utterson. "But if that be so, we may step into the court and take a look at the windows. To tell you the truth, I am uneasy about poor Jekyll; and even outside, I feel as if the presence of a friend might do him good."

The court was very cool and a little damp, and full of premature twilight, although the sky, high up overhead, was still bright with sunset. The middle one of the three windows was half-way open; and sitting close beside it, taking the air with an infinite sadness of mien, like some disconsolate prisoner, Utterson saw Dr. Jekyll.

"What! Jekyll!" he cried. "I trust you are better."

"I am very low, Utterson," replied the doctor drearily, "very low. It will not last long, thank God."

"You stay too much indoors," said the lawyer. "You should be out, whipping up the circulation like Mr. Enfield and me. (This is my cousin—Mr. Enfield—Dr. Jekyll.) Come now; get your hat and take a quick turn with us²."

"You are very good," sighed the other. "I should like to very much; but no, no, no, it is quite impossible; I dare not. But indeed, Utterson, I am very glad to see you; this is really a great pleasure; I would ask you and Mr. Enfield up, but the place is really not fit."

---

¹ Strange that we never learn how, though the possibility of gossip is a keen one, and Enfield's sharp reprimand might suggest that – like Enfield himself had been earlier – Utterson has not kept his tongue. Mr Guest might also be the culprit, for he very likely knows Enfield as a mutual acquaintance

² "Taking a turn" was a popular habit among upper middle class Britons. Whether it was walking and talking around a neighborhood or going on a walking holiday through the country, walking was a deep part of British masculine culture

"Why, then," said the lawyer, good-naturedly, "the best thing we can do is to stay down here and speak with you from where we are."

"That is just what I was about to venture to propose," returned the doctor with a smile. But the words were hardly uttered, before the smile was struck out of his face and succeeded by an expression of such abject terror and despair, as froze the very blood of the two gentlemen below[1]. They saw it but for a glimpse for the window was instantly thrust down; but that glimpse had been sufficient, and they turned and left the court without a word. In silence, too, they traversed the by-street; and it was not until they had come into a neighbouring thoroughfare, where even upon a Sunday there were still some stirrings of life, that Mr. Utterson at last turned and looked at his companion. They were both pale; and there was an answering horror in their eyes.

"God forgive us, God forgive us[2]," said Mr. Utterson.

But Mr. Enfield only nodded his head very seriously, and walked on once more in silence.

The Last Night

Mr. Utterson was sitting by his fireside one evening after dinner, when he was surprised to receive a visit from Poole.

"Bless me, Poole, what brings you here?" he cried; and then taking a second look at him, "What ails you?" he added; "is the doctor ill?"

"Mr. Utterson," said the man, "there is something wrong."

"Take a seat, and here is a glass of wine[3] for you," said the lawyer. "Now, take your time, and tell me plainly what you want."

"You know the doctor's ways, sir," replied Poole, "and how he shuts himself up. Well, he's shut up again in the cabinet; and I don't like it, sir—I wish I may die if I like it. Mr. Utterson, sir, I'm afraid."

"Now, my good man," said the lawyer, "be explicit. What are you afraid of?"

---

[1] It would appear that Hyde is returning

[2] What for I'm not sure, though interrupting a dying man's peace might be one possibility. Still, I feel as though the moral responsibility in Utterson's grave prayer and Enfield's solemn nod bespeak a much deeper, human guilt than mere lack of tact

[3] Like Stevenson, Utterson is a confirmed oenophile, drinking good, old wine in virtually every other sign. Wine can be seen as representing his time-weathered, mellow worldview – warming, comforting, honest, and (both literally and figuratively) transparent

"I've been afraid for about a week[1]," returned Poole, doggedly disregarding the question, "and I can bear it no more."

The man's appearance amply bore out his words; his manner was altered for the worse; and except for the moment when he had first announced his terror, he had not once looked the lawyer in the face. Even now, he sat with the glass of wine untasted[2] on his knee, and his eyes directed to a corner of the floor. "I can bear it no more," he repeated.

"Come," said the lawyer, "I see you have some good reason, Poole; I see there is something seriously amiss. Try to tell me what it is."

"I think there's been foul play[3]," said Poole, hoarsely.

"Foul play!" cried the lawyer, a good deal frightened and rather inclined to be irritated in consequence. "What foul play! What does the man mean?"

"I daren't say, sir," was the answer; "but will you come along with me and see for yourself?"

Mr. Utterson's only answer was to rise and get his hat and greatcoat; but he observed with wonder the greatness of the relief that appeared upon the butler's face, and perhaps with no less, that the wine was still untasted when he set it down to follow[4].

It was a wild, cold, seasonable night of March, with a pale moon, lying on her back as though the wind had tilted her[5], and flying wrack[6] of the most diaphanous and lawny[7] texture. The wind made talking difficult, and flecked the blood into the face. It seemed to have swept the streets unusually bare of passengers, besides; for Mr. Utterson thought he had never seen that part of London so deserted. He could have wished it otherwise; never in his life had he been conscious of so sharp a wish to see and touch his fellow-creatures[8];

---

[1] Wolf places the time in roughly March

[2] Utterson's guests are always cheerfully sipping his vintages. The fact that Poole ignores the – presumably – expensive and delicious beverage suggests that he cannot be pacified, like so many others are, by Utterson's typically effective comforts

[3] While "foul play" is a general term for crimes generic, here it is used synonymously with "murder"

[4] Utterson is shocked that Poole was able to resist his tempting treat – a testimony to the sheer quality of his wine collection

[5] Nature is out of sorts (or at least appears to be) which reflects the distortion that Jekyll has admitted into the world. Jekyll himself will later make reference to the stars looking down on Hyde, a new species, with wonder

[6] Fragmented clouds being torn and blown by wind

[7] Like "diaphanous," lawny means something made of translucent, gauzy fabric

[8] Enfield earlier felt an overwhelming need to see a policeman on the night he met Hyde. One might speculative that Hyde's power has grown so much that it is releasing contagions of fear, dread, and disorientation all throughout the neighborhoods surrounding his den in Jekyll's lab

for struggle as he might, there was borne in upon his mind a crushing anticipation of calamity. The square, when they got there, was full of wind and dust, and the thin trees in the garden were lashing themselves along the railing. Poole, who had kept all the way a pace or two ahead, now pulled up in the middle of the pavement, and in spite of the biting weather, took off his hat and mopped his brow with a red pocket-handkerchief. But for all the hurry of his coming, these were not the dews of exertion that he wiped away, but the moisture of some strangling anguish; for his face was white and his voice, when he spoke, harsh and broken.

"Well, sir," he said, "here we are, and God grant there be nothing wrong."

"Amen, Poole," said the lawyer.

Thereupon the servant knocked in a very guarded manner; the door was opened on the chain; and a voice asked from within, "Is that you, Poole?"

"It's all right," said Poole. "Open the door."

The hall, when they entered it, was brightly lighted up; the fire was built high; and about the hearth the whole of the servants, men and women, stood huddled together like a flock of sheep[1]. At the sight of Mr. Utterson[2], the housemaid broke into hysterical whimpering; and the cook, crying out "Bless God! it's Mr. Utterson," ran forward as if to take him in her arms.

"What, what? Are you all here?" said the lawyer peevishly. "Very irregular, very unseemly; your master would be far from pleased."

"They're all afraid," said Poole.

Blank silence followed, no one protesting; only the maid lifted her voice and now wept loudly.

"Hold your tongue[3]!" Poole said to her, with a ferocity of accent that testified to his own jangled nerves; and indeed, when the girl had so suddenly raised the note of her lamentation, they had all started and turned towards the inner door with faces of dreadful expectation. "And now," continued the

---

[1] This suggests Zechariah 13:7 "Strike the shepherd and the sheep of the flock shall scatter." A verse later taken up by Jesus to illustrate his coming death and the subsequent terror of his disciples, one could see the idea – especially with Stevenson's religious education in mind – being projected onto Jekyll's servants who huddle sheepishly after their shepherd has been struck down by Hyde

[2] Like Utterson – and Enfield earlier – the servants are desperate to see a symbol of authority. Hyde represents the loss of moral leadership, anarchy, and chaos. Jekyll has been his servants' darling – a worthy gentleman whose social standing reflects just as keenly on them as it does on himself – and his absence, or rather replacement, has left them quite unsettled

[3] The woman's hysterics suggest the approach of madness. In British culture, venting hysterics was seen as opening the door to insanity, and Poole doesn't need to worry about a madwoman as well as Mr Hyde

butler, addressing the knife-boy[1], "reach me a candle, and we'll get this through hands[2] at once." And then he begged Mr. Utterson to follow him, and led the way to the back garden.

"Now, sir," said he, "you come as gently as you can. I want you to hear, and I don't want you to be heard. And see here, sir, if by any chance he was to ask you in, don't go."

Mr. Utterson's nerves, at this unlooked-for termination, gave a jerk that nearly threw him from his balance; but he recollected his courage and followed the butler into the laboratory building through the surgical theatre, with its lumber of crates[3] and bottles, to the foot of the stair. Here Poole motioned him to stand on one side and listen; while he himself, setting down the candle and making a great and obvious call on his resolution, mounted the steps and knocked with a somewhat uncertain hand on the red baize of the cabinet door.

"Mr. Utterson, sir, asking to see you," he called; and even as he did so, once more violently signed to the lawyer to give ear.

A voice answered from within: "Tell him I cannot see anyone," it said complainingly.

"Thank you, sir," said Poole, with a note of something like triumph in his voice[4]; and taking up his candle, he led Mr. Utterson back across the yard and into the great kitchen, where the fire was out and the beetles were leaping on the floor[5].

"Sir," he said, looking Mr. Utterson in the eyes, "Was that my master's voice?"

"It seems much changed," replied the lawyer, very pale, but giving look for look[6].

"Changed? Well, yes, I think so," said the butler. "Have I been twenty years in this man's house, to be deceived about his voice? No, sir; master's made away with; he was made away with eight days ago, when we heard him cry out upon the name of God; and who's in there instead of him, and why it stays there, is a thing that cries to Heaven, Mr. Utterson!"

"This is a very strange tale, Poole; this is rather a wild tale my man," said Mr. Utterson, biting his finger[7]. "Suppose it were as you suppose, supposing

---

[1] A minor servant (typically a young man) whose jobs included sharpening and cleaning the kitchen knives and running for errands

[2] A British expression that means "take care of this matter"

[3] Used to ship delicate chemical equipment and bottles containing solutions

[4] He is reassured by the sound of Jekyll's living voice

[5] Cockroaches. London was absolutely infested with roaches at the time, which were then commonly though erroneously referred to as "black beetles"

[6] In other words, making eye contact. Utterson is pale from fear, not shame

[7] A childish comfort habit that suggests regression in the face of Hyde's anarchic destruction of paternal order

Dr. Jekyll to have been—well, murdered what could induce the murderer to stay? That won't hold water; it doesn't commend itself to reason."

"Well, Mr. Utterson, you are a hard man to satisfy, but I'll do it yet," said Poole. "All this last week (you must know) him, or it, whatever it is that lives in that cabinet[1], has been crying night and day for some sort of medicine and cannot get it to his mind. It was sometimes his way—the master's, that is—to write his orders on a sheet of paper and throw it on the stair. We've had nothing else this week back; nothing but papers, and a closed door, and the very meals left there to be smuggled in when nobody was looking. Well, sir, every day, ay

, and twice and thrice in the same day, there have been orders and complaints, and I have been sent flying to all the wholesale chemists[2] in town. Every time I brought the stuff back, there would be another paper telling me to return it, because it was not pure, and another order to a different firm. This drug is wanted bitter bad, sir, whatever for."

"Have you any of these papers?" asked Mr. Utterson.

Poole felt in his pocket and handed out a crumpled note, which the lawyer, bending nearer to the candle, carefully examined. Its contents ran thus: "Dr. Jekyll presents his compliments to Messrs. Maw.[3] He assures them that their last sample is impure and quite useless for his present purpose. In the year 18—, Dr. J. purchased a somewhat large quantity from Messrs. M. He now begs them to search with most sedulous care, and should any of the same quality be left, forward it to him at once. Expense is no consideration. The importance of this to Dr. J. can hardly be exaggerated." So far the letter had run composedly enough, but here with a sudden splutter of the pen, the writer's emotion had broken loose. "For God's sake," he added, "find me some of the old."

"This is a strange note," said Mr. Utterson; and then sharply, "How do you come to have it open?"

"The man at Maw's was main angry, sir, and he threw it back to me like so much dirt," returned Poole.

"This is unquestionably the doctor's hand, do you know?" resumed the lawyer.

"I thought it looked like it," said the servant rather sulkily; and then, with another voice, "But what matters hand of write?" he said. "I've seen him!"

"Seen him?" repeated Mr. Utterson. "Well?"

---

[1] Again, an archaic word for an office or consulting room

[2] Pharmacies

[3] Messrs. – pronounced meh-*syurz* – is the French abbreviation of the word for "misters" and was used in business when referring to a firm or members of a business (e.g. Messrs. Jobs and Cook). The chemist's shop is probably called "Maw and Sons" or "Maw and Maw"

"That's it!" said Poole. "It was this way. I came suddenly into the theatre from the garden. It seems he had slipped out to look for this drug or whatever it is; for the cabinet door was open, and there he was at the far end of the room digging among the crates. He looked up when I came in, gave a kind of cry, and whipped upstairs into the cabinet. It was but for one minute that I saw him, but the hair stood upon my head like quills. Sir, if that was my master, why had he a mask upon his face? If it was my master, why did he cry out like a rat, and run from me? I have served him long enough. And then..." The man paused and passed his hand over his face.

"These are all very strange circumstances," said Mr. Utterson, "but I think I begin to see daylight. Your master, Poole, is plainly seized with one of those maladies that both torture and deform the sufferer[1]; hence, for aught I know, the alteration of his voice; hence the mask and the avoidance of his friends; hence his eagerness to find this drug, by means of which the poor soul retains some hope of ultimate recovery[2]—God grant that he be not deceived! There is my explanation; it is sad enough, Poole, ay, and appalling to consider; but it is plain and natural, hangs well together, and delivers us from all exorbitant alarms."

"Sir," said the butler, turning to a sort of mottled pallor, "that thing was not my master, and there's the truth. My master"—here he looked round him and began to whisper—"is a tall, fine build of a man, and this was more of a dwarf[3]." Utterson attempted to protest. "O, sir," cried Poole, "do you think I

---

[1] Syphilis, or a similar venereal disease. Syphilis is capable of driving its sufferers to psychosis, and also of causing great disfigurement to the face. Wolfsuggests leprosy, but I can think of nothing more realistic or poignant than this (Robert Mighall agrees with this assessment). Utterson seems almost relieved because he supposes that this is what Hyde has been blackmailing Jekyll over. Syphilis was a fairly serious epidemic at the time, and was known for prowling around whorehouses and red light districts. Utterson assumes that Jekyll has been whoring, and has caught the disease in an indiscreet moment

[2] Mercury and potassium iodide were the standard treatments for syphilis, and these treatments were absolutely critical if madness and death were to be avoided – or delayed

[3] To the best of my knowledge, no adaptation has chosen to honor this all important detail – not to mention the only physical descriptor available – of Hyde's appearance. This results, of course from two things: 1. It is more convenient and more fun to have one actor play both roles, and although height difference is easily faked, this is usually ignored 2. It is more dramatically satisfying to make Hyde physically imposing. I however, think the idea of the broad shouldered Jekyll mouldering into a lithe adolescent to be highly disturbing. Hyde is dwarfish, slight, and undeveloped because his soul has been so long repressed and unseasoned. One might even suspect that he has the height of an adolescent because that was the time in Jekyll's life that he was run

319

do not know my master after twenty years? Do you think I do not know where his head comes to in the cabinet door, where I saw him every morning of my life? No, sir, that thing in the mask was never Dr. Jekyll—God knows what it was, but it was never Dr. Jekyll; and it is the belief of my heart that there was murder done."

"Poole," replied the lawyer, "if you say that, it will become my duty to make certain. Much as I desire to spare your master's feelings, much as I am puzzled by this note which seems to prove him to be still alive, I shall consider it my duty to break in that door."

"Ah, Mr. Utterson, that's talking!" cried the butler.

"And now comes the second question," resumed Utterson: "Who is going to do it?"

"Why, you and me, sir," was the undaunted reply.

"That's very well said," returned the lawyer; "and whatever comes of it, I shall make it my business to see you are no loser[1]."

"There is an axe in the theatre," continued Poole; "and you might take the kitchen poker for yourself."

The lawyer took that rude but weighty instrument into his hand, and balanced it. "Do you know, Poole," he said, looking up, "that you and I are about to place ourselves in a position of some peril[2]?"

"You may say so, sir, indeed," returned the butler.

"It is well, then that we should be frank," said the other. "We both think more than we have said; let us make a clean breast. This masked figure that you saw, did you recognise it?"

"Well, sir, it went so quick, and the creature was so doubled up, that I could hardly swear to that," was the answer. "But if you mean, was it Mr. Hyde?—why, yes, I think it was! You see, it was much of the same bigness; and it had the same quick, light way with it; and then who else could have got in by the laboratory door? You have not forgot, sir, that at the time of the murder he had still the key with him? But that's not all. I don't know, Mr. Utterson, if you ever met this Mr. Hyde?"

"Yes," said the lawyer, "I once spoke with him."

"Then you must know as well as the rest of us that there was something queer about that gentleman—something that gave a man a turn—I don't

---

through the punishing system of British education so famously depicted in *Pink Floyd's The Wall*

[1] If there is no pressing danger and Jekyll's butler chops his way into his master's office, Poole truly does stand to be a loser – he could lose his job, his social standing, even his ability to be hired. Utterson is assuring him that he will take the blame if they are mistaken

[2] As Wolfnotes, the dangers are twofold: of course the physical danger of the murderer Hyde, and perhaps less dramatically but just as concerning, the threat of being charged with breaking and entering

know rightly how to say it, sir, beyond this: that you felt in your marrow kind of cold and thin."

"I own I felt something of what you describe," said Mr. Utterson.

"Quite so, sir," returned Poole. "Well, when that masked thing like a monkey[1] jumped from among the chemicals and whipped into the cabinet, it went down my spine like ice. O, I know it's not evidence, Mr. Utterson; I'm book-learned enough for that; but a man has his feelings, and I give you my bible-word it was Mr. Hyde!"

"Ay, ay," said the lawyer. "My fears incline to the same point. Evil, I fear, founded—evil was sure to come—of that connection. Ay truly, I believe you; I believe poor Harry[2] is killed; and I believe his murderer (for what purpose, God alone can tell) is still lurking in his victim's room. Well, let our name be vengeance. Call Bradshaw."

The footman came at the summons, very white and nervous.

"Put yourself together, Bradshaw," said the lawyer. "This suspense, I know, is telling upon all of you; but it is now our intention to make an end of it. Poole, here, and I are going to force our way into the cabinet. If all is well, my shoulders are broad enough to bear the blame[3]. Meanwhile, lest anything should really be amiss, or any malefactor seek to escape by the back, you and

---

[1] Hyde's devolved status is brilliantly depicted by Stevenson when – like so many of his adaptors – he could have given Hyde a big, imposing, monstrous physique (the Hulk and the abomination from The League of Extraordinary Gentlemen come to mind). Rather, spring boarding off of Darwin's theories, he demonstrates that Hyde is not a man of power and masculinity and strength, but of decadence, degeneration, and primitivity. To what extent Hyde looks like a monkey is not clear, although I suspect he merely moves like one since it is never mentioned by witnesses of his face. This didn't stop the 1932 version of the story from depicting him as humanoid ape

[2] A moment of deep tenderness: gentlemen did not refer to one another by their first names, especially not by nicknames. They used the last name almost exclusively (Holmes, Watson, Van Helsing, Silver, Scrooge, etc.). This nickname, Harry, was likely the name that Utterson called Jekyll during their childhood. The Granada adaptation of the Sherlock Holmes story "The Devil's Foot" uses this to great effect when Jeremy Brett's Holmes breaks from canon: in a scene where Holmes has almost killed them both and has just been saved by Watson, he reaches his arms out, face twisted with childlike fear, and shouts "JOHN!" The effect is very moving coming from these formal friends

[3] Utterson's reputation can take the shame if there is nothing to fear, and he will accept responsibility if the servants are charged with breaking and entering or threatened with termination

the boy[1] must go round the corner with a pair of good sticks and take your post at the laboratory door. We give you ten minutes, to get to your stations."

As Bradshaw left, the lawyer looked at his watch. "And now, Poole, let us get to ours," he said; and taking the poker under his arm, led the way into the yard. The scud[2] had banked over the moon, and it was now quite dark. The wind, which only broke in puffs and draughts into that deep well of building, tossed the light of the candle to and fro about their steps, until they came into the shelter of the theatre, where they sat down silently to wait. London hummed solemnly all around; but nearer at hand, the stillness was only broken by the sounds of a footfall moving to and fro along the cabinet floor.

"So it will walk all day, sir," whispered Poole; "ay, and the better part of the night. Only when a new sample comes from the chemist, there's a bit of a break. Ah, it's an ill conscience that's such an enemy to rest! Ah, sir, there's blood foully shed in every step of it! But hark again, a little closer—put your heart in your ears, Mr. Utterson, and tell me, is that the doctor's foot?"

The steps fell lightly and oddly, with a certain swing, for all they went so slowly[3]; it was different indeed from the heavy creaking tread of Henry Jekyll. Utterson sighed. "Is there never anything else?" he asked.

Poole nodded. "Once," he said. "Once I heard it weeping!"

"Weeping? how that?" said the lawyer, conscious of a sudden chill of horror.

"Weeping like a woman or a lost soul," said the butler. "I came away with that upon my heart, that I could have wept too."

But now the ten minutes drew to an end[4]. Poole disinterred the axe from under a stack of packing straw; the candle was set upon the nearest table to light them to the attack; and they drew near with bated breath to where that

---

[1] This suggests that the "knife boy" is, like a bellboy, probably not a "boy" at all, but a young man
[2] Clouds and fog broken up and driven by the wind
[3] Lumbering and shuffling footsteps were the first things that Utterson noticed about Hyde
[4] The knife boy and footman are now in position to defend the backway

patient foot was still going up and down, up and down, in the quiet of the night. "Jekyll," cried Utterson, with a loud voice, "I demand to see you." He paused a moment, but there came no reply. "I give you fair warning, our suspicions are aroused, and I must and shall see you," he resumed; "if not by fair means, then by foul—if not of your consent, then by brute force!"

"Utterson," said the voice, "for God's sake, have mercy!"

"Ah, that's not Jekyll's voice—it's Hyde's!" cried Utterson. "Down with the door, Poole!"

Poole swung the axe over his shoulder; the blow shook the building, and the red baize door leaped against the lock and hinges. A dismal screech, as of mere animal terror, rang from the cabinet. Up went the axe again, and again the panels crashed and the frame bounded; four times the blow fell; but the wood was tough and the fittings were of excellent workmanship; and it was not until the fifth, that the lock burst and the wreck of the door fell inwards on the carpet.

The besiegers, appalled by their own riot[1] and the stillness that had succeeded, stood back a little and peered in. There lay the cabinet before their eyes in the quiet lamplight, a good fire glowing and chattering on the hearth, the kettle singing its thin strain, a drawer or two open, papers neatly set forth on the business table, and nearer the fire, the things laid out for tea; the quietest room, you would have said, and, but for the glazed presses[2] full of chemicals, the most commonplace that night in London.

Right in the middle there lay the body of a man sorely contorted and still twitching. They drew near on tiptoe, turned it on its back and beheld the face of Edward Hyde. He was dressed in clothes far too large for him, clothes of the doctor's bigness[3]; the cords of his face still moved with a semblance of life[4], but life was quite gone: and by the crushed phial in the hand and the strong smell of kernels[5] that hung upon the air, Utterson knew that he was looking on the body of a self-destroyer.

---

[1] The terrible noise of the axe

[2] Again, this is a cabinet with glass doors

[3] The very first suggestion that Hyde might be Jekyll, but even this would be explained away by a first-time reader as a clumsy attempt at disguise

[4] The death spasms that are animating his facial muscles as his neurological system is being ravaged by poison

[5] The tell-tale odor of cyanide: "Inhalation of high concentrations of cyanide causes a coma with seizures, apnea and cardiac arrest, with death following in a matter of minutes. At lower doses, loss of consciousness may be preceded by general weakness, giddiness, headaches, vertigo, confusion, and perceived difficulty in breathing. At the first stages of unconsciousness, breathing is often sufficient or even rapid, although the state of the victim progresses towards a deep coma, sometimes accompanied by pulmonary edema, and finally cardiac arrest. Skin colour goes pink from high blood oxygen saturation"

"We have come too late," he said sternly, "whether to save or punish. Hyde is gone to his account; and it only remains for us to find the body of your master."

The far greater proportion of the building was occupied by the theatre, which filled almost the whole ground storey and was lighted from above, and by the cabinet, which formed an upper story at one end and looked upon the court. A corridor joined the theatre to the door on the by-street; and with this the cabinet communicated separately by a second flight of stairs. There were besides a few dark closets and a spacious cellar. All these they now thoroughly examined. Each closet needed but a glance, for all were empty, and all, by the dust that fell from their doors, had stood long unopened. The cellar, indeed, was filled with crazy lumber, mostly dating from the times of the surgeon who was Jekyll's predecessor; but even as they opened the door they were advertised of the uselessness of further search, by the fall of a perfect mat of cobweb which had for years sealed up the entrance. No where was there any trace of Henry Jekyll dead or alive.

Poole stamped on the flags of the corridor. "He must be buried here," he said, hearkening to the sound.

"Or he may have fled," said Utterson, and he turned to examine the door in the by-street. It was locked; and lying near by on the flags, they found the key, already stained with rust.

"This does not look like use," observed the lawyer.

"Use!" echoed Poole. "Do you not see, sir, it is broken? much as if a man had stamped on it."

"Ay," continued Utterson, "and the fractures, too, are rusty." The two men looked at each other with a scare. "This is beyond me, Poole," said the lawyer. "Let us go back to the cabinet."

They mounted the stair in silence, and still with an occasional awestruck glance at the dead body, proceeded more thoroughly to examine the contents of the cabinet. At one table, there were traces of chemical work, various measured heaps of some white salt[1] being laid on glass saucers, as though for an experiment in which the unhappy man had been prevented.

"That is the same drug that I was always bringing him," said Poole; and even as he spoke, the kettle with a startling noise boiled over[2].

This brought them to the fireside, where the easy-chair was drawn cosily up, and the tea things stood ready to the sitter's elbow, the very sugar in the cup. There were several books on a shelf; one lay beside the tea things open,

---

[1] For chemists this means a chemical powder that is a compound made by neutralizing an acid with a base

[2] This scene was so effective and atmospheric – the cozy, warm, well-lit murder room with the body front and center and the kettle humming on the hob, its sudden overflowing into the fire jolting the men from their wonder – that it was employed prominently in the Frederic March movie

and Utterson was amazed to find it a copy of a pious work, for which Jekyll had several times expressed a great esteem, annotated, in his own hand with startling blasphemies.

Next, in the course of their review of the chamber, the searchers came to the cheval-glass, into whose depths they looked with an involuntary horror[1]. But it was so turned as to show them nothing but the rosy glow playing on the roof, the fire sparkling in a hundred repetitions along the glazed front of the presses, and their own pale and fearful countenances stooping to look in.

"This glass has seen some strange things, sir[2]," whispered Poole.

"And surely none stranger than itself," echoed the lawyer in the same tones. "For what did Jekyll"—he caught himself up at the word with a start, and then conquering the weakness[3]—"what could Jekyll want with it?" he said.

"You may say that!" said Poole.

Next they turned to the business table. On the desk, among the neat array of papers, a large envelope was uppermost, and bore, in the doctor's hand, the name of Mr. Utterson. The lawyer unsealed it, and several enclosures fell to the floor. The first was a will, drawn in the same eccentric terms as the one which he had returned six months before, to serve as a testament in case of death and as a deed of gift in case of disappearance; but in place of the name of Edward Hyde, the lawyer, with indescribable amazement read the name of Gabriel[4] John Utterson. He looked at Poole, and then back at the paper, and last of all at the dead malefactor stretched upon the carpet.

"My head goes round," he said. "He[5] has been all these days in possession; he had no cause to like me; he must have raged to see himself displaced; and he has not destroyed this document."

He caught up the next paper; it was a brief note in the doctor's hand and dated at the top. "O Poole!" the lawyer cried, "he was alive and here this day. He cannot have been disposed of in so short a space; he must be still alive, he must have fled! And then, why fled? and how? and in that case, can we

---

[1] Self-examination was certainly the horror of Jekyll's life – the realization of the monsters that lurked within him – and the discomfort with which he gazed so many times into that mirror seems to be contagious

[2] No kidding

[3] Jekyll's body has still failed to manifest, so Utterson fights against the instinct to use the past tense verb which would imply that he is dead

[4] Wolfnotes that Gabriel – the name of the archangel who was known for sending messages from God to mankind, most famously by telling Mary that she was pregnant with Christ – is a telling name: it belongs to an angel whose role was "reveal[ing] and explain[ing] ... truth"

[5] Being Hyde

326

venture to declare this suicide? O, we must be careful. I foresee that we may yet involve your master in some dire catastrophe[1]."

"Why don't you read it, sir?" asked Poole.

"Because I fear," replied the lawyer solemnly. "God grant I have no cause for it!" And with that he brought the paper to his eyes and read as follows:

"My dear Utterson,—When this shall fall into your hands, I shall have disappeared, under what circumstances I have not the penetration to foresee, but my instinct and all the circumstances of my nameless[2] situation tell me that the end is sure and must be early. Go then, and first read the narrative which Lanyon warned me he was to place in your hands; and if you care to hear more, turn to the confession of
"Your unworthy and unhappy friend,

"HENRY JEKYLL."

"There was a third enclosure?" asked Utterson.

"Here, sir," said Poole, and gave into his hands a considerable packet sealed in several places.

The lawyer put it in his pocket. "I would say nothing of this paper. If your master has fled or is dead, we may at least save his credit[3]. It is now ten; I must go home and read these documents in quiet; but I shall be back before midnight, when we shall send for the police[4]."

They went out, locking the door of the theatre behind them; and Utterson, once more leaving the servants gathered about the fire in the hall, trudged back to his office to read the two narratives in which this mystery was now to be explained[5].

---

[1] He fears that Jekyll has poisoned Hyde and may now himself be a murderer

[2] In that it is the first situation of its kind – who else can say that they are two people who might have two distinct destinies?

[3] His good name; social reputation

[4] Utterson wants to be prepared in case a cover up is necessary. As a fairly quick reader can tell you, it takes less than an hour to read Lanyon and Jekyll's narratives. Combined with the commute from Jekyll's to Lanyon's, this allows some time to shuffle the facts if needed in order to protect Jekyll

[5] It is noteworthy that this is the last we hear from Utterson. His response to the revelation is not recorded, and we are left to imagine his reaction – a masterful play on Stevenson's part which allows the reader to project their moral and psychological reactions onto Utterson without being guided. Knowing Utterson, however, I imagine that his response would be stoic pathos – to quote Coleridge, "He went like one that hath been stunned, And is of sense forlorn: A sadder and a wiser man He rose the morrow morn"

On the ninth of January, now four days ago[1], I received by the evening delivery a registered envelope, addressed in the hand of my colleague and old school companion, Henry Jekyll. I was a good deal surprised by this; for we were by no means in the habit of correspondence[2]; I had seen the man, dined with him, indeed, the night before; and I could imagine nothing in our intercourse that should justify formality of registration. The contents increased my wonder; for this is how the letter ran:

"10th December[3], 18—.

"Dear Lanyon,—You are one of my oldest friends; and although we may have differed at times on scientific questions, I cannot remember, at least on my side, any break in our affection. There was never a day when, if you had said to me, 'Jekyll, my life, my honour, my reason, depend upon you,' I would not have sacrificed my left hand to help you[4]. Lanyon my life, my honour, my reason, are all at your mercy; if you fail me to-night, I am lost. You might suppose, after this preface, that I am going to ask you for something dishonourable to grant. Judge for yourself.

"I want you to postpone all other engagements for to-night—ay, even if you were summoned to the bedside of an emperor; to take a cab, unless your carriage should be actually at the door[5]; and with this letter in your hand for consultation, to drive straight to my house. Poole, my butler, has his orders; you will find him waiting your arrival with a locksmith. The door of my cabinet is then to be forced: and you are to go in alone; to open the glazed press (letter E) on the left hand, breaking the lock if it be shut; and to draw out, with all its contents as they stand, the fourth drawer from the top or (which is the same thing) the third from the bottom. In my extreme distress

---

[1] This is when Lanyon must have realized that he was dying – only four days after his fatal shock

[2] Lanyon and Jekyll have a tremendously volatile relationship in spite of Utterson's diplomacy – this is likely due to Jekyll's intellectual progressiveness and Lanyon's conservatism

[3] Commonly considered a mistake on Stevenson's part. Likely he corrected one of the dates to align with his timeline and forgot – how I can't imagine – to amend the other

[4] Perhaps Jekyll is left handed, but if not, this demonstrates the reservation in their friendship – yes he would give a hand, but just his left one

[5] The cabs are easily grabbed as soon as one passes the house, but a carriage would have to be outfitted and taken out of the stable, a process that might take a half hour – time Jekyll doesn't have. This also demonstrates Lanyon's – a confirmed establishment insider – extreme wealth. A carriage was tantamount to a limo or a chauffeured town car – tremendously expensive both to buy and to maintain

of mind, I have a morbid fear of misdirecting you; but even if I am in error, you may know the right drawer by its contents: some powders, a phial and a paper book[1]. This drawer I beg of you to carry back with you to Cavendish Square exactly as it stands.

"That is the first part of the service: now for the second. You should be back, if you set out at once on the receipt of this, long before midnight; but I will leave you that amount of margin, not only in the fear of one of those obstacles that can neither be prevented nor foreseen, but because an hour when your servants are in bed is to be preferred for what will then remain to do. At midnight, then, I have to ask you to be alone in your consulting room, to admit with your own hand into the house a man who will present himself in my name, and to place in his hands the drawer that you will have brought with you from my cabinet. Then you will have played your part and earned my gratitude completely. Five minutes afterwards, if you insist upon an explanation, you will have understood that these arrangements are of capital importance; and that by the neglect of one of them, fantastic as they must appear, you might have charged your conscience with my death or the shipwreck of my reason.

"Confident as I am that you will not trifle with this appeal, my heart sinks and my hand trembles at the bare thought of such a possibility. Think of me at this hour, in a strange place, labouring under a blackness of distress that no fancy can exaggerate, and yet well aware that, if you will but punctually serve me, my troubles will roll away like a story that is told. Serve me, my dear Lanyon and save

"Your friend, H. J.

"P.S.—I had already sealed this up when a fresh terror struck upon my soul. It is possible that the post-office may fail me, and this letter not come into your hands until to-morrow morning. In that case, dear Lanyon, do my errand when it shall be most convenient for you in the course of the day; and once more expect my messenger at midnight. It may then already be too late; and if that night passes without event, you will know that you have seen the last of Henry Jekyll."

Upon the reading of this letter, I made sure[2] my colleague was insane; but till that was proved beyond the possibility of doubt, I felt bound to do as he requested. The less I understood of this farrago, the less I was in a position to judge of its importance; and an appeal so worded could not be set aside without a grave responsibility. I rose accordingly from table, got into a hansom, and drove straight to Jekyll's house. The butler was awaiting my arrival; he had received by the same post as mine a registered letter of

---

[1] A paperback notebook
[2] Was certain

instruction, and had sent at once for a locksmith and a carpenter. The tradesmen came while we were yet speaking; and we moved in a body to old Dr. Denman's[1] surgical theatre, from which (as you are doubtless aware) Jekyll's private cabinet is most conveniently entered. The door was very strong, the lock excellent; the carpenter avowed he would have great trouble and have to do much damage, if force were to be used[2]; and the locksmith was near despair. But this last was a handy fellow, and after two hour's work, the door stood open. The press marked E was unlocked; and I took out the drawer, had it filled up with straw and tied in a sheet, and returned with it to Cavendish Square.

Here I proceeded to examine its contents. The powders were neatly enough made up, but not with the nicety of the dispensing chemist; so that it was plain they were of Jekyll's private manufacture: and when I opened one of the wrappers I found what seemed to me a simple crystalline salt of a white colour. The phial, to which I next turned my attention, might have been about half full of a blood-red liquor, which was highly pungent to the sense of smell and seemed to me to contain phosphorus and some volatile ether[3]. At the other ingredients I could make no guess. The book was an ordinary version book and contained little but a series of dates. These covered a period of many years[4], but I observed that the entries ceased nearly a year ago and quite abruptly[5]. Here and there a brief remark was appended to a date, usually no more than a single word: "double" occurring perhaps six times in a total of several hundred entries; and once very early in the list and followed by several marks of exclamation, "total failure!!!" All this, though it whetted my curiosity, told me little that was definite. Here were a phial of some salt, and the record of a series of experiments that had led (like too many of Jekyll's investigations) to no end of practical usefulness. How could the presence of these articles in my house affect either the honour, the sanity, or the life of my flighty colleague? If his messenger could go to one place, why could he not go to another? And even granting some impediment, why was this gentleman to be received by me in secret? The more I reflected the more convinced I grew that I was dealing with a case of cerebral disease; and

---

[1] Lanyon's disdain is clear – he still refers to Jekyll's chemical lab as Denman's surgical theatre, as if not deigning to acknowledge it as legitimately Jekyll's

[2] As Utterson well knows

[3] There appears to be no scientific theory here in Stevenson's concoction: it is merely meant to sound science-y.

[4] This corresponds with Lanyon's assertion that Jekyll began to go "wrong" about ten years before. Jekyll must have been working on his research for the better part of a decade

[5] Hyde is then nearly one year old. Happy birthday

though I dismissed my servants to bed, I loaded an old revolver, that I might be found in some posture of self-defence[1].

Twelve o'clock had scarce rung out over London, ere the knocker sounded very gently on the door[2]. I went myself at the summons, and found a small man crouching against the pillars of the portico.

"Are you come from Dr. Jekyll?" I asked.

He told me "yes" by a constrained gesture; and when I had bidden him enter, he did not obey me without a searching backward glance into the darkness of the square. There was a policeman not far off, advancing with his bull's eye open[3]; and at the sight, I thought my visitor started and made greater haste.

These particulars struck me, I confess, disagreeably; and as I followed him into the bright light of the consulting room, I kept my hand ready on my weapon. Here, at last, I had a chance of clearly seeing him. I had never set eyes on him before, so much was certain. He was small, as I have said; I was struck besides with the shocking expression of his face[4], with his remarkable combination of great muscular activity and great apparent debility of constitution[5], and—last but not least—with the odd, subjective disturbance caused by his neighbourhood[6]. This bore some resemblance to incipient rigour, and was accompanied by a marked sinking of the pulse. At the time, I set it down to some idiosyncratic, personal distaste, and merely wondered at the acuteness of the symptoms; but I have since had reason to believe the cause to lie much deeper in the nature of man, and to turn on some nobler hinge than the principle of hatred.

This person (who had thus, from the first moment of his entrance, struck in me what I can only describe as a disgustful curiosity) was dressed in a fashion that would have made an ordinary person laughable; his clothes, that is to say, although they were of rich and sober fabric[7], were enormously too large for him in every measurement—the trousers hanging on his legs and rolled up to keep them from the ground, the waist of the coat below his

---

[1] It is very telling that Lanyon anticipates some sort of uncouth visitor

[2] At odds with cultural depictions of Hyde – timid, skittish, and flustered, he is no demon whacking his murderous cane on the door with flair and panache

[3] A tremendously bright lamp used by the police and made iconic by the Jack the Ripper murders

[4] The closest we come to a description of Hyde's face, but it seems to suggest insanity. Hyde is not necessarily ugly – hair and fangs and all that – but certainly revolts people with his facial expression

[5] Hyde is physically weak – likely hungry – but is filled with muscular animation. A starved, wild dog demonstrates the same combination of weakness and power

[6] By being near him

[7] Although these are Jekyll's clothes, Hyde's clothes tend to be of the same kind – plain but luxuriant

haunches, and the collar sprawling wide upon his shoulders. Strange to relate, this ludicrous accoutrement was far from moving me to laughter. Rather, as there was something abnormal and misbegotten in the very essence of the creature that now faced me—something seizing, surprising and revolting— this fresh disparity seemed but to fit in with and to reinforce it; so that to my interest in the man's nature and character, there was added a curiosity as to his origin, his life, his fortune and status in the world[1].

These observations, though they have taken so great a space to be set down in, were yet the work of a few seconds. My visitor was, indeed, on fire with sombre excitement.

"Have you got it?" he cried. "Have you got it[2]?" And so lively was his impatience that he even laid his hand upon my arm and sought to shake me[3].

I put him back, conscious at his touch of a certain icy pang along my blood. "Come, sir," said I. "You forget that I have not yet the pleasure of your acquaintance. Be seated, if you please." And I showed him an example, and sat down myself in my customary seat and with as fair an imitation of my ordinary manner to a patient, as the lateness of the hour, the nature of my preoccupations, and the horror I had of my visitor, would suffer me to muster.

"I beg your pardon, Dr. Lanyon," he replied civilly enough. "What you say is very well founded; and my impatience has shown its heels[4] to my politeness. I come here at the instance of your colleague, Dr. Henry Jekyll, on a piece of business of some moment; and I understood..." He paused and put his hand to his throat, and I could see, in spite of his collected manner, that he was wrestling against the approaches of the hysteria—"I understood, a drawer..."

But here I took pity on my visitor's suspense, and some perhaps on my own growing curiosity.

"There it is, sir," said I, pointing to the drawer, where it lay on the floor behind a table and still covered with the sheet.

He sprang to it, and then paused, and laid his hand upon his heart: I could hear his teeth grate with the convulsive action of his jaws[5]; and his face was so ghastly to see that I grew alarmed both for his life and reason.

"Compose yourself[6]," said I.

---

[1] Since Hyde is the manifestation of evil, Lanyon might just as easily be asking these questions about Satan or evil in general

[2] There is something of the alcoholic or junky in Hyde's thrilled anxiety

[3] A tremendously forward gesture between unacquainted gentlemen

[4] Interfered with – "my impatience got in the way of my manners"

[5] Hell is often described as a place that is known for the sound of "gnashing teeth." Hyde's own proclivity to gnash his teeth is suggestively diabolical

[6] That one gentleman would say such a thing to another (Hyde's wickedness and ludicrous appearance notwithstanding, his dress, sloppy as it is, and speech

He turned a dreadful smile to me, and as if with the decision of despair, plucked away the sheet. At sight of the contents, he uttered one loud sob of such immense relief that I sat petrified. And the next moment, in a voice that was already fairly well under control, "Have you a graduated glass[1]?" he asked.

I rose from my place with something of an effort and gave him what he asked.

He thanked me with a smiling nod, measured out a few minims[2] of the red tincture and added one of the powders. The mixture, which was at first of a reddish hue, began, in proportion as the crystals melted, to brighten in colour, to effervesce audibly[3], and to throw off small fumes of vapour. Suddenly and at the same moment, the ebullition ceased and the compound changed to a dark purple, which faded again more slowly to a watery green. My visitor, who had watched these metamorphoses with a keen eye, smiled, set down the glass upon the table, and then turned and looked upon me with an air of scrutiny.

"And now," said he, "to settle what remains. Will you be wise[4]? will you be guided? will you suffer me to take this glass in my hand and to go forth from your house without further parley[5]? or has the greed of curiosity too much command of you[6]? Think before you answer, for it shall be done as you decide. As you decide, you shall be left as you were before, and neither richer nor wiser, unless the sense of service rendered to a man in mortal

---

reveal him to be a gentleman) is a testament to Hyde's nearness to a hysterical fit

[1] Or graduated cylinder – a glass beaker with measuring marks on it to mark the "graduations" of liquid as it rises

[2] 1/480 of a fluid once. My suspicion is that Stevenson didn't quite understand how small a minim is, because this would be infinitesimal – less than a drop

[3] To snap, crackle, and pop as American cereal consumers might say

[4] Satan essentially asked Eve the same question in the garden of Eden. Suggesting that eating the fruit of the Tree of Knowledge of Good and Evil, the serpent told her that to eat it would make her wise like God. Of course, her indulgence lead her to losing Eden and inviting sin into the world, and Lanyon's acquiescence leads him to a similar understanding of the nature of sin which results in his death

[5] Discussion, but a word that has a wartime connotation, as in a meeting between enemies under a flag of truce. Lanyon, the conventional conservative, and Hyde, the enemy of order and decorum, are true enemies

[6] Lanyon had earlier named his besetting sin: "disgustful curiosity." Like Satan, Hyde is privy to the weaknesses that tempt others, and gleefully lures Lanyon with his pet temptation

distress may be counted as a kind of riches of the soul[1]. Or, if you shall so prefer to choose, a new province of knowledge and new avenues to fame and power shall be laid open to you, here, in this room, upon the instant; and your sight shall be blasted by a prodigy[2] to stagger the unbelief of Satan."

"Sir," said I, affecting a coolness that I was far from truly possessing, "you speak enigmas, and you will perhaps not wonder that I hear you with no very strong impression of belief. But I have gone too far in the way of inexplicable services to pause before I see the end."

"It is well," replied my visitor. "Lanyon, you remember your vows[3]: what follows is under the seal of our[4] profession. And now, you who have so long been bound to the most narrow and material views, you who have denied the virtue of transcendental medicine[5], you who have derided your superiors— behold!"

He put the glass to his lips and drank at one gulp. A cry followed; he reeled, staggered, clutched at the table and held on, staring with injected eyes[6], gasping with open mouth; and as I looked there came, I thought, a change—he seemed to swell—his face became suddenly black and the features seemed to melt and alter[7]—and the next moment, I had sprung to my feet and leaped back against the wall, my arms raised to shield me from that prodigy, my mind submerged in terror

"O God!" I screamed, and "O God!" again and again; for there before my eyes—pale and shaken, and half fainting, and groping before him with his hands, like a man restored from death—there stood Henry Jekyll![8]

---

[1] Hyde downplays the "riches" of good deeds, comparing them to the delicious acquisition of new knowledge and – he hints, though I know not why exactly – material wealth

[2] Something new and unheard of – a sign or wonder

[3] The Hippocratic oath which bars a doctor from disclosing information that could be considered rendered in doctor/patient confidence

[4] This, then, is Jekyll speaking out of Hyde's mouth. Unless he considers himself a doctor by proxy, Hyde is no physician. It is bitter, jilted Henry Jekyll himself who wants to stick it to his disapproving colleague and former friend

[5] Medicine concerned with metaphysics – the spirit and soul – rather than the body. Lanyon is probably a strict materialist and Darwinian – probably an atheist – and has no concern for the speculations of the mind when he can serve the body. This is the fundamental difference between the two men that leads to their split

[6] Bulging

[7] A beautiful, fantastical scene rendered in so few words, and yet so often imperfectly rendered in film – the imagination truly does this scene a greater service

[8] IMPORTANT TO NOTE: For first-time readers and for those who are not familiar with the story's cultural legacy (most of whom would have been reading the

What he told me in the next hour, I cannot bring my mind to set on paper. I saw what I saw, I heard what I heard, and my soul sickened at it; and yet now when that sight has faded from my eyes, I ask myself if I believe it, and I cannot answer. My life is shaken to its roots; sleep has left me; the deadliest terror sits by me at all hours of the day and night; and I feel that my days are numbered, and that I must die; and yet I shall die incredulous[1]. As for the moral turpitude that man unveiled to me, even with tears of penitence, I can not, even in memory, dwell on it without a start of horror. I will say but one thing, Utterson, and that (if you can bring your mind to credit it) will be more than enough. The creature who crept into my house that night was, on Jekyll's own confession, known by the name of Hyde and hunted for in every corner of the land as the murderer of Carew[2].

HASTIE LANYON

Henry Jekyll's Full Statement of the Case

I was born in the year 18— to a large fortune, endowed besides with excellent parts, inclined by nature to industry[3], fond of the respect of the wise and good among my fellowmen, and thus, as might have been supposed, with every guarantee of an honourable and distinguished future. And indeed the worst of my faults was a certain impatient gaiety of disposition, such as has made the happiness of many, but such as I found it hard to reconcile with my

---

story when it came out) this is actually the first time that we understand that Hyde is not a grubby blackmailer, and we are no longer wondering what he "has" on Jekyll – we now know that the two are one, and this revelation is seismic. In most movies (since we already know, there's not much point in hiding it, though I think it is an experiment worth trying), Jekyll's appearance is depicted in the second or even first act. Here it is in the penultimate paragraph of the penultimate chapter – *A CRIME NOVEL HAS SUDDENLY BECOME A SCIENCE FICTION HORROR STORY*

[1] He still refuses to believe what he saw because of his moral and philosophical opposition to the suggestion that men are both good and evil. A consummate conservative, Lanyon's worldview is organized by divisions of class, gender, birth, education, and race. There are good men who are good, and there are bad men who are bad – this is his basic understanding of evil. His friends are good, bad people live in bad parts of town. Perhaps more than anything, Lanyon is stricken by the understanding that inside of him lurks a Hyde of his own, and that he harbors just as wicked a soul as Jekyll's

[2] Here again we see how famous Carew is: he can be easily referred to by last name only, like Churchill, Thatcher, or Disraeli

[3] Productive work

imperious desire to carry my head high, and wear a more than commonly grave countenance before the public[1]. Hence it came about that I concealed my pleasures; and that when I reached years of reflection[2], and began to look round me and take stock of my progress and position in the world, I stood already committed to a profound duplicity of me. Many a man would have even blazoned[3] such irregularities as I was guilty of; but from the high views that I had set before me[4], I regarded and hid them with an almost morbid[5] sense of shame. It was thus rather the exacting nature of my aspirations than any particular degradation in my faults, that made me what I was[6], and, with even a deeper trench than in the majority of men, severed in me those provinces of good and ill which divide and compound man's dual nature. In this case, I was driven to reflect deeply and inveterately on that hard law of life, which lies at the root of religion and is one of the most plentiful springs of distress[7]. Though so profound a double-dealer, I was in no sense a

---

[1] Early on Jekyll battled with the instincts to do what he wanted, and to do what others expected of him – to be a free spirit and a man of high acclaim. This first impulse, mind, was NOT to be evil or to do bad things, merely – as he will later say – to do things which were not wicked but indiscreet. This makes the story all the sadder, since this is really just the conflict between childhood carefreeness and the rigorous performative training of adulthood. It is this repression – at first harmless – which, through decades of pressure, turns Jekyll's childhood gaiety into rebellious evil – a pressure which turns a diamond into a coal

[2] One might presume his thirties – the age the Stevenson was at the time of writing

[3] Openly displayed – Jekyll's "sins" are so tame that some reputable gentlemen (Enfield comes to mind) would have no trouble being open about them, but the pressure to be socially couth is so great that he finds these vices hateful. We could summon up such "embarassments" as a taste for show music, gambling, buying drinks for singers, and other such un-wicked but undignified habits

[4] "Had set before me..." By whom? This could either mean "that I myself had set before me," or "that I had had set before me." If the later, one might suspect parents of setting this standard. Such was certainly Stevenson's case

[5] That is, to the point that it consumed his thoughts and damaged his well being

[6] This is important: contrary to common mythology, Jekyll was tripped up by his repression, not by his hypocrisy, or – since the two things might seem too similar to distinguish – by his too-high standards, not by his desire to do evil. Jekyll was through and through a decent man, but his high expectations dammed up his wicked energies and the force of their release was unbelievable

[7] Certainly for Stevenson who was raised Calvinist, this was true. The distress of the Calvinist concept of the Elect – that you are either chosen or not, that you have no free will to determine your salvation, that your good deeds are the only proof of your election, and that if a man is elected, he can be the most rampant, hateful sinner without ever threatening his salvation, that a good and pious man

hypocrite; both sides of me were in dead earnest; I was no more myself when I laid aside restraint and plunged in shame, than when I laboured, in the eye of day, at the furtherance of knowledge or the relief of sorrow and suffering. And it chanced that the direction of my scientific studies, which led wholly towards the mystic and the transcendental[1], reacted and shed a strong light on this consciousness of the perennial war among my members. With every day, and from both sides of my intelligence, the moral and the intellectual, I thus drew steadily nearer to that truth, by whose partial discovery I have been doomed to such a dreadful shipwreck: that man is not truly one, but truly two. I say two, because the state of my own knowledge does not pass beyond that point. Others will follow[2], others will outstrip me on the same lines; and I hazard the guess that man will be ultimately known for a mere polity of multifarious, incongruous and independent denizens[3]. I, for my part, from the nature of my life, advanced infallibly in one direction and in one direction only. It was on the moral side, and in my own person, that I learned to recognise the thorough and primitive duality of man[4]; I saw that, of the two natures that contended in the field of my consciousness, even if I could rightly be said to be either, it was only because I was radically both; and from an early date, even before the course of my scientific discoveries had begun to suggest the most naked possibility

---

(if unelected) can go to hell, and a raging, sacrilegious man (if elected) can go to heaven – deeply disturbed Stevenson and this disparity in faith and intellect characterized most of his fiction

[1] Taking up the mantle of Frankenstein and Faust, and spurning the sober materialism of Lanyon, Jekyll's pursuits might today be called neuro-psychology, and dealt more with the mind and the spirit than the body. While Lanyon tries to save lives, Jekyll tries to understand them

[2] Among them C. G. Jung who developed the concept of the collective conscious – the internal, psychological world of human identity which is inhabited by thousands of archetypes and archetypal concepts (the hero, the warrior, the mother, the wise man, the lover, the priest, the seducer, the king, the virgin, and so on)

[3] He foresees that mankind consists of thousands of independent selves. This concept is explored beautifully in another Jekyll and Hyde tale, Hermann Hesse's Steppenwolf, inspired by the author's own Jungian psychoanalysis after a divorce

[4] Freud termed these types the Id and the Super-Ego, which are both regulated by the consciousness termed the Ego. The Id is the baser, animal, instinctive, reactive self – the brat, the rebel, the thief, the glutton – and the Super-Ego is the internalized parent which produces guilt and encourages socialized behavior – the teacher, the judge, the priest, the policeman. The Id resists the Super Ego, but the Super Ego fights back with shame and guilt and fear, and the two are locked in an ebbing and flowing struggle over the destiny of the Ego

of such a miracle, I had learned to dwell with pleasure, as a beloved daydream, on the thought of the separation of these elements. If each, I told myself, could be housed in separate identities[1], life would be relieved of all

that was unbearable; the unjust might go his way, delivered from the aspirations and remorse[2] of his more upright twin; and the just could walk steadfastly and securely on his upward path, doing the good things in which he found his pleasure, and no longer exposed to disgrace and penitence by the hands of this extraneous evil[3]. It was the curse of mankind that these incongruous faggots[4] were thus bound together—that in the agonised womb of consciousness, these polar twins should be continuously struggling. How, then were they dissociated?

I was so far in my reflections when, as I have said, a side light began to shine upon the subject from the laboratory table. I began to perceive more deeply than it has ever yet been stated, the trembling immateriality[5], the mistlike transience, of this seemingly so solid body in which we walk attired. Certain agents I found to have the power to shake and pluck back that fleshly vestment, even as a wind might toss the curtains of a pavilion. For two good reasons, I will not enter deeply into this scientific branch of my confession[6]. First, because I have been made to learn that the doom and burthen of our life is bound for ever on man's shoulders, and when the attempt is made to cast it off, it but returns upon us with more unfamiliar and more awful pressure. Second, because, as my narrative will make, alas! too evident, my

---

[1] That is, Egos – the executive function of the unconscious Self: choice, observation, and deliberation

[2] Again, the flaw in "good" Jekyll is actually the very real darkside of goodness: unnecessary remorse, regret, and shame. A person might be chided by an authority figure and brood over a small infraction for weeks. This is not healthy. Jekyll never sought to release evil – only the side which has no regrets

[3] Here he refers to temptations – that which we don't wish to do, but do anyway. Hyde isn't just a source of indulgence – he also brings things to Jekyll's life which doesn't even secretly want, things that he hates and could do without. Too often Hyde is viewed as a secret identity for getting away with bad stuff, but Hyde was originally intended to siphon that away, not to make it possible

[4] Bundles of sticks which are tied together for burning. Jekyll evokes the idea that these incompatible selves are shackled together and destined for torment (the idea of fire) which could be avoided if they could be separated to go their own ways

[5] This was the point of Lanyon's break with Jekyll. Lanyon, a staunch Darwinian materialist and possibly an atheist, is disgusted by Jekyll's fixation on the immaterial while there are material needs to be met

[6] Of course, this also spares Stevenson from having to justify the transformation with real science (and spares his readers from mumbo-jumbo). Mary Shelley similarly concealed her science in *Frankenstein*. Both novels benefit from this

discoveries were incomplete. Enough then, that I not only recognised my natural body from the mere aura and effulgence of certain of the powers that made up my spirit, but managed to compound a drug by which these powers should be dethroned from their supremacy, and a second form and countenance[1] substituted, none the less natural to me because they were the expression, and bore the stamp of lower elements in my soul.

I hesitated long before I put this theory to the test of practice. I knew well that I risked death; for any drug that so potently controlled and shook the very fortress of identity, might, by the least scruple[2] of an overdose or at the least inopportunity in the moment of exhibition, utterly blot out that immaterial tabernacle[3] which I looked to it to change. But the temptation of a discovery so singular and profound at last overcame the suggestions of alarm. I had long since prepared my tincture[4]; I purchased at once, from a firm of wholesale chemists, a large quantity of a particular salt which I knew, from my experiments, to be the last ingredient required; and late one accursed night[5], I compounded the elements, watched them boil and smoke together in the glass, and when the ebullition had subsided, with a strong glow of courage, drank off the potion.

The most racking pangs succeeded: a grinding in the bones, deadly nausea, and a horror of the spirit that cannot be exceeded at the hour of birth or death[6]. Then these agonies began swiftly to subside, and I came to myself as if out of a great sickness. There was something strange in my sensations, something indescribably new and, from its very novelty, incredibly sweet. I felt younger, lighter, happier in body; within I was conscious of a heady recklessness, a current of disordered sensual images running like a millrace in my fancy[7], a solution of the bonds of obligation, an unknown but not an

---

[1] Body and face

[2] A minute measure – an once, a grain

[3] Calling to mind the biblical idea that "the body is a temple" – a holy place formed by God and invested with a soul, and suggesting that to tamper with it is blasphemous and evil

[4] A solution of high proof alcohol which is used to draw the essential oils out of dissolved material, in this case a red liquor with traces of ether and phosphorous into which a mineral salt is dissolved

[5] This echoes Mary Shelley's description of Frankenstein's successful resurrection: "It was on a dreary night in November that I beheld the accomplishment of my toils"

[6] A beautifully poetic phrase that not only suggests the birth of Hyde, but also introduces birth and death as two other well-known polar opposites that plague humanity – the pains and disappointments of birth and the fear and regrets of death

[7] The 1941 version of the story adapts this scene in a ridiculously surreal manner. At one point Ingrid Bergman is pulled out of a champagne bottle like a cork. The

innocent freedom of the soul. I knew myself, at the first breath of this new life, to be more wicked, tenfold more wicked, sold a slave to my original evil; and the thought, in that moment, braced and delighted me like wine. I stretched out my hands, exulting in the freshness of these sensations[1]; and in the act, I was suddenly aware that I had lost in stature[2].

There was no mirror, at that date, in my room; that which stands beside me as I write, was brought there later on and for the very purpose of these transformations. The night however, was far gone into the morning—the morning, black as it was, was nearly ripe for the conception of the day—the inmates of my house were locked in the most rigorous hours of slumber; and I determined, flushed as I was with hope and triumph, to venture in my new shape as far as to my bedroom. I crossed the yard, wherein the constellations looked down upon me[3], I could have thought, with wonder, the first creature of that sort that their unsleeping vigilance had yet disclosed to them; I stole through the corridors, a stranger in my own house; and coming to my room, I saw for the first time the appearance of Edward Hyde.

I must here speak by theory alone, saying not that which I know, but that which I suppose to be most probable. The evil side of my nature, to which I had now transferred the stamping efficacy[4], was less robust and less developed than the good which I had just deposed. Again, in the course of my life, which had been, after all, nine tenths a life[5] of effort, virtue and control, it had been much less exercised and much less exhausted. And hence, as I think, it came about that Edward Hyde was so much smaller, slighter and younger than Henry Jekyll[6]. Even as good shone upon the countenance of the one, evil was written broadly and plainly on the face of the other. Evil besides (which I must still believe to be the lethal side of man) had left on

---

1932 version depicts it in a far more meaningful and less insane manner. Of course, however, Stevenson probably doesn't refer to "sensuous" in a sexual manner at all, merely meaning visions which employ the senses and overwhelm them

[1] Like Frankenstein, Jekyll has brought forth a new creation with the mind of a man but the perspective of a newborn: each sensation is new and thrilling

[2] Hyde's most distinguishing trait is also that which films are most loathe to show. His short stature is a metaphor for his stunted experience in the world, having been jailed by Jekyll's Super-Ego for forty years or more

[3] Symbols of the divine – God watches his job being performed by Jekyll

[4] The right of a government to produce currency (to "stamp" coins). Jekyll has handed the power of his Ego from his Super-Ego to his Id. It would make as much sense to say "I had handed over the keys"

[5] Jekyll asserts that he lost his shamelessness around the age of five or six

[6] Here again is the suggestion that Hyde is literally a young lad of less than eighteen – young Master Hyde, Harry Jekyll's protégée

343

that body an imprint of deformity and decay[1]. And yet when I looked upon that ugly idol in the glass, I was conscious of no repugnance, rather of a leap of welcome. This, too, was myself[2]. It seemed natural and human. In my eyes it bore a livelier image of the spirit[3], it seemed more express and single, than the imperfect and divided countenance I had been hitherto accustomed to call mine[4]. And in so far I was doubtless right. I have observed that when I wore the semblance of Edward Hyde, none could come near to me at first without a visible misgiving of the flesh. This, as I take it, was because all human beings, as we meet them, are commingled out of good and evil: and Edward Hyde, alone in the ranks of mankind, was pure evil[5].

I lingered but a moment at the mirror: the second and conclusive experiment had yet to be attempted; it yet remained to be seen if I had lost my identity beyond redemption and must flee before daylight from a house that was no longer mine; and hurrying back to my cabinet, I once more prepared and drank the cup, once more suffered the pangs of dissolution, and came to myself once more with the character, the stature and the face of Henry Jekyll.

That night I had come to the fatal cross-roads. Had I approached my discovery in a more noble spirit[6], had I risked the experiment while under the

---

[1] Our one hint that Hyde might have something of a ghoulish face, though most descriptions suggest that the malady is in his expression, not his physique

[2] Wolf remarks that "Here, if anywhere, is the thematic radium center of Jekyll and Hyde: Stevenson's recognition that the wholeness of mankind absolutely includes a Hyde.." He goes on to quote Stevenson's grim philosophy on human nature: "What a monstrous specter is this man, the disease of the agglutinated dust, lifting alternate feet or lying drugged with slumber; killing, feeding, growing, bring forth small copies of himself; grown upon with hair like grass, fitted with eyes that move and glitter in his face; a thing to set children screaming" ("Pulvis et Umbra")

[3] Undiluted by goodness, Hyde is a vigorous, unblemished expression of the human character, albeit the wicked side

[4] Again, Jekyll is not pure good and Hyde pure evil – Jekyll is evil-with-good; only Hyde is a pure distillation. Had – as he later suggests – Jekyll drawn out the good, he would be a veritable god or angel

[5] Enfield, Utterson, and Lanyon have all noted that they felt an instinctive disgust at Hyde – something vestigial and automatic – and each suggested that there was something inherent in mankind which reels at the presence of pure evil

[6] Jekyll suggests that at the bottom of his experiment was a genuine desire to uncage his repressed child-self, and that had he actually – as many of the film versions claim – been doing the tests to unshackle his better nature, that it would be his best self, not Hyde who appeared. One wonders if this third party

empire of generous or pious aspirations, all must have been otherwise, and from these agonies of death and birth, I had come forth an angel instead of a fiend. The drug had no discriminating action; it was neither diabolical nor divine; it but shook the doors of the prisonhouse of my disposition; and like the captives of Philippi[1], that which stood within ran forth. At that time my virtue slumbered; my evil, kept awake by ambition, was alert and swift to seize the occasion; and the thing that was projected was Edward Hyde. Hence, although I had now two characters as well as two appearances, one was wholly evil, and the other was still the old Henry Jekyll, that incongruous compound of whose reformation and improvement I had already learned to despair. The movement was thus wholly toward the worse.

Even at that time, I had not conquered my aversions to the dryness of a life of study[2]. I would still be merrily disposed at times; and as my pleasures were (to say the least) undignified[3], and I was not only well known and highly considered, but growing towards the elderly man, this incoherency of my life was daily growing more unwelcome. It was on this side that my new power tempted me until I fell in slavery. I had but to drink the cup, to doff at once the body of the noted professor, and to assume, like a thick cloak[4], that of Edward Hyde. I smiled at the notion; it seemed to me at the time to be humourous; and I made my preparations with the most studious care. I took and furnished that house in Soho, to which Hyde was tracked by the police; and engaged as a housekeeper a creature whom I knew well to be silent and unscrupulous[5]. On the other side, I announced to my servants that a Mr. Hyde (whom I described) was to have full liberty and power about my house in the square; and to parry mishaps, I even called and made myself a familiar object, in my second character. I next drew up that will to which you so much

---

could have shown up in the middle of this novel had Jekyll had a selfless heart at the time of his drinking

[1] A decisive battle fought between Brutus and Cassius and Mark Antony and Octavian for control of the Roman Republic after Caesar's assassination

[2] As a youth we know that Jekyll was something of a playboy, and he informs us that thirty years later, he still nurses a distaste for the quiet life

[33] Again, we don't know what Jekyll's vices are, other than to say that he enjoys a good time and gets bored. What excites him appears to be accessible in Soho – a poor red-light district – and although prostitution is a perennial favorite vice, it could be anything from gambling, to drinking lots of champagne, to watching burlesque shows, to wearing drag. Stevenson wisely holds back his cards

[4] Perhaps this is the phrase that forever linked Hyde with a billowing cape. In any case, he is described as plainly dressed in expensive fabric, so we can probably rule out a cloak in favor of a sensible greatcoat

[5] Which is to say, she could be paid off and felt no moral duty to inform the police if Hyde strayed on the wrong side of the law

346

objected; so that if anything befell me in the person of Dr. Jekyll, I could enter on that of Edward Hyde without pecuniary loss. And thus fortified, as I supposed, on every side, I began to profit by the strange immunities of my position.

Men have before hired bravos[1] to transact their crimes, while their own person and reputation sat under shelter. I was the first that ever did so for his pleasures[2]. I was the first that could plod in the public eye with a load of genial respectability, and in a moment, like a schoolboy, strip off these lendings and spring headlong into the sea of liberty. But for me, in my impenetrable mantle, the safety was complete. Think of it—I did not even exist! Let me but escape into my laboratory door, give me but a second or two to mix and swallow the draught that I had always standing ready; and whatever he had done, Edward Hyde would pass away like the stain of breath upon a mirror; and there in his stead, quietly at home, trimming the midnight lamp in his study[3], a man who could afford to laugh at suspicion, would be Henry Jekyll.

The pleasures which I made haste to seek in my disguise were, as I have said, undignified; I would scarce use a harder term[4]. But in the hands of Edward Hyde, they soon began to turn toward the monstrous. When I would come back from these excursions, I was often plunged into a kind of wonder at my vicarious depravity. This familiar[5] that I called out of my own soul, and sent forth alone to do his good pleasure, was a being inherently malign and

---

[1] Thugs, assassins, mercenaries

[2] Again, we have to give Hyde some credit: in the beginning, he was merely a means of experiencing the undignified pleasures that fulfilled Jekyll's soul. He wasn't Jekyll's henchman, going around and killing his enemies – just an outlet to help him experience the life that his society denies him. Queer studies have seen Jekyll's dilemma as possibly reflecting a man who is struggling to stay in the closet, whose "wicked" forays are more about living authentically than raping barmaids, although this is pure conjecture

[3] When the wick of an oil lamp became thoroughly charred, its light grew weak and it required trimming with scissors after which a new half inch of wick would be scrolled up and lit. A modern image might be "quietly at home, face illuminated by his computer screen"

[4] Considering Jekyll's vicious Super-Ego (which is, of course, directing his confession as a form of penance), I find no reason to doubt his claim that his vices were little more than improper for a man of his standing, but not particularly wicked. Hyde of course tightens the screws on these vices, however, turning them into deep sins

[5] Stevenson connects Hyde to witchcraft folklore (something he will probe in "Thrawn Janet"): a familiar is a witch's supernatural companion, minion, and henchman, typically a black cat, but also said to be bats, wolves (as in Dracula's case where he employs the zoo wolf), dogs, spiders, toads, owls, ravens, and vultures (hence the popular depiction of these animals at Halloween)

villainous; his every act and thought centered on self[1]; drinking pleasure with bestial avidity from any degree of torture to another[2]; relentless like a man of stone. Henry Jekyll stood at times aghast before the acts of Edward Hyde; but the situation was apart from ordinary laws, and insidiously relaxed the grasp of conscience. It was Hyde, after all, and Hyde alone, that was guilty[3]. Jekyll was no worse; he woke again to his good qualities seemingly unimpaired; he would even make haste, where it was possible, to undo the evil done by Hyde. And thus his conscience slumbered[4].

Into the details of the infamy at which I thus connived (for even now I can scarce grant that I committed it) I have no design of entering; I mean but to point out the warnings and the successive steps with which my chastisement approached. I met with one accident which, as it brought on no consequence, I shall no more than mention. An act of cruelty to a child aroused against me the anger of a passer-by, whom I recognised the other day in the person of your kinsman; the doctor and the child's family joined him; there were moments when I feared for my life[5]; and at last, in order to pacify their too just resentment, Edward Hyde had to bring them to the door, and pay them in a cheque drawn in the name of Henry Jekyll. But this danger was easily eliminated from the future, by opening an account at another bank in the name of Edward Hyde himself; and when, by sloping my own hand backward, I had supplied my double with a signature[6], I thought I sat beyond the reach of fate.

Some two months before the murder of Sir Danvers, I had been out for one of my adventures, had returned at a late hour, and woke the next day in bed with somewhat odd sensations. It was in vain I looked about me; in vain I saw the decent furniture and tall proportions of my room in the square; in vain that I recognised the pattern of the bed curtains and the design of the mahogany frame; something still kept insisting that I was not where I was, that I had not wakened where I seemed to be, but in the little room in Soho where I was accustomed to sleep in the body of Edward Hyde. I smiled to myself, and in my psychological way, began lazily to inquire into the elements of this illusion, occasionally, even as I did so, dropping back into a comfortable morning doze. I was still so engaged when, in one of my more wakeful moments, my eyes fell upon my hand. Now the hand of Henry Jekyll

---

[1] Pure Id, pure animal, pure Self

[2] It certainly sounds like Hyde is guilty of more physical cruelties than the trampling of the girl and the bludgeoning of Carew. Not likely murders – they would probably be mentioned – but cruelties that demean, harm, and humiliate

[3] False

[4] This defense is popularly – and derisively – called "the devil made me do it"

[5] Jekyll confirms the suggestion that the crowd that night had lynching on its mind

[6] Confirming Guest's analysis

(as you have often remarked) was professional in shape and size[1]: it was large, firm, white and comely. But the hand which I now saw, clearly enough, in the yellow light of a mid-London morning, lying half shut on the bedclothes, was lean, corded, knuckly, of a dusky pallor and thickly shaded with a swart growth of hair[2]. It was the hand of Edward Hyde.

I must have stared upon it for near half a minute, sunk as I was in the mere stupidity of wonder, before terror woke up in my breast as sudden and startling as the crash of cymbals; and bounding from my bed I rushed to the mirror. At the sight that met my eyes, my blood was changed into something exquisitely thin and icy. Yes, I had gone to bed Henry Jekyll, I had awakened Edward Hyde. How was this to be explained? I asked myself; and then, with another bound of terror—how was it to be remedied? It was well on in the morning; the servants were up; all my drugs were in the cabinet—a long journey down two pairs of stairs, through the back passage, across the open court and through the anatomical theatre, from where I was then standing horror-struck. It might indeed be possible to cover my face; but of what use was that, when I was unable to conceal the alteration in my stature? And then with an overpowering sweetness of relief, it came back upon my mind that the servants were already used to the coming and going of my second self. I had soon dressed, as well as I was able, in clothes of my own size: had soon passed through the house, where Bradshaw stared and drew back at seeing Mr. Hyde at such an hour and in such a strange array; and ten minutes later, Dr. Jekyll had returned to his own shape and was sitting down, with a darkened brow, to make a feint of breakfasting.

Small indeed was my appetite. This inexplicable incident, this reversal of my previous experience, seemed, like the Babylonian finger on the wall[3], to be spelling out the letters of my judgment; and I began to reflect more seriously than ever before on the issues and possibilities of my double existence. That part of me which I had the power of projecting, had lately been much exercised and nourished; it had seemed to me of late as though the body of Edward Hyde had grown in stature, as though (when I wore that

---

[1] The hand of a man not used to manual labor – soft, pale, well groomed

[2] The only direct physical description – to the point of conjuring a real image – that we have of Hyde, and one which has led to the cultural expectation of an ape-ish man, or at least one with monstrously thick body hair approaching the appearance of a werewolf

[3] In the Book of Daniel, the king of Babylon – a debauched playboy – desecrates the holy Jewish plateware and goblets stolen from the Temple by using them at a bacchanal. The wild party is interrupted by a ghostly hand which writes a death sentence on the wall in fiery letters that predict the downfall of the Babylonian empire to the Medes. Essentially Jekyll is saying that he now realizes that partytime is over

form) I were conscious of a more generous tide of blood; and I began to spy a danger that, if this were much prolonged, the balance of my nature might be permanently overthrown, the power of voluntary change be forfeited, and the character of Edward Hyde become irrevocably mine[1]. The power of the drug had not been always equally displayed. Once, very early in my career, it had totally failed me[2]; since then I had been obliged on more than one occasion to double[3], and once, with infinite risk of death, to treble[4] the amount[5]; and these rare uncertainties had cast hitherto the sole shadow on my contentment. Now, however, and in the light of that morning's accident, I was led to remark that whereas, in the beginning, the difficulty had been to throw off the body of Jekyll, it had of late gradually but decidedly transferred itself to the other side. All things therefore seemed to point to this; that I was slowly losing hold of my original and better self, and becoming slowly incorporated with my second and worse.

Between these two, I now felt I had to choose. My two natures had memory in common, but all other faculties were most unequally shared between them. Jekyll (who was composite) now with the most sensitive apprehensions, now with a greedy gusto, projected and shared in the pleasures and adventures of Hyde; but Hyde was indifferent to Jekyll, or but remembered him as the mountain bandit remembers the cavern in which he conceals himself from pursuit. Jekyll had more than a father's interest; Hyde had more than a son's indifference[6]. To cast in my lot with Jekyll, was to die to those appetites which I had long secretly indulged and had of late begun to pamper. To cast it in with Hyde, was to die to a thousand interests and aspirations, and to become, at a blow and forever, despised and friendless. The bargain might appear unequal; but there was still another consideration in the scales; for while Jekyll would suffer smartingly in the fires of abstinence, Hyde would be not even conscious of all that he had lost[7]. Strange as my

---

[1] The looming specter of alcoholics and drug users – the moment when a chosen release becomes a mandatory sentence. Although the story is not meant to be an allegory of substance abuse, it fits that end beautifully

[2] We recall Lanyon's having seen a note in his lab book that said "Total Failure!!!"

[3] The word "double" was constantly written throughout the book's pages

[4] Triple

[5] Like a drug user, the earliest doses are now impotent, and more and more dangerous increases are necessary to hit the original high successfully

[6] Oedipal readings of this story are tremendously popular. Jekyll – in defiance to his upbringing – revives the rebellious son that he never was, only to become father to that son, and suffer from his own riotous disobedience. Jekyll is more devoted to Hyde than most fathers to their sons, and Hyde has less love for Jekyll than most sons have for their fathers – the relationship is volatile and disastrous

[7] What makes chosing Hyde attractive is what made him summon Hyde from the beginning: freedom from the Super-Ego – freedom from guilt, remorse, shame,

circumstances were, the terms of this debate are as old and commonplace as man[1]; much the same inducements and alarms cast the die for any tempted and trembling sinner; and it fell out with me, as it falls with so vast a majority of my fellows, that I chose the better part and was found wanting in the strength to keep to it[2].

Yes, I preferred the elderly and discontented doctor, surrounded by friends and cherishing honest hopes; and bade a resolute farewell to the liberty, the comparative youth, the light step[3], leaping impulses and secret pleasures, that I had enjoyed in the disguise of Hyde. I made this choice perhaps with some unconscious reservation, for I neither gave up the house in Soho, nor destroyed the clothes of Edward Hyde, which still lay ready in my cabinet[4]. For two months, however, I was true to my determination; for two months, I led a life of such severity as I had never before attained to, and enjoyed the compensations of an approving conscience. But time began at last to obliterate the freshness of my alarm; the praises of conscience began to grow into a thing of course; I began to be tortured with throes and longings, as of Hyde struggling after freedom; and at last, in an hour of moral weakness, I once again compounded and swallowed the transforming draught[5].

I do not suppose that, when a drunkard reasons with himself upon his vice, he is once out of five hundred times affected by the dangers that he runs through his brutish, physical insensibility; neither had I, long as I had considered my position, made enough allowance for the complete moral insensibility and insensate readiness to evil, which were the leading characters of Edward Hyde. Yet it was by these that I was punished. My devil

---

regret. Even without Hyde, Jekyll will loathe himself for ever having called him forward, but without Jekyll, Hyde would be a content hedonist

[1] One need not have a Hyde to struggle – as Stevenson himself did – with this balance of pleasure and respectability – contentment or acceptance

[2] His overall desire is to be good, but he is too weak to maintain that resolve during moments of temptation

[3] Both figuratively and – as Utterson will attest – literally

[4] More behavior common among addicts, who will resolve to go clean, but will quietly permit a backdoor to remain unlocked to let them back in their addiction in the future: the shopping addict who preserves her credit cards, the sex addict who keeps his salacious phone contacts, the alcoholic who will not sell their basement bar

[5] Any addict will relate overwhelmingly to this moment of desperate, shameful surrender. Wolfnotes that, while not an addict, Stevenson frequently over relied on narcotics, red wine, and marijuana in order to combat his pathological insomnia, and understood the struggle of dependency

had been long caged, he came out roaring[1]. I was conscious, even when I took the draught, of a more unbridled, a more furious propensity to ill. It must have been this, I suppose, that stirred in my soul that tempest of impatience with which I listened to the civilities of my unhappy victim; I declare, at least, before God, no man morally sane could have been guilty of that crime upon so pitiful a provocation[2]; and that I struck in no more reasonable spirit than that in which a sick child may break a plaything[3]. But I had voluntarily stripped myself of all those balancing instincts by which even the worst of us continues to walk with some degree of steadiness among temptations; and in my case, to be tempted, however slightly, was to fall.

Instantly the spirit of hell awoke in me and raged. With a transport of glee, I mauled the unresisting body[4], tasting delight from every blow; and it was not till weariness had begun to succeed, that I was suddenly, in the top fit of my delirium, struck through the heart by a cold thrill of terror. A mist dispersed; I saw my life to be forfeit; and fled from the scene of these excesses, at once glorying and trembling, my lust of evil gratified and stimulated, my love of life screwed to the topmost peg[5]. I ran to the house in Soho, and (to make assurance doubly sure) destroyed my papers; thence I set out through the lamplit streets, in the same divided ecstasy of mind, gloating on my crime,

---

[1] In addiction lingo, this moment is called a binge: a behavior has been successfully resisted, but when that strength yields, the behavior is indulged in with unparalleled vigor and intensity

[2] The reference here is to Carew's inquiry, which we tellingly do not learn. The fact that Jekyll doesn't describe the conversation strongly suggests that it was something a bit untoward. As previously suggested, Carew may have solicited Hyde for sex, may have asked the way to a brothel, or may have even been a blackmail victim of Hyde's, asking for mercy and carrying a confession to Utterson in hopes of finding legal help, but in spite of the servant's suggestion that the old man was asking for directions, Jekyll never mentions such a trite reason for his death. In fact, he calls the query "pitiful." My strong impression is that Sir Danvers was involved in something tremendously scandalous and was killed by Hyde for reasons relating to the nature of the vice

[3] A scenario very familiar to Stevenson, who was an invalid as a child. This also has a fairly suggestive sexual connotation, as the "beautiful" old man becomes Hyde's helpless toy

[4] It is perhaps psychologically pertinent to note how indirectly Jekyll describes this event, never using the name of his victim – rather "the unresisting body" – and failing to describe the scenario (see previous comment). It brings to mind Buffalo Bill's dehumanizing command "it puts the lotion in the basket!"

[5] Hyde is a virtual toddler – life is his only concern: having it extend as long as possible, be as accommodating as possible, and serve him as devotedly as possible. While Jekyll may aspire to the higher calling of a noble character, Hyde just wants to live and live without restriction

light-headedly devising others in the future, and yet still hastening and still hearkening in my wake for the steps of the avenger. Hyde had a song upon his lips as he compounded the draught, and as he drank it, pledged the dead man. The pangs of transformation had not done tearing him, before Henry Jekyll, with streaming tears of gratitude[1] and remorse, had fallen upon his knees and lifted his clasped hands to God. The veil of self-indulgence was rent from head to foot. I saw my life as a whole: I followed it up from the days of childhood, when I had walked with my father's hand[2], and through the self-denying toils of my professional life, to arrive again and again, with the same sense of unreality, at the damned horrors of the evening. I could have screamed aloud; I sought with tears and prayers to smother down the crowd of hideous images and sounds with which my memory swarmed against me; and still, between the petitions, the ugly face of my iniquity stared into my soul. As the acuteness of this remorse began to die away, it was succeeded by a sense of joy. The problem of my conduct was solved. Hyde was thenceforth impossible; whether I would or not, I was now confined to the better part of my existence; and O, how I rejoiced to think of it! with what willing humility I embraced anew the restrictions of natural life! with what sincere renunciation I locked the door by which I had so often gone and come, and ground the key under my heel[3]!

The next day, came the news that the murder had not been overlooked, that the guilt of Hyde was patent[4] to the world, and that the victim was a man high in public estimation. It was not only a crime, it had been a tragic folly. I think I was glad to know it; I think I was glad to have my better impulses thus buttressed[5] and guarded by the terrors of the scaffold[6]. Jekyll was now my city of refuge; let but Hyde peep out an instant, and the hands of all men would be raised to take and slay him[7].

---

[1] That he was able to turn back into himself, and thus theoretically given a chance to banish Hyde

[2] Stevenson, whose relationship with his father was very dear until his radical philosophies broke the old man's heart and temporarily estranged them, surely invests a great deal of himself into Jekyll's fairly obvious father issues. Both devoted and rebellious, loving and disobedient, Jekyll, like Stevenson, could probably trace Hyde back to his mixed emotions surrounding his relationship with his father

[3] Found by Poole and Utterson

[4] Obvious, unquestionable

[5] Enclosed by fortifications – protected

[6] The only thing which could frighten Hyde is the threat of losing his life – the sole thing he cares about

[7] There is no doubt now in Jekyll's mind that if Hyde isn't captured by the police, he will be lynched by the mob

I resolved in my future conduct to redeem the past; and I can say with honesty that my resolve was fruitful of some good. You know yourself how earnestly, in the last months of the last year, I laboured to relieve suffering; you know that much was done for others, and that the days passed quietly, almost happily for myself. Nor can I truly say that I wearied of this beneficent and innocent life; I think instead that I daily enjoyed it more completely; but I was still cursed with my duality of purpose; and as the first edge of my penitence wore off, the lower side of me, so long indulged, so recently chained down, began to growl for licence. Not that I dreamed of resuscitating Hyde; the bare idea of that would startle me to frenzy: no, it was in my own person that I was once more tempted to trifle with my conscience; and it was as an ordinary secret sinner that I at last fell before the assaults of temptation.

There comes an end to all things; the most capacious measure[1] is filled at last; and this brief condescension to my evil finally destroyed the balance of my soul. And yet I was not alarmed; the fall seemed natural, like a return to the old days before I had made my discovery. It was a fine, clear, January day, wet under foot where the frost had melted, but cloudless overhead; and the Regent's Park was full of winter chirrupings[2] and sweet with spring odours. I sat in the sun on a bench; the animal within me licking the chops of memory[3]; the spiritual side a little drowsed[4], promising subsequent penitence[5], but not yet moved to begin. After all, I reflected, I was like my neighbours; and then I smiled, comparing myself with other men, comparing my active good-will with the lazy cruelty of their neglect. And at the very moment of that vainglorious thought, a qualm came over me, a horrid nausea and the most deadly shuddering. These passed away, and left me faint; and then as in its turn faintness subsided, I began to be aware of a change in the temper of my thoughts, a greater boldness, a contempt of danger, a solution of the bonds of obligation. I looked down; my clothes hung formlessly on my

---

[1] Measuring container – even the biggest bucket will eventually spill over

[2] Chirpings

[3] More subtle Victorian suggestiveness: critics agree almost unanimously that Jekyll is sitting here in the park fantasizing over a past sin. Whether it is a sin of Hyde's from recent days or one from his own youth we can't say, but it is clear that he is relishing this unsavory memory. Given that Stevenson overtly claims that some of Jekyll's sins have a basis in "sexuality," we might wonder what exactly he is doing while he drinks in this sinful memory... alone on a bench in the park

[4] Jekyll associates his better nature with the spirit, his baser with the flesh. This will come into play at the time of his "death" when he argues that he will die when his spirit is locked out of Hyde's fully claimed body

[5] Fully Jekyll, the good doctor sprawls out on a bench and gorges on this memory, promising to ask for forgiveness when he is finished. Without being too speculative, I have little trouble suggesting that Jekyll may be masturbating

shrunken limbs[1]; the hand that lay on my knee was corded[2] and hairy. I was once more Edward Hyde. A moment before I had been safe of all men's respect, wealthy, beloved—the cloth laying for me in the dining-room at home[3]; and now I was the common quarry[4] of mankind, hunted, houseless, a known murderer, thrall to the gallows.

My reason wavered, but it did not fail me utterly. I have more than once observed that in my second character, my faculties seemed sharpened to a point and my spirits more tensely elastic; thus it came about that, where Jekyll perhaps might have succumbed, Hyde rose to the importance of the moment. My drugs were in one of the presses of my cabinet; how was I to reach them? That was the problem that (crushing my temples in my hands) I set myself to solve. The laboratory door I had closed. If I sought to enter by the house, my own servants would consign me to the gallows. I saw I must employ another hand, and thought of Lanyon. How was he to be reached? how persuaded? Supposing that I escaped capture in the streets, how was I to make my way into his presence? and how should I, an unknown and displeasing visitor, prevail on the famous physician to rifle the study of his colleague, Dr. Jekyll? Then I remembered that of my original character, one part remained to me: I could write my own hand; and once I had conceived that kindling spark, the way that I must follow became lighted up from end to end.

Thereupon, I arranged my clothes as best I could[5], and summoning a passing hansom[6], drove to an hotel in Portland Street, the name of which I chanced to remember. At my appearance (which was indeed comical enough, however tragic a fate these garments covered) the driver could not conceal his mirth. I gnashed my teeth upon him with a gust of devilish fury[7]; and the smile withered from his face—happily for him—yet more happily for myself, for in another instant I had certainly dragged him from his perch[8]. At the inn, as I entered, I looked about me with so black a countenance as made the attendants tremble; not a look did they exchange in my presence; but obsequiously took my orders, led me to a private room, and brought me

---

[1] Hyde is truly a little man – it's a true pity that no adaptations attempt to present this physical difference. In my mind's eye it is a wildly shocking change

[2] Thickly muscular, ridged with muscle bands

[3] Viz. the table is set for his meal

[4] "The common quarry" – the universally sought after prey

[5] As Lanyon noted, albeit with the impression that the look was clownish bordering on ludicrous

[6] Two person cab driven by one horse with the cabbie mounted behind and above the passengers

[7] Again, gnashing teeth is closely linked to hell in Christian tradition, further underscoring his Satanic character

[8] That is, he *would have* dragged him

wherewithal[1] to write. Hyde in danger of his life was a creature new to me; shaken with inordinate anger, strung to the pitch of murder, lusting to inflict pain. Yet the creature was astute; mastered his fury with a great effort of the will; composed his two important letters, one to Lanyon and one to Poole; and that he might receive actual evidence of their being posted, sent them out with directions that they should be registered. Thenceforward, he sat all day over the fire in the private room, gnawing his nails; there he dined, sitting alone with his fears, the waiter visibly quailing before his eye; and thence, when the night was fully come, he set forth in the corner of a closed cab, and was driven to and fro about the streets of the city. He, I say—I cannot say, I[2]. That child of Hell had nothing human; nothing lived in him but fear and hatred[3]. And when at last, thinking the driver had begun to grow suspicious, he discharged the cab and ventured on foot, attired in his misfitting clothes, an object marked out for observation, into the midst of the nocturnal passengers, these two base passions raged within him like a tempest[4]. He walked fast, hunted by his fears, chattering to himself, skulking through the less frequented thoroughfares, counting the minutes that still divided him

---

[1] The necessary materials

[2] This is a dubious, though debatable point. We are naturally inclined to call foul and interpret Jekyll's self-distancing as a combination of denial and dishonesty, although (admittedly only through his own possibly compromised narration) we have evidence that Hyde may indeed be pure flesh while Jekyll is an amalgam of flesh and spirit. However, this STILL provides a link of responsibility on Jekyll's part: his Ego consists half of Super-Ego (spirit) and half of Id (flesh), and like a man who is father to a son, unlike a step-father, is represented in half of his offspring's body and mind. Although Hyde is all Hyde, Jekyll is undeniably himself half Hyde, so the argument that Hyde has "hijacked" their shared body, holds less water than Jekyll might imagine. What HAS lost ground is the third party – the unnamed Super-Ego. But even after Jekyll departs in spirit, half of him – the fleshly half – is still resident in the body now controlled by Hyde

[3] Stevenson continually implies that Hyde occupies the physical side of man – the animal, the hungry – while Jekyll strides both the physical and the spiritual. This portrait of Hyde as thoroughly inhuman, and his inhumanity as being founded in fear and hatred, says much about Stevenson's philosophical understanding of the differences between mankind and animals. At its route, he suggests, is the ability to transcend the mechanism of self-preservation (fear) and the instinct to dominate (hatred) – this transcendence (or attempt at transcendence), he argues, is the core of our humanity

[4] Again, Stevenson suggests that Hyde – and the worst parts of humanity – can be essentially distilled into fear and hatred, and that all which is shameful, cruel, or repugnant about mankind springs from one or both of these two elements. Hyde, who embodies all that they are capable of, is a virtual maelstrom of these emotions and all their tributaries

from midnight. Once a woman spoke to him, offering, I think, a box of lights[1]. He smote her in the face[2], and she fled.

When I came to myself at Lanyon's, the horror of my old friend perhaps affected me somewhat: I do not know; it was at least but a drop in the sea to the abhorrence with which I looked back upon these hours. A change had come over me. It was no longer the fear of the gallows, it was the horror of being Hyde that racked me. I received Lanyon's condemnation[3] partly in a dream; it was partly in a dream that I came home to my own house and got into bed. I slept after the prostration[4] of the day, with a stringent and profound slumber which not even the nightmares that wrung me could avail to break. I awoke in the morning shaken, weakened, but refreshed. I still hated and feared the thought of the brute that slept within me, and I had not of course forgotten the appalling dangers of the day before; but I was once more at home, in my own house and close to my drugs; and gratitude for my escape shone so strong in my soul that it almost rivalled the brightness of hope.

I was stepping leisurely across the court after breakfast, drinking the chill of the air with pleasure, when I was seized again with those indescribable sensations that heralded the change; and I had but the time to gain the shelter of my cabinet, before I was once again raging and freezing with the passions of Hyde. It took on this occasion a double dose to recall me to myself; and alas! six hours after, as I sat looking sadly in the fire, the pangs returned, and the drug had to be re-administered. In short, from that day forth it seemed only by a great effort as of gymnastics, and only under the immediate

---

[1] There is considerable speculation – especially considering Jekyll's tendency to self-censor (viz. the details of the Carew murder) – and combined with his hesitation in remembering the exact nature of the woman's request, that she was a soliciting prostitute. Stevenson himself acknowledges in several letters that (although he never addresses it in the text) one of Jekyll's besetting sins is of a sexual nature, and this may be his polite way of insinuating prostitution without being overt. Match girls were incidentally a common cover for prostitutes: poor girls offering matches to wealthy men for their cigars could easily be entirely innocent, but they could also be a very convenient disguise for a more insidious industry

[2] Wolf notes the circularity of the narrative: Hyde's first discussed victim is a small girl whom he crushes with his feet, and his last mentioned victim is a grown woman whom he strikes in the face with his fists

[3] We never know the dialogue between Lanyon and the transformed Jekyll, but his use of the word "condemnation" and Lanyon's hateful opinion of his former friend give us an idea of the acidic lecture that must have occured

[4] That is, throughout the entirety of the day

stimulation of the drug, that I was able to wear the countenance of Jekyll[1]. At all hours of the day and night, I would be taken with the premonitory shudder; above all, if I slept, or even dozed for a moment in my chair, it was always as Hyde that I awakened. Under the strain of this continually impending doom and by the sleeplessness to which I now condemned myself, ay, even beyond what I had thought possible to man, I became, in my own person, a creature eaten up and emptied by fever, languidly weak both in body and mind, and solely occupied by one thought: the horror of my other self. But when I slept, or when the virtue of the medicine wore off, I would leap almost without transition (for the pangs of transformation grew daily less marked[2]) into the possession of a fancy brimming with images of terror, a soul boiling with causeless hatreds[3], and a body that seemed not strong enough to contain the raging energies of life. The powers of Hyde seemed to have grown with the sickliness of Jekyll[4]. And certainly the hate that now divided them was equal on each side. With Jekyll, it was a thing of vital instinct. He had now seen the full deformity of that creature that shared with him some of the phenomena of consciousness, and was co-heir with him to death: and beyond these links of community, which in themselves made the most poignant part of his distress, he thought of Hyde, for all his energy of life, as of something not only hellish but inorganic[5]. This was the shocking thing; that the slime of the pit seemed to utter cries and voices; that the amorphous dust gesticulated and sinned; that what was dead, and had no shape, should usurp the offices of life[6]. And this again, that that insurgent

---

[1] Ironically, now the drug has become Jekyll's only conduit to his former self – the self he had at first delighted in throwing off. Now he is more Hyde than Jekyll – more Id than Ego, certainly more Id than Super-Ego

[2] It has become so effortless to shift from Jekyll to Hyde because Hyde now encapsulates the far greater portion of Jekyll's body-mind, like the man who at first feels great pains when he lifts weights because he is not a weightlifter, but after months and months of regularity, one day realizes that there is hardly any pain now at all – he has become a weightlifter

[3] Hyde hates without reason because he hates everything that is not him; he is a toddler on a rabid temper tantrum, loathing anything which refuses to apportion him his desires and submit to his Hyde-centric worldview

[4] As he drifts away from his former Ego, Jekyll, Jekyll-Hyde feels more comfortable referring to himself in the third person – not because he has become so much of Hyde, but because he has become so less of Jekyll

[5] Hyde is not so much another person – in spite of his physicality – but another spirit. This is why Hyde can be summoned without the drugs: he is not a chemical development, but a spiritual condition

[6] In the 2002 John Hannah adaptation, Jekyll commands Hyde to obey him, challenging that "the mind commands the body." Hyde sneers as he reminds his terrified host that while this is true, surely beneath even that layer, the body

horror[1] was knit to him closer than a wife, closer than an eye[2]; lay caged in his flesh[3], where he heard it mutter and felt it struggle to be born; and at every hour of weakness, and in the confidence of slumber, prevailed against him, and deposed him out of life. The hatred of Hyde for Jekyll was of a different order. His terror of the gallows drove him continually to commit temporary suicide, and return to his subordinate station of a part instead of a person[4]; but he loathed the necessity, he loathed the despondency into which Jekyll was now fallen, and he resented the dislike with which he was himself regarded. Hence the ape-like tricks that he would play me[5], scrawling in my own hand blasphemies on the pages of my books[6], burning the letters and

---

commands the mind. Jekyll is horrified to realize the very thing that he had so desperately argued with Lanyon: that man is both spirit and form, and that the spirit can be independent from the form – that the psychical can conduct itself divorced from the physical. As a theory it was thrilling, but as a fact – as he now finds himself at the beck and call of an incorporeal element that somehow derives from himself – it is terror

[1] A lovely phrase that encapsulates the horror of Hyde: a power that – vampire like – once invited in, makes itself uncomfortably at home. Again I revert to the A.A. adage that so succinctly describes Jekyll's degeneration: "Firs the man takes the drink; then the drink takes the drink; then the drink takes the man..."

[2] A wife being a spiritual bond, and the eye being a physical one. Hyde is closer than both because unlike a wife, he has a physical connection with his partner, and closer than the organ, because unlike it, his link also contains a spiritual coupling. He is part flesh – impulse and hunger: hatred – and part spirit – selfishness and paranoia: fear

[3] Wolf addresses this word image beautifully: "The imagery announces the imminent closure of a circle. Our story began with Jekyll's desire to separate the moral aspects of his self so that he might have vibrant, voluptuous, and wicked experiences without remorse. The cost of that pilgrimage, however, has been a deadly reversal of dominance – as we will soon see"

[4] Hyde's only reason for not taking over Jekyll – for remaining a part rather than a whole – is his parasitic use for Jekyll as a protective host. No one will hang Henry Jekyll, but Edward Hyde is quite vulnerable to destruction apart from his alter ego. Hyde keeps Jekyll around like the bandit who doesn't kill his hostage because he hasn't yet figured out an escape route – but eventually he will

[5] Again, we see signs of Hyde's unevolved or devolved status – a troglodyte, a cave man, a raging, unrefined predecessor to socialized man

[6] An act of intellectual rebellion, much like that which Stevenson enacted as a youth. Hyde's victims are probably books of theology and philosophy, and his violence against them symbolizes his (and Jekyll's) dismissal of the established order: the collective wisdom and mores of Western mankind. Imagine him scrawling curse words on the Bible and Koran, profanities on the works of Plato

destroying the portrait of my father[1]; and indeed, had it not been for his fear of death, he would long ago have ruined himself[2] in order to involve me in the ruin. But his love of me is wonderful; I go further: I, who sicken and freeze at the mere thought of him, when I recall the abjection and passion of this attachment, and when I know how he fears my power to cut him off by suicide, I find it in my heart to pity him[3].

It is useless, and the time awfully fails me, to prolong this description; no one has ever suffered such torments, let that suffice; and yet even to these, habit brought—no, not alleviation—but a certain callousness of soul, a certain acquiescence of despair; and my punishment might have gone on for years, but for the last calamity which has now fallen, and which has finally severed me from my own face and nature. My provision of the salt, which had never been renewed since the date of the first experiment, began to run low. I sent out for a fresh supply and mixed the draught; the ebullition followed, and the first change of colour, not the second; I drank it and it was without efficiency. You will learn from Poole how I have had London ransacked; it was

---

and Aristotle, and obscene drawings on the teachings of Hume, Kant, Kierkegaard, Burke, and Locke

[1] Not only does this represent a further psychological rebellion – an act of repressed aggression against the establishments which have resulted in Hyde's banishment (his jailers, as it were) – but there is a very telling Oedipal issue (repressed resentment towards a father's controlling guidance) here, one which Stevenson (a notoriously rebellious youth, whose Calvinist father's heart was broken when he learned of his son's belonging to an atheist club whose constitution required a complete swearing off and denouncement of the lessons of one's father) was keenly familiar with. There is a sense of rebellion by Hyde-the-Id against Jekyll-the-Ego (the executive center that willingly chooses good) as a father figure, much like the Creature's rage against Victor Frankenstein, but also a sense of Jekyll-the-Hyde (the bad part of Jekyll already extant in his consciousness) joining the pure Id-Hyde in revolution against his father, a man for whom he nourished fond memories. Both the Id and the Ego – the bad and the neutral – rally against this symbol of their common enemy, the Super-Ego – the internalized parent – by destroying the portrait

[2] That is, become an object of public shame – he would have brazenly invited scandal into Jekyll's life, had Jekyll not provided him a convenient hiding place

[3] Jekyll loathes Hyde – as he testifies in the last paragraph, once Jekyll's soul has left their body, he doesn't care what happens to him – and yet there remains a pitying (and might I add, HUMAN) element that has always distinguished Jekyll from Hyde: the virtue of nobility. Jekyll maintains his noble nature to the end, looking after Hyde paternally – perhaps as a grown man sadly reflects on the bitter frustrations of his adolescence, with tears on his face and mercy in his heart – and cannot bring himself to destroy himself

in vain; and I am now persuaded that my first supply was impure, and that it was that unknown impurity which lent efficacy to the draught[1].

About a week has passed, and I am now finishing this statement under the influence of the last of the old powders[2]. This, then, is the last time, short of a miracle, that Henry Jekyll can think his own thoughts or see his own face (now how sadly altered!) in the glass. Nor must I delay too long to bring my writing to an end; for if my narrative has hitherto escaped destruction, it has been by a combination of great prudence and great good luck[3]. Should the throes of change take me in the act of writing it, Hyde will tear it in pieces; but if some time shall have elapsed after I have laid it by, his wonderful selfishness and circumscription to the moment will probably save it once again from the action of his ape-like[4] spite. And indeed the doom that is closing on us both has already changed and crushed him. Half an hour from now, when I shall again and forever reindue[5] that hated personality, I know how I shall sit shuddering and weeping in my chair, or continue, with the most strained and fearstruck ecstasy of listening, to pace up and down this room (my last earthly refuge) and give ear to every sound of menace. Will Hyde die upon the scaffold? or will he find courage to release himself at the last moment? God knows; I am careless[6]; this is my true hour of death[7], and what is to follow concerns another than myself.

---

[1] This is brilliant irony – the first drug which he had considered the premium wellspring of Hyde was just a mistake, an unrepeatable mistake. All the "impure" samples that he has been throwing away have been perfectly fine; it was the first batch that was a mistake, and now nothing can be done to bring back Jekyll. That mathematical irony, that incalculable twist of chemical fate that handed him the keys to Hyde was a mere whim, like finding a wormhole to another dimension in a pile of leaves: at first the trips seemed wonderful, but when the pile was blown to the four corners by the wind, he finds himself now trapped in an inescapable joke of Fate

[2] He now has to take the drugs to keep Hyde AWAY

[3] Hyde – even if dying – would surely wish to ruin Jekyll's last hope of peace by destroying his testimony

[4] Another simian reference that suggests a devolved, troglodytic mind

[5] Readopt, to take on

[6] Literally – I don't care

[7] At the end of his existence as Jekyll, Jekyll claims that when his Super-Ego (his unnamed spiritual-half) fades away, leaving only his Id (the fleshly-half, Hyde) in control of his executive consciousness – a poor soul called Jekyll – his death has been effectively accomplished. Without a Super-Ego, Jekyll ceases to be himself – ceases to be human – for what is a human but an animal with a conscience, and what is an animal but an ego governed by an Id? What happens to Jekyll's body after the spiritual part of his consciousness departs means nothing to him

Here then, as I lay down the pen and proceed to seal up my confession, I bring the life of that unhappy Henry Jekyll to an end.

THE END.

—FURTHER READING—
Critical, Literary, and Biographical Works

Bell, Ian. *Dreams of Exile: Robert Louis Stevenson: A Biography.* Mainstream Publishing, 2014.

Furnas, J. C. *Voyage to Windward: The Life of Robert Louis Stevenson.* Faber and Faber, 1952.

Hammond, John Richard, and Robert Louis Stevenson. *A Robert Louis Stevenson Companion.* Macmillan, 1984.

McLynn, Frank. *Robert Louis Stevenson: A Biography.* Pimlico, 1994.

Stevenson, Robert Louis, and Leonard Wolf. *The Essential Dr. Jekyll & Mr. Hyde: The Definitive Annotated Edition.* Plume, 1995.

Stevenson, Robert Louis. *Dr Jekyll and Mr Hyde and Other Strange Tales.* Arcturus, 2012.

Stevenson, Robert Louis., and Robert Mighall. *The Strange Case of Dr Jekyll and Mr Hyde and Other Stories.* Penguin Books, 2007.

Michael Grant Kellermeyer -- OTP's founder and chief editor -- is an English professor, bibliographer, illustrator, editor, critic, and author based in Fort Wayne, Indiana. He earned his Bachelor of Arts in English from Anderson University and his Master of Arts in Literature from Ball State University. He teaches college writing in Indiana where he enjoys playing violin, painting, hiking, and cooking.

Ever since watching Bing Crosby's *The Legend of Sleepy Hollow* as a three year old, Michael has been enraptured by the ghastly, ghoulish, and the unknown. Reading Great Illustrated Classics' abridged versions of classic horrors as a first grader, he quickly became enthralled with the horrific, and began accumulating a collection of unabridged classics; *Edgar Allan Poe's Forgotten Tales* and a copy of *The Legend of Sleepy Hollow* with an introduction by Charles L. Grant are among his most cherished possessions. Frequenting the occult section of the Berne Public Library, he scoured through anthologies and compendiums on ghostly lore.

It was here that he found two books which would be more influential to his tastes than any other: Henry Mazzeo's *Hauntings* (illustrated by the unparalleled Edward Gorey), and Barry Moser's *Great Ghost Stories*. It was while reading through these two collections during the Hallowe'en season of 2012 that Michael was inspired to honor the writers, tales, and mythologies he revered the most.

Oldstyle Tales Press was the result of that impulse. Its first title, *The Best Victorian Ghost Stories*, was published in September 2013, followed shortly by editions of *Frankenstein* and *The Annotated and Illustrated Edgar Allan Poe*.

In his free time, Michael enjoys straight razors, briarwood pipes, Classical music, jazz standards from the '20s to '60s, sea shanties, lemon wedges in his water, the films of Vincent Price and Stanley Kubrick, sandalwood shaving cream, freshly-laundered sheets, gin tonics, and mint tea.

ABOUT THE FOREWORD WRITER

Nathan Hartman (M.F.A.) is a multi-award winning screenwriter and producer with university level experience in teaching film classes pertaining to screenwriting, broadcasting, story development, sound design, equipment usage, and post-production. Currently he acts as the "Studio Supervisor" of Huntington University's Digital Media Arts (film, animation, broadcasting) department as well as a film instructor. He also has acted as director of the "Fandana Film Festival."

Nathan performs screenwriting and project consultation through his "Hartman Creative" venture.

Nathan has received degrees in film studies and broadcasting as well as worked in development in Los Angeles. In 2016 he earned his Masters of Fine Arts in screenwriting from National University, a renowned private institution based in California, while continuing to write, consult and create for a multitude of mediums.

A multi-award winning screenwriter and producer, Hartman currently teaches film at Huntington University.

Made in United States
North Haven, CT
01 September 2022

23484536R00221